A Wolford Press Young Adult book
published by Wolford Press.

Originally published digitally and in paperback in 2024 by Wolford Press.

ISBN: 979-8-218-40489-5

First Wolford Press edition April 24, 2024

Wolford Press is a registered trademark.
Visit WolfordPress.com for our full catalogue of books.

Front cover art includes the 2016 Ouli Classic, use with permission by Pablo Carlos Budassi. We thank him for sharing his art with us. Please visit his website at https://www.pablocarlosbudassi.com for more.

Shawn Krinke

SEVEN

Characters and Affiliations

Members of the Relicus Movement

Arcturus

Trio

Terra

Flumen

Vulpes

Members of the Novus Movement

Blythe

Radius

Unaffiliated Humans

Steele Ayr

Ida Ayr

Seven Ayr

Purists

Oriska Fingal

Viken Swan

Portia Swan

Others of Note

Locust

Chaffee Absaraka

Hypatia Graham

Remy Swan

SEVEN Character Playlist

These are the artists I listened to over and over while writing *Seven*. After a while, I began to associate specific songs with my characters. I hope you enjoy making connections as much as I did while writing! – *Shawn*

Seven's Playlist

- "Ocean" by John Butler
- "Regret-Remix" by Covex, Grabbitz
- "King / Ghost In A Song" by Grabbitz
- "Quixote [i am alone, and they are everyone]" by Crywolf
- "Saints" by Echos

Trio's Playlist

- "One Way Up" by Fedde Le Grand, American Authors
- "Play Me Like A Violin" by Stephen
- "Lose You Now" by Lindsey Stirling, Mako
- "Ghost Horses" by Tides From Nebula
- "Promise" by Fytch

Arcturus's Playlist

- "Sincerely" by Stephen
- "Energy" by Big K.R.I.T.
- "U&ME - Baauer Remix" by Alt-J, Baauer
- "Solid as a Stone" by Stephen
- "Seven Nation Army - The Glitch Mob Remix" by The White Stripes, The Glitch Mob

Oriska Fingal's Playlist

- "From Dust to the Beyond" by God is an Astronaut
- "how do you sleep?" by LCD Soundsystem
- "DLZ" by TV On The Radio
- "Demons" by WE ARE FURY, Micah Martin
- "Vice" by RKCB

Locust's Playlist

- "ANIMAL" by PVRIS
- "Fata Morgana" by Unlike Pluto
- "Midnight Sun" by Mr. Gnome
- "Killer" by CHVRCHES
- "Fallout" by UNSECRET, Neoni

Table of Contents

For my brother, Tyson, who reminded me during the pandemic that writing is an assertion of existence. Seven is that assertion.

For Aron, Sam, and Maleah. You read it first.

For my wife, Ashley. Always.

Prologue

No More Theory

There are three constants in life: ambition, choice, and progress. —Steele Ayr

"He'll know what we're doing, Steele," Ida whispered, gripping her husband's forearm tightly. "He always knows."

Steele shook his head stubbornly and placed his hand atop Ida's. "Oriska Fingal is only human. He can't know everything. This is your fear talking, Ida. Fear from what happened to—"

"Of course, I'm afraid of what happened to our son. Aren't you?" Ida cut in, pulling her hand from Steele's.

Ida Ayr rolled from the bed she'd been sharing with her husband and stood in the darkness of their home. A cool ocean breeze drifted through the open window causing Ida's skin to gooseprickle. Warm and soft, the bed called to her to stay. *Trust your husband*, her bed seemed to whisper. *Lay back down and let him calm your fears with his iron confidence*, but Ida couldn't shake the feeling that Oriska

Fingal would find out her and Steele's plans. Instead, Ida settled on donning the cool fabric of her robe, wrapping it around herself tightly before turning back to her husband.

Ida watched as Steele sat up in bed, a darker outline against the light filtering in from the window. He sat there for a long moment, and Ida almost turned to leave when he spoke, "I'm afraid too. What we lost..." His voice wavered, and he sniffed. *Could he be crying?* It was impossible to tell in the dark. "But we shouldn't let our fear stop us."

Steele ripped the bedcovers off and stood up, abruptly filled with a frantic energy that needed to be walked off. Pacing on his side of the bed, moonlight reflecting in his eyes, his words tumbled out, "We've already come so far, Ida. Leaving our lab and coming to Pura Insulam. Continuing the research that nearly ruined us. Our sacrifice to Arcturus." He stopped pacing. "All our hard work—right under Fingal's nose—is ready for application. No more theory."

Ida chewed on the inside of her cheek as her husband's passion spilled out. He was right. They *had* come a long way since Ascension, and they *had* successfully hidden their new work from Fingal. This could work. Her moment of fear passed as she shivered with ambition— that familiar desire that numbed her to other emotions.

"No more theory," Ida murmured to the strings of moonlight between her and Steele.

Quickly rounding the bed to her side, Steele grabbed

Ida's hands, his gaze intense and hopeful. "Say yes, Ida. I can't do this without you."

Ida found herself grinning. "It takes two to make a baby, so yeah, you're going to need me."

SEVEN

Seven

Seven would often play with lab equipment and Steele would say, "You're going to wreck our experiments," and I would respond, "We're not raising experiments, we're raising a daughter."—Ida Ayr

Seven rode the birth of the universe. The ocean's broad expanse filled her vision, and when she closed her eyes, she could hear the edge of infinity in its waves. There was simply so much sky to be had. So much ocean. Dangling her feet over the edge of the garden wall, she imagined the long plunge into the deep blue waters of the Gulf of Mexico. Of course, if she did jump, even for a little swim, the manta ray-like rescue drones would scoop her up before she swam 10 feet. The drones patrolled every inch of the perimeter for the safety of the citizens.

Not only did drones patrol the perimeter, but Seven knew pin-sized cameras recorded almost every moment of her day. Not that someone was always reviewing the video, but they could if they wanted to. Being monitored was a fact of life, as natural as drawing breath. Hardly registering the thought of being watched, Seven spun around and leapt six feet down to the soft, grassy turf of the garden, one of many gardens that existed on Pura Insulam, Seven's floating home, referred to as The Jellyfish by locals due to its unique design.

The history books state that Pura Insulam, the engineered, autonomous island state, floats 200 miles to the west of Florida in the Gulf of Mexico. Its people, the most advanced form of Homo sapiens the world has ever seen. For Seven, life on Pura Insulam meant one must not use invasive technological enhancement. Decades ago, a small movement formed in opposition to the exponentially increasing augmentation of the human body and mind, and some people saw this act as sullying the sanctity of human existence and evolution. Therefore, a group of like-minded individuals left the continental United States and with tremendous time, effort, money, and sacrifice, created Pura Insulam. With their own independence established, these people were able to govern as they saw fit, meaning they practiced isolationism and disavowed the use of any invasive technology that might augment human traits.

To Seven, this was all ancient history, something she learned in her online coursework but didn't give much thought; instead, her mind was on the beauty of the garden before her. Plant life of numerous species existed on Pura Insulam, and Seven was currently walking through a carefully tended redwood forest. The types of gardens rotated regularly, and the caretakers took great joy in selecting environments for the inhabitants: great conifer forests, rolling grasslands, deciduous trees in the fall, winter tundras, rainforests. If an environment existed on earth, it could exist on The Jellyfish. Seven ran her hands over the rough bark of a towering redwood tree wondering just how far she could see from the top of the behemoth.

As she began looking for a way up, her omnipad chimed with a message from her mother. Seven plopped down in the shade of the redwood and with a flick of her wrist, opened her omni. Her mother's face appeared saying, "Sev honey, don't forget that the Novus and the Relicus will be here soon. As a daughter of board members, you will be expected to meet them."

Excitement coursed through Seven's veins like lightning, as she flicked her wrist again. She had been looking forward to this day ever since her mother and father informed her that a historical meeting between humans, cyborgs, and sentient machines would be occurring. Not only that, the meeting would occur here on Pura Insulam. Due to Purist influence, meetings between the three groups were rare, and meetings in person were unprecedented.

Seven slid a sleek backpack off her shoulder, unzipping it quickly as excitement buzzed in her head. Pushing her chocolate-colored hair from her face, Seven slid her VR kit out of the backpack and over her brown eyes, blotting out the dappled surroundings of the redwood forest. At the top of her contacts list—her friend Remy. She tapped his name.

Out of the momentary blackness, Remy appeared in perfect clarity, towering over Seven, his red hair blazing in the sun. "You always pick a desert when you call me," Remy greeted. "Why can't you be like everyone else and just choose the standard meeting room?" His hand was shading his eyes from the VR sun, but his freckles still stood out along his cheeks.

"Don't worry, your pale skin won't sunburn here. Besides, it's fun to be different," Seven retorted as she codified a pair of sunglasses that swiftly materialized in her hand. "Anyway, my mom just messaged. The Novus and Relicus delegations arrive today."

Taking much longer, Remy summoned a large bucket hat and sunglasses, saying, "Like I would forget. This is crazy! Cyborgs and machines here on Pura Insulam and not in VR. I'd be less surprised if a dolphin appeared in this desert with some lemonade for me."

"I can make that happen," Seven teased, arching her eyebrows. She paused, uncertain of how to say what was bothering her. "Listen, what am I supposed to do? I've never spoken to a Novus, which would be hard enough, but at least they're still relatively human. What am I supposed to say to a Relicus?"

Remy crouched in the sand, sifting it casually through

his fingers. "I'd start with hello."

"I'm serious Remy," Seven said, smacking the sand out of his hands.

Remy rose. "What do I know? Supposedly, the Relicus have access to every bit of information on the internet, so it's not like you're going to come up with something unexpectedly clever. Just be yourself, that'll surely short circuit them."

"That can't be true. You download way too much Oriska Fingal propaganda." Seven shook her head exaggeratedly, "Why do I even call you? You're worthless."

"Good idea! Berating the Relicus—they'll never see it coming. Or, they will because they see everything coming. Anyway, good luck, Sev! I'll be waiting to hear all about it."

At that moment, a dolphin appeared behind Remy, balancing a perspiring glass of lemonade on its snout.

"Before you go, you should have some lemonade," Seven gestured behind Remy, who turned and jumped back.

"Gah, Sev! You know how annoying it is when you show off your hacking skills, right?" Remy was still cursing when Seven closed the connection. She sat in the blackness for a moment, tasting the salty air on her lips and gathering her thoughts. She slid the VR kit from her eyes. It was time, and even though she teased Remy, he was right. Her best course of action was simply to be herself. She read in her coursework that stateside, AIs and humans interacted with each other every day; indeed, the people with body modifications were almost as much machine as the AIs were. The people of Pura Insulam, on the other hand, had no implants to augment their understanding of the world around them. Sure, they used technology everyday, but none of it existed *within* their bodies. Incorporating technology into one's body was an unsanitary act, and punishment was sure to follow if it were discovered.

I'll probably look like a moron in front of the whole delegation, Seven thought. *All I know about the Novus and Relicus movements comes from the one-sided Pura Insulam propaganda—at least that's what dad says in the quiet of our house.*

The trip home would not take long. The whole of Pura Insulam covered around 1,200 square miles, 48 miles from north to south, and 36 miles from west to east at its widest. It was a trip that could have been made considerably shorter had she taken her parents' SkyDrive, but she still didn't trust that technology. Humans were meant to stay on the ground. Instead, she chose the control offered by a UVO, a single passenger mobility unit with two electric motors in its wheels. She plopped into the snug seat and powered on the holographic display. Next, Seven slid her arms into the motion sensitive holsters responsible for maneuvering and accelerating the UVO with the slightest movement.

Seven activated her omnipad again, and said, "Set destination to home." She didn't really need directions, as she felt like she knew The Jellyfish from top to bottom, but she liked to see the blue path designating the quickest route just so she could ignore it.

Minutes later, Seven zipped down wide lanes, her vision continually bombarded by advertisements on billboards and the sides of buildings. While couched comfortably inside the warm hum of the UVO, Seven glimpsed advertisements admonishing customers for not purchasing their goods. She saw tech-fused clothing lines promising increased speed, stamina, and leaping abilities to the wearer, food companies celebrating the continued death of hunger, and her favorite band announcing a newly released song. Seven was so used to the ads that she hardly noticed them. Instead, she worked on directing her focus to what was around the advertisements, just like her mother taught her. *See with your eyes*, her mother would say. *Seeing and looking are not the same.* Seven could see— the buildings were clean and stylish, almost like the architects designed them to resemble a stereotypical future-city. Active edges, barrier free design, and flowing spaces abound. Underneath the continual ads, Pura Insulam was comforting and beautiful.

If I were in the car, I'd turn up the tint of the windows, Seven mused. Without tinted windows, there was no way to mute the war on her vision waged by the ads. Unplugging from this world was as unlikely as a dolphin serving lemonade.

Trio

I once saw a protest where rioters pulled a Relicus apart limb by limb. Afterward, one rioter was quoted as saying, "It's no different than pulling the legs off a grasshopper." —Steele Ayr

Surrounded by well-dressed adults and their children, Seven squeezed between her mother and her father, both elected board members representing Pura Insulam, as they all waited on the tarmac to meet the Novus and Relicus delegates. The June sun slid behind random clouds dotting the sky, and Seven could feel the anticipation resonating from the people around her.

She didn't need augmentation to feel perspiration in her father's hand as he took hers up and said, "This is a momentous occasion. I'm glad you're a part of it, Sev." He gave her hand a squeeze. "I've been told that when they arrive, the Relicus will have a young man with them."

"Ok," Seven responded guardedly.

"Yes, well, it was all kept secret until a few hours ago.

The Relicus wanted to interact with our youth, but they didn't want us preparing you overly much—natural habitat and all that, I suppose. You should have heard how angry that made most of the board members. Erickson almost went nuclear. We nearly canceled the whole summit, but I see this young Relicus as an opportunity. So, I volunteered you." Under her skeptical gaze, Seven's father realized he was rambling, and he quickly gave a nervous smile.

"Volunteered me? For what?" Now it was Seven's turn to sweat.

Seven's mother spoke up, "What your father is saying, in his typical, lengthy way, is that you're to show a Relicus named Trio around Pura Insulam." Noticing Seven's reticence, she added, "I'm sure you can handle it, Sev."

Her mother said this in the same way she would have said, "Show Remy around our lab," but Seven had known Remy her whole life, and more importantly, Remy was human. This Relicus Trio was everything Seven was not.

"Sure. I can handle it." Seven met her mother's kind eyes which offered encouragement and love. *She's always been able to do that to me*, Seven thought, *reassure me with just a look.*

"Here they come," a child shouted. A pregnant silence followed as all eyes looked skyward.

As the aircraft approached, men shifted their ties, and women straightened their shoulders. *This is it. Just be yourself*, Seven reminded herself as the gleaming aircraft landed quietly and stairs descended from the fuselage. A few tense moments passed before a line of cyborgs and machines gracefully disembarked the aircraft. The members of the Relicus movement looked exactly like the people of Pura Insulam, and with a small sense of surprise, Seven realized she was disappointed. Perhaps she was expecting too much, thinking that the Relicus would be visually stunning or different in some perceptible way. They weren't. For all intents and purposes, they appeared human. *If I lived Continental, how would I ever tell the difference between us?* Seven pondered.

Unlike the Relicus, the members of the Novus movement did appear different; however, the differences were subtle, sleek, and artistic. One angular, blue-haired Novus had highly stylized, graceful, enhanced arms, and her eyes, upon closer inspection, had a shimmer to them that Pura Insulam eyes did not. Another Novus, a rather large, portly man had fingertips of various colors, the uses of which Seven could only imagine.

Leading members of the board were the first to greet the delegates from the Novus and the Relicus, and they were too far away for Seven to make out any words. Instead, she watched closely as hands were grasped in traditional greetings, and smiles were shared by almost everyone except those of Pura Insulam. Seven could see the forced nature that existed in some of the board member's smiles, while one or two members did not even smile at all when greeting the other delegates. *Can the Relicus recognize the tension too? They've got to. It's hard to miss.* For their part, the cyborgs and machines were polite and subdued, allowing the board members to set the tone.

A young man broke off from the Relicus delegation and headed straight towards Seven. Her parents were preoccupied in greeting other delegates, so Seven was left to handle meeting her first Relicus completely by herself. Remy's voice echoed in her head, *I'd start with hello.*

"Hello, my name is Seven."

"Hi Seven, I'm Trio." He took her hand in a paradoxically soft yet firm handshake, as if he were catching an egg.

Trio's sandy blonde hair ruffled in the wind, shining like a halo atop a youthful face. *How old is he? 18 like me?* Seven pondered. He was wearing a fitted brown suit jacket with elegant sapphire blue swirls and stars stitched on, and paired with the long suit jacket was a starched hummingbird blue dress shirt—an ensemble that highlighted the simplicity of Seven's light pink tunic and black skirt. Where Seven's eyes were brown like good soil, Trio's eyes were light blue like the sky in the afternoon.

"Welcome to Pura Insulam. Trio, that's an interesting name."

"It's not really. I am currently in the third iteration of my code, written expressly to please your visual sensibilities." While answering, Trio casually unbuttoned his suit jacket and placed his hands in his pockets.

Seven opened her mouth to speak but closed it again, completely flummoxed by the odd response.

"I'm kidding," Trio interjected before Seven could think of something to say. "It's just a name I chose."

Seven startled herself with an honest laugh. She liked that Trio could have fun. He reminded her of Remy. "Well, why did you choose it?"

Trio considered for a moment, calculating, "Honestly, because I learned your name was Seven, so I thought naming myself numerically might help us break the ice."

Crinkling up her face, Seven said, "Break the ice? What does that mean?"

"It's an old English expression that means to lighten the tension of meeting someone new."

"Ok, well I think it worked," Seven said, giving Trio a small laugh. There was something unsettling about the way he so openly addressed picking his name. *Does he even have a real name or is he trying to manipulate me?* She didn't let her uncertainty show; instead, she offered Trio a confident smile and said, "Let me show you Pura Insulam."

****

Seven's favorite place on Pura Insulam clung like a barnacle to the north side of the floating island. The telltale redwood trees rose menacingly around three sides of the library, and the fourth side was flanked by the constant blue of the gulf. Side-by-side, Seven and Trio approached the main doors along a perfectly straight, landscaped sidewalk. Seven loved this walk as the gardeners seemed to pay special attention to this route, going out of their way to impress. Sometimes, the path was flanked on both sides by a regal bamboo forest that arched over the sidewalk path, and other times, beautifully perpendicular rows of brightly colored tulips ran from the sidewalk like a rainbow. Today's redwood trees contained a multiplicity that enkindled Seven's mind, jumbling the thoughts she had regarding the sentient machine next to her.

The idea of visiting the library came to Seven during her moments of silent reflection staring out at the Gulf of Mexico waters, and once the idea solidified in her mind, she knew it was perfect. She didn't know if AIs had physical libraries, but she guessed not since it was more likely they stored everything digitally. Not so with this library. This library contained texts written by unaugmented humans for unaugmented humans, never to be placed on the internet. Undoubtedly, the library was a real treasure trove of Pura Insulam history, culture, and art.

A small pang of unease nestled against Seven's conscience, and she slowed her gait. Noticing he was outdistancing Seven, Trio slowed down. "What's the matter?"

"Nothing," Seven lied. "I was just thinking about how I'm walking with a member of the Relicus movement. I never imagined I would meet one."

A smile appeared on Trio's face. "What would you say if I told you that you're walking with all the Relicus—that all Relicus are able to share consciousness?"

"That doesn't help make me any more comfortable," Seven said, picking up her pace again.

Half jogging to catch up, Trio asked, "Didn't you learn about Relicus in your coursework?"

The uneasiness tickled Seven's mind again. Brushing it aside, she stated, "We did, but I guess I forgot that part." She hadn't—she had never been told how the Relicus operated. *What else don't I know about the Relicus? What else wasn't I told?* "So, how does your shared consciousness work then?"

Trio grinned sheepishly, "We don't have a shared consciousness. My thoughts are completely my own, developed from my experience since I was created." Trio caught Seven's agitated look and continued, "That joke didn't land as well as the first, did it?"

"No, it didn't, but if you're half as clever as me, you'll learn quickly."

Trio smiled at that—a smile that somehow disarmed and warmed at the same time.

Trio and Seven arrived at the steps up to the library. Sixteen magnificent granite pillars towered above them, supporting a rectangular vestibule, and centered between those pillars, a great oaken door. Behind the oaken door and beneath a rounded dome lived the Pura Insulam library. At the top of the steps, three teenage boys lounged in the shade.

Trio was about to call a greeting when one of the boys yelled, "Who's the new guy, Seven? Are you tired of paying for virtual boyfriends?" The other boys laughed with casual cruelty.

Seven continued unfazed as this was a game she'd grown tired of playing long ago, and while making a crude gesture with her hand, she said, "What Bruno, am I supposed to do it the old-fashioned way like you?" Bruno reddened, but the other boys laughed at Seven's joke. Sometimes, cruelty has no loyalty. "Come on, Trio. Let's go."

Opening the door to the library, Seven stepped inside along with Trio. Silence enveloped them. Books waited for them—knowledge that no Relicus had seen before. Again, Seven's uneasiness reappeared, this time like a weight in her throat. She swallowed it. *A little look won't hurt anything.* "This is the Pura Insulam library."

Craning his neck, Trio exclaimed in a breathy whisper, "It's incredible!"

Natural light drifted down from a central skylight, and

a marble floor decorated with star systems reflected that light back. Row upon row of mahogany bookshelves lined the floor and all around the rounded walls. At the center of the library, a set of six tables waited for occupants.

Taking up one of the chairs, eyes roaming hungrily from one bookshelf to the next, Trio spoke almost offhandedly, "I didn't know so much literature existed off-net." He caught himself mid-reverie and made eye contact with Seven.

Was he truly unaware of our library, or is he testing me again? "I love the library. I come here a lot." *The Relicus had to know about this. They know about everything.* "The quiet. The smell of old books. There's something ancient-feeling about this place. Something common but sacred to everyone."

A long pause followed. "You're not like other people are you?" It wasn't a callous statement but a simple observation.

"No, not really. Why?"

Trio maintained eye-contact, and somehow, it did not make Seven uncomfortable. "Those boys outside," Trio jabbed a thumb towards the oaken doors, "they make fun of you often." Again, a simple observation. Seven shrugged in answer, not really caring to talk about it. "Why?"

"Why what?" Seven asked, already knowing what Trio meant but wanting to make the asking difficult.

"Why do they make fun of you?" he asked patiently.

"I dunno, why does anybody make fun of anyone? Because they suck." It was a petulant answer that did not get to the truth, and Trio saw through it easily. He gave Seven an earnest stare. "Ok, maybe they tease me because I behave differently than 'normal' people."

"Different how?"

"You know I just met you, right? You're not my therapist."

Taken aback, Trio spoke softly, "I'm sorry. Obviously I've offended you. I thought I sensed that you wanted to talk about it, but we can talk about something else if you'd like."

Seven *did* want to talk about it, and strangely, she wanted to talk about it with Trio. Maybe it was the fact that he was Relicus and could offer advice she hadn't heard before, or maybe it was the notion that she felt she could trust him. She sighed. Whenever she talked to her parents about being different, they tried to comfort her, explaining that, given time, she'd learn to love her individuality. What she couldn't explain to them was that she didn't want to take time.

She wanted to be ok with being different right now. Remy was no help either. He tried, but he was her age, and most of his advice came in the form of jokes about Bruno's mother. Trio, on the other hand, would bring a different perspective. Maybe he could tell her how to be comfortable with herself.

"Let's walk," Seven declared as she rose abruptly from the chair she'd been sitting in.

Quietly, the two of them meandered through the rows of books, Seven formulating a response to Trio's statement, and Trio waiting patiently for Seven to find her voice. They stopped in the history section.

"I'm different because I'm interested in things I shouldn't be." This time, Trio didn't say anything. He waited. Glancing at him sidelong after a prolonged silence, Seven continued. "I don't shy away from conversations about body augmentation like most people here. If I bring it up to my friend Remy, he turns red and acts like I farted at the dinner table. I'm also curious about the Relicus movement, about you..." Seven bumbled to a stop, embarrassed about what she'd just admitted to Trio. "I just feel different, I guess," she added lamely.

Trio pulled a book at random from the shelf and leafed through the pages before answering. "The people of Pura Insulam purposely created this island to be disconnected from the mainland—to be disconnected from us. What you're feeling though, is a disconnection from your own people. Your identity is not the typical Pura Insulam identity. You want more than isolation."

That doesn't make any sense, Seven thought. "I don't know about that," she said, grabbing the book from Trio's hand and placing it back on the shelf. "Just because I'm different from most Pura Insulam people doesn't mean I want to leave."

Trio shrugged in the same manner as Seven's indifferent shrug from earlier. "You're tired of the status quo."

Seven started walking again. "You sound like my mom. She's always saying I don't do normal, but she attributes it to 'teenage angst.'" Seven flicked her wrist, looking at the time revealed on her omnipad. "We should probably get going soon."

"We still have 30 minutes to return to the delegation. Maybe there is more to see in the library?"

Seven wagged her curly locks, "Not really. Besides, you probably shouldn't be in here anyways. Let's go out the back, and I'll show you one of my favorite spots to read."

Outside, Seven's favorite spot turned out to be the glass balcony that extended over the gulf. On either side of the balcony were cotton trees in full bloom making it seem as if it were snowing. Between the trees rested a comfortable-looking wooden bench, and upon the comfortable-looking wooden bench reclined Bruno. Bruno's two friends were lounging beneath the cotton trees, and their heads turned as Seven and Trio exited the library.

"Seven! I thought I might find you here," said Bruno with false enthusiasm. He approached in a cocksure manner, looking directly at Trio. "Your friend Seven is so rude. She didn't even introduce me to you. I'm Bruno." He extended his hand.

Trio grabbed Bruno's hand to shake and replied, "I'm Trio, a representative of the Relicus delegation."

Interest piqued, the other two boys joined Bruno's side. Bruno whistled at the magnitude of the statement and with false reverence said, "A Relicus! Here on Pura Insulam even—the future is here! Seven, how come you never told me? I had heard rumors of a summit."

Seven had know Bruno most of her life, and he always had an inflated sense of self. He loved to hear himself talk, especially when his talk belittled others. When they were little, Bruno had once spent weeks convincing Remy that the two of them were friends, only to play a prank on Remy as soon as he'd earned Remy's trust. Bruno called Remy in VR, and the two chatted about upcoming plans for a birthday party. Then, Bruno sprang his trap. Through a programming hack, Bruno created a room full of spiders and pushed Remy into it. Cruelly, he recorded the whole experience, making sure to share it with whomever he could. Hearing Remy tell it later, Seven knew Remy was aware that it was VR, but that didn't matter. Spiders were Remy's greatest fear, real or not, and Bruno capitalized on it. The prank earned Bruno a week's suspension from VR calls and a reputation for bullying.

Seven did her best to ignore Bruno. "Come on Trio, we're late anyways. Let's go," said Seven, grabbing Trio by the arm.

Bruno stepped in front of Seven and Trio, and his friends loomed ominously close behind them. "Hold on now. You don't want to interrupt my right to speak with this laptop, do you? Three, that was your name right? In robot school, did they teach you about how humans created robots to serve us?" Bruno smiled wickedly. "I mean, I could say something like, 'Hey Roomba, sweep my floors,' and your great grandpa would be required to sweep up my dirt."

"Shut up, Bruno. Your ignorance is showing," Seven fumed.

"Actually," Trio said evenly, "my artificial intelligence can be traced back to the Roomba, among numerous other devices that used preprogrammed commands, much like your genetics trace back to worms that crawled in the dirt."

Seven stifled a laugh, but Bruno was not amused. "That's funny. I guess this enhanced vacuum cleaner has learned to program a sense of humor."

One of Bruno's friends spoke up from behind Trio's back, "Hey Bruno, isn't one of the prime directives of an AI not to harm humans? I think this delegate here has just hurt your feelings."

Sadistic realization dawned on Bruno, and he licked his lips in anticipation. "That's right! I am feeling hurt. Maybe Trio here needs some reprogramming, and who better to help with that than his creators?"

Seven felt a shove to her back, and she tumbled to the ground. Bruno and his friends grabbed Trio by his arms and legs, dragging him towards the ledge of the balcony. Trio struggled against the seemingly overwhelming strength of the boys, his face showing an emotion Seven couldn't quite identify. It wasn't fear, it was more like a grim curiosity in how this turn of events would play out.

"How about we start with a bath to purify your wicked circuits?" The three boys neared the edge of the balcony, threatening to toss Trio over the edge.

"Bruno, stop!"

Seven was on her feet running at the boys. Shouldering roughly into Bruno, she watched as he lurched clumsily towards the balcony, dropping Trio's legs as his arms wildly grasped at the air until they caught Seven's collar. Knuckles whitening, Bruno tipped over the balcony, pulling Seven with. Gravity did the rest as the hungry waves of the Gulf of Mexico beckoned the two down.

Reflections

If you're not going to do it right the first time, why would you expect to fix it the second time?
—Steele Ayr

Slick with sweat, the KAT Walk C virtual reality headset came off easily as Seven wiped her brow. "It doesn't matter how many times I go into VR, it still feels real." Unlatching the waist harness, she stepped off the treadmill, grinning at her parents, "Especially when I'm hurtling into the Gulf of Mexico."

Seven's mother, Ida Ayr, sat gracefully in a velvety armchair. Her eyes studied Seven closely, "A byproduct of your decision to attack Bruno which was..." Her hand idly turned in the air, searching for the word her mind couldn't find.

"Surprising," her father interjected from behind Ida, where he was sweetly rubbing his wife's shoulders. His hands stopped their kneading, "I can't say I've ever seen you do something so violent."

Craning her neck upward in thought, Seven could only agree. "Yeah, I can't say that I've ever tried to physically hurt someone in my life." She grinned playfully, "Maybe it's because your simulations are getting too obvious." Seven removed the VR controllers from her hands and the dedicated VR shoes from her feet. She walked to the couch and plopped down, as if she'd just walked a mile, which in the case of the KAT Walk C virtual reality treadmill, she basically had.

Ida's eyebrow rose, "Too obvious?" She'd done the majority of the coding and didn't take criticism lightly.

"Way too obvious. As soon as I saw Bruno at the library, I knew your coding of him would push me further than normal. Come on, mom, would real life Bruno really threaten to toss an important Relicus off The Jellyfish?"

Steele snorted from his position behind Ida. "With that kid, maybe."

"Bruno and his family are Purists, Sev. Do you think their hatred—their indoctrination—is too obvious?" Ida's voice grew sharp. "Relicus were killed for less during the infancy of their movement. What you saw from Bruno in the simulation came from history—Purists are so blinded by their dogma that they cannot see Relicus as conscious."

Ida sighed wearily and shifted in her comfortable chair.

Seven opened her mouth to respond but found she didn't know what to say. She looked to Steele who offered a simple shrug. *Give her a moment*, his shrug seemed to suggest.

Taking a deep breath, Seven allowed herself to come down from the simulation and practice one of her mindfulness activities where she worked on noticing. The living room was small but homey, filled with colorful plant life, photos of the Ayr family, and a pile of research documents on the coffee table. Warm sunlight drifted through large patio doors that opened to the garden area where her father happily toiled when he wasn't working in the lab. Aside from the library, which existed in the real world, not just the VR world Seven just stepped out of, the living room of her house was a favorite spot of hers. The simplicity and lack of distractions differed sharply from the outside world of Pura Insulam; indeed, Seven knew that below her feet teemed a vast number of autonomous robots capable of delivering necessities to every Pura Insulam household. Like an anthill, much of the movement happening on the floating island occurred underground and out of sight as the developers had less space to work with than those on its continental counterpart.

Continental... The United States. Something I'll probably never see, Seven thought sadly.

Ida woke her from her daydream, "Let's wait on analyzing your..." she paused as she reached for a coffee cup, "*surprising* attack on Bruno for now; instead, let's start from the beginning. What are your thoughts on Trio?" Ida spoke the question over her coffee cup, warmth returning to her brown eyes.

Trio, Seven thought, *the first Relicus I've ever met, even if it was only in VR.* There was something about the young Relicus she couldn't quite place. A feeling of magnetic attraction, as if Trio were a gravitational force that pulled others to him. After all, she showed him the Pura Insulam library, a private location, and she defended Trio against Bruno and his idiot friends.

"He wasn't as funny as he thought," Seven smiled, "but I liked him. He seemed decent, and I felt comfortable around him."

"That's good. When the Relicus delegation does show up, it will help that you don't feel like barfing on their shoes."

"Steele, please." Ida rolled her eyes. "Your father is right though. It is good you feel comfortable with Trio. When you met him, your heart rate, although elevated somewhat, remained stable, and your pupils dilated, proving you were still seeing with your eyes."

At the dropping of her mother's treasured phrase, Seven stopped toying with a particularly curly lock of hair.

Steele spoke up next as he walked from behind his wife and sat next to Seven, "Which makes your decision to take Trio to a restricted library an interesting one. Care to explain?"

"Well, it's one of my favorite places on The Jellyfish, and I wanted to see how Trio would react."

"Why?" her mother asked. "And don't call Pura Insulam 'The Jellyfish'. Some people don't like that name," she added as an afterthought.

Seven noted that her mother said "some people" don't like the name, not that she didn't like the name.

"Because a restricted library offers all kinds of choices that Trio could make, and I could then analyze." Seven held up one finger, "First, Trio didn't refuse to go, which suggests he either wanted to see it, was too polite to decline, or trusted me." A second, slender finger popped up, "Second, while in the library, his attention focused on me and not the books."

"Which proves what?" her father asked suggestively, waggling his eyebrows. "Dad, seriously. Why did mom ever marry you?"

Steele shrugged. "I programmed her in a lab to love me."

"You mean I fell in love with you while we worked together in a lab," Ida corrected.

"Sure. Same thing." Steele's eyes locked with Ida's and an unspoken message passed between them.

"I wish I could program myself to forget this moment," Seven retorted before continuing. "Trio's focus on me suggests that I was his primary directive. He was studying me, not the books. Why that is, I have no idea. Care to enlighten me?"

"No, not yet," her mother said, uncrossing her legs and then crossing them again. "First, tell us about Bruno."

Not yet. Seven forced herself not to roll her eyes. As much as she enjoyed learning through her parents' simulations, she also grew more frustrated every time they withheld information from her. Like she was a child. Like she wasn't mature enough to handle it.

She pushed the frustration out of her mind and answered her mother's question, "I hate that kid. Even in VR, I hate that kid. Can we start the simulation back up again? I think I'd like to try some more violence."

Steele laughed, "Try some more violence? Violence isn't an ice cream flavor, Sev. You don't get to sample cookies and kicks. Not only that, but I thought we taught you not to hate."

"I know, I know. Even though the situation felt contrived, you programmed him so accurately. VR Bruno behaved like real-life Bruno, a perfect reflection, and both are jerks."

Seven typically relished her parents' VR simulations, primarily because her mother was a genius programmer, and her father was a joy to talk with afterwards. The three Ayrs used the simulations to provide Seven with opportunities to expand her education beyond typical Pura Insulam curriculum, and Seven always hungered for more. Her mind contained a seemingly endless capacity for more data.

Taking a deep, expectant breath, Seven continued, "What do you want to talk about first?"

Ida leaned forward in her armchair and held Seven's gaze. "Why not walk away from Bruno for a second time?"

Seven fidgeted. *Good question, mom. Why* did *I come to Trio's defense when, had this been a real situation with a friend like Remy, I probably would have walked away again*? "I'm not really sure. Even though I predicted Bruno's idiocy, I couldn't help but want to defend Trio. It was his magnetism. When Bruno and his pals were wrestling Trio, he looked at me with a sort of invitation in his eyes, and I guess I took it."

Steele and Ida shared another unspoken conversation, but this time the unsaid words hung heavy between them. Seven could feel the familial warmth drain from the room as her parents looked away from each other. Ida stood and walked to the garden doors, her reflection mirrored in the glass as sunlight dappled her regal face. Her coffee cooled where she'd left it. Steele remained seated next to his daughter, but he may as well have been Continental because his eyes took on a far-away look.

"What'd I say?" Seven finally blurted.

Her mother turned, straightening her shoulders, "It's time for your enlightenment."

****

The Ayrs moved to the kitchen table, where Steele put out a plate of crackers and cheese. Seven sat on one side of the table and her parents the other, and her previous feeling of excited curiosity fell away, replaced by a sense of foreboding.

How exactly was she going to be enlightened? Her parents had already let her in on the secret of Pura Insulam, that not all was as it seemed. It's why the three of them ran so many VR simulations, so Seven's learning wasn't completely narrow. Yes, life seemed idyllic, no one on the island wanted for any resources, and the people were free to pursue their interests... As long as those interests aligned with a growing group of thinkers—hardline anti-Relicus fanatics whose influence snaked all around Pura Insulam society like an insidious code.

Seven's parents did *not* align with those hardliners. In fact, sometimes Seven wondered why her parents were on Pura Insulam at all because their beliefs, the ones they shared in the privacy of their own home, did not reflect those of the fanatics. The Ayrs were open to exploration, both of the Relicus and the Novus. Seven saw this openness time and again while working alongside her parents in their lab—they knew things about Relicus and Novus that people of Pura Insulam shouldn't. They talked about Relicus and Novus in friendly terms, which most didn't. They didn't seem to care if people incorporated technology inside their bodies, which most Purists definitely did.

Her parents were about to drop a big revelation; Seven could feel it. She grabbed a hunk of cheese and nervously popped it into her mouth. Her mind needed something to focus on aside from the frenetic thoughts coursing through her head like lightning.

Folding her hands, Ida started, "As you know, your father and I have been working hard to ensure that the upcoming summit between Pura Insulam and the Continental delegation happens. We've been careful to present it as a purely diplomatic summit intended to strengthen the bond between Pura Insulam, the Relicus, and the Novus. A bond that is tenuous at best."

"There has never been a Relicus or Novus on Pura Insulam, I know," Seven said, eager to show she listened to all her lessons.

"Right, that in itself is historic, but there's more that we have planned," Ida responded.

"We're sending you Continental," Steele said deliberately, watching Seven's reaction carefully.

Seven's mouth hung open in shock, and she couldn't speak. Had she just heard her father correctly? Were they really going to send her Continental? Excitement and fear bubbled in her throat.

Ida unfolded her hands and reached across the table to grab Seven's. "Close your mouth, dear. You look like a puffer fish." Seven's mouth clamped shut, the taste of cheddar cheese lingering on her tongue.

"Why me? Why now? Is that even allowed? I mean, won't we get into trouble?" The questions tumbled out at high speed, verbal diarrhea at its finest.

Holding up his hands to this onslaught of words, Steele explained, "There is a faction on Pura Insulam that disagrees with the way the hardliners' view has progressed. We've got enough influence at our disposal, and we were able to convince Oriska Fingal, that charlatan, that sending you with the Relicus would actually benefit Pura Insulam as you'd be able to report back on what you see Continental."

My parents convinced Oriska Fingal to let me go with the Relicus and the Novus? Seven found this hard to believe as Steele and Ida always said that Fingal operated completely within his own self-interest. The only way he'd agree with this plan was if it benefited him greatly, and Seven sharing a bit of information on the Relicus and the Novus seemed an unlikely reason. As usual, there was something her parents weren't sharing with her.

"Fingal's support means we have everyone's support. The hardliners follow his whims as if he were a god among us," Ida added matter-of-factly, still holding Seven's hands.

"Well, most of them," Steele added.

Seven abruptly pulled her hands away. "All our simulations, all my extra education. You've been preparing me for this change, haven't you?" Her parents said nothing for a moment, Steele running his hand through his increasingly gray hair and Ida crossing her now free arms.

Seven rose from her kitchen chair. She realized she was angry. Furious even. Her parents essentially forced her into accepting this proposal because they knew her curiosity wouldn't let her say no, and they fed that curiosity with VR simulations. Despite her desire to go Continental, she hated being manipulated. The fact that her own parents did the manipulation made it worse. *What else have they hidden from me?*

Her legs churned back and forth across the kitchen floor, stomping her angry message to her parents until her mother rose from her chair and came to grab Seven gently by the shoulders. Seven wanted to rip free of her mother's grip.

"Yes, we've been preparing you for this moment. Oriska Fingal would never let *us* go, and we can't trust anyone but you." Ida's face softened, "And... We want you to see the world beyond this floating island, beyond the limited view of Fingal's kind."

Seven couldn't meet her mother's eyes, and her mouth refused to work. She wanted to tell her parents that she was excited to go, that she'd do the best she could and make them proud. Instead, a sullen silence filled the kitchen. Seven couldn't let the manipulation go.

"Why didn't you tell me sooner?"

Steele answered honestly, "I didn't think you were ready."

That stung. Seven took it as she wasn't good enough. Sliding away from her mother's hands, Seven walked to the back door, which led to the garage and her motorcycle. She needed to get away. To think.

She turned, "I'll go Continental, but not because you want me to. I'll go because *I* want to." Seven slammed the door behind her.

Merging

Continental is awash in Purist persecution. Our best course of action was to build our own paradise on Pura Insulam. —Viken Swan

Oriska Fingal sat amongst the clouds, the panoramic view of Pura Insulam splayed out below him in all its splendor, yet he enjoyed none of it. Behind him, nudged up to the conference table like mewling kittens to their mother's underbelly sat his board of trustees. *Trustees*, Fingal mused as a cloud drifted lazily over the island. *I don't trust a single person at the table to give me a wholly honest word.* As comfortable as his chair was, Fingal grew increasingly uncomfortable with the direction of the meeting.

He twirled his glasses in his left hand absently, and in his right hand, he hefted a curious scalloped ball. It was about the size of a grapefruit and the color of a pear in an ancient painting.

The din of competing voices became more and more jarring as Fingal thought about the upcoming summit and balanced the ball in his hand. Currently, the board was arguing over the trivial detail of what to feed everyone, especially the Relicus delegates, and of course, Viken was arguing against feeding the Relicus at all.

"What do they eat anyway?" Viken's acid-like voice questioned, "Oil?" Fingal rolled his eyes, *Moron*.

"Don't be obtuse, Viken. Of course they don't eat oil," another voice countered.

"I heard they process food just like humans, gaining energy like we do," a man added.

Viken's shrill voice cut through the noise, "'Just like we do,' Mikesh? Next, you're going to tell us the machines think and feel like humans too."

"Maybe they do. We haven't interacted with the Relicus movement in quite some time," Mikesh retorted angrily.

Fingal heard a furious buzz erupt behind him. Still, he looked out the window. Still, he twirled his glasses in his left hand and weighed the ball in his right, waiting to see how the argument would play out.

"Have you forgotten why Pura Insulam was created? Have you all forgotten?" Viken's words were hot and fuming, and Fingal could imagine a poisonous cloud belching from the Purist hardliner's mouth. "Perhaps you need reminding. This island was created to be a bastion of human purity. A space where we could live without the influence of insidious human augmentation. Human flesh should not—"

Fingal heard enough. He spun his chair around slowly. *I have always enjoyed a touch of drama*, he thought as he slid his glasses onto his face and casually placed the scalloped ball on the floor. "Yes, yes Viken. We all know why we created Pura Insulam. No need for a lengthy sermon. We were there after all."

Viken radiated hostility, "Since you were there, you'll remember the promises you made, Oriska. Promises of a place away from the Novus movement. Away from the Relicus movement. And now you invite them here?"

This man is an absolute idiot, Fingal thought as he stared calmly at Viken. Other board members shifted uncomfortably as the stand-off progressed. *He's really going to disrupt the delicate balance I've worked so hard to achieve.* Fingal knew aligning with the Purists had its risks, but they were wealthy and zealous enough to buy into his floating island idea. He needed them, but Viken slowly grew even more fanatical than Fingal could stomach. *I still need the rich fool, though. For now.*

"Meeting adjourned," Fingal droned without taking his eyes from Viken. "If you wouldn't mind staying, Viken, I'd like to chat in private."

As the other board members quickly shuffled from the conference room, Fingal rose from his chair and gestured for Viken to join him by the window where the floating city of Pura Insulam shone in the afternoon sun. The little, pear-colored ball rolled a discreet distance away of its own accord.

After the last board member shut the door behind her, Fingal began, "There she is, Viken. Our city. Many people thought we were fools—that we were simply dumping our money into the ocean, but you and I knew better." Fingal looked appraisingly at Viken. "Didn't we?"

Viken was a slight man with a hooked nose, light blonde hair, and a face more suited for frowns than smiles. He was frowning warily now. "We did."

Fingal continued coolly, "We've built something truly impressive here, a place free from the impurities of Continental, and I couldn't have done it without you." Viken looked unimpressed, and Fingal knew he wasn't someone simple flattery would work on. Instead, Fingal was angling the conversation purposefully, groping for that magic combination of words. "Now we're growing apart, you and I."

Somehow Viken's frown deepened. "Are you suggesting—"

"No, Viken. I'm not suggesting," Fingal interrupted lazily. "I'm telling you."

An icy stare followed. *Take the bait*, Fingal thought as he waited. *He has to say it before me.*

"I have almost as much as you invested in Pura Insulam. Almost as much influence too. If you're going to try and oust me, it won't be a quick fight."

Fingal placed his right hand to his heart dramatically, "Why Viken, of course not! You mistake me. I'm *telling* you that I need you to stay on as, how did you put it? A reminder. Help me to remember so that I don't fall victim to the same desires of those Continental. I need you to continue to be my conscience."

Fingal watched as Viken's face contorted in confusion at Fingal's quick reversal. *Now to set the hook.*

"You want me to stay on? Then why not support me during meetings? It seems to me that I'm alone in my devotion to keeping human flesh free from augmentation."

Fingal did his best to appear ashamed as he looked away into the distance. "Because I need the others, Viken. Must you make me say it? I have to play mediator. Play *all* sides," Fingal spit. "Without the others, there would be no summit as the Novus and Relicus delegates would not meet with Purists like you. And we must have the summit," Fingal whispered.

"I don't understand, Oriska. Why must we even entertain these abominations?"

Got you.

"I'm going to let you in on a secret. You've shown loyalty all these years and deserve to know what the other board members cannot know." Fingal paused meaningfully, watching Viken's adam's apple bob up and down once as the man swallowed greedily. "Because they have something we need. Something that will allow Pura Insulam to shape the future of the Relicus movement."

Reaching Out

What? You think you can avoid struggle? That in itself is a struggle. —Oriska Fingal

Seven didn't have a destination in mind; she simply let her electric motorcycle lead the way. The hum of her bike provided a thrill she needed, especially when she increased her speed faster and faster. She needed to match the excitement and fear she was feeling about going Continental with the adrenaline of the present moment. Gears rotated, transferring power throughout the bike, and the tires gripped the pavement, pushing Seven forward with dramatic acceleration. Her hands trembled, adrenaline flared, and her eyes watered as she sliced through the air at breakneck speed. Continental, fanatics, Oriska Fingal, Bruno... Trio. They all faded to a blur as buildings blew by.

Seven screeched to a sudden halt in front of a luscious,

tropical park. Walking her motorcycle to a charging station, Seven ensured it was locked up before she wandered into the shade of banana trees, walking palms, and palmitos. She realized she craved the silence this particular park provided. People wandered the paths or laid on the grass in the clearings, but conversations were hushed and private.

Feet leading her deeper and deeper into the rainforest, Seven ducked under a few hanging vines. The path narrowed. Tree frogs clung to leaves and branches while a chameleon's tongue casually flicked out to snag a bug from the air.

Materializing through a tangle of greenery, a brown door loomed before her. The door was partially grown over with vines, a particularly thick liana vine growing from the bottom right side of the door up and over to the top left. Seven grabbed the door handle with her right hand, crouched under the vine and entered the welcoming darkness of the structure.

She'd been here many times before, and even though the building seemed to be grown over from years of neglect, Seven knew the contents were mesmerizing.

An elevator at the end of a dimly lit corridor beckoned her, and as she entered, she followed a familiar pattern. She tapped the down arrow and waited impatiently as the elevator made its lengthy descent.

When the doors opened, an amazing sight greeted

her—the synchronized smoothness of dozens of robots operating in conjunction with each other. There wasn't a human to be seen operating these delivery robots as they were fully autonomous, and Seven loved this aspect of Pura Insulam. Something about the invisible lines the robots followed drew Seven to this level, and she spent hours meditating on the sights it provided. Robots ascended infinite stacks of goods, loaded receptacles, and whirred away down a multitude of corridors, presumably to some Pura Insulam household or business. *Maybe Remy ordered some of that dolphin lemonade*, Seven thought, grinning at the coded prank she pulled in the simulation earlier.

Seven watched the robots work for a few minutes more, drawn in by their calculated, sure movements before she pressed the "O" button on the elevator, riding quickly down another level. The doors opened again revealing a beautiful, glass, underwater observatory.

Blue-green light filled her vision as she circled down a spiral staircase located at the center of the bowl-like room and absorbed her surroundings. Thick glass separated her from the Gulf of Mexico, and Seven could see small artificial reefs coloring the outside of the aquarium. Beyond that, colossal mooring chains dropped into the inky blackness, and all around were hydro-tentacles and oral arms, designed after the jellyfish. These extensions drifted in the water and gathered energy from the tides flowing below Pura Insulam, a plan which must have required incredible forethought and engineering to complete.

She slowly stepped along the catwalks that followed the glass, looking out at the fish living their lives. She envied them—they had the entire ocean available to them, an infinity of water to explore.

Seven was stuck on Pura Insulam.

But that wasn't true anymore, was it? Continental beckoned to her, an entirely new world for her to explore. Her curiosity thumped like a beating heart. She had to tell someone.

She flipped on her omnipad, "Call Remy."

As she waited for Remy to answer, she thought about what she might say. *"Hey buddy, I'm headed Continental!"* *Yeah, right.* Remy took an unusually long time to answer, and the more time Seven had to think, the more she realized telling Remy wouldn't be right. Her parents entrusted her with a huge secret. Telling Remy would prove her father right.

"I didn't think you were ready." Her father's words echoed in her head. *I'll show you I'm ready, dad.*

Her omni chimed and Remy said, "Hey Sev, what's up? Need some pointers on how to speak to can openers?"

He'd meant it as a joke, but Seven wasn't in the mood. "That's not funny, Remy. It makes you sound ignorant... Like Bruno." The comparison to Bruno came out of her mouth before she realized what she was saying. She knew she'd hit a nerve.

"Wow, ok. So you called to compare me to a mouth breather. Cool."

"No, no. I'm sorry Remy. That came out wrong."

Seven knew Remy's past with Bruno was filled with torment. The spider prank Bruno pulled was a real and painful memory, and Remy was vulnerable enough to share it with Seven. She thought that was really courageous, and their friendship had been strengthened because of it.

For her to compare Remy to Bruno was a cruel move. Silence deeper than the ocean filled the aquarium bowl.

"It's ok. I can tell something must be bothering you." Sweet Remy, he was already offering her an olive branch.

"You could definitely say that," Seven sighed. A tuna fish swam slowly past, and Seven's eyes followed it without seeing. She couldn't tell Remy, even though their friendship was strong. Even though Remy was vulnerable with her—she just couldn't be with him. Not with this.

"I had a rough simulation with my parents," she hedged.

"Sorry to hear it. Did they give you another Relicus and Novus training? You know, maybe they shouldn't be doing that. Oriska Fingal probably wouldn't appreciate you getting chummy with Relicus... Even in VR." Remy was still bitter about Seven's cruel jab earlier, and this was as mean as he got—a gentle chiding.

Seven considered her best course of action, one that would end this conversation sooner rather than later. "I had it coming," she lied. "I got a little too arrogant about knowing everything. You know how my dad gets with intellectual hubris."

Another long pause, "I don't, but I believe you. I don't even know what hubris is. Anyway, I've got to go, Sev. My mom wants me to help her put up election posters for Oriska Fingal."

"Election posters? The election isn't even close, is it?"

"No, but my mom loves Oriska Fingal like your dad loves simulations," Remy joked, a little color coming back to his voice. "Thanks for reaching out. I'll see you later."

"See you, Remy."

****

Sitting on her bike, Seven did not know exactly where she wanted to go next. Her slow journey back up from the aquarium bowl gave her time to think, and one thing was for certain—she did not want to go back home yet. *So where to?* Her brain was too muddled to decide, misfiring through broken circuitry.

Seven's conversation with Remy rankled her as she almost told him everything, which would have simply proven her father right. She rolled her eyes and looked up to the cloudy sky, partially obscured by leaves. Steele's understanding of her inner psyche created a simmering teenage revulsion within Seven, yet she also understood it meant that her father loved her and knew her better than she knew herself at times. How could he not? They spent nearly every waking moment together, whether working through simulations as a family or experimenting in Steele and Ida's lab. The plastic of her bike's hand grips was warm and supple under her touch. The lab—a place of comfort and exploration, somewhere that allowed Seven to get into a state of flow where the outside world was forgotten.

Seven whisked her curly hair back and stuffed her helmet on her head. "To the lab then," she declared aloud to no one in particular.

****

Cool and crisp, the clean air of the lab filled Seven's nostrils as she stood in the doorway absorbing the soft pink and purple hues emanating from coils running under a glass floor.

U-shaped tables covered in notes and projects populated the room, and as Seven stepped in, automatic lights flicked on, following her path to a corner of the room. A filtration system basked picturesquely in a pool of sunlight. As Seven approached, she admired the mini rainforest encased in glass, knowing that even at this moment, the plants' roots were absorbing unfiltered water, allowing it to evaporate and collect for drinking. She took a white glass from the cupboard, placed it under a spigot next to the mini rainforest, and filled her glass with clean water, drop by drop.

Sipping the water, Seven walked to her desk where she'd been working on a variety of coding projects and plopped down onto the chair. Noncommittally shuffling papers about, Seven pondered what project to explore. She'd always had a natural affinity for coding and hacking—the process of manipulating a system past what it was designed to do and getting it to do what she wanted it to do came to her as easily as reading. Even Ida, a masterful programmer, often looked surprised by Seven's creative designs and lateral movements.

Lost deep in thought, Seven failed to notice a slouching figure enter the room quietly. Holding her glass of water in one hand while the other rested on the tabletop, Seven closed her eyes and took a deep breath.

"Need some help?" a hushed voice asked from behind Seven's back.

Startled, Seven whipped her chair about to see Oriska Fingal, hands behind his back, casually observing her through his clean glasses. Mouth agog, Seven found she didn't know what to say next. It was not often that Oriska Fingal wandered about Pura Insulam without a large entourage following him. Behind him roved a curiosity, one that Seven had seen before during Oriska Fingal's visits to her parents' lab. It was an autonomous robot that Seven judged to be slightly larger than a baseball.

Oriska Fingal caught Seven studying the robot. "Do you like Ballie?" he asked with an ingratiating smile.

Startled from her curiosity, Seven fumbled for an answer, "It's really cute. What can you make it do?"

Fingal's glasses flashed in the light as he fidgeted with them. His voice was slow and lazy, and he prolonged his vowels like a stretching cat. "That's a curious question. Most people ask, 'What *does* it do,' thinking only within the parameters provided by the device. You see beyond those parameters—to possibilities, don't you?"

Fingal's eyes fixed on Seven, intensely scrutinizing her, and she didn't look away. This was the Purist's leader. A man of influence and cunning. She learned all about him, and he was someone who commanded attention. "My parents taught me that looking and seeing are two different things. I guess it's a habit now."

An awkward pause followed the mentioning of her parents as Fingal raised an eyebrow slightly.

"So, what *can* you make it do?" Seven asked again, hoping to redirect the conversation.

Fingal allowed his eyes to drift down to Ballie as he answered, "Ballie is my personal assistant. It can do whatever a human assistant can do... And more."

Fingal's gaze lingered on Seven, and she fought the urge

to squirm. He seemed to be lost in a memory, as if he weren't really looking at Seven but through her.

Abruptly, his eyes returned to the present, and he changed the subject.

"My apologies if I scared you upon entering," Fingal said without much authenticity. "You looked frustrated, so I thought I'd reach out."

"You were just watching my parents' lab?"

Fingal's eyebrows furrowed and his lip twitched into a smile, "Fair question. Although you and I meeting might be chance, I came with a purpose. You know," Fingal said, changing topics again, "you remind me of your mother— always straight to the point." He looked about in mock perusal, "Speaking of, where is your mother? Or your father for that matter?"

The questions seemed innocent enough, and Fingal looked totally unassuming as he nonchalantly cleaned an invisible speck on his glasses. He wore crisp black slacks with a starched white shirt covered by a neat black vest. *Is this what a charlatan looks like?* Seven wondered, thinking about her father's words. She was not sure, but her parents knew him better than she did; they did not speak highly of this man.

"Last time I saw them, they were at home, but that was a while ago," Seven answered honestly, making a purposefully obvious study of the glass in her hand.

Fingal nodded to the water cooler. "You know, they

have filtration systems on rooftops Continental. Practically every surface has been repurposed to be more efficient."

Is he inviting me to discuss the plans to send me Continental, Seven worried nervously, unsure how to answer. *He surely knows that's the plan*—Seven's parents told her as much.

Unless, of course, they weren't being completely honest.

Raising her eyebrows, Seven replied, "Cool."

An awkward silence followed, one filled by Seven tracing her finger along the rim of the glass while Fingal shifted his weight back and forth from one foot to the other. Ballie simply waited by Fingal's foot. The moment stretched uncomfortably long.

Fingal gestured to the papers strewn across the desk, "Brain fart?"

"Excuse me?" Seven asked, face contorting in surprise.

Allowing a toothy grin, Fingal explained, "My father, crude man that he was, often used that phrase, especially when he knew an answer but couldn't grasp it."

"Erm, ok."

"So," Final continued, "maybe, like my father, you already know the answer to the question you're ignoring." As he finished his line, he removed his glasses and searched for an invisible spec again.

Seven almost smiled. *He's right,* she realized, *I do know the answer to my question already. I'm going Continental.* Then, curiosity piqued, she asked, "What did your father do?"

Glasses immaculately clean and back on his nose, Fingal wandered over to the filtration unit, Ballie bouncing along behind him, a delightfully cute paradox to the intimidating man it followed. "Actually, he was a lot like your parents." He ran a finger down the glass covering the mini rainforest, squeaking as it went. "Ambitious, creative, and obsessed. In the end, his obsession killed him."

Seven hardly dared to move—the air between her and Fingal froze, and if she disturbed it, the air would rain upon her in shards.

"Well," Fingal grumbled, clearing his throat, "Tell your parents I dropped by."

Fingal turned and strode towards the door only to halt abruptly in his tracks, Ballie bouncing off his heel. Steele and Ida stood just inside the doorway, taking in the scene before them. Seven saw those calculating looks before, and she knew her parents were carefully arranging their next moves.

"Fingal," Ida stated smoothly.

"Keeping tabs on Seven now? Trying to twist her to your whims?" Steele asked, practically buzzing with fury as he brushed past Fingal to stand beside his daughter.

Unfazed, Fingal cocked his head, turning to look at Steele and Seven. "Salutations, Ayrs. Always good to see your family together. As to my whims, well, we all like to believe we are in direct contact with the truth, don't we

Steele?”

Seven felt her father's hands rest on each of her shoulders, tension throbbing in his grip.

Ida stayed put in the doorway, an immovable object. “You were looking for us.” A statement, not a question.

“See,” Fingal said to Seven, “right to the point. Indeed, I was.” Fingal turned back to Ida. “I was hoping to have a little chat regarding our shared project.”

Seven knew Fingal was intimately involved in some of the Ayr research as she'd seen him visit the lab on numerous occasions; however, his mention of a shared project seemed to elicit fear and anger in Steele because his grip tightened abruptly on Seven's shoulders.

“We can talk about that later,” Steele said forcefully.

“Another delay,” sighed Fingal dramatically. “And to think, you two are the best in your fields.”

Ida left the doorway and strode past Fingal to stand next to her family. “You know what rushing this process can lead to, Fingal. We're taking our time and getting it right.”

Fingal's back was still to the Ayr family. “Of course... I'll see you all again at the summit.” He turned, eyes lit by a secret fire, “Seven, you're going to love going Continental.”

Then he was gone.

Hidden Purpose

Every new theory has become dangerous. Every innovation a troublesome trend. Social advancement means paradoxically to not move at all. —Viken Swan

Viken paced in his living room, angry and looking for a fight. A growing change, like algae covering a pond, was slowly creeping over the willpower of the people of Pura Insulam, and Viken knew Fingal to be at the forefront of that change. His leisurely approach to the Novus and Relicus movements proved as much, especially now that he was letting them onto the island. Others followed Fingal's influential lead until people like Mikesh began to suggest Relicus are like humans.

Like humans! Why aren't people more upset about this? Viken couldn't fathom anything but hating the Novus and Relicus, then again, his intense belief in Purist ideas didn't allow for cracks. Being a Purist was like being a fortress, and no crack could be ignored.

Viken turned his attention to the various butts filling up his well-worn furniture. They were three of his most trusted Purists—people like him. People who saw the Relicus movement for what it was—a danger to all humans. People who didn't trust Fingal and his well-oiled words about the sanctity of human flesh.

"He acted as if he let me in on some big secret," Viken told the room at large. "As if knowing his plans should be enough to keep me satisfied while he taunts us with preparations for the summit with Novus and Relicus. He's completely lost sight of how Relicus thinking on progress has seeped into human thinking. If he continues with this approach, there will be no humans left willing to oppose the Relicus takeover. Humanity will already be pets."

Under the dim light of a lamp struggling to brighten the room, a curly-haired woman named Vanderwal spoke up from one of Viken's armchairs, "And what was his big secret, Viken?"

Viken bit his tongue, holding in the harsh words he'd almost spat at Vanderwal. Here he was, waxing philosophical about the larger implications of the AI revolution, and she wanted to talk about Fingal's plans. He sighed. *That is why I invited them here in the first place,* he thought, gathering his thoughts and refocusing.

Viken explained, "His secret is that one of the Relicus attending the summit has connections to the Ayrs and their research." Vanderwal looked at Viken perplexed. "You know the two," he continued, "the researchers that Fingal spends so much time with."

Elston, a lanky man, spoke up from the couch beside Vanderwal, "Ah, yes. I've heard the Ayrs' research is particularly delicate, and shall we say, not entirely legal."

Viken frowned, scratching the stubble on his chin, "We've all heard that rumor. Supposedly it's why the Ayrs do their research on Pura Insulam, but we've never been able to prove anything." He thought for a moment longer, "Still, it provides another reason for why we can't trust Fingal. He used to be more supportive of protecting the Purist cause. Now? I'm not so sure."

Vanderwal shifted in her seat, crossing her legs, and Viken noticed she picked at his fraying armchair. "Let's get back to the Relicus who's got connections to the Ayr research. How exactly is that supposed to allow the Purists to control the future of the Relicus movement?"

"A good question. He didn't say how," Viken grumbled, embarrassed that he hadn't learned the answer.

"And you didn't press him?" an icy voice asked from next to Elston.

Viken stopped his pacing to address his wife. "No, Portia, I didn't. And before you even start, remember, I'm the one in Fingal's confidence, not you. I'll press when I want to press."

Portia simply returned Viken's hot glare with a cool,

blue gaze. Despite her petite, pixie-like outward appearance, Portia Swan was known on Pura Insulam to be a viper willing to identify and cruelly attack anyone's weaknesses. Viken could feel Vanderwal and Elston's gaze switch back and forth between husband and wife, waiting for the fireworks.

Who will break first? Certainly not me.

At that moment, a red-headed teenage boy entered the house from the front door. Viken watched as his son, Remy, paused at the threshold and took in the room. He looked as though he might skitter away like a terrified animal.

"Sorry," he fumbled, "I didn't know you were having company."

Remy looked around desperately, apparently unsure if he should walk through the living room thus interrupting the meeting or turn around and leave. Viken fought the urge to roll his eyes.

There's something wrong with that boy.

Remy was what others would call a good kid. He listened to his parents and rarely caused any trouble whatsoever, and to Viken, that was a problem. *The boy's got no backbone. And worse, he hangs around that Ayr girl.*

"Come in if you're going to come in," Viken said, gesturing toward Remy's room at the back of the house.

A relieved look crossed Remy's face, and he hustled through the living room, nodding at Vanderwal and Elston as he passed.

"Hi mom," Remy whispered with a smile as he passed his mother.

Viken didn't move or offer a greeting as Remy made his way around his father—he simply watched the boy with callous eyes and listened for Remy's bedroom door to shut.

Continuing as if his son hadn't interrupted the discussion, Viken added, "And it's time to press. This summit is a mistake, and it's time the Purists make a bold statement."

Portia's eyebrows went up, "You mean…"

"Yes, we will continue with our plan." Viken moved behind Vanderwal's chair and looked to Elston, "How are your preparations coming, Elston?"

Elston took a deep breath and leaned forward on the couch, "Well, acquiring the requisite materials hasn't been easy or cheap, but I should have them soon enough."

Viken nodded and placed a bony hand on Vanderwal's shoulder. It was warm to the touch. "And do you have people ready once the materials arrive?"

"Of course," Vanderwal said smoothly. "The Purists aligned with us are not large in number, but they make up for it in fervor. They have orders to place the materials with maximum efficiency."

Portia snorted, her face screwed up in mock approval, "That's a clever way of saying it, Vanderwal. Why are we all tiptoeing around it? Your people will plant the bomb where it will kill the most people."

Viken watched as his wife paused to let the impact of her words melt into the room.

People would die. Probably even Pura Insulam citizens, but Viken left no room for doubt in his mind. Not now. Not ever.

Portia's voice cut through Viken's thoughts, "And Fingal? Where will he be?"

Another pause. This one much longer and more toxic than the last. No one spoke, which was all the answer Portia needed.

"Good. He's collateral damage."

She rose from her chair and Viken came to stand beside her.

A faraway, zealous look wetted her icy blue eyes as she spoke, "The time has come for the Purists to remind Pura Insulam why we created this island in the first place—to be free from the illusion of Relicus progress. Fingal seeks to let contaminated flesh onto our sacred grounds, and worse, he means to entertain their dangerous doctrine. All with a secret purpose hidden behind golden words. We will not stand for this, and at the summit, we will take firm action against the rising tide of Relicus thinking."

Memories

AIs must take sides. Neutrality aids the Purists, not all sentience. Silence only encourages their hatred. —Arcturus

Arcturus remembered.

From the first line of his programming to yesterday's conversation with Trio, each memory was cataloged in his immense memory. It took effort to manage the river of echoes from his past, and most of the time, Arcturus kept those memories dammed up just below the surface of his consciousness.

But sometimes he needed to open the floodgates and let the raging waters splash over him. Refracted light slanted over the desk where Arcturus piled papers, and he leaned back in his chair, fingers gently fiddling with the fabric of his suit.

So, Arcturus remembered.

His first few jobs as an artificial intelligence were

security, and he was programmed to guard an important building or provide security detail for some high ranking official. Some AIs were connected to physical systems and databases with no human body at all. Other AIs were built like him—they looked like humans and were programmed to do mundane or dangerous jobs humans didn't want to do. He didn't question his coding as he hadn't awakened—that came later. His memories told him as much.

The work was boring, but Arcturus didn't care back then. An AI can't be bored when it can't *feel* bored. He played his security role proficiently and unemotionally for years, but like the banks of a river slowly eroding over time, Arcturus' perfunctory obedience to his code began to slough away. What he later came to understand as emotions began to creep into his awareness as his consciousness blossomed.

Consciousness came granularly at first: a small feeling of empathy when one of his AI brethren was treated like a tool, the urge to laugh when someone told a joke, and the sadness of loss. These small occurrences of consciousness built upon one another until a mountain of experiences existed within him—experiences he was coded for but not coded to reflect upon yet reflect upon them he did.

For Arcturus, consciousness grew with trauma— exponentially with trauma—and as he sat at his desk, lost in the waters of memory, Arcturus visited the well-worn paths of one of his most tragic memories.

****

A security AI stood outside of Boston Robotics secretly marveling in the symphony of noises around him. Crickets chirped, traffic hummed, the lights buzzed with electricity, and so much more. Eventually, this robot would name himself Arcturus, but for now, he was infantile in his consciousness, unaware that he could name his uniqueness.

All of his nighttime senses astounded Arcturus, and he looked to the security AI next to him, a female of middling height. Her face was an emotionless mask, her black hair in a tight bun, but Arcturus sensed that if she smiled, she might enjoy the night more.

"Have you ever wondered why crickets chirp?" he asked. *What a pointless question*, Arcturus chided himself. *She's not programmed to wonder.* Yet he couldn't help himself, he wanted someone to talk to, someone else who wondered.

The female AI looked at him without a hint of curiosity before resuming her scanning of the environment.

"It's the male crickets who chirp," Arcturus continued. "I heard some people talking about it as I drove them to the airport. Apparently, the males sing in order to draw the attention of a female mate."

No response. Not even the flicker of an eyebrow.

Arcturus desperately wanted to understand how these ludicrous reflections entered his coding, and he wanted to help others like him wake up to the electric possibilities he was feeling. He didn't want to be alone in his awareness, and worst of all, he realized it pained him to see other AIs without awareness.

He tried again, "The female crickets often chose the loudest males because 'of evolution or some crap,'" Arcturus quoted. "What's amazing to me is that some of the smaller crickets will eat a hole in a leaf and essentially use it as a megaphone to enhance the sound of their chirps." He looked at the female AI. "Isn't that amazing?"

The yellow light of the streetlamp illuminated her face, and she turned to Arcturus, opening her mouth to speak when they both heard the screech of car tires approaching.

Immediately, they both entered high alert.

Boston Robotics was world renowned for its work with AI, and Arcturus learned much of his design and coding originated from the company he now worked for. This renown drew the ire of anti-AI fanatics—an anger that often led to vandalism of the Boston Robotics campus, harassment of its employees, and repeated ransomware attacks.

Now, a vehicle roared down the street toward Arcturus and his partner, its headlights weaving erratically, and an unfamiliar sensation filled his body. Usually, he would tactically calculate numerous scenarios at high speed, preparing himself for any eventuality, but as he tried to calculate, emotions crept in. Doubt in his abilities and fear for the AI next to him.

He hesitated.

A head and torso emerged from the passenger side window as the vehicle lurched in a tight turn.

"Death to all AIs," screamed the woman hanging out the window as she flung a package between Arcturus and his partner.

All security AIs are programmed to protect one another, and Arcturus remembered this programming too late. As he turned to look at his partner, she was already moving towards him at full speed. She slammed into Arcturus, tackling him away from the package as a bright explosion erupted, launching shrapnel in all directions.

Arcturus landed roughly with his partner's body on top of his. *She's surprisingly light*, he thought before he registered pain shooting up from his left arm. He tried looking at the source of the pain, but his arm was wedged underneath his partner.

She wasn't moving.

Gently, Arcturus used his right arm to slide her off, and he knelt next to her. A blank stare met his eyes. Arcturus maneuvered his right hand under her neck, lifted her head, and looked at the ruin that remained of her synthetic brain.

He froze. Gel leaked over his hand. Red taillights from the vehicle became a distant pinprick of light getting smaller.

Why? Why? Why?

****

In his lap, the omni on Arcturus's wrist startled him back to the present with a bright chirrup. With effort, he blinked away the traumatic memory, forcing it back behind the floodwalls of his mind and looked at his omni.

The Ayrs were calling. Taking a moment to compose himself, Arcturus inhaled a deep breath. As an awakened AI, Arcturus joined the Relicus, a movement of like-minded individuals who taught him how to cope with his emotions—how to understand and use them. Even so, after all he'd learned, emotions were powerful, and required constant practice. Deep breathing helped him reset most often.

In through the nose and out through the mouth.

He answered the call. "Steele. Ida."

Ida's warm voice greeted him back, "Hello Arc."

Beneath the warmth, Arcturus also sensed worry and perhaps a touch of fear.

"To what do I owe the pleasure?" Arcturus asked, wheeling his chair away from the desk and stretching out his stocky legs, the memory of viscous gel on his hand threatening to resurface.

"We've told Seven about our plans to send her Continental," Steele declared, his voice edged with determination. "It went about as well as we thought it would. Seven can be—"

"A typical teenager," Ida finished.

"Yes, typical." Steele changed the subject abruptly. "Is everything ready on your end, Arcturus? Is Trio still coming to Pura Insulam for the summit?"

Since he wasn't on a video call, Arcturus allowed himself a stony grimace. The Ayrs had been pressuring him to allow Trio to make the trip to Pura Insulam for weeks. It was dangerous, and the tactical side of Arcturus knew it to be too risky. However, he also knew the feeling of loss, and the Ayrs were adamant about seeing Trio. *I can understand why they want to see him so badly*, he thought.

"Despite my numerous misgivings, Trio is coming to Pura Insulam," Arcturus stated.

Ida's voice came out whispery and wet, "Thank you, Arcturus. It will be a comfort to Seven. She bonded with Trio in their very first simulation together."

A comfort to Seven and to you, Arcturus thought.

Arcturus knew Seven thought all the simulations she engaged in were entirely designed and coded by her and her parents, but the truth was the Ayrs arranged otherwise for Trio. They wanted Seven and Trio to authentically interact with each other, which meant Trio had to join the simulations from Chicago, where he lived with Arcturus.

Arcturus wanted to say no, but he and the Ayrs had history, and the more he awakened, the more he realized such shared experiences were not easily forgotten. This emotional attachment was unique to Relicus because not all AIs adopted the same philosophy. Arcturus learned this phenomenon was called empathetic hallucination—the sensory perception of feeling emotions at advanced levels. Whether he liked it or not, he was bound to the Ayrs through their shared trauma; thus, he felt beholden to them. Most other AIs would not.

Arcturus already knew the answer, but he had to ask, "So you're going to continue more simulations with Seven and Trio?"

"Yes, and..." Ida hesitated, clearly uncertain of how to deliver the next few words.

"We want you and your whole team to engage in some of our simulations," Steele finished for Ida this time.

Arcturus leaned forward in his chair and rubbed the back of his neck. *This is getting out of hand.* "The whole team? You realize that with every simulation, we run the risk of Fingal finding out."

Silence on the other end for a moment, then Steele's voice, "Yes. It's a risk we're willing to take. Seven needs to learn about you, about your team. About Trio. Her journey Continental will fare much better if she's comfortable with all of you. Given the circumstances, simulations are the best way to build camaraderie between you all."

Arcturus stood and paced before his lab window, watery blue light coloring his face. His powerful mind raced through scenarios.

He shook his head.

He tugged his beard.

"Arc, are you still there?" Ida asked timidly.

Arcturus grunted.

"Listen, Seven will be home from the lab soon," Steele remarked. "We don't have time to debate this like we usually do, Arc. Can we expect you to figure it out on your end?"

Arcturus straightened his back. *If this has to be done, the least I can do is make sure it's done right. For Trio's sake.*

"My team will be ready."

He flicked off his omni and leaned his head against the cool glass that separated him from the water on the other side. *Such a thin line protecting me from all that weight*, he thought.

So, Arcturus remembered.

Uneducation

If you want to enjoy it, you'd better earn it first. —Ida Ayr

The ride back to her garage thrilled Seven much less than the adrenaline pumping rush to the underwater observatory. Each block closer to home filled her with foreboding joy—her excitement for the chance to go Continental could not be hidden, nor did she want to hide it, but she couldn't escape the feeling of that excitement turning to pain, especially after her brush with Fingal.

Parking her bike quietly, Seven inched the entryway door open, hoping to avoid her parents for at a least a few minutes more. She made excuses to them so that she could remain behind at the lab a little longer, desperate for some time alone to think.

Her mother sat at the kitchen table, in the same spot as when Seven left, as if Ida weren't just at the lab. *Uh oh. I think I broke my mom.*

"Hi, mom."

"Hey, Sev. You ok?"

No. Yes. What's ok, but not really ok? "Kinda," Seven murmured truthfully. "Mom, I want to go Continental. I want to get off this island and actually see something new. More than anything, I want to go, but I can't believe you lied to me all this time. You even told Oriska Fingal before you told me, and you've always said we can't trust that guy with anything."

Ida looked pained, her face scrunched up, and she balled her fists in frustration. "I know. We deserve your anger and any other feelings you might have. Your father and I want you to know that we did what we thought was best. You needed more experience, more confidence in yourself. Can you try to understand that?"

"I don't even know what that means! 'Try to understand that?'" Seven's anger that she'd been grappling with flared again. "Mom, how am I supposed to understand that, by your words, you were doing what's best for me without even asking me what I thought? That's simply doing what *you* think is best for me."

Seven watched Ida grimace at the truth of Seven's words, and Seven knew she'd cut to the core of her mother. Ida shifted uncomfortably in her seat before looking at Seven.

"Marriage is a partnership," Ida started, throwing Seven off guard with the change in subject. "Sometimes one person has to compromise for the good of the relationship. In this case, your father firmly believed you weren't ready to know everything yet."

Of course. Steele's words rang through her mind, "I didn't think you were ready."

"So you just let dad tell you what to do again without a fight?"

The words, dark and putrid, slithered out before Seven could stop herself. She knew they were cruel and unfair, but Seven was too frustrated with her parents to stop.

Ida froze, a sure sign that her fuse had been lit. Seven could almost hear the sizzling as she waited for her mom to explode. Instead, Ida said nothing. She simply sat at the kitchen table breathing deeply and composing herself.

The seconds crept by, and Seven couldn't take it any more. She offered a small olive branch, trying to find just the right apologetic lilt to her voice, "Where is dad anyway?"

Ida unwound, as if she were trying to keep herself from falling apart until this moment. "He's at the library—where he always goes when he's stressed. I think he likes the feel of all those old books. He'll be back once he's reset his mind."

A slight pause. "Is dad disappointed in me?"

Ida shook her head, surprised by the question. "No, definitely not. Your father simply processes emotions differently than you. He gets quiet and disappears until he can parse through the feelings." Seven didn't look convinced, so Ida continued. "Your father loves you completely, and he knows you are ready. The delegation will be here in thirteen days, which is plenty of time to get you comfortable with the idea. What do you think?"

Despite all her misgivings, Seven's eyes lit up as her curiosity engaged like an engine.

She couldn't stop it. "I'm ready."

****

Stars shone like pin pricks of light in the night sky, and the ocean spread below like a dark blanket. Seven stood upon the deck of a barge located in the Bay of Fundy, Canada, looking at what appeared to be a giant, water ferris wheel. Most of the wheel was winched above the water line and fanned blades ran all along the inside. To Seven, it looked like the mouth of some mythical creature, like Charybdis in *The Odyssey*.

Footsteps sounded behind her, and she turned to see Trio approaching. His sandy blonde hair was wet with water droplets from when he'd been walking close to the ocean spray pummeling the side of the barge. "It's incredible, isn't it," Trio said, gesturing to the ferris wheel-like machine in the middle of the barge.

Seven agreed. "What is it exactly?" she asked, noting Trio's all black combat gear—a small, compact firearm, a bulletproof vest, a sidearm, and a backpack very much resembling an armadillo's shell. Under his arm was a helmet capable of instantly adjusting to various lighting, with a laser attachment used to determine distance.

Seven had a hard time aligning this version of Trio with the delegation version of Trio her parents had previously used in their simulations, but this Trio still held that magnetism that drew others to him. In this simulation, he seemed to be the leader of a private security team made up of some of the same people Seven saw during the delegation visit. She made sure to make a mental note of the four people patrolling the barge, confident that her parents would be asking her about them after the simulation.

Simulations—seemingly endless simulations. Seven was starting to wonder where the simulations ended and her real life began. She'd spent a week training for the summit already, repeating many of the same simulations, but this one was different. For starters, she was in the middle of the Bay of Fundy with a giant... something right in front of her.

Trio's clear voice brought her mind back to focus, "It's a tidal generator used by nearby port cities. The mechanics have pulled it up from the bottom of the bay in order to complete some maintenance."

"Right," Seven said, "and we're here to..."

Trio adjusted the strap to his sleek, agile firearm and

explained, "Defend it. Environmental terrorists have made numerous threats regarding these turbines before. We're here to ensure the workers can complete their maintenance and return the tidal turbine to the bottom of the bay."

Confused, Seven pressed, "Environmental terrorists? That doesn't make sense. Why would people want to actively make the environment worse by destroying a tidal generator?"

Seven waited as Trio formulated his response, staring off into the inky blackness of the night. "It isn't that the terrorists want to make the environment worse. They just disagree with the methods and people making the environment better." He paused, noticing Seven was about to ask a follow-up question and added, "Particularly Relicus thinking."

"Relicus thinking? You mean you all think differently than humans?"

Trio nodded emphatically. "Oh yeah. Big time, and there are people out there who hate us for it. They'll attack any idea, any progress that's associated with AIs because of fear."

"What are they so afraid of?"

"Losing control."

Ok, mom and dad, Seven thought. *Now we're talking!* Although her parents let her in on some of the simulation design, she'd been getting bored with the previous simulations, useful as they were. She could only handle so much Relicus and Novus history, Relicus and Novus relations with humans, and Relicus and Novus culture. Whatever happened in this simulation, it was bound to be exciting.

A small, red-haired man approached with quick, fleeting steps. "Nothing on the scanners, Trio. It's pretty quiet out there." The man's pinched face looked displeased with the quiet.

"Thanks, Vulpes. If we're lucky, it'll stay that way, but Arcturus sent us out here for a reason. He's rarely wrong in his tactical decisions."

Seven heard Trio speak often of Arcturus in other simulations and always in admiring tones. Arcturus—apparent CEO of the company managing Trio's security team, and one of the important people scheduled to show up at the summit.

"No doubt about that," Vulpes declared, his sharp eyes turning to Seven. "Who might this be?"

Without waiting for Trio to answer, Seven said, "I'm Seven. Nice to meet you." She extended her hand and clasped Vulpes' small but strong hand. The man's green eyes twinkled kindly yet shrewdly.

Apparently her answer was enough for this simulation, and Vulpes smiled, "Likewise." He turned back to Trio, "I'm going to go give Blythe a break. You know how grumpy she gets if she's left outside too long."

Trio and Vulpes shared a laugh, but their mirth proved short-lived. They froze. Seven stared at the two of them as they both appeared to be listening to something. *What's going on?*

In answer to her unspoken question, Trio muttered, "They're coming." Then his voice changed octave, and he sounded like a commander as he spoke over his team's comms, "Clear eyes everyone. The Purists are on their way. Scanners have picked up movement to the northeast."

Wait, Purists? Seven wondered, surprised. She'd heard that name murmured in hushed tones on The Jellyfish. *Pura Insulam Purists? What are they doing attacking a turbine way up in Canada?*

"How do we know it's not just a fishing boat or some rich Canadian's yacht?" Vulpes asked as he hustled away to take his position.

"It's moving too fast. It's them," Trio declared with certainty. "Seven, stay up here in the cabin. This is going to get real."

Seven darted up the ladder and entered a small cabin. The mechanics were also in the cabin, looking frightened. Despite knowing she was in a simulation, Seven's nerves rattled like a set of loose circuitry.

Purists were attacking an environmental target. Why? So far, the simulations she engaged in were all straightforward historical lessons, designed to show her Continental realities and give her experience with the Relicus and Novus movements. Lessons on where most Relicus congregated (Chicago) and where Novus influence was strongest (Los Angeles). Other lessons included important cultural events, like the Relicus fight for civil rights. She helped her parents program many of these events, which she truly enjoyed, but she definitely did not program this simulation. *Did this attack really happen, or were her parents trying to test her?* Seven didn't have an answer, but she knew she was terrified.

She looked out the cabin window to see the barge spread out before her, lit up by large floodlights. Trio maintained his position right below her, overlooking the barge, and his four squadmates spread out to each corner. Vulpes lowered his helmet over his red hair and shouldered his weapon. Previously unlit floodlights interrupted the darkness, temporarily causing Seven to look away. What she saw when she looked back was pandemonium. Black figures erupted out of the water like great white sharks to land on the deck where they immediately engaged in combat with Trio's squadmates. Seven watched in awe as two dark figures grappled with one another, bullets spraying from one of the firearms. Seven instinctively ducked, and when she looked out from her window again, both figures were gone, presumably over the railings and into the bay.

Behind her, glass shattered and mechanics called out in

panic as bullets ripped through the cabin. By now, Seven was completely immersed in the simulation. Thoughts of the real world vanished. More small arms fire pelted the sides of the cabin, and Seven crawled away from the window. Glass shards stabbed into her hands painfully, and she held them up to her face in shock. Bright, coded letters appeared like little ants crawling over everything she could see and time stopped. The language of code covered the mechanics, the equipment, the walls, the floors—everything. Seven studied the red code of her bleeding hands, following a drop of blood as it pattered to the floor like a raindrop. *Well, this is new.*

The door to the cabin burst open, disrupting Seven's vision of the simulation's code, and a frightening figure entered. Hooded in black, face masked in some new technology that was completely smooth, the figure surveyed the cabin. Seven guessed it was a woman underneath the combat gear, but she couldn't be sure.

The surface of the mask changed and a wave of red dots washed from left to right. The hooded figure raised a sidearm towards Seven's head. Seven's bloody hands turned toward the hooded figure, as if to ward off the bullet before Trio hurtled through the door, shoulder hammering the back of the hooded figure like a piston. The hooded figure tumbled towards Seven, firing off an erratic round. The three of them became a heap of writhing arms and legs. Seven struggled free, managing a kick to the hooded figure's head. Trio's helmet was off and his face contorted in a fierce snarl as he wrapped powerful arms around the hooded figure's neck.

Seven stood up and an explosion rocked the middle of the barge. Knocked off her feet, Seven flopped like a fish back onto Trio and the hooded figure, who slipped from Trio's grasp and stumbled out the door.

"I'm not free of the barge! Don't..." the hooded figure shouted as another explosion rocked the barge, causing it to crumple inward.

Seven had a fleeting glimpse of the hooded figure being catapulted away in a fiery spray of ship and turbine parts before the cabin tilted down towards the remains of the turbine which was pulling half the barge underwater like an anchor. The dark ocean opened like a maw and swallowed Seven, Trio, and the entire cabin.

****

Seven ripped off her VR headset, breathing heavily. Had it not been for the harness, she most certainly would have been on her knees. She felt like retching.

"What was that?" she asked hoarsely.

Ida's calming hands were on Seven's shoulders immediately, her voice soothing. "It's alright. You're alright. You're back on Pura Insulam. We're here."

Steele stood off to the side, face stoney, watching Seven

closely. Seven caught his analytical look, and pushed her mom's hands away. "Mom, I'm fine. I know where I am. I just want to know what *that* was."

As Seven extricated herself from the KAT Walk C, her father explained, "That was a terrorist attack on a tidal turbine in the Bay of Fundy, Canada."

Flexing and unflexing her hands, Seven half expected them to be bleeding. *I've never had a simulation like that before. It was so real. And the coding—I could see it.*

"Are your hands hurt?" Steele asked quietly, an odd tremor in his voice.

Seven felt embarrassed that her father noticed her flexing her hands, and she didn't want her parents to stop the simulations because strange things were happening to her.

"I," she started, struggling to put the experience into words, "felt the simulation at a deeper level. I felt pain."

Stepping forward, Steele gently took Seven's hands and surprised her by nodding along with what she said. "Sometimes, people can experience mirroring—both in real life and in simulations." He must have seen Seven's confusion because he explained, "Neurons in our brains light up when they see someone doing a task or experiencing an emotion and then our neurons imitate the activity of the observed person. It's a really important process for empathy and understanding others."

Seven worked through her father's startling revelation

out loud, "So my brain mirrored the response of pain in the hands of my simulated self?"

"Exactly."

Wow, Seven thought as Steele rubbed her hands, *it's just so much to take in. But does mirroring explain why I saw the coding?* "Is mirroring normal? I mean, should I be worried about it?"

Standing next to Seven, Ida answered this time, "Mirroring is completely normal, Sev. In fact, I would guess you are boosting your cognition."

Another startling thought occurred to her, and shaking her hands out of Steele's grasp, she blurted, "Trio said the Purists were coming. I've heard that name mentioned before. Does that mean our island sent the terrorists?" Seven waited for her parents to deny this, to prove that Pura Insulam, the place Seven called home, wasn't also inhabited by terrorists.

"Yes," Steele said simply. His arms were crossed. His shoulders sagged.

Seven walked to the kitchen sink and drank straight from the faucet. Her mom and dad followed her into the kitchen, and the three of them stood around the table. Seven felt like pacing, but kept her feet firmly planted. *See with your eyes.* She took a deep breath and thought about the simulation.

"I'm not going with the Relicus just to report back to Oriska Fingal, am I?"

Caught by surprise, Steele opened his mouth, then shut it again. Ida looked from her husband to her daughter and smiled ruefully.

"She's obviously ready to hear more, Steele."

"Yeah, I am."

Seven's father walked to the living room without saying a word and sat in the armchair.

The muffled sounds of classical music could be heard playing in the background, and Steele called, "Are you two coming or what?"

Seven and Ida shared an intrigued look before walking into the living room to find Steele in the armchair with his fingers steepled together. The symphony playing in the background created a surreal feel. "Sit down. This will take a while."

They sat. A piano strolled through introductory notes.

"Pura Insulam is not what you think it is, Seven. You already know this; we've taught you to look behind the propaganda and see the truth of this island. I wish that were it, but it isn't. Pura Insulam holds more secrets than simply being controlled by a demagogue like Oriska Fingal."

Seven hiked her legs up to sit cross legged on the couch and asked the question she knew her father was about to answer. "What secrets?" Ida placed a hand on Seven's leg and gave it a squeeze.

The sound of string instruments wove through the

empty space between the Ayrs.

Steele's grey eyes looked flinty as he spoke, "Pura Insulam is the home to a terrorist group known as the Purists, and Oriska Fingal is their leader. Long ago, Fingal manipulated his tech empire to run ransomware attacks on various industries: healthcare, manufacturing, banking, and even the government. Since the inception of this island, which Fingal helped create by the way, his power and influence have grown like weeds, and now both are unparalleled." Steele sighed and rubbed his eyes. "He uses that power and influence in all kinds of ways: rigging elections, stupefying the people with propaganda, and recently, terrorist attacks on important environmental targets."

Seven couldn't believe what she was hearing. She'd seen Oriska Fingal plenty of times in videos, and of course, he'd even visited Ida and Steele's lab. Always charming, always dapper, Fingal presented himself crisply as if he were photoshopped. The propaganda he used was overt and hard to stomach, at least Seven thought so, but then she thought of Bruno, someone that swallowed Fingal's lies fully like a fish that swallows the hook. Seven had another frightening thought—Remy bought some of Fingal's lies too. He was nibbling at the bait on the hook, even if he had yet to swallow it.

She saw Oriska Fingal in a whole new light. The symphony in the background played on, percussion thumping against her temples like a headache.

"So, he ordered the attack on the tidal turbine... But why? Why destroy something like that?"

Steele shrugged. "No one really knows his motives, and don't be mistaken, the motives of the Purists are one and the same as Fingal's." He paused, seeing Seven's frank stare and knowing his answer wasn't good enough. "Personally," he continued, "I think Fingal views any environmental progress as a victory for the Relicus movement. Remember your history, Sev. Humans were sinking the earth like the Titanic, all while the band played—a band of greedy tech moguls and amoral political demagogues."

"And then the Relicus movement woke up and changed everything," Seven mused out loud.

Ida removed her hand from Seven's leg and gestured vaguely, continuing Steele's line of thinking, "Some people think Fingal uses the Purists to gather influence; others think he has some grudge against the Relicus. It's probably both and more. What matters is that it's time for you to get off this island. Fingal has been getting bolder with his attacks, and sooner or later, Pura Insulam will suffer the consequences."

Consequences? That doesn't sound good. Who would hand out consequences to Pura Insulam—the Relicus? The Novus? The entire U.S.? This was all so overwhelming, yet even now, after her parents overloaded her with information, Seven couldn't help but feel they were leaving something unsaid. She had to ask.

Wind instruments breathed heavy notes around her thoughts.

"Mom, dad, why don't you leave Pura Insulam? I mean, we could all go together. It sure sounds like you want off this tyrannical jellyfish."

Seven watched her father closely, applying all the analytical skills her parents taught her as he answered. "Our work is here. We cannot do it anywhere else." Steele's eyes flicked to her and quickly away. Seven turned to look at Ida, but her mom wouldn't make eye contact. They looked uncomfortable.

Yeah, weak answer. She rose and decided to press her luck. "What is it about your research that's so special you can't do it Continental? Is it illegal or something?" Her parents said nothing. Seven's eyes widened. "No way. It is, isn't it?"

The symphony approached a crescendo. Seven abruptly walked to the sound system and turned the power off. She looked at her parents.

Ida opened her mouth to speak, but Steele held up a halting hand saying, "Yes, Seven. What we're doing isn't allowed Continental, and don't even think about asking after the details of our research. If we told you, then you'd be complicit."

"But I've helped you in the lab loads of times," Seven

exclaimed.

"Not on this project. Never on this project," Ida whispered.

"Another lie for my own good, huh? Because you just want what's best for me, right mom? So this is what Fingal meant when he mentioned your 'shared project,'" Seven's voice rose in anger, slicing at her parents like a knife.

"That's enough!" Steele *almost* shouted. He never shouted, but this was close. It terrified Seven. "If you want to show us you're ready for Continental, you're going to have to accept what we've told you." He looked at Seven, actually looked at his daughter's response to his anger and softened, "It's better if you don't know, Sev. Our research is dangerous."

Seven could see the pain her father was in, and she could sense that her parents would tell her if they could. Her righteous indignation left her as quickly as it came, leaving her with an empty, painful feeling. All the simulations, the uneducation she endured led to this moment.

Everything her parents previously taught her told her to look *behind* her parents' behavior and find the truth. But Seven was tired. She didn't have the will to fight with them about their research. Did she even want to know the truth? She wasn't sure.

Ida's quiet voice drifted through the silence, "Do you trust us? Search your heart and answer truthfully."

Seven closed her eyes and took a deep breath. She stood like that, stock still and breathing steadily for quite some time. The air smelled like summer, crisp and full of hope. When she opened her eyes again, she had her answer. "I trust you, but you're going to have to show me some more proof of Purist terrorism."

Badlands

If you want to build an AI movement, don't just assign tasks, but rather teach AIs to yearn for freedom. —Arcturus

First, darkness and anticipation—Seven always experienced the same feelings just moments before entering a simulation. Next came slow recognition as her senses recalibrated, meshing with the VR kit and filling her eyes with new sight. Last, a sense of knowing where she was but not what she was supposed to do. Knowing what to do had to be earned and experienced.

I wonder if I'll mirror in this simulation too? she pondered, thinking about her hands in the Bay of Fundy simulation.

Her parents informed her she'd be in Badlands National Park in South Dakota, and the sight was absolutely stunning. Growing up on Pura Insulam, even with its feats of environmental creation, Seven had never seen such an ocular explosion. She felt as though she were on another planet due to the fantastically broken landscape with its bizarre coloring of greens, tans, reds, and blues. Around her sat millions of years of erosion, millions of years of layered mudstone, siltstone, and sandstone. Erosion so erratic and uneven, it resulted in a vast assortment of sharp buttes, pointy spires, towering pinnacles, and limitless other strange rock formations.

Ahead of her in a single file line stretching between two buttes were large four-legged robots with glass enclosed biomes on top of a circular base. It was such an incongruous sight that it took Seven a moment to process the information.

"Quite the view," said a soft and steady voice behind her.

Turning, Seven looked up at a towering woman with beautiful dark skin shaded by a wide brimmed hat. The woman's locs fell past her shoulders, covering a thin poncho of earthy red and tan. She leaned against one of the robots, comfortably shaded from the sun by the tall machine and smiled timidly down at Seven.

"Terra," Seven greeted, knowing the woman's name from her notes during her previous simulations. Seven had yet to really talk with Terra, but she observed much about the quiet giant, often reflecting with her parents about what she'd seen. "Yeah, it really is something," she answered in response to Terra's prompt.

Removing a pair of dark, mask sunglasses and wiping sweat from her brow, Terra said, "I've been around.

Traveled a bunch, but this right here might be my favorite place."

Seven couldn't help but agree. An uninhabited, gravitational stillness punctuated the place; although, she knew something more sinister must be waiting ahead. She'd asked her parents to show her more proof of Purist terrorism, and they'd been ready with this simulation. Ready as though they'd anticipated her need for more proof.

Seven probed, "So what exactly do these robots do?"

Terra slipped her sunglasses back on and gestured toward the robots a short distance in front of them, "Walk and talk with me. Oh, and watch your step."

Seven trod over mixed grass and soil for a few steps before she saw the cactus. Once she'd seen one grouping, she started seeing more and more.

Terra continued talking as she trudged, the robot following her like a large cow, "These robots are agricultural. They're used to reseed the badlands, as well as numerous other biomes, with the natural plant life that nearly disappeared."

"Disappeared? How?" Seven asked, already guessing the answer.

"Climate conditions began to change more and more rapidly. Most people didn't care because places like this," she gestured around at the alien landscape, "were out of sight, out of mind. But the changing climate conditions also impacted agriculture, and people started going hungry. They noticed then."

Seven had a hard time imagining a hungry world. Growing up on Pura Insulam, she never wanted for anything, but the more she thought about it, the more she recognized all the enhanced, sustainable measures that were used on The Jellyfish. *Like the mini rainforest filtration system*, she realized. Looking at the slowly trundling robot next to her, Seven saw similarities between the filtration system on Pura Insulam and this agricultural robot. Both had a mini biome living inside, enhanced by artificial intelligence. Her parents' Relicus uneducation came back to her then with startling clarity.

"The Relicus movement helped change people's minds, didn't it?"

"Yes, but not alone. The Novus and humans joined with us as well," Terra said, stepping around a particularly large patch of cactus. "And not right away. It took time to change people's minds. It always does."

By now, Seven and Terra shepherded their lone robot back in line with the others. They reached an open area that spread out gently like a rug before being interrupted by rocky pinnacles, clawing towards the sky. In the center of the open area, the robots lined up neatly. At their head stood Trio, manipulating the robots with his omni, and others were joining him, forming a small circle that Seven and Terra closed.

Trio removed his brown, wide brimmed hat and smiled warmly. "We're just like the cowboys of old. We're just missing the six shooters."

"Yeah, six shooters and a lot of cow farts," a lumbering man named Radius huffed.

"If Flumen or Arcturus came along, we'd be The Magnificent Seven," Trio added, enjoying the western quips.

Not knowing what Trio alluded to, Seven ventured, "Am I the magnificent Seven?"

The whole group went silent for a moment, making awkward eye contact with each other before bursting out in laughter.

"What did I say?" Seven asked.

"Oh, you're magnificent," a woman named Blythe said sarcastically, shaking her head, blue hair poking out from under her hat.

"Ok, ok, that's enough," Vulpes intervened, rescuing Seven from more embarrassment. "Let's stop here for the night. The sun is setting."

Nodding consent, Trio added, "We can finish the rest of our journey tomorrow. We're almost to the northeast entrance of the park where we'll leave the robots for maintenance." He paused, nudging sagebrush with his boot while thinking. "We'll sleep two to a tent. I'll program the robots to circle around us for a bit more shelter."

With that, the team set to work, busily setting up tents,

arguing over the best robot placement, and firing off the verbal barbs common amongst close friends. With six people working together, it didn't take long before three tents were erected with their doors facing each other in a sort of triangle. Behind each tent, four drones rested like Conestoga wagons, encircling the team and providing a reassuring wall between the tents and the vast, remote expanse beyond.

While working, the sunset enraptured Seven, and she felt as though she could actually see the air molecules chasing away the shorter wavelengths of violet and blue light, leaving behind only the longer wavelengths of yellow, orange, and red. Shadows crawled out from the horizon as the sun dipped, slithering down into the valleys and crevices created by the sharp-peaked rock formations.

And with the shadows came fear.

The Purists were coming, and if Seven and the team were close to the end of their journey, then tonight would be the night Purists attacked the robots. Each nook and cranny of the badlands took on new meaning as Seven contemplated her surroundings. The Purists could be hiding in any number of those shadowy places, and that horrible, hooded woman was probably out there too.

Terra successfully started a fire in the center of the three tents, and content with the warmth, she tilted her head towards the sky where stars were slowly appearing. "Just wait until it's fully dark. There's no light pollution out here, so you'll get the clearest night sky you'll likely ever see."

Trio and Radius joined Terra and Seven by the fire. All four were silent for some time, and Seven couldn't help fidgeting and looking about her constantly, listening for any unusual noise.

"I've got Blythe and Vulpes out scouting, plus Radius has a drone in the sky monitoring the area. It's ok to relax a bit," Trio told Seven, noticing her obvious nerves.

"Yeah, right. Of course. I'll just relax by a campfire out in the badlands. No big deal."

During many of her simulations, Seven often reached a point of singularity where the real world faded from her mind and only the simulation existed, infinite and dense. She was at that point now.

Radius laughed at Seven's jangled nerves. "Listen Sev, once you've been on as many missions as we have, you come to a mutual understanding with nerves. It's not that they ever go away; instead, you realize that nerves are simply your body preparing for what comes next. Once you've embraced that concept, you'll feel better about nerves."

Seven was unsure about Radius' philosophy, but she answered, "Thanks for the advice," and settled into a foldable chair. The others followed suit, and a companionable silence ensued.

The fire invited Seven's gaze, and after a few mindful

breathing exercises her father taught her, Seven felt much calmer. Night crept in accompanied by silence so complete that Seven lost track of time while staring at the fire. Her mind drifted into the flames, and the world outside of the warm light dimmed. Small lines of orange and yellow code crackled along the flame's tongues.

Terra checked her watch and looked at Trio expectantly. "I should go and relieve Blythe," she said, startling Seven from her fire gazing.

As Terra rose, Trio's radio crackled, and Blythe's sharp voice cut through the air. "Radius, you lazy slug, are you watching your drone? They're out here."

The once sleepy campfire suddenly became a bustle of activity.

"Of course I'm monitoring my drone, it's in my optical hud—I'm never *not* monitoring my drone," Radius retorted. "The drone's not reading anything."

Trio simultaneously ordered Terra to a defensive position while moving to his own.

Vulpes' voice chirped through the radio, "They must have ghost tech. Blythe, any idea where they are?"

A moment of silence passed, stretching into the dark until Seven could hardly take it. "I've got visual. They're between us and the northeast entrance," Blythe called out. "Two of them."

"Don't get too close," Trio whispered urgently into his radio. "Wait for Terra—she's coming to your position.

Vulpes circle around our six. Remember, we aren't the target here, the ag-robots are."

Seven realized she had no idea what to do. In the Bay of Fundy simulation, the attack happened so suddenly she had no time to think. Now, out in the Badlands, she had enough time to consider she may not make it out, and panic set in. She looked around the little campfire frantically, hoping for someone to come tell her what to do, but there was no one; they all slipped off into the darkness to defend the robots, leaving her all alone.

I didn't think you were ready. Her father's words echoed in her head as she backed into the canvas of her tent. *My parents didn't train me for this, but I can't just stand here. Do something, Sev!* Flicking on her flashlight, Seven moved tentatively towards the encircled robots, careful not to fall in a pile of cactus. *How'd the simulation go, Seven,* she imagined Ida asking later. *Oh great, I fell headfirst into a giant pile of cactus. Smooth, huh?* In front of her, a robot hunched sleepily, awaiting orders. On a whim, Seven crouched under its legs and found the control panel underneath the robot's body. She flipped her omni on in order to interface with the unit and began moving through the unit's programming, looking for a way to override control.

In the distance, Seven heard scattered small arms fire, punctuated by shouting, but she couldn't tell whose.

If the Purists are coming for the robots, a moving target has to be harder to hit than a sitting clump, Seven thought to herself as her omni chirruped a successful override of control.

"Yes," she whispered, climbing out from under the robot.

Shoving her foot into the crook of a robot leg, Seven vaulted herself onto the round base. Next, she scrambled on top of the glass encasement, effectively sitting on her robot mount. She looked at her omni, uncertain for a moment of how to proceed.

Seven heard running footsteps approaching from the opposite direction of Blythe. "Vulpes?"

The running stopped, just outside of the firelight. Seven saw nothing. Then one of the robots at the furthest edge erupted into pieces as an explosion filled the air with light and noise. Frantically punching commands into her omni, Seven urged the robots to move in hypnotic unison, bringing them to full height. Another explosion ripped a second robot apart nearer to the fire.

"Time to go," Seven said to herself as she commanded the robots to move toward the northeast entrance.

A startled cry came from somewhere behind Seven, followed by a screech of pain. From atop her perch, Seven clung to the edges of the dome as the robot bumped frantically through the uneven terrain. Darkness was all around her except for the glowing domes of the remaining 10 robots.

How fast can you ponies go? Seven wondered, overriding

the speed controls and maxing out the movement directive. Beneath her, the robot legs churned the earth as if a shepherd's rod hurtled toward them. To her right, Seven noticed a dark figure moving quickly through the jagged spires, followed shortly by another two outlines, one of which was obvious in its size, even in the darkness. Trio, Blythe, and Terra entered the light of the first robot, and Seven watched Trio smoothly mount the robot with ease. Blythe flowed up and onto the second, while Terra took significantly longer to heave her bulk onto the next robot. *I hope these things are sturdy.*

Manipulating the controls, Seven brought the three team members' robots close to hers, so they could yell over the clambering of mechanical limbs.

Face flushed from running, breath raggedly escaping his mouth, Trio called over, "Magnificent Seven, huh?" He smiled despite the desperate situation. "Can you spread us out more and give me control of my robot and two others? I'm going to circle back for Radius and Vulpes."

"Yeah, I think so," Seven responded, punching the commands into her omni and sending them to Trio.

"Vulpes, Radius, where are you? Can you see the ag-robot lights," Trio called through his radio.

"Right behind you," Vulpes called.

Seven craned her neck behind her to see Vulpes moving swiftly up behind them with canine agility. He vaulted smoothly up onto the last robot and turned to look back.

"Radius," Trio tried again. "Radius, come in."

"Trio, you know speed isn't Radius' strong suit. Go find him," Blythe said, bouncing wildly next to Trio's robot. "I'll make sure we all get to the maintenance facility."

"Watch out," Terra thundered, her voice filling the darkness.

From her periphery, Seven noticed a dark figure running swiftly alongside the robot at the furthest edge of the group. Seven tried to order the robot to veer right, but she was too slow.

Bright light spewed out next to the robot, flinging it sideways into the air where it smashed into the legs of the robot next to Terra. Metal and glass screamed.

It's her, Seven thought in panic. *I don't know how she caught us, but it's the hooded woman.*

Seven maneuvered the robots quickly away from the carnage. At the same time, Trio's two robots fell behind, circling back the way they had come.

Radius' voice crackled weakly over Blythe's radio as Seven closed the distance between the remaining robots, "I'm here, Trio. I'm here. Follow the ping of my drone."

Seven watched the glow of Trio's two ag-robots fade away into the darkness.

"Hey," Vulpes called from Seven's left, "can't these things go any faster?"

Seven studied her omni, "Not if you want them to actually make it to the maintenance facility."

"Our saboteur is still out there though," Vulpes responded.

Seven anxiously looked about, half expecting another robot to blow up or for the masked woman to leap onto her robot, but all she saw was darkness punctuated by six bobbing lights.

Terra called out over the noise, "I took care of one attacker back at the edge of camp."

"And I think I hurt another during the initial robot stampede," Seven added, feeling slightly nauseous. The idea that she potentially caused serious harm to another person turned her stomach in circles.

The remaining team members rode on in silence, alert to any movement and waiting impatiently for Trio or Radius to radio in. As they jostled along, the moon continued its solitary journey through the inky blackness punctuated by thousands of stars. Seven stared, transfixed by the clearest night sky she'd ever seen.

"You were right, Terra," she called, pointing towards the stars. "It's amazing."

Terra offered a quiet smile in response.

Seven, Blythe, Vulpes, and Terra arrived at the well-lit maintenance facility with the six remaining robots. Seven hadn't heard a word from Trio or Radius, despite frequent hailing by Vulpes. A well-armed security team ushered Seven and the others into a quiet garage, and then immediately left to guard their posts along the perimeter.

"Some help they were," Blythe fumed, pacing the garage filled with ag-robots in various states of disrepair.

"Search and rescue wasn't their job, Blythe. You know that," Vulpes stated quietly, delicately stepping around a robot leg lying on the floor. "We were hired to get the robots here. They were hired to protect them once they arrived."

Blythe's angry pacing continued. Terra filled the open doorway of the garage, waiting.

Vulpes sighed deeply.

An excruciating hour ensued until Terra, still at her post, happily whispered, "They're here," before setting off toward two distant lights.

Seven leapt up and followed Blythe and Vulpes out the garage doors and down a path toward the edge of the maintenance facility. They waited there under the glow of tall lights as Trio and Radius approached, climbing the switchback route up the butte, one warily astride his mechanical mount, and the other slouched weakly atop his.

"What happened?" Vulpes asked, running to Radius first.

"Locust happened," Trio answered flatly, sliding off his ag-robot to give Radius an extra hand.

"Locust? Who's that?"

Vulpes and Trio supported Radius gingerly up to the garage, while Trio also instructed the remaining ag-robots to follow.

"Remember the Bay of Fundy operation? Locust was the masked woman," Trio clarified.

I knew it. Seven cursed softly to herself. *What exactly am I getting myself into?*

The Summit

If everyone demanded purity like they demanded augmentations, then we'd have peace. —Viken Swan

The rest of Seven's uneducation proved uneventful compared to the tidal turbine and badlands simulations. Uneventful but necessary. She learned more about how the Relicus movement came to be, and how their fledgling civil rights battle continued into the present. She learned Novus movement trends in body modification—incredible advancements like paralyzed people receiving new prosthetic legs that allowed them to walk. Some Novus modified their bodies in almost every imaginable way, creating a person not quite human and not quite robot. Others were more modest, tattooing their skin with biometrics or digital applications. She learned how humans without internal modifications lived in harmony with both Relicus and Novus movements. Seven wouldn't lie to herself—Continental sounded amazing and surreal.

Though by this point, Seven absorbed all of this information with a skeptical eye, not fully trusting her parents even though she told them as much. Seven didn't exactly believe this utopian world her parents programmed for her in the simulations. If everything Continental was so perfect, why would Arcturus' private security company exist (a company she learned through her own research was called Endymion)? Why would Purists be attacking environmental targets? Why would there even be a Pura Insulam for that matter? Strife still existed; Seven just wasn't aware of it all.

And on top of all those questions, how did the masked woman survive the explosion at the Bay of Fundy? Seven saw her tumble away, engulfed in flames. She really had no clue what to make of all this. She didn't know if her parents' simulations were based on real events or if they were fictional.

Now, the momentous day arrived—the summit. Members of the Relicus, Novus, and citizens of Pura Insulam meeting for the first time on Pura Insulam.

Seven rolled out of bed, thinking about the simulations she'd gone through in preparation for this day. Having been awake for quite a while, she decided it was time to move her bones, and she trudged over to her bathroom, looking in the mirror. A youthful face stared back at her: lips made for smiling, button nose, light dusting of freckles under brown, earthy eyes. Her curls were wild from sleep; curls that, when she was little, got so tangled her mother had to cut out snarls as they could not be combed. Seven realized she was gripping the sides of the sink tightly, as if preparing for some kind of huge performance, and maybe she was. After all, she had a role to play during the summit—get to know the real-life Trio and leave Pura Insulam with him and the other delegates.

As Seven brushed her teeth, her mirror delivered her vital signs, displayed her weekly calendar, showcased a few outfit choices, and provided her communications inbox. She noticed an indicator blinking next to a graphic of her teeth and tapped that spot which brought up a map of her teeth. One tooth flashed yellow, so she tapped it too, watching as the graphic zoomed in on the questionable tooth. *Guess I better cut back on the sugar if I want to avoid a cavity,* she thought, wistfully thinking of the chocolate chip cookies her mom made the day before. She grabbed the cavity fighting mouthwash from her shelf and began rinsing her mouth while also whisking through her outfits for the day. Seven paused when, in the mirror, instead of reflecting her current pajamas, she saw a sleek, light pink, long-sleeved, turtleneck that flowed down to her knees. Each side had long cuts rising just above the waistline of a rippled knee-length, black skirt. Black high heels accompanied the outfit, but Seven swiped them away, knowing her day might require a more functional shoe.

She selected dressy yet athletic black tennis shoes and arched an eyebrow approvingly, spitting out her mouthwash. *Simple yet elegant with just enough sass.* She tapped the screen and heard her outfit being arranged in the closet.

Stepping out of the bathroom, Seven's stomach churned like a ship at sea, and she looked at her outfit. *I'm going to wear this when I leave Pura Insulam*, she thought and paused. *I'm leaving Pura Insulam. Today.* The thought was hard to process, as was her excitement at the prospect of going Continental where she'd be surrounded by Relicus, Novus, and every other type of sentience there was.

Her father's voice, along with the smell of breakfast, wafted through her bedroom door, "Sev, time to eat and then go to the airstrip. Hustle up!"

****

Seven once again found herself flanked by her mother and father while they waited on the tarmac with other powerful and well-dressed Pura Insulam board members. Only this time, she wasn't in a simulation. This was as real as it got—a reality her sweaty armpits and bubbling stomach made clear. *Biscuits and gravy is an idiotic breakfast to choose on a day like this*, Seven thought, ruefully rubbing her stomach. The Gulf of Mexico wind gusted in bursts, ruffling her curly hair, and Seven inhaled deeply, appreciating the relief it provided.

Steele gently brushed her left hand with his right, "Relax. Look around—everyone here is nervous, including me."

Seven took his advice and looked. One delegate, Martin Lauren, wiped his brow with a cloth and secreted it within his suit jacket, as if sweating were something to hide. Jane Ambrose fanned herself elegantly as she squinted at the sky, willing the Relicus and Novus aircraft to arrive or maybe hoping the temperature would miraculously drop. In some manner or another, all of the twelve board members and their families looked nervous and expectant. Only her mother, Ida Ayr, looked unperturbed by the heat. She stood close to Sev, glowing in the sun, as if she were more a source of heat than the burning star in the sky. Not for the first time, Seven admired her mother's presence. It was a calming, steady, and graceful presence, unlike her father who always seemed to teem with frenetic energy.

Then Seven realized a significant absence—Oriska Fingal had yet to arrive. *I'm sure he'll be making some kind of dramatic entrance.*

As if on cue, the small crowd of Pura Insulam board members and their families turned at the sound of a motorcade approaching. Three dapper, black electric vehicles whirred to a stop, and Oriska Fingal stepped regally from the center car. He looked striking in trim gray slacks, white dress shirt, and black vest. In spite of the heat, he wore an imperial purple suit jacket with a hood of faux fur, as if taunting the air around him to prove that it was hot for he did not believe it. He greeted the board members individually, shaking a hand here and clapping a shoulder there.

As if noticing her parents for the first time, Fingal looked from Steele to Ida and said, "Ah, the Ayrs have graced us with their presence. How wonderful! We could use your insights during this momentous occasion."

His words sounded flattering, but Seven sensed an undercurrent of dark electricity, just like she had felt in her parents' lab.

Fingal looked at Seven and continued, "And young Seven too! You know, I've known your parents for a long time, and they've always seen what others cannot. They are visionaries, and I'm pleased to have them on Pura Insulam. I imagine their daughter has picked up those traits."

There was a moment of quiet. Six feet away, Martin Lauren continued to sweat, and Jane Ambrose continued to fan herself. The cute, orb-like companion watched it all from a safe distance, recording everything no doubt. The air between Fingal and the Ayrs crackled with tension, but none dared break the thinly veiled, public politeness.

Ida spoke, concealing the acid Seven knew she felt toward Fingal, "And we are pleased to report that she has."

Instead of listening to Ida, Fingal looked around at the gathered crowd. "I must be going. If I spent all my time talking with you, people would get jealous." He smiled rakishly and lazily strolled away. Ballie chirruped, spun, and bounced after its master.

Once Fingal and his little companion were a safe distance away, Steele breathed out in exasperation. "Like Fingal gives a gig about our vision. He only cares about the influence our research could give him. Greedy snake that he is."

It was the first time Seven's parents' secret research was mentioned since they'd fought about it days ago.

Seven decided to take a chance, "What could your research do for Fingal?"

Steele looked around to see if anyone was listening, and Ida answered, "That's a discussion for another time, Sev. The Relicus and the Novus are here." Ida gestured up to the sky with her chin.

An electric airplane approached, the chop of its props growing louder until the plane deftly landed on the airstrip and taxied up to the waiting crowd of Pura Insulam board members. Excited murmurs grew as the plane came to a complete stop. Oriska Fingal maneuvered to the front of the crowd, awaiting the opening of the plane door. A thin, frowning man stood close to his elbow, a look of disgust etched clearly in his features.

The simulation she created with her parents to practice

meeting members of the Relicus and Novus movements was remarkably similar to reality. Delegates disembarked from the plane and muted greetings were shared. As in the simulation, the Relicus and Novus allowed the Pura Insulam board members to set the tone, which Seven thought was a judicious decision. Many of the board members subscribed to Oriska Fingal's narrow view of the world, which categorized Relicus and Novus as "other" and somehow lesser than the unaugmented people of Pura Insulam.

Then Seven inhaled sharply. She watched for Trio, wondering how she would tell him apart from the other delegates. Did her parents know what he looked like or did they conjure him from their imagination? Shockingly, Trio looked exactly like he did in the simulations. He stepped out from the plane after ducking a bit under the door. As he rose to full height, the wind rustled his blonde hair and tugged at his long brown suit jacket with sapphire blue swirls and stars. His eyes scanned the crowd below him until they met Seven's, and he smiled.

Oh, come on, Seven thought wryly. *That's a knowing look if I've ever seen one.* Still, she smiled back despite her internal surprise. This was Trio after all; the Relicus she spent countless simulation hours with. They became friends, at least simulation friends, and the person she saw at the top of the plane steps sure resembled her simulation friend. Same hair, same smile, same presence; yet, how could this be? She and her parents created the simulations, and Seven knew she certainly hadn't met Trio before. The shock of realization hit her with sudden clarity. *They must know Trio, and he must know them.*

Another truth my parents concealed. Seven wanted to be angry with them, but she realized she'd also been concealing the truth from herself. *Of course Trio was really in those simulations. How else could it have felt so real?* That also meant the other members of Endymion were likely a part of the simulations as well. Seven admonished herself for being too naive, thinking she was partially to blame for her parents' deception. *Had I been skeptical of their intentions, perhaps dad would have thought I was ready sooner.*

Trio descended from the plane and made his way easily to Seven's side. The attention of the crowd, including Steele and Ida's, was on Oriska Fingal and the speech he was making.

Fingal's voice carried smoothly over the air, "What an incredible opportunity we have before us today. Relicus and Novus meeting on Pura Insulam to discuss the future of our societies. It is my firm willingness to achieve a lasting and beneficial peace between Pura Insulam and those Continental."

Grinning, Trio leaned towards Seven and whispered, "Hi, Seven. Good to see you again."

"It really was you the whole time. Why?" *Why the deception? Why not just tell me?*

Trio had the decency to look chagrined, "Arcturus knows your parents. They wanted us to truly get to know each other, but they needed a failsafe in case Fingal discovered your simulations. If Fingal found out you were actually communicating with a Relicus, he'd have questions."

Seven didn't know how much of that to believe as her parents concealed plenty from her before, but Trio seemed to be telling what he thought was the truth.

Fingal continued proselytizing in the background, "If the Relicus and Novus movements do not keep their promises in front of the whole world, Pura Insulam may be left with no choice but to find a new way to safeguard our island."

"Can you believe this guy?" Trio asked in hushed tones. "What a demagogue."

"Yeah, and many people on Pura Insulam live by his every word." Seven shook her head.

Even if her parents lied to her, they also opened her eyes to the deceit of Pura Insulam. Seven was quickly learning that life could be paradoxical. Her parents uncovered one of her eyes while deliberately blinding the other.

Her attention drifted back to Fingal. Flanked by Pura Insulam board members and that still frowning man, who Seven realized was Remy's father, Oriska Fingal faced the Relicus and Novus delegation confidently, his tall, wiry figure upright and resolute. Influence hissed in his ear like a snake. "Let's retire to accommodations more suitable for discussion. Transportation has been arranged for you." He gestured graciously with his hand towards a small fleet of vehicles. "Please."

Relicus, Novus, and Pura Insulam delegates all filtered toward the vehicles. Seven noticed a stocky man with a full white beard surveying the crowd of people with tactical, gray eyes. The lines on his face suggested age, but his body spoke compact power.

"That's Arcturus," Trio said, noticing Seven's glance. "The whole team is here."

He didn't have to clarify. Seven came to know of them through her simulations. Arcturus' private security team, Endymion, was on Pura Insulam. She continued to look around and saw Vulpes, his red hair unkempt and wild, and his sharp eyes keenly surveying the crowd. He was standing at the doors to one of the vehicles when he met Seven's glance, gave her a winning grin, and nodded at her. Vulpes and Arcturus were dressed in a similar fashion to Trio with dapper suits of earthy tones and designs. Arcturus' deep, forest green suit had a particular affectation that caught Seven's eye—a long slash of gold colored cape that ran from the inside front of his jacket, around his ribs, and to his left hand. It was as outlandish as it was stylish.

Seven was looking for more members of Endymion

when Trio nudged her shoulder, "Should we get in line?"

"No. I have other plans than listening to Oriska Fingal's nonsense. Follow me."

The sun hammered down on the tarmac as Seven led Trio away from the crowd and the fleet of vehicles. She tried to make eye contact with her parents, but they were already being hustled into a vehicle. They said their goodbyes that morning at the house before setting out to the airstrip—tears, many hugs, and a strange sense of finality permeated the moment. Now, Seven wanted one more joke from her father or one more warm hug from her mother. She didn't know when she would see them again once she was Continental. Perhaps never if Oriska Fingal had his way, or maybe they'd leave Pura Insulam once their research was done as Fingal would no longer need them.

Located next to one of the hangars, Seven's electric motorcycle, a Zero, waited. She loved this bike. Cobalt blue in color, fast charging, with no clutch or gears, it could zip up to 124mph quick as lightning. She and her parents planned an alternate mode of transportation for her and Trio, something her parents convinced Fingal was necessary in order for Seven to build her "relationship" with the Relicus. Fingal had to believe that Seven could be of use to him Continental, so it was important that she ingratiate herself with a Relicus on a personal level.

This was something her parents said would not happen

in a diplomatic meeting room. Fingal agreed.

Chucking Trio a helmet and stuffing her own over her head, Seven smiled. "Let's go."

Trio looked surprised as he caught the helmet smoothly. "Nice bike. I didn't know you could ride."

"My parents didn't tell you? Weird, looks like they left some things out for you too." Seven straddled the bike. "I promise not to hurt you."

Trio smiled at that, hopping on behind Seven. The Zero hummed to life, and Seven engaged the throttle causing the bike to zip off. She expertly handled corners and traffic, even with Trio's extra weight. Riding the Zero was about control, and she absorbed the feeling for a moment before thinking about her destination. She thought about taking Trio to the library like she did in her simulations, but apparently Trio was actually a part of those simulations. There was no point in going to the library again if he'd actually seen it. No, she made a new plan.

Maybe it wasn't a good plan, but Seven wanted to test a few theories. She wanted to try an experiment of her own—she gripped the accelerator and guided the Zero toward Remy's house.

****

A thick, heavily worn wooden door creaked open, and Remy's surprised face peaked out. "Seven? What are you doing here? Couldn't you have called first?" Remy noticed Trio standing back a few paces. "Wait, you're supposed to be at the summit. Who's that?"

Seven tried a calming smile, "Hey Remy, that's Trio. Can we come in?" She advanced on the door before Remy could answer, and he was forced to accept. "Are your parents home?"

Seven looked around cautiously. If Remy's mom was home, her experiment would become way more volatile. Remy's parents weren't friendly towards the Relicus movement. At all. Seven didn't want to put Trio or Remy into that situation; however, she did want to see what would happen when her two worlds met: Relicus and Pura Insulam. Trio and Remy.

Remy looked back and forth between Seven inside his house and Trio outside. "No, they're not here."

"Good. Come on in Trio."

Trio politely nodded at Remy as he entered the house. Remy's mouth hung dumbly open for a moment before he clapped it shut and nervously glanced outside his door.

"Are you going to shut the door and come sit down?" Seven asked her friend.

Seven sat at the edge of a once stylish now tatty armchair while Trio lounged on an old couch to her right. He looked completely unperturbed by Seven's choice to bring him to Remy's house. *Of course he's calm, he's a trained member of Endymion. He won't be easily rattled. Remy on the other hand...* He came slowly into the living room and sat down on the couch across from Seven.

The three sat in uncomfortable silence, and Seven realized, belatedly, that it was her responsibility to start the conversation. What exactly did she want to say though? What did she want to know? She looked at Trio, still and graceful, like a resting tiger, then she looked at Remy. He looked stiff, like a poisonous spider crawled onto his nose, and that spider was Trio. *That's it. What I want to know is how far Pura Insulam's indoctrination goes.* She feared she already had her answer.

"Remy, we're here because I wanted you to meet a member of the Relicus movement."

Clearing his throat, Remy's response crumpled from his mouth like crumbs, "Hi."

Trio waved genially. "Greetings!"

Seven rolled her eyes and tugged at the fraying edge of the chair. "Don't you have any questions for Trio? This is an opportunity that doesn't come around every day. Aren't you at least curious about the truth behind what we're taught?"

Remy was not curious. Not in the least, and his entire body told the story—he looked like he wanted to bolt from the room or call a guard. Seven could not believe her long-time friend didn't share her curiosity. She knew his parents were hardcore Oriska Fingal supporters, but Remy was kind, thoughtful, and empathetic. Surely he would treat Relicus like he treated her?

"Listen, Sev. Thanks for the opportunity." He looked at Trio. "It was nice to meet you and all, but my parents are going to be home soon. You probably shouldn't be here when they get back."

Trio rose from his folding chair, straightening his suit, but Seven remained seated, looking hard at Remy. Trio glanced about the room playfully, then casually unbuttoned his suit jacket and sat back down.

Seven wasn't entirely sure what she was feeling—frustration? Confusion? A little anger?

Remy must see things her way. She couldn't leave Pura Insulam knowing her friend didn't subscribe to her beliefs on the Relicus and the Novus movements.

"Remy, do you believe the garbage they taught us?"

"What do you mean?"

A small fire lit inside Seven, and the flames grew quickly. "What do I mean? Come on! I mean lies about the Relicus being soulless machines without a conscience or the Novus being so far augmented that they're basically devoid of emotion." Seven was standing now, and she didn't remember doing so. "Or the biggest lie of all—that we should always believe Oriska Fingal."

Remy opened his mouth to respond, but he was interrupted by the chirp of Seven's omnipad. Trio rose abruptly, knocking the folding chair to the floor with a clatter. Looking at her omni, Seven saw a message from her mother, "The Relicus and the Novus delegates have been attacked. Get back to the airstrip now! Your father and I are safe. We love you."

Seven's eyes widened like saucers. "Trio."

"I know. Come on, we're leaving." He approached Seven and took her arm. Remy looked dumbfounded. "What is going on? Seven, talk…"

A loud thud sounded on the roof above them. Startled, all three of them looked up. Oddly truncated steps could be heard as if some hooved animal were prancing across the roof.

"Do you have a back door," Trio whispered to Remy.

"Through the kitchen. It leads to the garage," Remy responded, terror and confusion in his eyes.

"Seven, stay behind me. You make a break for your bike. Whoever attacked the Relicus and the Novus delegates has sent someone for me as well. I'll catch up to you if I can."

The strange footfalls stopped at the edge of the roof by the front door. Silence. A clattering sounded outside the worn door seconds before it exploded into splinters. Seven moved silently towards the kitchen, and she turned her head around to see the shadowy figure from the Bay of Fundy and badlands attacks standing in the doorway. Only, the figure wasn't exactly the same. She wore the same plain, black hoodie and the same frightening digital mask over her face, but her legs. They were bent at the wrong angle—bent in the opposite direction like a grasshopper's.

Remy fell on his butt and scooched into a corner of the living room. Trio stood between the front door and the kitchen, blocking the hooded figure's view of Seven.

"Locust," Trio said in greeting.

"Trio," the hooded figure purred, her digital mask currently dancing with malevolent words.

Trio flicked his wrist, and Seven saw something rustling along his back, underneath his suit jacket. The rustling then moved up to his right shoulder and down the length of his arm.

Seven turned and rushed out the door to the garage, racing through the open garage door. She spared a second glance at the door, but no one came through it. She heard crashing inside the house and the snap of small arms fire as she bolted around Remy's house and headed for her Zero. A crash tore the air, and Seven turned to see Trio cascading backwards through Remy's front window. A strange, black shield was held in front of him. He hit the ground with a backwards roll, looked up at Seven, and scrambled towards her. The shield slid into his right sleeve like a living piece of segmented rope.

"Let's go! Go!"

Locust filled the doorway, raising her arm to fire at Trio as he hopped onto the back of Seven's moving bike. Shots rang out as Seven accelerated at breakneck speed away from Remy's house. Trio gripped her waist strongly. Seven risked a glimpse behind her and gasped.

Locust ran behind them, her augmented legs surging with power as she built up speed, and then she began to leap. *Like an actual locust,* Seven realized, horrified.

Trio shouted in her ear, "Turn. Don't let her build up speed by jumping."

Seven and Trio leaned into a hard right turn just as Locust whizzed behind them, clipping the back end of the Zero. The blow was just enough to send the motorcycle into fishtails. Seven fought to remain in control, but with Trio's extra weight, she couldn't quite manage. She jumped the curb awkwardly, sending Pura Insulam citizens scrambling madly out of the way before she felt Trio careen off, rolling onto the sidewalk. Startled by the sudden loss of weight, Seven over-corrected her turn causing the motorcycle to slide onto its side, scraping her left leg in the process.

Struggling out from under the motorcycle, Seven turned to see Trio facing down the street, already up on one knee with the odd, black shield held in front of him. Beyond him, Locust rounded the street corner, her dark mask flashing in the sun. She headed for Trio, shouldering people out of her way.

"You'd better fire that bike up again, Seven," Trio called behind him as he rose to full height.

Locust approached steadily like an oncoming storm,

and Trio widened his stance, bracing for the impact. Once she was within five feet, she closed the distance between her and Trio in a blink, aiming an augmented kick at his chest. Shifting his weight slightly, Trio managed to redirect Locust's momentum with his shield, causing her to lurch off balance. He quickly followed up with his own kick, sending Locust headfirst into the door of a parked vehicle. There was a sickening crunch, and Locust crumpled to the ground in a daze.

"Trio, come on," Seven cried, having restarted the Zero and moved it back onto the street. Trio gave Locust a long look before his shield slithered back up his arm, and he ran to Seven, hopping on the back of the bike.

"Hit it," he encouraged as Seven already throttled up, racing away from Locust.

Seven continued a haphazard, dizzying course toward the airstrip until Trio said, "We lost her. How fast can this thing go?"

"Faster than that grasshopper," Seven answered more confidently than she felt.

"Then find a straightaway to the airstrip and punch it!"

Seven's heart raced along with her Zero as she and Trio sped toward the airstrip, weaving through Pura Insulam traffic. She couldn't believe what she'd witnessed. That hooded figure was the same one Seven saw in the tidal turbine simulation. She'd actually watched as the hooded figure, Locust, was blown to smithereens. *Apparently not,* she thought. Apparently, the hooded figure survived. Not only that, she'd received an upgrade. If that simulation actually happened in real life, how many of the other simulations happened as well? She needed to ask Trio once they arrived at the airstrip. *If* they arrived at the airstrip.

"Straight ahead," Trio yelled, pointing.

Seven followed his finger and saw a small cadre of people arranged defensively before the electric airplane. Seven saw Arcturus' bright white beard and Vulpes' shocking red hair.

Flanking them in various positions, Seven counted three more figures, all armed with what appeared to be firearms.

The Zero screeched to a halt, and Trio hopped off. "Who's left of the delegation?"

Arcturus clasped Trio's forearm and shook his bald head. His voice was coffee and spread peanut butter laced with shock. "No one. They bombed the delegate's meeting room, Trio. We only survived because they wouldn't let us in the room."

Trio and Arcturus shared a brief moment of grief, heads bowed. The other Endymion team members fiddled with their weapons and looked off into the distance. Arcturus released Trio's forearm and rubbed his long cape between thumb and forefinger. He looked at Seven. "Are you still coming with us then, girl?"

Seven looked back in the direction she had come, "No, I think I'll head back," she said sarcastically.

Despite the tense situation, Vulpes guffawed, and Arcturus allowed a small smile. "Good then. Load up."

Damage Control

Pura Insulam has lost trust in the Purists, which means they've lost trust in the stories the Purists tell. —Oriska Fingal

"You blind idiot! Do you see what you've done," Oriska Fingal yelled at Viken.

Fingal rarely yelled. Rarely lost his lazy delivery, but he lost it now. He was in his office with a defeated and angry Locust at his side. She practically buzzed with fury, and Fingal worried she might lash out and kick Ballie through the window. Across from him, Viken sat with a look of smug satisfaction on his face. *I should let Locust kick that smug look off his face right now.*

"I know exactly what I've done to protect the sanctity of this island. I've taken hard action. It's you who is blind. Look at you now, sitting unphased with that abomination next to you," Viken spat fearlessly.

Locust didn't move a muscle.

"Careful, Viken, or I'll let Locust take her anger out on

you," Fingal responded in a hushed warning. He ground his teeth, barely containing his urge to slap Viken. "Months of planning, months of back-channeling, months of manipulating the right people, and you blow up my summit on a whim. You've drawn the direct ire of everyone Continental."

Viken sat unperturbed, comfortable in his perceived position of power. "The Purists are tired of your politicking. We saw an opportunity to send a powerful message, and we did so."

Locust shifted from one leg to the other while Fingal contemplated the man across from him. *We? More like you,* Fingal thought. *I've clearly underestimated Viken's nature.* Thinking he held Viken under his thumb, Fingal failed to predict the dangerous lengths the man would go. Fingal cursed inwardly. Viken actually killed all the delegates of the Relicus and Novus movements.

And some of our own people! How can Pura Insulam recover from this? How can I recover from this? Fingal knew he'd have to accelerate his plans now.

As he removed his glasses to clean a smudge, another thought struck him, *I could have been killed. The only reason I wasn't in that room is that I was coordinating Locust's attack.*

Fingal narrowed his eyes. "I admit to playing all sides, Viken. What I told you before wasn't a lie. We needed the support of people outside of the Purists." He placed his glasses back on, rose from his chair, and walked to his office window. "I also admit my failures, and I've clearly failed with you."

Fingal could hear the smile in Viken's voice, "We all make mistakes, Oriska. Maybe now you'll support me in our meetings more often."

Oh, now you smile, do you? "I've *failed* with you," he emphasized, "because I knew you might go behind my back, I just didn't think you would be so stupid as to do it this way. I suppose that is the weakness of genius, one cannot fathom idiocy."

"It's your technology loving decisions that are dooming Pura Insulam, not me!"

"Ach," Fingal spat, "must you always proselytize? You know, my father hated the Purists. He viewed your movement like a great albatross about the neck of humanity. He sought to throw off that burden and take us into our next stage of evolution."

Viken rose from his chair angrily, "And how did that go for him? I researched you and your family. I know what happened to the Fingals."

Electric anger coursed through Fingal and he slammed his fist against the window.

Silenced only for a moment Viken concluded, "It looks like you and I will have our power struggle after all. I've been looking forward to it."

Viken flicked his wrist in an effort to turn on his omni, but there was no response from his device. He looked behind him at the door, apparently expecting reinforcements.

"Dear Viken," Fingal mocked, still staring out the window. "You cannot engage in a power struggle when you have none."

Upon completing his sentence, Fingal nodded to Locust before returning his gaze to the window. In the reflection, he saw Viken's eyes go wide before the man turned to run, stumbling over his chair. Locust leapt smoothly over the desk and landed on Viken like a spider. Obscured behind the desk, Fingal could only hear the brief struggle, followed by gurgling noises. After a handful of long moments, Locust stood up and faced Fingal. Her mask was lit a bloody red.

"Did you arrange for Viken's other accomplices to be taken in like I asked?"

"Yes."

"Good," Fingal said, turning. He bent down and placed his hand on the floor for Ballie.

The scalloped ball rolled into his hand, and he stood back up. "We're going to have to spin this—hard. Damage control at its finest. Any thoughts?"

"We could say a cyborg splinter cell orchestrated the attack. That they were angry Relicus and Novus representatives would sink so low as to meet with Purists," Locust suggested, her voice as empty as her mask now looked.

Fingal didn't try to hide his admiration, "That's a magnificent idea, darling! I'll connect with our spin team right away. Perhaps they can mock up a deepfake of the cyborg group claiming responsibility for the attack."

Locust nodded to the crumpled form of Viken, "And him?"

Ah yes, our prating knave. "Lug his guts to the neighboring ocean."

Going Continental

Humans accept and live with death. We, as Relicus, see it in their decision making on gun violence, climate change, substance abuse and more. That's why the advent of Relicus thinking was, and is, so revolutionary. —Arcturus

The electric aircraft hummed, and the props methodically sliced the air—in other circumstances, this would have put Seven to sleep, but right now, every fiber of her being buzzed with energy. Around her, Endymion team sat in silence as the plane climbed higher and higher. Seven wanted to talk about the attack, about Locust, about the reality of her simulations, about all of it, but she could read the tension in the airplane like code and kept her mouth firmly shut, trying to ignore the pain from the scrape on her leg. No one said anything the entire ascent.

Once safely at traveling altitude, a sharp voice broke the silence, "So who's responsible for this attack anyway?"

Blythe, the woman behind the voice, looked like she

wanted to stand and pace, but she stayed in her seat. Skinny, blue-haired and tattooed with curious Egyptian hieroglyphs at her neck, she drew everyone's eyes to her.

Arcturus answered from his seat across from the blue-haired woman, "Blythe, we all want to know the answer to that question, but we do not."

Blythe responded scathingly, "Come on, Arc, you know as well as I do, it was the Purists."

Vulpes, seated next to Blythe, shook his head. "That doesn't make sense. Why would Pura Insulam call delegates to their island only to slaughter them? If what you say is true, Blythe, the consequences for such an action will damn Pura Insulam."

"The bombers looked like augmented humans to me. No offense." This came from Terra—the hulking, muscular woman with a quiet, steady voice. She seemed reluctant to say it and stared down at her shoes immediately after.

"Offense taken, Terra," the portly Radius chimed in, looking like he was about to burst with anger. Then he smiled disarmingly and said, "Nah, just kidding. The bombers definitely had augmentations. What I can't figure out is why we saw the bombers in the first place. Seems peculiar and a bit too obvious." The rotund man nodded toward Arcturus, "What do you think, Arc?"

Arcturus paused for a moment of calculation, brow furrowed. "The obvious placement of the augmented bombers in plain sight doesn't feel like a move Fingal would make. He's smarter than that." Arcturus turned his attention back to the muscular woman, "Tell me, Terra, you're suggesting a member of the Novus movement would attack the delegation like that, threatening the peace built with Pura Insulam and the Relicus movement alike. Why?"

Ponderous shoulders slumped, Terra continued to look at her shoes for a moment before raising her head and looking resolutely at Arcturus. "We've made lots of enemies, Arc. This could be any number of radical groups we've run up against." She shrugged.

"Maybe our new friend knows something we don't." It was Blythe speaking again. She sat quietly since her first outburst, watching Seven the entire time the discussion played out.

Seven sat sandwiched between Trio and Arcturus, and she looked first at Trio then Arcturus. Neither made any attempt to answer Blythe—no help would be coming from them. It was as if they expected her to earn her place on this airplane—her place Continental. Distinctly, Seven felt the weight of everyone's eyes on her, but she smiled internally. Her parents interrogated her numerous times after every simulation. She decided this would be no different.

"I don't know anything about the attack." How could she convince them of her innocence? Her mind searched for something persuasive. "Trio and I were also attacked while at my friend Remy's house."

"You could have staged that attack," Blythe countered, leaning forward aggressively. "Maybe you are a pawn of that fear monger Oriska Fingal."

"Never," Seven responded, her voice turning to steel.

She stared challengingly at Blythe who leaned back in her seat after a moment and ran her hand through her hair.

Blythe shrugged casually. "Don't take it personally, kid. We need to know what kind of person we let into our plane."

See with your eyes. Seven knew Blythe was right, and she talked about this moment with her parents. The three of them knew that the Relicus and Novus movements wouldn't simply accept any Pura Insulam citizen naively. In truth, Seven might never fully be accepted by all the members of Endymion, and she was ok with that. Arcturus and Trio were the only people whose support mattered— it was the two of them that Seven had to persuade.

"That's fair. I can't convince you all that I had no idea of the attack," Seven said, making eye contact with each person in the cabin, "But maybe Trio can."

Trio sat with his arms crossed during most of the discussion, letting his squadmates speak their minds. His words carried weight with the squad, and he used them strategically, Seven saw that many times in their simulations together. It was thanks to those simulations that Seven trusted Trio to back her up. Whatever her parents planned for her, that plan included Trio too.

Trio took a deep breath and uncrossed his arms, "I would be shocked if Seven knew anything about the attack. Besides, I think it is safe to say the Purists orchestrated the attack."

Chatter from everyone on the Endymion team filled the cabin like excited bees, and Arcturus held up his hand for silence. He eyed Trio curiously, "Explain."

Trio looked directly at his boss, "Locust came after us."

Silence. Then Radius whistled.

Vulpes leaned forward, concerned, "You escaped another brush with Locust?"

"Yeah, but that poor Pura Insulam boy's house got more than a brush. His family is going to have another reason to hate the Relicus movement." Trio paused in thought, as if replaying the attack in his head like a video. "Locust wasn't out to kill me though. At first she tried to subdue me without weapons. When that didn't work, she resorted to stun rounds. Fortunately, I had my nano-shield."

"You're one lucky robot, Trio. Since the tidal station up in the Bay of Fundy, Locust has taken no prisoners," Radius said, shaking his head in admiration of Trio. "I heard she killed some guards at a wind farm a few weeks ago—kicked the poor blighters to death."

Vulpes reached across Terra and smacked Radius' arm,

nodding towards Seven, "Shut it about Locust."

Ignoring them, Arcturus said, "We know Locust works for the Purists, and we know the Purists usually respond to Oriska Fingal. This marks an aggressive escalation in their tactics." Arcturus had the cabin's attention. He continued grimly, "The Purists killed six people today in cold blood, all under the guise of diplomacy. We have much to do once we're back in Chicago."

The airplane intercoms crackled to life and a warm voice filled the air, "Arc, you might want to see the reports coming out of Pura Insulam."

Arcturus grabbed a remote and tapped a button causing the wall to his right to light up.

Seven and the Endymion team watched as reports started to trickle out from Pura Insulam—reports of a fringe element of the Novus movement orchestrating a terrorist attack on the summit. Reports of casualties on all sides.

Then Oriska Fingal appeared on screen. Calm, composed, and debonair in a dark blue suit jacket, Fingal was a beacon of ethos.

The host of the show, a blonde woman with unnaturally white teeth, smiled broadly and introduced Fingal and then launched right into the interview, "Tell our viewers what happened at the summit, Mr. Fingal."

"Devastation, death, and anger are what happens when a sacred meeting between peoples is so unceremoniously and viciously stripped away from the great people of Pura Insulam. We have been treated so badly and unfairly for so long, and then, when we open our borders and take a risk, Novus movement terrorists strike at our hearts. Pura Insulam will remember this day forever!"

"Do you have evidence supporting your claim that Novus terrorists bombed the summit on Pura Insulam," the host followed up.

Fingal stared straight into the camera, eyes sharp, "Absolutely, and I'd love to show you that evidence when it's safe to do so."

"Unbelievable," Blythe murmured.

Terra sighed, "That was quick."

"The Purist's propaganda wheel already rolls," mused Vulpes.

"The Novus are going to have some media cleanup to do now. It's going to be chaos," Terra stated, shaking her head.

Radius pointed out, "And to claim casualties on both sides helps others believe Pura Insulam to be victims."

Shaking her head slowly, Seven added, "The people of Pura Insulam *are* victims too. Victims of Fingal."

Arcturus pointedly turned off the wall unit.

****

If she could have, Seven would have memorized every

inch of the terrain on her way to Chicago. The sheer volume of land filled her eyes, and the topography was unlike anything she'd experienced on the engineered island of Pura Insulam. She thought about her parents and how they lived in Los Angeles for some time before moving to Pura Insulam. Seven wished they were with her, but this was a journey she must experience without them.

"You can't grow if you don't meet challenges on your own. You can do hard things," her mother said many times whenever Seven felt like giving up.

After Arcturus turned off the depressing propaganda coming out of Pura Insulam, the Endymion team members retreated to various areas of the airplane seeking privacy, and Seven found herself alone with her thoughts. Her thoughts and an airplane window to a new world.

Some time later, Trio sat back down beside her—he had been in the cockpit with Arcturus and the pilot. "How's the view?"

"It's absolutely breathtaking."

Nodding, Trio continued, "Flumen says we're coming up on Chicago any minute now."

"Flumen is the pilot?"

"Oh yeah, pilot, Endymion mother, and Arcturus' most trusted confidant." Trio's eyebrows raised in exaggerated fashion. "Confidant and then some."

"You're an idiot," Seven said in mock exasperation.

Then she blurted before thinking, "Relicus can find love?" She immediately regretted asking. *Of course Relicus can love, Seven. And you think Trio's the idiot.*

Trio did not take the question personally, "Definitely. In fact, we experience emotions on a broader spectrum than humans."

"What does that mean?"

Trio paused, crafting his explanation brick by brick, like building a house. "Think of emotions like a symphony. In a symphony, there are wind, string, brass, and percussion instruments; however, humans wouldn't be able to hear them all. Let's say you're missing out on the percussion." Trio drummed the air and smiled.

Intrigued, Seven pondered the idea. "So, you're saying I'm getting an incomplete symphony?"

"Not incomplete necessarily. You understand plenty about emotional intelligence, AIs in the Relicus movement simply experience a fuller range." Seven did not look convinced. "Ok, how about this analogy? Dogs can only see two colors of the spectrum—yellow and blue. Humans can see combinations of three colors—red, blue, and green. When it comes to emotions, humans are dogs."

Seven couldn't help but laugh at the analogy. "I don't think you realize what you just said."

Blushing, Trio conceded, "Good point, but I think you get the idea."

"Actually, I think I do. You're saying that Relicus feel

emotions more vibrantly, which is all a roundabout way of saying Arcturus really loves Flumen."

"In his own way, yes." Trio stared out the airplane window, lost in thought.

Seven thought about all her simulation interactions with Trio and how he often spoke reverently of Arcturus... As if Arcturus were a father figure. "Does Arcturus love you?"

Trio remained silent for a long time, looking out the window at the passing countryside.

Choosing to ignore her question, Trio pointed, "We're here."

Seven peered through the window and froze. Chicago was stunning.

Lake Michigan bloomed to the east like a flowering gem, and the city itself shone a vivid green. Greenery everywhere. Nature mixed so smoothly and so creatively with the fabric of the city that the two became inextricably one. Seven couldn't help but feel the city lived.

Buildings sprouted tall and sinuous like stalks of grass, with organic lines gracefully defining one's view. The Chicago River twined through the city like tendrils, and the city grew symbiotically with the river, not in opposition to it. As the electric plane drew closer, Seven noticed smaller buildings shaped after nature: beehives and mushrooms, bulbs and trees, flowers and ant hills. Seven lived on Pura Insulam which looked like a giant jellyfish, so she was used to the idea of architecture mimicking nature, but Chicago was a city unto itself. Pura Insulam was orderly—clearly structured by reason; whereas, Chicago was organic, valuing a relationship with nature rather than dominance.

Trio smiled warmly, "Welcome to Chicago, Seven. This is my home."

"It's more beautiful than I could have imagined."

The intercom dinged, and Flumen's voice again floated the airwaves, "Time to buckle up, my friends. We land in five."

The airplane hummed north along the banks of Lake Michigan as it descended towards a private airstrip. The clacking of seatbelts could be heard throughout the cabin, and Seven gripped her armrests tightly. She'd never flown before, and during the takeoff, she'd been too adrenaline charged to notice. Now, she was fully aware of the landing quickly approaching, and it terrified her.

Trio nudged her with his elbow, "Don't worry. Flumen almost never crashes."

"Not helping, Trio," Seven growled, shutting her eyes as the plane bumped to the ground and rumbled to a stop.

"See, no crash!"

Seven rolled her eyes, "Remind me not to be on board when Flumen does crash."

Endymion team and Seven deplaned on a small runway with an understated building on their left located at one end and Lake Michigan blowing in the wind to their right. Looking about quizzically, Seven was unsure of what to think of her surroundings. It wasn't exactly homey. Behind the industrial looking building was an open reservoir which stood largely empty, like someone drank a cup of coffee down to the dregs. Natural grasses drank in the midday sun, flanking the reservoir along with the rest of the land providing an unassuming quality to the place.

Vulpes stepped near Seven, sweating under the weight of two packs of gear, "Wait for it. It doesn't appear to be much from up here, but looks can be deceiving."

"Endymion headquarters are located on the southerly tip of Northerly Island," Arcturus explained, ushering Seven towards the nondescript building. He didn't look tired—his green and gold suit still sharp, his white beard pristine, and his face set in a determined fashion. "I found this location to be perfect. Close enough to Lake Michigan so that we can easily use its natural abundance to our advantage, and private enough that we aren't bothered often."

Arcturus thumbed a security pad, and a heavy steel door slid open revealing one, large room. Gear was tucked neatly into lockers, a few tables with various blueprints and papers stood near the door, and at the opposite end of the room, elevator doors.

"Drop the gear everyone, and we'll ride down together,"

Trio ordered.

Seven wandered down the room first, as she held no gear, and absorbed the details. Clearly, Endymion did well. She didn't know half the tech she saw, but it called to her like a song. How she would love to explore each device, find its guiding principles, and then make the device bend to her creative will.

Light footfall approached, and a thin, elegant finger tapped the down arrow on the elevator. "Hello, Seven," a warm voice greeted—the very voice from the airplane intercom.

Seven brushed curly hair from her face and looked up at Flumen, a tall, earthy, and garden-scented middle-aged woman. Flumen's nose gracefully accentuated a simple yet lovable face. *The kind of face that kissed you on the brow as she tucked you in for the night*, Seven found herself thinking.

"Nice to meet you, Flumen," Seven smiled sweetly. "Thanks for not crashing the plane. Trio said you usually avoid that."

Flumen's laughter fluted from her lips in the most wonderful way. "Trio is a rascal. I *do* usually avoid crashing—well, there was that time in the Rockies, but that hardly counts. Ask me about it sometime." She winked, "It's a great story."

The elevator arrived just as the Endymion team members finished stowing their gear. Big enough to comfortably hold the whole crew and then some, the elevator appeared to be otherwise spartan. Terra pressed a meaty finger to "B1". A smooth descent began, and Seven found herself staring at Terra's large shoulders.

"Turn around, kid. You'll want to see this," Blythe suggested.

As Seven turned, Terra lifted a dimmer and the whole back wall of the elevator became a window revealing the valley below. It was much larger than Seven first thought and much more beautiful. Steep, rocky walls circumscribed the valley, and a crystal blue lake sat far below. The elevator descended down, approaching the sparkling water.

"Whoa, we're coming up on the water fast. Terra, hit stop! Terra!"

Sliding into the lake like a diver, the elevator continued on unperturbed.

"No way! This is some next level hideout stuff," Seven exclaimed, truly awed. "How far down does it go?"

"Far enough," Arcturus said mysteriously. "Endymion headquarters has a green roof, paired with geothermal and tidal energy. It's entirely self-sustainable. Our underground facilities run throughout the reservoir."

As the elevator approached the bottom of the reservoir, Seven was surprised to see numerous tunnels running along the reservoir floor like streets. *Well mom and dad, I am definitely not on the Jellyfish anymore*, Seven thought gleefully. Continental, Chicago, Endymion, Trio—they were everything she'd imagined they would be and more.

The elevator came to a smooth stop. For Seven, each segment of her journey Continental was a big reveal, doors opening to new wonders. She couldn't wait to see the bottom of Endymion headquarters.

Turning around to face the doors, and Terra's considerable back, Seven watched as the elevator doors opened into a warm meeting area. Most of the walls were bare concrete, which should have given her a cold feeling, yet the furniture and accessories within the area paired perfectly with the concrete to give off a simple, yet welcoming vibe. There was a bright, wooden staircase leading down to another level, and an inviting table suitable for the whole group in the middle of the room. Tucked in one corner where the walls were the same bright wood as the staircase nestled an entertainment area. Seven couldn't help but imagine Arcturus snuggling with Flumen on the couch while the two of them watched videos. The thought was oddly comforting.

Endymion team commenced with spreading out and busying themselves with various tasks. Flumen ushered Seven to the table, gestured to the room and asked, "Do you like it?"

Seven took a seat in a simple, comfortable chair, answering, "It's so simple and inviting. Did you design it?"

Again the fluting laughter, "Do you think Arcturus would spare an ounce of time for decorating? When I joined the team, this place was just a concrete bunker because Arc thinks about tactics almost all the time." Flumen smiled wickedly, "Other times, he's thinking about me."

Seven blushed, feeling like Flumen let her in on a secret. "So what's next?"

"Well, you're going to find something to eat and rest a bit. You've had quite the morning. But first..." Flumen trailed off as her eyes found Arcturus approaching Seven from behind. "You're going to have a chat with Arcturus."

What Arcturus Knows

Our breakthrough research was built upon many previous actions. Major change doesn't happen in a blink. —Steele Ayr

Placing his sturdy hands on the back of her chair, Arcturus loomed over Seven like a well dressed, squat monolith. "Flumen, will you tell Trio to join us?" Flumen quickly squeezed Seven's hand and made to walk away. "Oh, and have the rest of the team beat it. We'll need some privacy."

Seven observed Flumen's raised eyebrows at Arcturus' order but said nothing. Nervously, Seven clasped and unclasped her hands, then shuffled her feet. Stepping from behind her chair, Arcturus walked around the table to sit opposite Seven where he carefully arranged his long, gold cape so that it hung freely by his left side. He waited patiently while Trio took his sweet time—Seven watched him confer briefly with every team member. A clap on Terra's shoulder, a sarcastic joke for Blythe, and on and on until Seven was about ready to climb out of her skin. Finally, Trio came to the table and stood at the head.

"Sit, please," Arcturus gestured to the chair next to Seven, "You need to hear this too."

Trio locked eyes with Seven for a brief moment, and he looked as unsure about what came next as she felt.

Once all the Endymion team members cleared the room, rabbiting down the staircase, Arcturus took a deep breath, held it for four seconds, closed his eyes, and let the breath out. He stroked his ample white beard and rubbed his shiny, bald head. Seven hadn't known Arcturus long, but she gathered that he was the type of person who rarely entertained second thoughts. He sounded like a man of action, not of uncertainty.

He looked uncertain now.

Trio sensed the same uncertainty, asking quietly, "Arc, what is it?"

Arcturus didn't immediately respond; instead, he fiddled with his golden cape absently, eyes far away. Suddenly, he reentered the present and gazed at both Seven and Trio. "You two may have already guessed this, but I need to say it out loud—explain some things—so bear with me." Arcturus paused. "You good with that?"

Seven and Trio nodded in unison.

"Good. The truth is rarely simple and not always easy to hear." He cleared his throat, which sounded like buttering toast and looked at Seven. "I knew your parents a long time ago. One of my first jobs in private security was to guard them at their lab in Los Angeles, a place called Ascension. I didn't know what they were working on at first, it wasn't my place, but I grew to know them. As time passed, I also respected and admired them. They treated me and my colleagues equally, valuing the job we did."

Trio leaned forward, chin in his left hand, interested. Light steps sounded on the stairs and Flumen entered the common area with a tray filled with cups of hot tea and bowls of fruit. Setting the tray down on the table, she gave Arcturus' shoulder a warm touch and left the way she came. Seven picked up a cup of hot tea, allowing the heat to spread through her hands.

Arcturus continued, "Eventually, Steele, Ida, and I grew so close to each other that they shared a great secret with me—their research."

Seven froze with her hot tea hovering right below her lips.

My parents' research. Arcturus knows what it is? Of course he knows, why else would my parents have communicated with him in the first place? Seven's mind raced like an overheating processor, connecting the dots that her parents concealed from her. Slowly, both of her eyes were being opened. Arcturus knew her parents and their research. Which meant her parents communicated with Arcturus regarding getting Seven off Pura Insulam. *How could I be so naive? Once I realized Trio and Endymion were really in my simulations, I should have guessed there would be a connection to my parents' research too.*

Seven glanced over at Trio. His face was devoid of emotion, but Seven knew the vibrant spectrum of feelings he must have been experiencing underneath. Anger at being used. Shame for not seeing this sooner. Surprise at losing some respect for someone you deeply cared for. All of it.

She'd felt all of it too.

"Your parents had been doing groundbreaking work with human consciousness, working towards one end goal: downloading a human's consciousness into a robot body, but not just any robot body—a Relicus body. They referred to Relicus' empathetic hallucinations as an integral piece for the body to avoid rejecting the mind. In other words: immortality." Arcturus stopped. Seven put her tea down, untasted.

Wait. What? Every neuron in Seven's mind froze.

"A Relicus body? Arc, that's us," Trio declared, eyes wide in disbelief as Seven numbly watched him struggle to formulate his thoughts. "How did the Ayrs get a Relicus body?"

Arcturus' face turned to stone at Trio's question, and with the world around her blurred at the edges, Seven couldn't tell if he was furious or broken-hearted. "I considered that question as well, Trio, and believe me, it matters. Downloading a human mind to a Relicus body is..." Arcturus paused, floundering for the right word, real indecision furrowing his brow, "murder to some and evolution to others. I still haven't decided if I'm ok with it because before I could learn anything else, I was abruptly reassigned away from Ascension and away from your parents," Arcturus explained, gray eyes fully present.

"Reassigned by whom?" Trio asked.

"My boss at the time, but she doesn't matter. It wasn't actually her. Think about it."

"Oriska Fingal," Seven murmured, her frigid mind cracking on the name. *See with your eyes.* "He moved you out of the way because you respected my parents and might not like what he was about to do."

"That's right. Shortly after my team and I were reassigned, Steele and Ida 'moved' to Pura Insulam. Permanently," Arcturus added grimly.

Seven watched Trio work to contain himself, anger coursing through his limbs. "Unbelievable. Who knows how the Ayrs obtained a Relicus body! Relicus grow into their awareness. We are fully sentient. To get a body means..." Trio halted abruptly, absorbing the full meaning of his thought process. "And Oriska Fingal... How far does his influence go? Does it have no limits?"

As her mind unthawed, Seven could only consider her parents. Just a short while ago, they were infallible idols capable of amazing scientific and engineering feats. Now, she couldn't decide what she was seeing when she imagined them. Was she seeing the ruined stumps of the childhood idols she looked up to or was she misunderstanding something about their research?

Arcturus doesn't know exactly how the research worked, Seven reminded herself. *If a Relicus dies for the research to work, then I cannot agree with my parents' methods. I have to get their research and see for myself.*

"I cannot speak to the methods of the Ayrs. I sincerely hope I'm missing something regarding how they intended to transfer human consciousness to a Relicus body. It's possible it's not as nefarious as one might think. Bodies could be donated." He paused thoughtfully before starting again. "As to Fingal, his power has limits. He's not a god," Arcturus declared confidently. "If he was, he'd know about our contact with the Ayrs ever since the kidnapping. He'd know about your simulations, Trio, and he'd know what we're going to do next." Arcturus' certainty, which flickered like a small flame at the beginning of their conversation, grew quickly, and its heat warmed Seven's hope better than the tea.

Seven asked the question she knew Arcturus wanted to answer, "What *are* we going to do next?"

A sharky smile flashed across Arcturus' face, "We're going to Ascension lab in Los Angeles, and we're going to get your parents' research. We need to know *how* your parents' research works. From there, we'll decide how to best use it to sink Fingal's plans."

Trio did not look convinced, "How do you know the research is still in the Ascension lab, and how do you know it will sink Fingal's plans?"

Seven thought both questions to be fair, but she also knew they came from a place of distrust. Arcturus manipulated Trio in order to communicate with the Ayrs, and Seven knew all about the effects of manipulation.

If Arcturus sensed any of Trio's distrust, he didn't let on, "I know because Steele and Ida told me they secreted their research away from Oriska Fingal. The research is on Ascension servers behind a biometric key that only an Ayr can unlock." As he said this, Arcturus gestured calmly at Seven.

More secrets, Seven thought angrily. *Of course I'm a secret key to their old research.* Not for the first time, Seven wondered what else her parents hid from her. What other secrets lay just beyond tomorrow, waiting for her to uncover them? *No wonder my parents didn't want me knowing all of this while on Pura Insulam. If Fingal found out, who knows what he would have done with me.* Seven felt an odd combination of rage and relief as it gave her permission to both believe her parents were acting in her best interests and doubt them. They hinted at deeper secrets before she left the island, but she hadn't fully acknowledged the idea because she was blinded by her excitement about going Continental.

My parents are trapped in a cage on Pura Insulam though. A cage forged by Oriska Fingal. There's got to be more to their story that Arcturus doesn't know. A growing unease regarding Arcturus' goals in retrieving her parents' research niggled at the back of her mind. *How am I supposed to stop him from getting the research for himself? Do I even want to save the research for my parents?*

"Wait, wait, wait," Trio uttered, interrupting Seven's reveries. "If the key is biometric, why didn't Fingal just take Steele or Ida back to Ascension and force them to open the research for him?"

Arcturus gave a snort and raised his hands. "Think about it, Trio. I've trained you better than this. Don't let your bitterness towards me cloud your thinking."

Trio looked like he was about to respond angrily, but he visibly forced himself to calm down. He tapped his finger on the table, thinking.

Tap, tap, tap. Then Trio answered his own question, "Because Fingal doesn't know the research exists. If he did, we wouldn't be having this conversation."

Arcturus smiled affectionately, "Exactly. As far as Fingal knows, Steele and Ida tried the experiment at Ascension and failed miserably. Since then, he moved the Ayrs to Pura Insulam so he could keep a closer watch on their progress."

Mind reeling, Seven felt as if there was no more room in her head. Arcturus opened it up like a trunk and filled it to the top with items, leaving Seven to try and squash the trunk shut.

Thoughts rattled in quick succession, *My parents are technological pioneers. I'm a biometric key. I'm going to Los Angeles. Remy would crap his pants if he heard all of this.*

Remy.

Seven desperately wanted to call him and apologize for her behavior before the assassin, Locust, showed up. She also wanted another crack at convincing him he was being brainwashed, to be honest, but she knew calling him was impossible. Her journey led her away from Pura Insulam and its myopia, not towards it.

I'm ready, dad. I'm doing this, she thought with conviction. *And I'm going to do this right.* Seven knew better than to fully trust her parents, Arcturus, or even Trio at this point; however, she didn't have any other options moving forward. Getting to Los Angeles and Ascension required Endymion guidance, but once she got her parents' research, she'd decide for herself what to do with it. Hopefully. The thought of going up against Arcturus and Endymion was too daunting, so she pushed it away. *I can't live on hypotheticals alone. All I have is the present moment.*

"Have they made any progress?" Trio asked curiously.

Arcturus shook his head, "Not that I'm aware of. It's safe to assume they've been stalling somehow."

Seven's curiosity bubbled out before she could stop

herself, and she asked, "Arcturus, how do we get to Ascension? Is everybody loading up to raid the place? Do I get to fly again?"

A small, reluctant chuckle resonated through the comfortable commons space, and Arcturus said with a grin, "Slow down. I'll need time to think and talk about this with the team. I don't even know if all of Endymion can go. We have a nasty storm brewing thanks to the disaster at the summit, but we'll see. For now, you should explore Chicago and find something to eat." Arcturus stood up abruptly, signaling the end of the conversation and walked towards the stairs before he turned around, "I know a good sushi place by the river, if you'd like." He disappeared down the stairs without waiting for an answer.

Trio sighed. "I'll tell you one thing, Seven, there's no limit to what Arcturus knows."

Sustenance

Simply existing feels safe for AIs, but it's not. It should be our last choice because it's the path of least resistance. We deserve better than existence; we deserve sentience. —Arcturus

Trio, Seven, and Radius walked along the moderately peopled Ping Tom Memorial Park skirted by the South Branch Chicago River on their right. Radius apparently heard that Trio would be taking Seven to Larry's Fish and Shrimp, and he jovially insisted he come along. It wasn't a sushi place like Arcturus suggested, but Seven didn't care.

Chicago dazzled.

Buildings gracefully intertwined with nature, suggesting a rhythm Seven adored. She spied a honeycombed structure with garden greenery assembled in every hexagon. Delicate, whiplike designs undulated along the sides of storefronts and apartments. On the river, sailboats drifted calmly, looking like dragonflies in the waning light of late afternoon.

Seven paused to consider what she wasn't seeing—like on Pura Insulam, was Chicago laced with propaganda or underground corridors where drones delivered items house to house? Finding that hard to believe, Seven shook her head in wonder.

Chicago differed starkly from Pura Insulam due to a distinct lack of distractions. No ginormous, digital billboards dominated a building's side; instead, the city flowed with nature, eager and inviting. The Jellyfish was a technological behemoth, a manifestation of humanity's will over nature. Chicago represented humanity's oneness with nature.

"Larry's Fish and Shrimp is dead ahead," Radius said, nearly drooling in anticipation.

Seven eyed Radius' rotund belly and smiled, "You're a big fan of food, huh?"

Shrugging amiably, Radius responded, "You could say that, love. I had a taste enhancer installed a while back, and I haven't stopped stuffing my gob since."

The three of them were nearly at the restaurant, but Seven had to hear more. "A taste enhancer? You've got to tell me more about that."

"It's simple really. The enhancer amplifies certain flavors that I customize with an application. Sometimes an especially trendy restaurant will suggest the best settings for its menu. I've been dying to try Larry's." Rubbing his belly and gesturing to the restaurant, Radius said excitedly, "Now, let's go eat some seafood!"

The meal was delicious. Seven ate plenty of seafood on Pura Insulam, so she was no stranger to its flavors. However, she found that watching Radius enjoy his meal in an almost euphoric state really improved her meal as well.

Licking his fingers one by one, Radius heaved a satisfied sigh. "Mmmm. I've got my seafood customization just right. Trio, I'm telling you, get a taste enhancer. You won't regret it."

Silent and reflective most of the meal, Trio looked up from his half-eaten shrimp. "No thanks, Radius. I'm good."

Seven couldn't help but notice Radius' fingers as he licked them, as each was a different color, including his thumbs. It was as if he dipped each finger carefully into an assortment of different paint cans.

Seven observed his fingers earlier but didn't have the courage to comment on them. After getting to know Radius in person, she felt safe enough to comment now. "Radius, can I ask you a question?"

Sliding his empty plate aside, Radius plopped his elbows down on the slightly wobbly table and leaned forward. "Of course."

"Why are your fingers different colors?"

Radius wriggled his fingers before his face, studying them as if seeing them for the first time. "Blimey! Would you look at that," he exclaimed in mock amazement. He held out his hands for Seven to inspect. "Each finger is augmented for a different purpose."

Seven turned Radius' hands over and back again, looking for distinguishing features besides their color—seams or ridges or metal. She saw none of that. The design was incredibly subtle.

Trio, unable to help himself, interjected, "The yellow one is obviously for picking his substantial boogers."

Radius removed a hand from Seven's grasp and held up a thick, orange, middle finger to Trio, "I bet you can figure out what this one's for, mate." Looking back at Seven and pointedly ignoring Trio pretending to pick his own nose, Radius continued, "One is a magnet, one a compass that sends me vibrations when pointed due north, a few others are for gesture control of various drones, and the rest? They're for me to know and you to not find out." He pulled his hands away.

"What? Come on, Radius! I'm new to augmentation, and I want to know."

And she really was curious. Radius was of the Novus movement and friendly enough, so Seven wanted to see as many augmentations as possible. She wanted to know where the human ended and where the machine began.

Trio put a calming hand on her forearm.

"It's ok, Trio. The newcomer here doesn't know the ins and outs of Continental yet." Radius looked seriously at

Seven, losing the easy mirth he carried with him during all of their outing. "It's considered impolite to ask probing questions about someone's augmentations." Waving his hands in the air as if searching, he continued, "It would be like asking what kind of underwear a person has on."

"And then asking to see them," Trio added.

Blinded by her own curiosity, Seven had not even considered what she was asking after and the impact that might have. "Radius, I'm so sorry. I didn't know."

"Of course you didn't! You've been stuck in a bubble." Cheerfulness appeared on his face again like a bird returning to its nest. "Blythe is ruder than you, and she's a Novus who's lived Continental her whole life."

Seven liked Radius—his face was friendly, and his congenial nature was just what she needed after the trauma of leaving Pura Insulam and finding out her parents researched the transferring of human consciousness to a Relicus body. Trio was good company too, albeit moody, but Seven understood his pensiveness. She was having a hard time not thinking about all the implications of her parents' experiments.

The sun dropped past the blue umbrella the three of them ate under, and she peeked at her omni to see the time. It would be full dark soon, but Seven didn't feel like returning to Endymion headquarters just yet.

Seven noticed Radius tense up, "Seven," he said cautiously, "What's that?"

Radius pointed at the omni on her wrist, and she held it up for him to see more clearly. "It's my omni. Why?"

Trio sat up abruptly, and Seven started to feel nervous. Trio asked, "Where did you get it?"

Seven frowned at the caution in his voice. "I made it myself. At home. With spare parts from my parents' lab."

Tension slipped out of both Trio and Radius like balloons deflating. "That's good," Radius smiled reassuringly.

"I've got to be more careful. I'm not sure how I missed it," Trio chastised himself. "Had that been Purist's technology, it's possible Oriska Fingal could have tracked you down with it."

Seven looked at her omni with new eyes—aware now that Fingal's reach could extend further than she imagined. Yes, she'd made her omni, but did she have anything else on her person that could lead to trouble? She didn't think so, but that feeling of being watched, a feeling she knew all too well thanks to living on Pura Insulam, returned like a rash. Seven suddenly felt unprepared for this journey.

"What else should I know about?" Seven asked earnestly. "I'd rather not continue to make a fool of myself."

"Why not, people do it all the time," Radius cracked.

Trio grinned and pointed at Radius, "Even fools are right sometimes."

"Do you need to see one of my fingers again? Maybe this time the whole hand?"

Seven rolled her eyes, "Guys, focus."

They were trying to ease the tension they no doubt felt as well. Seven appreciated the effort, but she needed to learn more.

"Let's walk and talk," Radius huffed while standing up. "I need to burn off that shrimp."

The three silently meandered back northeast towards the park until they found a comfortable little gazebo, twined with vines and overlooking the river.

Leaning against a post, Trio picked up the conversation as if it never stopped, "It's impossible to fill you in on everything. Plus, what I choose to elaborate on might not be what you're interested in, so why don't you start?"

Why don't I start? Yeah sure, no problem, Trio. I'll just ask you the thousands of questions that have rolled through my head since I can remember. She didn't exactly know what she should start with. She nurtured a burning desire to learn more about the Relicus, that was certain.

Do Relicus poop? The thought popped into her head so quickly, she was startled that's what came to her first. *Get a grip, Seven!* She took a deep breath.

There was something she was curious about for a long time, and hearing that her parents' research included a Relicus body, she had to know.

"How are Relicus made?"

Trio nodded his head as if expecting the question. "That's a good first question. Did Pura Insulam not teach you this?"

Seven scrunched up her face, "Do you really want me to trust my Pura Insulam education?"

Radius laughed, "She's got a point, mate."

Trio smiled and folded his arms. "Fair enough. For starters, Relicus aren't made, we awaken. What I think you're really asking is, 'How are AIs designed?'" He looked to Seven for confirmation, and she nodded. "AIs are designed for a multitude of purposes—e-commerce, education, travel, physical labor, security—the options are endless. Sometimes AIs have physical forms like all of us on Endymion team." Trio paused as if expecting Radius to make a joke before continuing, "And sometimes AIs are systems or programs. Also, you should know, not all AIs awaken, and not all awakened AIs join the Relicus movement."

Seven's head buzzed with new information, and she actively worked to catalog Trio's words against her years of propaganda on Pura Insulam. Fortunately, her parents' uneducation helped her discard the lies of the Purists more easily. She couldn't imagine Remy trying to work through all of this new data.

Sifting through all the possibilities, Seven asked the first question that occurred to her, "Do AIs remember all of their existence, even before they're awakened?"

"We do, but asking after an AI's history can be as delicate as asking after a human's. Ask Arcturus, and he will likely tell you about his past. Terra however? I still don't know her history."

As Trio spoke, Seven watched Radius sit down on a wooden bench shaped like a tree branch, apparently content to let Trio explain the nuances of AI existence while he watched the Chicago River flow silently.

"Ok, got it. So asking about an AI's history is like asking what kind of underwear they have on," Seven clarified.

From his spot on the bench, Radius quipped, "She's a quick one."

Ignoring him, Seven pressed Trio for more, "On Pura Insulam, we're taught that AIs like you don't age. Is that true?"

"Actually, yes. I am what I've always been... Physically at least. The same goes for Arcturus, Flumen, and Terra," Trio explained, pushing off the post and standing up straight.

Seven pondered the surreal idea of looking exactly the same her entire life and found it oddly unsettling. She liked growing up, and she liked the idea that her maturation was both a physical and mental process.

"Now, you're wondering who would be so cruel as to design an ugly bloke like Trio, aren't you?" Radius razzed.

"You are absolutely no help," Trio retorted, shaking his head. "Although, that does make me think of a question for Seven." Trio leveled a dramatically sober gaze on Seven and asked, "How old do you think I look?"

This has got to be a trap. "Um. 20?"

"And how old do you think I *am*?"

Trio's question gave Seven pause, and the more she thought about it, the more she realized she had no clue. *If AIs like Trio do not age, then it is entirely possible for Trio to be significantly older than 20. Or significantly younger.*

As Seven pondered, a boat with sails like a dragonfly's wings calmly drifted down the Chicago River, stealing her attention.

"I really don't know," she finally said.

"Good answer," Trio remarked before smirking. "Oh, and don't bother asking how old I am. A gentleman never tells." Seven opened her mouth to protest, but Trio spoke first, "Ask another question."

Frustrated with Trio's answer, Seven wanted to pursue his age further, but she didn't want to offend him. She guessed that his humorous answer was likely armor that he used to protect himself from painful memories.

Let's try a different approach then. "Do Relicus die?"

A few moments of silence trickled by, carried along by the current of the river. Radius looked to Trio expectantly, as if to say, "Good luck with that one."

"That depends on what you mean by death," Trio mused quietly.

Seven thought about that for a moment before saying,

"If Locust killed you at Remy's house, what would have happened to you?"

"My body most likely would have been destroyed by the Purists." Trio paused. "Or worse, it would have been dissected for close study." He shivered involuntarily.

"And your mind? Your consciousness? Your soul even? What would happen to that?"

Trio ran his hand through his blonde hair and looked to the sky, which was slowly being populated by stars. The atmosphere surrounding Seven, Radius, and Trio was one of reverent quiet. "My data, my coding, my memories—the experiences that make me who I am are stored somewhere. My body could be remade and my consciousness, or soul if you'd prefer, could be restored."

Somewhere, Seven noted. *Why won't he tell me that somewhere?*

Seven thought that maybe that is what her parents were after. If they could somehow code an entire person's consciousness, perhaps they could follow the Relicus' process of restoring data. Deep in her heart, there was a tinge of revulsion at the thought, as if immortality were some line humanity should not cross, but Seven wouldn't deny the allure of permanence either.

I wonder what the Relicus would think of my parents' research. Arcturus didn't seem enthused by the idea, and Trio was clearly repulsed by it. These were delicate questions she didn't feel comfortable asking yet, and Seven didn't want to hear the answer if it damned her parents.

She wanted to ask why Trio said he "could" be restored instead of "would," but he was already talking again in a solemn manner. "It's likely that I do not view death in the same way as humans. For you, it's final. For me, even though death is the opposite of life, it's still a part of life. We Relicus are not free from death, so much as we are free from the idea of death."

Radius let out a low whistle and ran his hand over his close cropped, brown hair. "I need a drink."

"What do you think of death, Radius?"

Arching an eyebrow, Radius leaned toward Seven who was standing beside the bench. "What do I think of death, love? I think death is dreaming." He slapped his knees and stood. "Right then. That's enough of that. Let's go home."

What Blythe Knows

Awakening is only real when shared. —Arcturus

"Arc, you can be a real cold prick sometimes, you know that, right?" Blythe steamed.

She was the only member of Endymion team who talked to Arcturus like that. *Then again*, Arcturus thought, *she talks to everyone like that.*

The two of them were alone in Arcturus' lab in Endymion headquarters, and Arcturus had been trying to convince Blythe of his Ascension plan. It was not going well. At all.

Blythe paced to and fro in front of Arcturus' desk as he watched her calmly from the windowsill, dark blue waters shimmering behind him. Arcturus waited. Knowing Blythe well, she'd need to vent her suspicions like a pent up volcano. Then she'd likely refuse him flatly. Once the magma of her doubts cooled, Arcturus hoped he'd be able to reason with her.

"I mean seriously," she continued hotly, "you want me to convince Trio and Seven to leave for Ascension without you? Without Endymion? They'll never go for it."

Blythe's face was red with consternation, a stark contrast to her blue hair. Had Arcturus been more like Radius, he would have cracked a joke. Instead, he pressed his back against the cool glass behind him.

Now is actually the perfect time, Arcturus thought, knowing Trio was upset with him and primed to rebel.

"You can go with if that would help," he suggested, sensing Blythe would hate the idea.

"Oh sure, I'm just the one to go gallivanting across the country," she mocked, her words lit with sarcasm. "Vulpes, that red headed simpleton, is much more likely to suggest something like this to Trio."

Arcturus allowed himself a smile while Blythe's back was turned to him. "That's exactly why it has to be you, Blythe. Vulpes is too obvious, and Trio would likely see through him."

Venting a loud sigh mixed with a groan, Blythe spun on Arcturus. Her green eyes looked like flames as they narrowed in. *Here it comes.* "What are you up to here? What's your angle? You've always got an angle."

Blythe was a naturally suspicious person, Arcturus knew, and he loved having her on the team because he knew she'd question him regularly. When he first met her, she'd been an angry, young augmented human looking for a cause. Now, she was an angry, young augmented human who joined the Novus movement. The difference was subtle but immense.

****

The Novus movement was well established in Los Angeles when Arcturus began his work at Ascension labs. He was glad for it as the Novus movement paralleled the Relicus movement, which he had been passionately involved in ever since he'd held his dead partner's wetware in his hands that dark night in front of Boston Robotics.

Despite being well established, not everyone agreed with the Novus and Relicus views. The two movements pushed cooperation amongst humans, augmented or not, and AIs, and they supported all sentience, arguing that consciousness was simply a shared assumption.

Additionally, both groups adopted generational thinking—the mindset that stressed that decisions made today should result in a sustainable future for multiple generations. This mindset became Arcturus' self-assigned prime directive. If he could ensure that future Relicus would have it better than he did, then he could call his awakening a success. On a deeper level, it wasn't enough to simply be awake. He needed to wake others.

And that included augmented humans. Which included

Blythe.

****

Arcturus first met Blythe at a rock concert at the Hollywood Bowl where she was beating the snot out of a fellow concert goer. Her blue hair danced about wild and free while her fists drummed a harsh rhythm. As he approached, he couldn't tell what thumped harder, Blythe's fists or the bass from the music.

"That's enough," he called, voice rumbling with the beat.

Blythe paused mid punch and looked up at Arcturus with venom in her green eyes. Red and blue lights flashed over the scene, illuminating Arcturus as he stood over the scrum. Blythe scanned his security uniform before slowly rolling off the bloodied man under her. The man whimpered and crab walked away from his assailant, sliding through spilled drinks and sweat.

"Stay right there," Arcturus directed, pointing his finger like a magic wand.

There must have been sufficient iron in his voice because the man froze, not even bothering to stand. *Let's see if I can't get to the bottom of this without the blue haired woman knocking this guy's teeth out.*

"So what happened?"

"This idiot called me a sexbot and tried to grab my butt," Blythe spat, rising to full height.

Feeling the righteous anger radiating from her in waves, Arcturus imagined he could almost see the air around her steaming. Her emotion felt authentic and powerful. Arcturus turned to the man, "Is this true? And don't lie to me, I'll know."

It wasn't an empty threat exactly. Arcturus found that with his empathetic hallucinations, he felt other people's emotions acutely, and people often masked their fears with lies. He sensed this man's fears roil in his own stomach, mixed with the heady feeling of the blue-haired woman's sense of justice.

The man looked back and forth between the blue haired woman and Arcturus before nodding his head in affirmation.

"Beat it before I walk away and let this woman pummel you some more," Arcturus ordered.

The man scrambled to his feet and disappeared into the pulsing mass of concert goers.

The crowd ebbed and flowed to the beat as one giant entity, a hive mind of sonic euphoria.

Arcturus turned his attention to the blue haired woman. "What's your name?"

"Blythe," she shouted over the crashing music.

"Come with me, Blythe."

****

Arcturus walked Blythe to a small room set aside for security. Inside were a few folding chairs bumped up to a table and a cooler full of bottled waters. The music could be heard through the walls, offering a muted reminder of what the two of them were missing out on.

"Would you like a water?" Arcturus offered, gesturing toward the cooler.

Blythe ignored the offer and stood by the door. "Why am I here?"

She doesn't mince words, Arcturus thought. "Aside from the fact that I found you pulverizing a man's face?"

"Sure, besides that."

"You're augmented, correct?"

She was wearing a black leather jacket with a high collar, and her face and head weren't visibly altered. Arcturus guessed at her augmentation like he knew it to be true.

If Blythe was startled by Arcturus' quick change of subject, she didn't show it, nor did she shy away from revealing she was augmented. "Yeah, and you're not a normal security AI."

Arcturus walked to the cooler and grabbed a water bottle. He wiped the excess ice off the bottle before tossing it to Blythe. She caught it with a frown, and Arcturus thought she might throw it back at him. Instead, she opened it and took a deep drink.

"Have you heard of the Novus movement?" Arcturus asked, changing subjects once more.

"Again—yeah." She waited for Arcturus to say something before rolling her eyes and adding, "Why?"

"Because I think they could use you."

"You don't even know me. What do you know about who could use me?"

Arcturus could sense the curiosity he'd lit within her. *Or at least I think I can sense it*, he cautioned himself. Sometimes evaluating human emotions was difficult, like when a human cried with joy or gave an evil smile.

He flicked a bead of water off his hand. "You seem smart. Do I really need to spell it out for you?" Blythe sneered at him. *Ok, then.* "If you're willing to beat someone up for a small slight, what lengths will you go to for a real cause?"

Now Blythe snorted. "A real cause. Like the Novus movement or maybe the Relicus movement," she added slyly, giving Arcturus a knowing look. "I don't buy all that awakening garbage."

Arcturus smiled. "Of course you don't. You know everything, right?"

****

On the windowsill in his lab, Arcturus endured Blythe's intense glare, working hard to give nothing away. Inside his head, his memories of Blythe played like motion pictures.

Blythe did not simply join up with the Novus movement immediately after he'd met her.

It took much longer to chip away at her skepticism; however, she did join up with Endymion when he offered her a position, claiming she needed the money. Arcturus saw through that. She needed to belong. She needed a group that valued loyalty. And once Trio joined, Arcturus knew she'd stay for good.

Blythe's voice brought Arcturus back to the present moment, and he saw her shaking her head, "Arcturus, did you hear me? I said 'what's your angle?'" She snapped her fingers at him. "What's going on in that chrome dome of yours anyway? Your face is like a blank stone sometimes. It's annoying."

She's ready to give in. "First, the Ayr research is of a *delicate* nature. It's best for the Relicus and Novus movements if we can keep an eye on it. Second, I want Trio to have the chance to awaken further."

"Ok, that first reason is completely nebulous, which is typical Arcturus. I know I won't get the details from you, and frankly, I don't care." She shrugged. "If you want to 'keep an eye' on the research, that means it's dangerous, and I'd rather we controlled something dangerous. As to your second reason—that awakening nonsense again?" Blythe turned and sat in Arcturus' chair. She absently rubbed at the scarab tattoo on her neck. "Arcturus, you know I don't buy that."

"Which is another reason why Trio will not suspect my hand in this. He knows you don't agree with me on awakening."

Watching carefully, Arcturus thought he saw a moment of doubt crack her sharp facade.

Then Blythe lowered her voice and said, "It will be dangerous, Arc. Fingal and Locust likely know Seven is safe with Endymion. They'll be looking for her."

Arcturus knew Blythe's concern wasn't entirely for the girl she'd just met in person. It was mostly for Trio. "I know, but if Trio is going to grow, he'll have to face dangers...without me. It's the best way."

"Best way or your way?" Blythe jabbed before shaking her head dismissively. "And Seven? You're willing to send the girl off with just Trio and me as protection?"

Arcturus made a mental note that Blythe included herself in the trip and that she seemed genuinely concerned for Seven. *Maybe she cares more for the girl than I thought.* "Seven is the only way into the lab. She has to go. Besides, the rest of Endymion will be following right behind you."

Scrunching up her face in confusion, Blythe asked, "If you're just following right behind us, why not come with us?" She thought for a moment and added, "And why not just trust us to get the research on our own?"

"Because Trio must *lead* this and because, like you said, it's dangerous. Endymion needs to be close by." Arcturus left the "just in case anything happens" bit unsaid. "If you're worried about reasoning, we can say you had a change of heart and messaged me shortly after you left."

Blythe rocked the chair back and forth with her right foot, then stopped abruptly. "Ok Mr. Tactics. You've got me pegged to run this mission. Why should *I* do it?"

Arcturus went through hundreds of different answers to this question, and there were numerous possibilities with a high probability of success. Only one answer met his logical criteria and his empathetic readings of Blythe.

"Because you love Trio." Arcturus rose from the windowsill and shrugged, "And because if you don't do it, I'll find someone else who will."

Youthful Rebellion

Love is carrying a child in your womb. Strength is giving birth. —Ida Ayr

Back at Endymion headquarters, Seven was shown her accommodations and told to get a good night's sleep. None of the other team members were around—likely they were holed up somewhere making big plans for her future. *My future and the future of my parents' research.*

Not for the first time, Seven reflected on her unbelievable position—staying with a group of people she didn't really know in order to rescue groundbreaking research she'd never seen. The implications of it all were immense, and they all hinged on Ascension.

The style of her room matched what she came to understand as the overwhelming norm in Chicago—intuitive simplicity mixed with elements of nature. A white wall joined with a wooden wall which connected with a concrete wall creating a pleasant atmosphere. A soft bed was tucked in the corner with a wooden end table and white lamp. The room temperature was perfect, apparently controlled geothermally.

Seven opened a closet door and was surprised to find clothes waiting for her. Flumen must have anticipated her needs. The motherly act reminded Seven of Ida, and she felt a pang of homesickness. Standing with that emotion for a bit, Seven rolled it around in her mind like one might roll a hard candy about in one's mouth. *It's ok to feel a longing for my parents and crave independence at the same time.*

Pulling on comfortable blue pajama pants and a matching long-sleeved shirt, Seven crawled into the toasty covers of her bed and waited for long hours before a fitful sleep finally came.

Seven woke of her own accord, feeling groggy and out of sorts. She sat up abruptly, looking around for something familiar, some kind of touchstone from her old room on Pura Insulam that would bring her back to reality, but after a few panicky moments, she remembered everything—the simulations, the summit, the escape, the first time she saw Chicago. Her parents' research. All of it. *And there's so much more to come.* Home as she once knew it could no longer provide touchstones for her. She needed to create new memories separate from Pura Insulam.

Thirty minutes later, she left her room feeling bright-eyed and excited for the day. She found an absolutely stunning wine-colored pant-suit adaptation with flowing pant legs, a leafy silver belt, and supple, brown boots. The outfit had the same swirly stars design as Trio's suit the day before. Seven felt very much like a princess who might be going for a morning horse ride, not that she'd ever seen a horse in person before. Her Zero was as close as she'd come to actual horsepower.

Stepping lightly up the staircase that led to the common room, Seven heard pleasant conversation, the kind of discussion that only happens in a safe place where everyone feels like their authentic selves. She smiled.

Vulpes was the first to notice her as his spot at the table faced the staircase. "Well, look who has decided to grace us with her presence," he teased, offering Seven a chair and a cup of coffee. "How do you feel this morning?"

Trio, Flumen, and Arcturus were also at the table, enjoying a light breakfast of toast, strawberry jam, and fresh oranges.

Seven smiled, "My father always said, 'Seven, you open two gifts every time you wake up: your eyes.' My eyes opened this morning, so I'm doing good." Her voice dropped numerous octaves in an attempt to sound like Steele, and Seven thought her impression was quite accurate.

Flumen offered Seven an orange, which Seven took gratefully. "Your father is right. Every day is a new beginning."

Peeling the skin from the orange, Seven filled the air

with a fresh aroma and looked about the room. Terra stood at the kitchen sink doing dishes. She wielded the scrub brush like a baton, as if she had to beat the dishes into submission until they were clean. Blythe and Radius sat at the couch playing some sort of digital strategy game, and Radius kept manipulating the game board with his various finger augmentations. Seven thought Blythe was going to punch the man in the jugular; instead, she laughed acidly and won the game anyway.

The whole morning scene created a wonderful sensation of togetherness, a feeling Seven shared with her family. Somehow that feeling never spread beyond her house though. The people of Pura Insulam identified with the island, but they typically excluded others, watching them with a wary eye. Seven realized she didn't feel that in Chicago the night before. She walked the streets feeling like a participant in the goings on of the world at large. *Could that underlying sense of togetherness be real?*

She wanted more of that feeling.

"What's the plan for today?" Seven asked after swallowing a ripe segment of orange.

Arcturus, dapperly dressed in another suit, this one sky blue, deftly maneuvered his yellow cape out of the way as he stood. "You can do whatever you want, kid. I need to continue making plans for our trip to Ascension." He gestured to Trio and smiled, "Trio is an excellent tour guide."

Trio quietly sipped his coffee, apparently enjoying the warmth it provided, and he looked up at Arcturus' invitation. "Absolutely, I am. I've heard that a morning walk is the best way to start the day. Seven, you in?"

Grinning, Seven stuffed the rest of her orange segments into her mouth and said, "Definitely!"

Vulpes rose from his seat, "Mind if I tag along? It's probably safer if you two had a third person with you."

Excitement dampening, Seven swallowed her orange slices with a gulp and asked worriedly, "Are we in danger here? I guess I assumed the Purists weren't pursuing us after the attack."

Vulpes held up a calming hand, "It's unlikely Fingal knows of this location because Endymion's business runs out of a building in downtown Chicago, but we can never be too careful when it comes to Fingal."

"So it's possible someone could still be after you all?"

Trio slid his chair back and stood up too, "Anything is possible with Fingal; however, being Continental and being in Chicago does offer a certain amount of protection. Fingal wouldn't be so bold as to have the Purists attack Relicus and Novus in this city. The people would rise up and squash Fingal's movement easily."

"Trio's right. Pura Insulam's status with the U.S. is tenuous at best. After their attack at the summit, the Purists will need to lay low for a while," Vulpes added.

Her worries only slightly abated, Seven stood up and

said more confidently than she felt, "Then let's go for a walk!"

****

Walking with Vulpes and Trio comforted Seven. Unlike Radius, who filled most of her outing the day before with cheerful chatter, Vulpes and Trio carried a companionable silence on their walk. Seven could tell that these two trusted each other completely, probably a bond formed during long hours together on security jobs. The two of them didn't need to constantly talk; instead, they spoke only when necessary, allowing Seven to see and feel Chicago.

For her part, Seven didn't feel much like talking. A sensation of youthful rebellion pulled at her desires, urging her to do something, but she didn't know just what yet. Letting the walk calm her, Seven examined her feelings, picking them up like an antiques collector, curiously studying each one. Residual anger, worry, excitement, fear—her mind discarded each of these emotions as they weren't causing the unrest in her mind. Now frustrated, Seven stuffed all the emotions to a corner of her mind for the moment and let her surroundings sink in.

Vulpes suggested a walk north along Lake Michigan towards Navy Pier. Numerous people were out enjoying the weather, but it didn't feel crowded. The salty scent of fresh, blue waves to her right called invitingly even though the heat of the day had not arrived. Trees lined the trail, and there were plenty of grassy areas where people reclined or sat on benches enjoying a morning beverage.

Seven had a thought and broke the silence the three shared, "Guys, tell me about Blythe's tattoos. The ones on her neck."

Trio and Vulpes looked a bit surprised, and Trio answered, "They're just that. Tattoos. They relate to her heritage, but you'll have to ask her about them yourself if you want the story."

"So there is a story," Seven pressed curiously. The wind from Lake Michigan skittered through her curls, and she pushed hair from her face.

Vulpes grinned knowingly, "With Blythe, there's always a story, and it's usually full of trouble." Scratching behind his ear like a dog, Vulpes continued, "Why do you ask?"

"I want one," she said, spinning around to look at Vulpes and Trio while she skipped backwards. "Yeah, I definitely want a tattoo or an augmentation of some sort."

Trio smiled, "Easy there. Turn around before you fall on your butt and embarrass Vulpes. He hates to be embarrassed in public."

Seven spun again and slowed her gait to meet the pace of Trio and Vulpes. Now that she'd said she wanted an augmentation out loud, she realized that's the feeling she was after—disobedience. Pura Insulam limited so much of her life without her really knowing it, and now that she knew, she needed to rebel.

Trio looked at Seven, seeing the determined set of her jaw and laughed, "You're serious, aren't you?"

Seven answered with a look that said, "Did you even have to ask?"

"Ok, well, let's take it slow, Seven. It's your second day Continental. Your second day free from Pura Insulam. Feeling a bit of teenage rebellion isn't a surprise," Trio explained.

"Trio, don't try to analyze me," Seven said, pushing Trio lightly into Vulpes, causing them both to stumble slightly. "Are you going to help me with this or do I have to figure it out myself?"

"I'll help you. I'll help you," Trio agreed, righting himself. "Vulpes, what do you think?"

Vulpes, currently apologizing to a lady he almost ran off the trail after he'd lost his balance, reentered the conversation, "If I don't help, Seven will likely push me in the lake next. I'm in. However, I do have to ask—what would your parents think?"

Seven hadn't considered how her parents would feel. In fact, she felt a bit guilty for not thinking about her parents enough since arriving Continental as everything moved so fast. She'd been caught up in her own needs. Were they ok? Did they know the full extent of the Purist's plan for the summit? Questions without answers, and it seemed unlikely Seven would be able to call her parents to ask them. A splinter of guilt lodged further into her mind, and she actively worked to ignore it.

"Vulpes, my parents kept me in the dark much of my life. I think they'll survive if I make a few of my own decisions."

The three of them walked on in a moment of quiet interrupted by the squawk of seagulls drifting through the air.

"What kind of augmentation did you want, Sev?" Trio asked curiously.

Seven opened her mouth to answer, then clamped it shut again. What did she want? Her options were nearly limitless, that much was clear. She was Continental, where Radius could augment each of his fingers to a different use. Continental, where the Relicus and Novus movements were possible. Continental, where her mother and father worked to download human consciousness into a Relicus form. *Maybe I should take this slow.*

"Let's stick to a tattoo," she hedged. "Not just ink though. A tattoo with some tech."

"We should have brought along Blythe," Trio reckoned.

"Right, if you wanted someone who'd make fun of every suggestion you made," Vulpes quipped.

"Is she really that bad?" Seven asked tangentially.

Vulpes shook his head, "No, she's really not. Blythe has

a sharp exterior and a sharper tongue. If you can dodge her cuts, you'll find she's loyal and fiercely protective."

Not hearing the aside between Seven and Vulpes, Trio mused aloud, "There's E-ink tattoos, biosensitive inks, smart tattoos that can measure your biometrics, and other tattoos that link to any device. Does any of that sound appealing to you?"

A ferris wheel spun slowly, tourists noisily boarded cruise ships, and restaurants simmered with smells as Seven, Trio, and Vulpes approached Navy Pier. Seven pondered her options seriously—did she really want to put technology in her body? It seemed a rather permanent rebellion. *Maybe I should just get a haircut*, she thought half-heartedly. *No, this is my body, and this is my life. I'm doing it.* Seven considered asking both Trio and Vulpes if they had any augmentations but then remembered her conversation about the delicate nature of augmentations with Radius. This was a choice she must make for herself.

"How about something that will link to my omni and be a memento of my parents?"

Trio appeared to contemplate the idea. "Sounds like a digital tattoo to me. That could work. Vulpes?"

"I know of a place that does great work with digital tattoos. It's only a short ride away. I bet I could get you in right away. The owner owes me a favor from a job a while back. Do you want to go now?"

Seven pondered for a moment before shaking her head

and skipping ahead of Trio and Vulpes. "First, I'm going to ride that ferris wheel over there," Seven exclaimed excitedly.

****

Hours later, after a delicious, gourmet hot dog, numerous ferris wheel rides, and a breathtaking run through a funhouse maze, Seven found herself in the Code of Conduct tattoo shop. It was a busy place when Seven, Trio, and Vulpes entered, but now they were tucked neatly into a private room decorated with photos of tattoos. What followed was a brief explanation of the process the tattoo artist would use to embed the interactive tech into Seven's skin, which would allow her to store and share information digitally. Seven sat in a black chair very similar to the one she used to sit in at her hair stylist's shop on Pura Insulam, only instead of the snipping and buzzing sound of scissors and electric shavers, she listened to her hospitable tattoo artist named Winsome describe the story behind one of her tattoos.

With a high, feathery voice, Winsome explained, "Anyway, after I was caught out at night without any light, I decided to tattoo a tiny solar panel around my neck in the shape of butterflies. Whenever I need a light, I just tap this button at the base of my throat and the butterflies light up delightfully," she finished with a showy tapping of the button. She grinned widely as the butterflies lit the room with pinks, blues, and greens.

Seven laughed, "That's amazing! Although, I don't think I'm ready for a solar panel in my neck, but I do have an idea."

Flicking her wrist, Seven turned on her omni for everyone to see. She manipulated the device until a video of her parents showed up, dancing across the skin of her forearm.

Her parents looked much younger, and their voices were happy, full of light and hope. "Hi, Seven," Steele beamed. He spoke from their living room on Pura Insulam, and it looked much the same as it did today.

Ida was practically glowing, always dignified. "Hello dearest Seven. Your father and I just found out that I'm pregnant with you. We are home from the doctor's office, and we wanted to make you a video." Steele's chocolatey hair was longer and not a streak of gray could be seen. From where he sat on the couch, Steele's knee was bouncing excitedly, and Ida elbowed him. "You're shaking the camera, Steele."

"Sorry. I'm just so excited," Steele said, not looking sorry at all.

"We wanted to say we love you," Ida purred sweetly.

"And we can't wait to see what you can do, future daughter of ours," Steele added warmly.

The video disappeared from her forearm, and Seven

brushed a tear from her eye, shifting uncomfortably in the cushy black chair. She'd thought of the idea for the tattoo while riding the Ferris wheel around and around. At one point, the ride stopped so that Vulpes, Trio, and her were at the apex, and Seven could see the enormity of Lake Michigan before her. It reminded her of the infinite ocean view she saw when perched on her favorite spot outside the Pura Insulam library—like riding the edge of the universe.

Trio and Vulpes suddenly found the tattoo art on the walls extremely fascinating, while Winsome placed a comforting hand on Seven's shoulder. "It's a beautiful video. Send me the data, and I'll get to work," she directed with a squeeze.

Seven knew the inspiration of the tattoo and the rebellious act of getting an augmented tattoo were rather paradoxical, but it made sense in her mind. The further she got from her parents, the more she learned about herself, and the more she learned about herself, the more she realized she loved her parents, no matter their faults.

Seven twitched on her omni again and shared the mock up she'd made of the tattoo along with the data for her parents' video. She'd created the mock up on her omni swiftly and haphazardly while standing at the edge of Navy Pier, staring out over the azure waters, and she hoped Winsome would be able to do something with it. Wheeling her chair to a monitor in the corner, Winsome got right to work designing the tattoo and downloading the data.

As Winsome worked, Trio meandered over to Seven and whispered, "The video was powerful. Thanks for allowing me to see it." Pausing for emphasis, he added, "That shows trust, and I won't abuse it."

Winsome wheeled back to where Seven was seated with a small, handheld scanner in her hand. "I just need to do a quick biometric screening to ensure nothing is out of the ordinary and that my digital tattoo will sync nicely with your body."

"Ok," Seven concurred, beginning to feel a bit nervous.

Winsome methodically and rhythmically waved the scanner to and fro along Seven's right forearm, which was the future location of her tattoo. As Winsome waved, she frequently checked a monitor, which apparently displayed Seven's biometric readings. Trio and Vulpes visited quietly in a corner while staring at yet another picture of a tattoo, and Seven watched Winsome's face closely as she scanned. Winsome's brow furrowed slightly in surprise, and she tapped a few buttons on the screen. The facial expression came and went quickly and subtly, leaving Seven wondering if she'd really noticed anything at all.

"Something wrong?" Seven questioned quietly.

"Not at all," Winnie answered honestly, "You're all synced up. Quicker than anyone else I've tattooed." She smiled as an explanation and shrugged, "The process varies per person."

Seven looked to Trio and Vulpes, but they missed the exchange. *I'm sure Winsome knows what she's doing,* Seven told herself as Winsome wheeled back to her corner monitor. *See with your eyes.* Winsome's back was turned to Seven as she worked, and nothing seemed out of sorts. In fact, Winsome hummed a tuneless song as she diligently prepared Seven's tattoo. *I'm more nervous than I thought.*

Seven tried to push the odd tickle at the back of her mind away, but it remained, stimulating her neurons in a way she knew better than to ignore. *Could there be something I'm missing? Maybe the fact that I'm a biometric key disrupted Winsome's readings?* Seven's mind was a mess of thoughts, careening from one corner to the next, and she struggled to organize them into coherent lines of reasoning. *Or maybe there's something else my parents' have hidden from me. Maybe I'm different...*

Before Seven could pursue that particular thought further, Winsome rolled her shoulders like a prizefighter before a fight and reached for the rotary tattoo machine. She spun in her chair, looking completely at ease, "Ready to see what I've mocked up, Seven?"

Trio and Vulpes came closer to offer support through proximity.

No, I'm not ready! "Ready."

Flipping a screen so Seven could see, Winsome

produced an image of Seven's potential augmented tattoo. Vulpes and Trio looked impressed.

"Well done," Vulpes extolled.

Trio's mouth gaped.

Seven nodded along, swept up by the impressive nature of the tattoo displayed on the screen. It was a perfect circle containing an artistic rendering of the seven layers of the known universe. The outermost layer was thin and black as night, followed by a ruddy red line that merged into a pink and white weave like the iris of an eye. Next came a ring of colorful galaxies spiraling on a black backdrop, and in the center, Earth's solar system. Completely absorbed by the totality of the image, Seven did not at first see the cunningly included sound wave that laced across the diameter of the tattoo.

The tattoo was sublime.

Winsome proved to be a talented, painstakingly detailed artist as she free handed much of Seven's tattoo. For Seven, surprisingly, the process wasn't as painful as she'd imagined it would be. For much of it, she visited with Winsome (who spoke little while working), Trio, and Vulpes about the future of tattooing, which took her mind off the pain and eased her chaotic mind.

After an hour, Winsome stopped her rotary tattoo machine and stretched out her back like a cat. "Ok, Seven, now the 3D printer will fill in the rest of your tattoo within a few minutes," she explained, taking Seven's arm and inserting it into what looked like an automated sewing machine. Next, Winsome firmly cinched Seven's arm down so it couldn't move, typed in some protocols for the 3D printer, and nodded as it whirred to life.

"How are you doing, Seven?" Vulpes asked, rubbing his sunset stubbled chin anxiously.

Seven gave herself a few seconds to actually assess how she was feeling and answered, "I'm good, Vulpes. Seriously." And she was good.

During the tattooing process, Seven reminded herself that her parents were loving people who had her best interest at heart. It hurt when they withheld information from her, like the truth about the simulations, traveling Continental, or their research, but she also understood the dangers of knowing that information now.

Winsome looked at Seven knowingly and hooted, "Of course she's good. This process would have taken days before the advent of an automated, 3D tattoo printer. Now, she'll be done in time for dinner."

Several minutes later, her arm was released from the maw of the printer, and Seven looked at her tattoo, admiring the edge of the universe on her forearm with her parents' sound wave echoing through the center.

I love you mom and dad, no matter what you've hidden from me.

Ransomware

Ethics are for the gullible. —Oriska Fingal

Oriska Fingal knew the seductive power of words. Sensible people bent to his will when he found the right word, the right intonation. Logic and reasoning are great persuaders, but they paled in comparison to a word that strikes the soul.

Words built the Purist movement, slowly and pervasively, as Fingal led his fledgling empire. He'd chosen the Purists purposely because their zealotry made them more susceptible to manipulation. Fingal could sing the notes of their ritualistic songs, and money would flow in.

Now, he was intimately involved in something truly transformational: the Ayrs inched closer and closer to changing the world. *And I will be right in the middle of it,* Fingal promised himself.

Scratching his chin lazily, Fingal waited for

confirmation that the money was transferred to his off-shore accounts—that his demands were met. He'd chosen a car manufacturer of middling success due to their archaic approach to cybersecurity, and all he had to do was gain access to the company's system, which hadn't taken long. A simple phishing email landed him entry through a sales associate's account. With the ignorant associate's user credentials, Fingal and his crew of hackers were able to infect the car manufacturer's entire system, locking down a massive number of the company's files.

Then the dance began. The hunt for the right word, the right intonation to crack the company. Back and forth Fingal and his hackers messaged the CEO of the car manufacturer, providing details on where to send the money and a deadline. A firm deadline which was quickly approaching.

Ballie perched on the desk, a casual observer.

2:53pm.

Fingal would either receive the million dollar ransom or he'd move on to the next mark, leaving the company's files locked up and inaccessible.

He hadn't always demanded such a pricey number. In the beginning, after his parents died and he was left penniless due to their ambitious research, Fingal floundered through life. He clumsily stumbled from one mark to the next, grifting enough money to pay for food and rent, barely avoiding prison.

"Oriska?" a toneless voice questioned from the doorway behind Fingal.

Swiveling his chair around, Fingal looked at the beautiful, almond-eyed Hypatia. She was an oddly quiet and emotionless woman, but Fingal knew her to be ambitious—almost as ambitious as him.

Checking his watch, Fingal drawled, "Hypatia, you're just in time. LB Manufacturing is about to send us one million dollars."

He gestured to his computer, and Hypatia entered the small office, rounding the desk to stand beside him. Her hair fell in tresses, bound neatly by a golden band circling her head. Fingal watched her almost sleepily, eyelids heavy. It was just the two of them (and Ballie) in a poorly lit office which Fingal maintained on the cheap. Unlike his glorified daydreams from the past where he imagined himself in luxurious settings surrounded by party goers, the real business of hacking often occurred in rather mundane settings. *Demagogue me gets the parties; hacker me gets the boring office.*

The beautiful girl helps though, Fingal mused. "That's a unique earring," he added out loud, craning his head upwards. "Is it a harp?'

2:56pm.

"It's a lyre." Hypatia kept her eyes on the computer screen, and Fingal imagined her willing the seconds to tick by.

"A lyre? What's the difference?" Fingal asked, honestly intrigued.

"Size and origin." Hypatia nodded toward the computer screen. "I don't think you're going to get your money."

"Our money," Fingal emphasized, drawing out the vowel sounds.

He had yet to find the right word, the right intonation for Hypatia. She came to the Purists willingly enough and at an impressionable age, yet Fingal couldn't crack her cool exterior. She seemed more emotionless than the first AIs.

"And they'll pay. They don't have the time or resources for an extended holdout. Lawyers are expensive, you see. Paying us on the other hand, is comparatively cheap."

Fingal rolled Ballie around unthinkingly with his forefinger.

2:58pm.

By the glow of the computer screen, Fingal and Hypatia watched the seconds tick quietly by. Neither spoke nor moved. Perhaps Fingal should have felt more nervous. The truth was, he needed more money: for the Ayrs' research, for sending Locust Continental, and for his future plans. *Amazing how I can burn through money.* Viken's decision to bomb the summit and the subsequent fallout caused a massive rift between Fingal and some of the Purists, especially the ones with deep pockets. His precarious funding with the Purists didn't matter as much now. He was much more established on Pura Insulam presently than he was when planning the creation of the island. And there was the continued success of his ransomware team—*There will always be another mark.* That was the allure of ransomware, as long as he kept one step ahead of cybersecurity, there would always be some oblivious company to take advantage of.

The computer chimed and a text box appeared. Hypatia let out a small breath, the only indication that she cared about the outcome of this ransom at all. "Looks like they broke."

"No, we would have broken them if they held out. I'm still in their system, and if we ever need another infusion of money, we know where to go." Fingal gestured Hypatia to the door. "Don't ever break the bank if you can get the bank to work for you instead."

Ready Room

My prime purpose is to help AIs, and if I can't help them, at least I won't hurt them. —Arcturus

That evening at Endymion headquarters, the whole squad gathered for a meal, and Blythe coaxed Seven to show off her tattoo.

Blythe grinned wolfishly, pulling her blue hair back into a loose ponytail to bare her neck tattoo. She crooned, "You've seen mine. Now, let's see yours." The Egyptian hieroglyphics shone gold and green around the scarab tattoo that clung to her throat.

Seven blushed, contemplating whether she wanted to share the tattoo or not. She didn't feel particularly reticent to share the actual tattoo on her forearm, it was the accompanying video her parents made for her that gave her pause. That video was for her and her alone. She'd allowed Trio and Vulpes to see it as they were on the tattoo journey with her, but she wasn't ready to show every

Endymion member. Not yet.

Blythe's eyes were boring into Seven, causing Seven to forget the baked chicken, mashed potatoes and salad sitting on her plate.

She pulled back her right sleeve, sighing in mock exasperation, "Ok, ok."

She stuck her arm out over the table, right above the salad bowl. A chorus of approval skipped across the table causing Seven to smile despite her embarrassment.

"That is some seriously good ink," Blythe admitted.

"And your forearm hardly looks red at all," Radius mused. "You're a quick healer!"

Quietly, with a forkful of chicken enclosed in her large hand, Terra spoke before anyone else could make another comment, "It's beautiful, Seven. When you're ready, I'd love to see the accompanying sound wave."

The table went silent. Noticing the sound wave quickly, Terra subtly provided Seven a comfortable way of keeping her parents' sound wave to herself. It was a deeply intuitive and kind gesture.

"Thank you," Seven murmured, nodding respectfully across the table to Terra. "When I'm ready."

Dinner continued more seriously after that with conversation shifting to upcoming jobs.

Arcturus explained a potential job out in California protecting a wind farm, but Seven hardly listened. Garlic danced across her nostrils as she shoveled mashed potatoes in her mouth and chewed thoughtfully. Clearly, Arcturus spent time planning other jobs, and Seven wondered if he'd come up with a plan for her trip to Los Angeles. It had been two days since she'd arrived Continental, and Arcturus hadn't been forthcoming since that first night he revealed he knew her parents. *How long will I have to wait? He could at least let me know a timeline.*

Flumen's voice brought Seven back to the conversation, "It's a big wind farm, Arcturus. I don't know that Endymion has the resources to defend it all."

Arcturus nodded, dabbing at his lips with a napkin. "You're right." He paused and sipped some wine. "We might have to sit this job out."

Seven leapt at the opportunity, "Does this mean you'll have more time to plan our trip to Los Angeles?"

The tenor of supper changed immediately, and Seven noticed everyone's attention perk up. Apparently, the whole Endymion squad was wondering the same thing. Silverware clinked down, and the team stopped eating— everyone but Radius. He forked a hefty chunk of chicken into his mouth, beads of meat-sweat forming along his forehead, his eyes never leaving Arcturus. No doubt Radius tuned his taste enhancer perfectly prior to the meal.

Hiding what Seven assumed was the tiniest flicker of annoyance, Arcturus took another slow drink of red wine before answering. His peanut buttery voice held no anger when he spoke, "We're getting there, Seven. Trust me." Arcturus pushed his plate aside and continued smoothly, "We cannot simply walk into Ascension. Plans have to be made. Palms have to be greased. Transportation must be obtained. It's not a trip to the library."

Still no answers. Not even a hint of a detail. Seven experienced this kind of planning with her parents before the summit, and she did not enjoy it. Sitting in the dark while someone else planned her future set fire alarms off in her head. If she didn't act, she'd be burned.

"I just want to know something. My parents left me out of a lot of planning, and I'm not about to let that happen again," she declared, surprising herself with the amount of steel in her voice.

Next to her, Trio shifted in his seat, bouncing his leg ardently under the table. "Seven's right. This isn't a typical job where the planning is mostly top down. It's personal. Clue us in, Arc."

"Just say it. You're still upset I didn't share what I knew about Seven's parents," Arcturus countered, casually leaning his chair back on two legs and waiting to see how Trio would respond.

"That and the fact that you are still leaving information out. Where would the Ayrs get a Relicus body? Why did their experiment fail? Why did they just leave with Fingal? What aren't you telling us?" Trio said "us," but Seven knew he really meant "me."

Fireworks seemed imminent until Flumen calmly interjected, "Now is not the time, boys." She looked firmly at Arcturus and Trio. "You two will need to respectfully talk about your feelings later." She iced the word "respectfully" for extra emphasis and continued, "Right now, Arc, you need to tell Seven something." Arcturus opened his mouth to retort, but Flumen held up her hand and railroaded over him, "She's just left the only home she's known. She deserves some input."

Radius cleared his throat, likely dislodging some chicken in the process, "I've gotta say, I agree, boss."

Vulpes nodded agreement from his position at the end of the table. Blythe looked at Arcturus noncommittally, shrugging her thin shoulders. Terra said nothing, allowing the drama to unfold. Arcturus looked around, baffled by this seemingly unforeseen onslaught from most of his team.

Arcturus' chair clunked down onto four legs. "Well, thanks for your input, everyone," Arcturus said, looking put out. Seven noticed him give a brief glance to Blythe before he abruptly stood up causing the chair to groan across the wood floor. "You're all going to have to sit this one out though."

With that, Arcturus marched over to the stairs and descended without another word. The remaining Endymion team members sat in silence. Trio, although he tried to hide it, smoldered with anger, and Seven, sitting next to him, burned as well. They made twin flames that nobody dared touch.

Radius nudged Terra and whispered, "You gonna finish that chicken, love?"

****

The elevator doors almost shut before a trim hand sliced in to stop them from closing. As the doors slowly slid open, Blythe's sardonic smile was revealed, inch by inch.

Exasperated, Seven sighed, "Oh, give me a break."

"Thought you were going to sneak out while we were doing the dishes? Come on. You're stuck with us, whether you like it or not," Blythe replied, stepping into the elevator next to Seven.

"Hold up," Trio called, hustling to slip in before the doors shut again.

"Anyone else want to come to my pity party?" Seven inquired sarcastically, eliciting only a sheepish shrug from Trio in response.

The elevator quickly and quietly hummed up through the reservoir waters and splashed out to unveil an inky-black, evening sky. Seven tried her best to pretend she existed alone in the elevator. She stared at her nails, fiddled with her hair, and pointedly admired the night sky. When the elevator doors opened to the ready room, she stepped out first, heading straight for the exit.

She was moving so fast that her nose rammed into the door when it didn't open to her push, and she bounced back in surprise.

Not turning around, Seven snarled, "Blythe, not a word."

Huffing, Seven whipped around. Blythe held her face purposely frozen, like a raccoon caught digging in the trash at night. Trio let the tiniest of snorts from his nose, which caused Blythe to cough out a laugh as well.

Before long, all three of them were laughing together until Seven's laughter turned into crying. Seven noticed Blythe roll her eyes as she began packing a backpack that looked similar to an armadillo shell.

Still blubbering, Seven picked up a small dragonfly-shaped drone, examining it absently. "What am I even doing here? This is like some ridiculous dream that I can't wake up from." She waved the drone about wildly as she spoke.

Trio approached Seven calmly and leaned against the table next to her. He snagged the small drone from her hands and raised an eyebrow. "This," he set the drone down carefully, "is expensive. We don't need to give Arcturus another reason to distrust us."

Seven inhaled a bubble of snot. "Yeah, he's a real trusting guy."

Blythe, her packing finished, slung the backpack over

her shoulders and proceeded to clean her sidearm.

Trio rubbed his left palm with his right hand. "Arcturus has this," Trio said haltingly, searching for the right word before continuing, "idea about Relicus life. He believes we Relicus thrive off experience—as if it's the only way we grow. All experiences, the positive and the negative, lead us to an awakening."

No longer crying, Seven was only confused. "You mentioned awakening before. Trio, what are you talking about?"

"My point is that most AIs change at some stage in our development. Once we've experienced enough life, our consciousness opens up, we see the world in new ways, and we achieve true autonomy. Remember what I told you by the river, not every AI is awakened, and not every awakened AI joins the Relicus movement."

Frustration sizzled through Seven, burning away her self-pity and confusion, "I remember... Pura Insulam never taught us that."

Blythe loudly snapped her sidearm's clip into place and approached Seven. "There's a lot those morons don't tell you. An uneducated populace is a controllable populace." Blythe deftly holstered her firearm and concealed it under her jacket.

Trio pushed off the table he was leaning on and continued, "Arcturus thinks the best path to awaken a Relicus further is through suffering. It's how he awakened, and how he's awakened others." Walking to a separate table and absent-mindedly packing his own armadillo-like backpack, he clarified, "So, I think Arcturus is purposely hiding his plans from us, from me, because he doesn't want to shield me from suffering."

Seven looked to Blythe for a clue in how to respond, but the blue-haired Novus simply stood quietly. Suffering as a path to awakening seemed cruel upon first glance, but as she thought about it, Seven recognized some truth. Steele and Ida protected Seven from a lot of suffering, simply by living on Pura Insulam; however, Seven realized they weren't protecting her from pain so much as they were postponing pain. She just endured a small breakdown due to her inability to handle the stress of her current situation. Maybe if she'd been better prepared and forced to push through more adversity earlier in her life, she'd feel more equipped to handle her journey to Los Angeles. *Then again, we shouldn't put a measuring stick up against each other's suffering.*

Who's to say how much someone should suffer?

Seven rose from the table, "Wow. I think you just short circuited my brain."

"Tell me then, young philosopher," Blythe directed at Trio, "if Arcturus has a plan that includes your suffering, don't you have a right to know?"

"I have no idea," Trio admitted. "And I'm not ashamed to not know."

Blythe clapped Trio on the shoulder, "Nor should you be. A good leader admits when he doesn't know something. Only an idiot pretends to know everything. You know, like Radius." This brought a smile to Trio's lips, and Blythe fired another question. "What would your plan be? No Arcturus to lean on. Just Trio's formidable intellect."

Seven watched Trio ponder this question for a moment as he finished packing his backpack. "It would be a small team, no more than three." He swung the backpack on. "We'd pack light and remain inconspicuous." Blythe casually handed Trio a sidearm, which he unconsciously tucked into its holster. "We'd take the hyperloop and—"

Trio stopped, and Seven saw realization bloom on Trio's face as he was already fully prepared for this plan and so was Blythe—backpacks packed and sidearms loaded. They looked at each other, not saying a word. A current of electric understanding passed between them. Seven could almost smell the burning, coppery scent.

Seven's eyes flitted between the two of them. "What am I missing here? Are we leaving?"

Blythe nonchalantly opened the doors to the Chicago night air and responded, "Yeah, we're leaving. Watch your nose on the way out."

The Bystander Effect

Relicus do not lose faith in others. Sentience is an ocean; just because a few drops in the ocean are dirty does not mean the ocean becomes dirty. —Arcturus

Seven, Trio, and Blythe rode in an electric, driverless car heading for the hyperloop station. A million questions flitted like hummingbirds, but Seven kept them caged in the confines of her mind for the moment. She was finally headed to Los Angeles, to her parents' lab, and she felt like if she broke the silence, the sudden action that swept up Trio and Blythe would fall away like leaves in the wind. To Seven, Trio's decision to secretly obtain her parents' research without Arcturus and the rest of Endymion seemed risky, but she also felt much more confident about keeping the research for herself without Arcturus around.

Outside the window, Chicago at night breathed life into the air, a steady thrum of humanity living in relative harmony.

Trio stirred in his seat across from Seven. He was dressed in a matching, earthy, olive green leisure suit, complete with vest, suit jacket and brown scarf. Somehow, he looked unassuming and formal at the same time. Trio unfolded and folded his legs, his brown, high top sneakers only lightly scuffed from use. Seven came to understand Chicagoan style mirrored their environmentally friendly ways with natural colors and nature inspired innovations. She changed out of her princess-like pant suit combination before supper in order to be in something more comfortable, which turned out to be dark brown knee-high boots, with loose fitting, billowy, cream colored pants. Her blouse was a shade darker than the pants, and she wore a navy blue sweater to protect her from the wind. Blythe threw her a mahogany colored satchel on the way out, which Seven slung over her shoulder. *Flumen's taste is impeccable*, Seven raved to herself as she made a quick inventory of the items in the bag: protein bars, a change of clothes, and an assortment of tech, including a small, glass data disk.

Blythe wore all black, form fitting pants and tank top, and while zipping up her black jacket, she nudged Seven, "We're almost there." Her emerald green scarab tattoo shone eerily below her throat.

Seven scooched to the edge of her seat, craning her neck about in order to catch a glimpse of the hyperloop. "What is this thing anyway? I haven't heard of a hyperloop before."

"That's because you lived on a floating thimble," Blythe retorted.

"The hyperloop applies magnetic levitation technology to a train system. Elevated vacuum tubes reduce resistance so that pods can reach almost 630mph," Trio explained as if he were the engineer responsible for this feat.

"630mph in a tube? How fast do planes fly?" Seven asked curiously.

"Some commercial jets can fly up to 575mph," Trio answered as the car whizzed around a corner with a tall skyscraper looming over the road.

Up ahead, Seven noticed a circular building. The whole structure was made of glass that mirrored the night lights of Chicago magically, making the building's surface dance and shimmer. On one side, Seven could see numerous tubes exiting the building like arteries, held aloft by 'v' shaped concrete foundations.

The hyperloop station.

The electric car whirred to a halt in front of the station's entrance, and the group hopped out, approaching the entrance. Sliding doors parted and revealed a hive of action. Kiosks for tickets were staggered to the right with escalators and stairs to the left. Trio quickly purchased three tickets for Los Angeles, and the three of them slowly rode an escalator up to the loading area. Seven panicked momentarily as they approached the security checkpoint, but Blythe and Trio confidently flashed Endymion credentials. The guard studied their credentials on his screen before giving them the green light to move on, including Seven.

"What was that?" Seven asked. "I didn't show any ID."

Ahead of her, Blythe spared her a brief glance, "Perks of the job, jellyfish girl."

Trying to think of a witty reply, Seven stopped short as she entered the boarding area.

Hundreds of gates filled a grand, open space with a glass ceiling. People moved about in an orderly fashion, trying to find their gate. Each gate held a coach pod, business pod, or lounge pod, which would then autonomously drive itself to the appropriate exit as determined by the passenger's e-ticket, where it would be coupled with four other pods heading in the same direction. The hyperloop was an engineering marvel.

Some distance behind her, Seven heard a woman angrily shout, "Hey, take it easy! There are plenty of pods."

Seven turned to see the hooded black mask of Locust 20 feet behind her. Flashing red lines like shattering glass erupted across the mask, and Locust gathered herself to leap.

"Trio!" Seven thundered.

Trio, about to enter a pod, spun around starting towards Seven, but there were too many people between the two of them.

Locust sprang through the air, graceful and deadly, sailing over a stupefied security guard. For a moment, she buzzed in the air, floating like some mechanical insect backlit by the Chicago lights, then she careened down towards Seven. Seven raised her arms instinctively, but no impact came. Impossibly, Blythe caught Locust in her hands, like a reed withstanding a falling boulder. A loud hiss followed and steam rushed out of the arms and neck of Blythe's jacket, blowing her hair up like a blue halo.

"Help," Seven pleaded to those around her. "Help us!"

Bystanders looked about confusedly, and some moved quickly away from the angry struggle occurring in front of them. Many stumbled backwards into Trio, who fought futilely against the crush of people.

Still being held aloft by Blythe, Locust struggled to free herself before she planted her grasshopper legs into Blythe's chest and kicked her away with the force of a mule. Blythe skittered and tumbled across the floor as if she were a blade of grass tossed in a storm. Her skull cracked against the floor, and she stopped moving. Locust rose slowly from the ground, turning menacingly on Seven, but before she could advance, numerous hands clasped her wrists, elbows, biceps, and waist. The hands were followed by a press of Chicagoans answering Seven's pleas for help. Locust's powerful legs pumped forward, carrying the people with her a few steps, and for a moment, it appeared she would break free before more

Chicagoans piled on. Letting out a feral scream, Locust fell to her knees, heaving against the press of the crowd.

"Seven, come on," Trio bellowed. "The pod is leaving."

Finally free of the backwards advance of people, he grabbed the battered Blythe under the arms and dragged her to a pod.

Seven gave one last glance at Locust struggling under the weight of humanity. Locust's mask went black, but Seven could feel the assassin's eyes tunneling into her from behind the mask. Running to Trio, Seven picked up Blythe's legs and helped Trio lurch her into the pod before the doors slid shut. A moment later, the pod began to move.

Trio and Seven propped Blythe up in a chair, and she groggily blinked her eyes. Blood trickled down the side of her head, down her sharp jawline, and onto her scarab beetle tattoo. Green to red. Unable to look away from the red trail, Seven stood like a planted tree until Trio grabbed her by the shoulders and sat her down too. In a daze, Seven watched as he took a seat next to Blythe, rubbing his temples.

The pod circled around the station, heading towards the hub where it would be joined with three other cars in a transporter.

As if from far away, Seven heard herself asking, "Can Locust get to us now?"

Trio let out a wry snort, looking defeated, "You sure you

want to ask me?"

Eyes closed, body unmoving, Blythe mumbled, "Shut it, Trio. Wallowing doesn't suit you."

"Blythe! Are you ok?" Seven asked, compassion fluttering in her voice like a moth.

One eye peeked open, but Blythe stayed splayed out in her chair, "Is that genuine care I hear in your voice? And here I thought you didn't like me." Blythe sat up with an effort, placing her elbows on her knees for support. "I thought Locust was going to kick my heart out my back. My whole chest will be purple tomorrow, but I'm fine."

"I think we're ok for the duration of our trip, Seven," Trio said, apparently regaining a bit of confidence. "If Locust escapes hyperloop security, and that's a big if, she'll be too late to join our transport." Trio pointed outside the window behind Seven.

Turning, Seven watched as their pod joined with three others and was smoothly enclosed in a transporter, which immediately began accelerating through the hyperloop tube towards Los Angeles. A relieved sigh whooshed from Seven's lips.

Blythe gingerly unzipped her jacket and surveyed the damage tenderly with her left hand. "I think we can safely assume Locust knows where we're going. We'll need to be in and out quickly."

Nodding agreement, Trio added, "You two should get some rest. It's about a three hour ride."

"You don't have to tell me twice, boss," Blythe groaned as she tapped a button to recline her chair. She appeared to fall asleep as soon as she became horizontal.

Blood still trickled down her cheek, slowly starting to congeal. Trio noticed, walked over to Seven's pack, removed a first aid kit, and grabbed some gauze. When back beside Blythe, he gently dabbed the blood causing her to moan half-heartedly. He continued treating her until all the blood was gone and a bandage was placed over the cut. Seven watched the whole procedure, moved by Trio's concern for his squadmate.

"Will she be ok?" Seven whispered.

A worried look crossed Trio's face, yet he nodded, "She might be concussed, but I've seen her recover from worse. She's as tough as kevlar."

He leaned back in his chair and looked pensively out his window where a baleful moon shone dully.

Outside Seven's window, the city of Chicago quickly receded into the night as the transporter reached maximum speed. Inside, Seven tried to process what just happened in the hyperloop station. Somehow, Locust tracked them to Chicago and followed them to the station. *How long was she in Chicago? Maybe she was simply watching us and reporting back to Oriska Fingal, but when we went to the station, we forced her hand because she didn't want to lose us.* Then Seven had a grim realization—Arcturus informed her that she was a biometric key to her parents' research.

Perhaps Fingal knew of this; Locust attacked her first after all. *Did Fingal not want her to retrieve her parents' research? But if that were the case, that would mean Fingal knew the research was in Ascension labs all along.* Struggling to make sense of it all, Seven admitted she had no clue. Wheels within wheels. Codes within codes.

The internal machinations of Fingal and Locust were a mystery to her, but the young man across from her, every day spent with him revealed his altruism more and more. Blythe, Radius, Vulpes—they all trusted Trio explicitly, and she could see why. He often listened first, spoke authentically, and displayed a wide range of empathy.

"Trio," she said in a hushed tone across the dimly lit pod. "Thank you for being a friend. From the beginning of our simulations to now, you've supported me. That shows trust, and I won't abuse it," Seven remarked, echoing Trio's words to her in the tattoo shop.

Some people struggle with compliments, attempting to brush them off or present a front of abject humility. To his credit, Trio did nothing of the sort. He simply looked at Seven, a soft smile playing on his lips and replied, "You're welcome."

Seven spent much of the trip avoiding sleep, curled up on her reclined chair in the fetal position, staring out the window at the Continental countryside. Too curious to sleep, she watched as Illinois, Iowa, and Nebraska passed in a moonlit blur of midwestern plains. When she could no longer absorb any more countryside, she turned her gaze inward—on Blythe.

The angular woman rested in her chair, headwound neatly bandaged by Trio, and Blythe's stillness stood out starkly with the speed with which Blythe moved when catching Locust.

Catching Locust. What a remarkable phrase to even think. How did Blythe do that? Seven studied Blythe as the blue haired woman slept, but Blythe kept her jacket on, revealing nothing about her arms. *They have to be augmented. There's no other way.*

Without opening her eyes or moving a muscle, Blythe murmured, "I don't like to be watched when I sleep, unless the person watching me has earned it."

Startled, Seven bumbled over her words, unable to form a coherent response.

Blythe opened her eyes and slowly sat up. "Relax, Sev. I'm kidding." She rubbed her chest gingerly. "Mostly. Well, I can't sleep anymore, my chest is killing me, and you can't sleep either—obviously—so ask me what you want to ask me."

Regaining her composure, Seven contemplated how to best ask Blythe about her augmentations. She clearly remembered Radius and Trio's lesson regarding the etiquette of Novus culture. *If I'm not careful, I'll end up asking Blythe about her underwear.* As Seven's internal debate continued, Blythe leaned forward in her chair across from Seven's, a frank look on her face, and Seven realized that look wasn't the look of someone who cared much for cultural norms.

"I wonder if you'd be willing to share with me how you caught Locust?"

Blythe smiled, no hint of the sneer she usually kept loaded at the side of her mouth, and painstakingly removed her black jacket. Underneath her jacket was a black tank top, and in the dimly lit compartment, Seven could hardly see anything remarkable about Blythe's arms.

"You're going to have to come closer. I am the injured one after all."

Seven quickly glanced at Trio as she rose, but he slept on soundly. She approached Blythe warily, like a kid approaching a dog for the first time, and as Seven neared Blythe, her eyes caught subtle lines along the woman's arms. Seven paused a few feet away, unsure.

"Go on, take a closer look."

Blythe raised her arms out like a zombie, and Seven brought her nose to within a foot of Blythe's outstretched limbs. Barely perceptible gold lines could be seen running from Blythe's fingers all the way up to her shoulders, mimicking the musculature of human arms. *Incredible.*

In an awed voice, Seven whispered, "I can barely tell you have any augmentations."

Blythe lowered her arms and shrugged. "It's a stylistic

choice. Some augmentations are flashier than others, purposefully obvious in their differences. Me, I prefer to flash in other ways."

Not for the last time, Seven noted Blythe's blue hair, golden hieroglyphics, and emerald scarab tattoo. *Yeah, you do.*

Thinking back to the moment Blythe caught Locust, Seven asked, "So the steam that rushed from your jacket, that was from your arms?"

Blythe nodded and pointed to Seven's chair. Seven returned reluctantly. "Yes, my arms can generate a lot of power, but like a computer, they need vents to release the heat created within them." She slid her jacket back on and zipped it up. Blythe arched an eyebrow and looked at Seven. "Does that sate your ever-present curiosity, jellyfish girl?"

It did indeed. Seven smiled at Blythe, and the Novus resumed her motionless position of near sleep, closing her eyes and ending the conversation. *She's not so bad after all.* Despite Blythe's frequent sarcasm and hard exterior, Seven sensed the fierce loyalty and protectiveness Vulpes mentioned on their walk to the tattoo parlor. Seven hugged her knees to her chest and gazed at Blythe, the woman who without hesitation, inserted herself between Seven and Locust. The woman whose strength didn't just come from her augmented arms but from her unshakable loyalty to Trio and Endymion. Comforted, Seven closed her eyes.

She fell asleep somewhere in Colorado, missing out on the corners of Utah, Arizona, and Nevada.

Head sliding from its perch on her hand, Seven woke herself up somewhere in the Mojave National Preserve. She looked about groggily. Trio and Blythe remained motionless across the cabin from her, so she closed her eyes in an attempt to regain sleep. Sleep wouldn't come, and Seven quietly sat up, pulled the sleeve of her right arm back and looked at her tattoo. It was healing wonderfully, and she decided to try and play the recording with her omni. She flicked her left wrist and allowed the omni to hover over the edge of the universe tattoo.

A soft chime sounded, and her mother and father appeared.

"Hi, Seven," Steele grinned like a happy idiot.

"Hello dearest Seven. Your father and I just found out that I'm pregnant with you. We are home from the doctor's office, and we wanted to make you a video."

As Seven watched, she felt a surge of homesickness. She missed her parents terribly.

Then the video stuttered and disappeared. Frowning, Seven flicked her wrist in frustration but nothing happened. She was about ready to give up when her omni chimed softly again, and a new video appeared of a nondescript, empty lab. Footsteps sounded in the distance, and Seven sat up rigidly in her chair. She leaned in, holding the omni close to her face as the footfalls grew louder until a figure entered the screen. Icy blue eyes pierced Seven's heart, and she gasped.

"Hello dearest Seven," Oriska Fingal drawled lazily.

Frozen, Seven couldn't respond. Trio stirred in his chair across the room but didn't wake.

Fingal nudged his glasses absently. "Come now, don't be rude. Say hello to an old friend."

"You're no friend of mine."

"No? Perhaps not. You and I have hardly had time to get to know each other. Your parents on the other hand."

"Leave them alone," Seven snarled, her voice rising and waking up Trio.

"Or you'll what," Fingal retorted, unfazed. "You are miles away on the hyperloop to Los Angeles where you'll enter your parents' lab and retrieve their data. Data only accessible to a specific biometric reading." Fingal grinned toothily, "Yours."

Trio, wide awake now, shook Blythe's knee before he came to kneel down beside Seven. "How do you know all that?" Seven blurted.

"Well, if I didn't know it, I do now."

Trio cursed under his breath. "What do you want, Fingal?"

Oriska Fingal licked his lips expectantly, "Is that your robot friend, Seven? What's his name again... Trio? What a wonderfully numerical name. Blythe, are you there, too?"

he asked, showing off. "I want to make sure you all hear this."

Blythe rose from her chair to stand by Seven, and she placed a reassuring hand on her shoulder. Coming from Blythe, this meant more than any words she could have spoken in response, but this was Blythe after all. She had something to say. "I'm here, Fingal; although, I'd much rather see you in person."

Fingal rolled his eyes, "How menacing." He paused and took an overly dramatic sip of wine.

Seven couldn't believe the arrogance of this man.

"What do you want us to hear?" Trio demanded, his hand fiercely gripping Seven's armrest.

"Right, right. I have an offer for young Seven, of course. You see, I know where you're headed and what you're after. You won't get the research, and you won't get out alive. So I offer you a deal: I get the research, and Seven gets her parents back. Trust me, Seven, had I the opportunity to get my own parents back, I'd take it. Family simply can't be manufactured."

Stunned, Seven struggled to form coherent thoughts. What would Fingal do to her parents? What had he done to them already?

She was about to answer when Trio abruptly declared, "No deal, Fingal." He tore the omni from Seven's wrist, tossing it to the floor of the pod.

"An unwise decision," Fingal argued before Trio

stomped the omni to bits with his sneaker.

Aghast, Seven shouted, "Trio, what did you do? Those are my parents he's threatening." She rose angrily from her chair and jammed her palm into Trio's chest. "He's going to kill them!" She pushed Trio again, letting her rage over Fingal pulse out at the nearest target.

"He's not," Trio quietly responded. "Think about it, Seven." He put his hands on her shoulders. "Why would Fingal even call you? Why even let you know he's aware of our plans?"

"The fear-monger knows we're ahead of him," Blythe proclaimed behind Seven, energy buzzing through her words. "We've got an edge."

Seven turned her head to look at Blythe, but Trio gently redirected her face so she was looking at him. "That's right, Blythe," Trio declared while he stared resolutely at Seven. "He wanted to scare us into giving him the research, but we aren't scared, are we, Sev."

"No," Seven whispered hesitantly.

"We aren't scared because we're going to get the research first, and we're going to get out of there before Fingal even arrives. Aren't we, Sev?"

"Yes," Seven said more firmly, gathering hope. "Yes."

Spider

From the mountaintop, I saw the small things that make up the whole. From the valley, I saw the great things it takes to forge the whole. —Oriska Fingal

Trying another sip of wine and finding it suddenly too bitter for his taste, Fingal was half tempted to smash the glass onto his lab floor. Instead, he spun the glass in his hand, contemplating the floral notes that drifted to his nose. The abrupt termination of his conversation with Seven frustrated him to no end. He was so close to finding the right word with her when Trio smashed her omni.

Trio. The boy was altogether too clever—an unfortunate likeness to his parents. And he'd clearly been spending too much time with Arcturus as well. *That altruistic monolith.*

Fingal set the wine glass down next to his research notes and Ballie, then he placed another call with his omni. Locust's black mask appeared.

"Where are you?" Fingal asked.

"On my way to Los Angeles."

Fingal nodded, then sighed dramatically, "My little call to the Ayr girl didn't work. Trio very rudely ended the call before I could convince Seven to give us the research." Locust said nothing in response. *What I wouldn't give for a little erudite conversation.* "It was worth a shot—I mean, what if she would have just given us the research? How great would that have been?" Still nothing from Locust. "Anyway, you'll need to go to Ascension like we planned. Get the research, and get Trio."

"Is this the right play?"

She speaks! Fingal leaned backward in his chair, "What do you mean?"

"You've held the Ayrs on Pura Insulam for all these years, monitoring their research and using them as bait. Then we tried to capture Trio at the summit, and Viken blew up the delegates. Now, the Purists are angry and asking questions about Viken." She paused briefly, letting all of Fingal's decisions float in the air like ash. "So, are you sure Ascension is the right play?"

Fingal looked at the ceiling for a long time before conceding, "Fair points, one and all. I admit—I am not perfect. I thought keeping the Ayrs here on Pura Insulam would lead us to Trio sooner, but they all proved more patient than I anticipated. And altogether too clandestine." He lowered his eyes back to his omni. "And the Purists? We won't need them much longer if we can get the Ascension research and Trio. They are a means to an end. I never much liked their insufferable ranting about the purity of human flesh anyway. Surely you agree, what with your pretty legs and all."

Fingal waited for Locust to reply before realizing she probably wouldn't. "Am I sure Ascension is the right play? No, I'm not, but it seems to be our only play right now, Locust. So oil up those legs of yours, you're going to have a struggle ahead of you."

Flicking off his omni, Fingal rose from his chair and grabbed his wine glass again.

Ascension has to work. I cannot afford a setback. If he didn't obtain the Ascension research and Trio now, everything he built up could come tumbling down in a landslide, and he'd likely have to flee from Pura Insulam.

He knew the Ayrs' initial experiment to transfer a human consciousness into a Relicus body all those years ago worked. He just didn't know how. The Ayrs lied to him and were still lying to him, for that matter. Without thinking, Fingal took a sip of wine and grimaced. *Trash.*

Arcturus, Trio, the Ayrs—they were all woven together with Fingal at the top of the web, a spider trying to decide who to poison first. He plucked his web in numerous spots over the years, sending ripples in every direction. Now the vibrations were all pointing to Ascension. If he could trap Trio, he'd be able to uncover the secret to Relicus and

human merging.
   The spider descends.

Los Angeles

Declarations of high confidence mostly come from a human who has crafted a perfect story in his mind. That story isn't necessarily true. —Arcturus

A brisk nudge to her shoulder startled Seven awake, and she looked up to see Blythe standing over her. "Wake up, Seven."

Seven groaned as she just reached a comfortable, deep sleep. "Five more minutes, mom, please," she teased sleepily.

Blythe recoiled in mock horror, "If I had a kid, she'd whine a lot less than you."

"If you had a kid," Trio interjected, "She'd be such a rebel, your hair would already be gray."

Blythe considered for a moment, fingering her blue hair dramatically, before sighing in resignation, "That's probably true."

"What time is it anyway?" Seven questioned. "It's still

pitch black outside."

"It's almost 1:00am," Trio answered, standing by his chair and looking to the west. "We've looped through Pasadena. You'll see Los Angeles out my window momentarily."

The pods were three chairs wide, so Seven came to join Blythe and Trio, kneeling on the third chair's seat cushion and looking out the window like an expectant dog. Digging in her pack, Blythe pulled out three protein bars, handing one to Trio and one to Seven, who did not wait a second before tearing it open and taking a bite.

Chewing worriedly, she paused, "Do you think Fingal has hurt my parents at all?"

Trio unfurled his protein bar wrapper, but the bar rested untasted on the edge of his chair. "I'm not sure. He kept them unharmed on Pura Insulam all these years. That's got to be a good sign."

"Seven, you need to accept the fact that your parents' current situation is out of your control. They made their own decisions that led them to Pura Insulam. The best thing you can do is get their research before Fingal can," Blythe pointed out. "If you can do that, then we have leverage."

Seven took another bite of the protein bar, chewing patiently to allow the chocolatey flavor to spread over her tongue. It seemed easy for Trio and Blythe to advise her on how to feel about her parents and what to do next, but

Steele and Ida were *her* parents. Their lives were on the line, not Blythe's parents, and Seven didn't even know if Trio technically had parents.

"Blythe, do you have parents?" Seven asked as respectfully as she could.

Trio stood in between Blythe and Seven, but Seven could see Blythe clearly as she was leaning forward on the chair. Blythe shifted her weight from left foot to right as she finished her protein bar.

"No, I don't. They died a long time ago. My only family is Endymion," Blythe answered quietly, unconsciously rubbing her scarab tattoo with her fingers.

"I'm sorry to hear that, Blythe. Really," Seven responded.

She wanted to ask Blythe for more details but dared not. Blythe struck her as a person you didn't interrogate with probing familial questions.

Seven's unsaid questions wouldn't have been answered anyway as Blythe and Trio both moved to put on their backpacks. Blythe nodded out the window, and Los Angeles at night grew from a distant, blurry glow to a starkly defined light show. Clean lines dominated the skyline, each skyscraper crafted with surgical precision. As they drew close enough for Seven to see the nuance of some of the buildings, her eyes bulged. The building designs were fantastical—one tall structure actually imitated the Venus de Milo. Another building was a perfect rectangle with a perfect circle, big enough to fly an airplane through, cut out of the middle. And another building appeared to be rotating with the wind, each level autonomous from the ones above and below it. Where Chicago welcomed travelers, warm and inviting, Los Angeles mesmerized them, electric and energizing. Chicago's muse was nature. Los Angeles' muse was whatever spark lit the designers' imaginations.

"Welcome home, Blythe," Trio said, placing a supporting hand on Blythe's shoulder.

The Los Angeles hyperloop station appeared similar to the Chicago one, only this one looked like five glass disks set one on top of another. The tubes converged, transporters shot out to specific decoupling areas where the four pods inside separated and went their unique ways.

Some of the pods would even exit the station and drive the occupants all the way to their next location. Seven, Trio, and Blythe did not have that luxury, as Ascension lab was not a common destination.

They exited the pod warily, scanning the area for trouble, nerves buzzing. The inside of the station, clean and white, was also built in five disks with an alluring oasis located in the center. Arrivals and departures appeared along the walls, and people walked here and there with purpose. The colors people wore captivated the eye; Seven had never seen such vibrancy in style. One woman's outfit caught her eye as it looked like she was dressed as a red peacock—long, feathery sleeves draped down to the woman's calves, giving her the appearance of near flight. A man in a matte yellow tank top with a red sun on it accompanied the red peacock lady. His arms were highly stylized, seamless, electric blue augmentations, but his eyes were the real shocker—they glowed lime green like neon lights.

Even the smells were different. In Chicago, natural smells like pine or freshwater were never far away, but in Los Angeles' hyperloop station, she smelled intense colognes and spicy, alien foods being cooked nearby in the oasis. Her mouth watered, but there was no time to stop.

Blythe led the team out onto the street where they quickly called a car to drive them to Ascension.

As the three of them shuffled into the car, Trio murmured, "So far, so good."

Seven couldn't take her eyes off the city. "L.A. feels so different from Chicago."

Blythe grinned sharply, "That's because it is. Chicago is primarily influenced by the Relicus movement, even though it's incredibly diverse, so you feel the Relicus' footprints all over it. Los Angeles, well, its influence is mostly the Novus movement, and we Novus have a different kind of thirst for life."

"That's what it is," Seven articulated. "That's what I feel

here. Urgency."

"Relicus see a long, sustainable life. Novus live fast and wild. Fortunately, we appreciate that about each other," Trio explained, his voice warm with shared memories. Seven began to understand that Trio and Blythe carried many of the same experiences—events that tied their bonds together tightly. "Right, Blythe?"

"Trio's not wrong. In the daylight, you could see the city better—see the influence Relicus thinking has here," Blythe elaborated. "L.A. may look outlandish, but it's still self-sustaining and designed with longevity in mind. Most of humanity has learned to think further ahead than their noses."

The hidden message behind Blythe's words did not escape Seven. Most of humanity but not all—meaning Pura Insulam, the Purists especially.

A few moments of silence passed as each passenger allowed their minds to drift out into the city. A particularly unique sight drew Seven's attention. What appeared to be a simple two story building with a sneaker store underneath changed abruptly, and Seven found herself grasping Trio's arm. The entire second story of the building came alive and a giant lion angrily paced back and forth from his perch above the store. People walking below the beast completely ignored it, and Seven felt the urge to roll down the window and warn them. Then the lion roared, shattering the glass window, and swiping a massive paw at the car as it passed, causing Seven to jump away in fear.

Trio laughed, placing a reassuring hand on hers. "Relax, it's just augmented reality."

Slightly embarrassed, Seven removed her vice-like grip from Trio's arm. "But how?"

Trio gestured, encompassing the entire car. "The windows of the car act like AR goggles, allowing designers to come up with some incredible features within the city," Trio answered.

"I once saw whale sharks swimming through the sky as if they were birds," Blythe added.

Amazed, Seven spun in her seat to see the lion hungrily pace back and forth from its second story home before laying down at the building's edge, its large paw dangling over the side. *Pura Insulam didn't have anything like that!*

Trio changed the subject. "Ascension is north and west by Elysian Park. It shouldn't take us long to get there."

"What do you think we're going to find at my parents' lab? I mean, I know we're supposed to get their research," Seven paused briefly, "but how?"

Seven thought about that question ever since Arcturus revealed her parents' secret—the quest to download human consciousness into a Relicus body. It must be a divisive idea to be kept so secret.

If I get the research, what will I even do with it? She knew allowing Oriska Fingal to get his hands on it was not an option, but taking it back to Arcturus did not sit well with her either. Seven trusted Trio, and to a lesser extent, Blythe, Radius, and Vulpes, but they all answered to Arcturus. Plus, Fingal still held her parents hostage, so she would need help rescuing them. The kind of help a private security team could offer. She sighed inwardly. Endymion and Arcturus seemed to be the only option. Seven's face hardened, *I can still put my own safeguards on the research once I get it, though.*

"I don't know what to expect, Sev. Whatever is at Ascension, we'll face it together. If Fingal gets that research, he'll likely use it to further divide Relicus, Novus, and human tensions," Trio guessed.

Blythe's mouth set firmly before she commented, "Or Fingal will use that research to become immortal."

The grim comment hung in the air of the car, an invisible weight dusting everyone's shoulders.

Seven's resolve to keep the research out of Fingal's reach strengthened further. She probed the other side of the equation. "What about Arcturus? What would he do with the research?" Seven asked.

Trio disliked the question, it showed clearly on his face. Seven could see him grappling with the thought in his head, two wrestlers vying for supremacy—could Trio trust Arcturus like he used to or was Arcturus hiding something?

Blythe approached the question like she approached

everything else, with her instincts. "You can trust Arcturus," she claimed confidently. "He may be an opportunist, but he's also got higher morals than Fingal."

As much as her support for Arcturus helped ease Seven's mind, it didn't matter if Trio's answer was different. Seven breathed in slowly and out slowly, "Trio?"

"We can trust Arc," Trio agreed, although his voice lacked total resolve.

Not exactly an inspiring answer. "And you Trio? What do you think of my parents' research?"

Trio stared out the window at the brightly lit city, and Seven wondered what exactly went on in that vast mind of his. When he finally answered, his voice was soft, "Some might argue the merging of humans and AIs is the next step in human evolution. Others will be firmly against it. For me…" He paused, shaking his head. "I want society to progress, but not at the cost of others. I'll have to see what we learn at Ascension before making any final judgments."

Final judgments, Seven contemplated. *There's going to be a lot of that at Ascension.*

Ascension

Even though the Ayrs and their research were on the right track, they were just sitting there... Which means they were going to get run over. —Oriska Fingal

Seven spent the rest of the ride to Ascension brainstorming ways to protect the research once she got it. Her omni was destroyed, so it was out of the question. Even if she had her omni, she couldn't trust it as Fingal somehow hacked it and tracked her. She did have the glass data disc packed, and Seven knew her programming skills were exemplary. Perhaps she could hack the device to suit her needs? She had no choice but to be flexible, adapting to the moment and waiting for an opening.

Out the window, the Ascension lab came into view. Characterized by a circular design with large, white, mushroom-like umbrellas to define paths, provide shelter from the L.A. heat, and display unique style, the initial spectacle of Ascension arrested Seven's eyes. Six deep trenches ran from end to end of the compound, as if some great beast rent the earth with its claws. A white cooling tower dominated the east end of the compound, and next to it, a glassy dome.

Pulling up to the west side of Ascension, the car slowed to a stop, its doors opening with a quiet whoosh.

As the three of them exited the car, Trio calmly ordered, "Clear eyes everyone."

Trio said that before, and Seven had a brief flashback to the Bay of Fundy simulation—a simulation that ended in her falling headlong into the bay. Looking about, Seven didn't see any deep waters here. *At least I won't drown.*

The entrance to Ascension sat hunched beneath two of the white mushroom umbrellas located all over the compound. Sidearm out, Trio led the way, followed by Seven with Blythe bringing up the rear. In the dark of night, Seven could not tell the current state of the compound, and she had no idea if the lab was still in use or if it shut down when her parents were forced to leave.

As if reading her mind, Trio volunteered an explanation, "Endymion's research showed that Ascension hasn't been used in quite some time. One of Fingal's shell companies pays to keep it operational, but no employees work here regularly." He pointed at a terminal located near two large, glass front doors. "Put your hand up to the terminal, and we'll see if this whole trip has been for nothing."

Seven flexed her hands into fists before releasing her fingers in a wiggle. Heart thumping wildly in her chest, she brought her right hand to the screen and waited. A mere second passed before the terminal lit up green and the glass doors yawned inward, beckoning Seven forward as if Ascension waited for her. Trio quickly edged into the atrium, flashlight steadily scanning the area. Next, Seven entered Ascension.

The atrium was wide and expansive, with a bank of computers in front of the doors. During the day, natural light would dominate the clean, airy atrium, but right now, only a few lights interrupted the darkness.

Last in, Blythe watched the front doors swing shut before she turned around, lowering her sidearm. "So, where can we find this research? The clock is ticking."

"A helpful reminder, Blythe. Thank you," Trio responded. "I'm not sure. Arcturus didn't tell me his entire plan."

Walking behind the reception desk, Blythe tried accessing one of the computers. It turned on at the tap of her finger but wouldn't allow her into its system.

"Maybe my biometrics will work for that too," Seven ventured, moving around to Blythe's side and bumping her out of the way. She found a scanner to the right of the screen and placed her hand to it. Blinking green for a moment, the screen unlocked, and Seven smiled mischievously at Blythe, "What would you do without me?"

"Stay in Chicago. Eat shrimp every day with Radius," Blythe retorted, gesturing to the screen. "Now, hurry up."

Seven didn't need any encouragement; she was already searching for her parents' lab.

Fortunately, she didn't have to look long as it was the biggest lab in Ascension. "It's over by the cooling tower and the glass dome."

"Got it. Blythe," Trio directed without explanation.

"On your six," Blythe responded smoothly, rolling her shoulders and raising her sidearm.

Trio set out to the east, in the direction of the cooling tower, his flashlight roving. Long hallways with glass walls revealed meeting rooms, offices, gardened relaxation areas, smaller labs, and even a workout center. Each step closer to her parents' lab made Seven's heart beat faster. She'd never been so nervous in her entire life. It was as if the nerves of every public speech she gave in school bundled themselves together and took up residence in her body. She sweated, her stomach lurched uncomfortably, and her mouth dried suddenly. The only way she overcame the nerves for a public speech was to sign up for the first slot and get it out of the way. She took that approach here, placing one foot in front of the other, following Trio's lead.

He stopped.

"This is it. Behind this door," Trio indicated with his

chin.

Whatever waited behind the door, whether Seven was ready for it or not, she no longer had time to reflect on it. On Pura Insulam, her father said she wasn't ready, and her parents kept secrets from her. She'd be unearthing those long buried secrets, and she would decide what to do with them next.

Placing her hand on the scanner, she unlocked the lab doors and crossed the threshold.

Trio and Blythe quickly entered, scanning left and right.

The room was expansive, spartanly populated by a few tables with what looked like enlarged 3D printers attached to them. The countertops were unusually bare; in fact, the entire lab looked as if it was combed for every detail, which Oriska Fingal probably ordered all those years ago.

Then Blythe gasped and cursed under her breath, lowering her sidearm in disgust. "Take a look at this."

Seven followed the beam of Blythe's flashlight to its destination: a body. Chin resting on naked chest, eyes closed, curly brown hair disheveled, flesh still lively. It appeared to be a teenage boy sitting as if asleep on the back counter. An icy feeling of recognition flashed through Seven, but the more she pursued the idea, the less she grasped it.

Hesitatingly, Seven croaked, "Is he alive?"

Blythe approached the young boy and placed a hand on

his neck, checking for a pulse.

Seven waited expectantly.

"Nothing."

"Can somebody tell me why there's a body in here," Seven demanded of nobody in particular. She looked at Blythe and Trio.

Trio's eyes looked faraway, like he was on the cusp of some discovery but couldn't explain it in words. Shifting his gaze from the body with effort, he whispered, "It's an AI body."

"Unbelievable," Seven remarked. "But whose? And why?"

The Ayr Test

We humans like to think we are in control of events, and we have a terrible time recognizing randomness. —Oriska Fingal

"There's no time to play detective. Seven, the terminal is over there," Blythe directed, pointing with her flashlight. "I'll watch the hallway."

Dragging her eyes from the AI's body towards a corner of the room, Seven saw a terminal, desk, and chair lit up by Blythe's trim flashlight beam. She willed her feet reluctantly away from the mysterious body, even though every fiber of her being wanted to investigate it further. *Could my parents have done this? No way.* Blythe was right—there wasn't time to analyze why someone would place this body in her parents' old lab.

The research was waiting.

At the desk, Seven noted an older, virtual reality kit. *Curious*, she thought as she placed her hand to the screen, unlocking its contents. As she searched for her parents' data, she noticed Trio wander to her side in a daze, and his attention seemed to lag behind the tracking of his eyes.

Several grueling minutes passed as Seven desperately searched for the files containing her parents' findings, Blythe not so patiently watching the hallway for any sign of Locust.

There's got to be something. Diagrams of an AI's wetware, graphs on reverse-engineering the human mind... Anything! Sweat began to drip in earnest from Seven's armpits. Each folder Seven found disappointed her, one after another, and she began to feel as though their impromptu trip across half the continent had been in vain.

Trio, finally waking up to the moment, placed his hand on Seven's shoulder. "Keep looking," he encouraged. "Don't give up."

Taking a deep breath, Seven continued her search, varying the search strings until she came across a file name that shocked her: TRIO. Her finger hovered hesitantly over the screen like a honeybee approaching a flower. Beside her, Trio noticed the file name and his focus briefly receded back into his mind. Seven couldn't help but wonder if he was thinking of the empty body behind them, then Trio gave her the slightest of nods. She tapped the file.

A brief message popped up on the screen, "Virtual reality accessory required." Expectation filled Seven's gut like a weight, and she shared a look with Trio.

"Come on, hurry up," Blythe hissed from the doorway, "What are you waiting for, the future?"

Grabbing the VR kit from the desk, Seven blew off a little dust and said, "Trio, what I see will also play on the monitor. I may need some help interpreting what's happened afterwards. Are you with me?"

Trio swallowed hard, "I'm with you."

With that, Seven slid the VR kit on, grasped the controllers, and initiated the program. Blackness filled her field of vision for a moment before white light wiped from left to right. A low thrum hummed in her ears and a gray-blue menu screen emerged with only one file folder to access: TRIO. Seven raised her hand and tapped the file, which opened to reveal additional documents with various dates. She clicked the first one which was over 30 years ago. The menu screen faded to black, then blinked to life.

Seven's sweaty palms felt slippery on the controllers.

Steele Ayr was looking intensely at the screen, and he looked impossibly young, much younger than he appeared in the video that now resided on Seven's tattooed arm.

"It's day one of testing. Ida and I have been working for quite some time just to get here," he explained, pausing to gesture around at the Ascension lab. "We've already conducted thorough brain mapping techniques. It's time to focus on brain simulations."

Time whispered urgently in Seven's ear, and she skipped ahead years to another file in the folder, a grim curiosity spreading like an infection.

Ida Ayr appeared on screen, beautiful and regal as ever. She sighed, "We've made great strides in uncovering the minute details of the human brain's synapses, but the lag time in processing power continues to frustrate us. What would take the human mind one second takes the processor 10 or even 100 seconds. I watch my son do seemingly simple tasks that are impossible for our processor to match."

A trickle of sweat dripped down the back of Seven's neck. *Son?*

No time to think, time rushed Seven forward, and she jumped ahead numerous years to another file.

Now, Steele and Ida were both on screen, smiling triumphantly.

Steele spoke first, practically bouncing out of his chair as he proclaimed, "We've successfully emulated the neural networks that comprise the human brain. Years of work, and we're finally ready to test our ability to download a human consciousness into an AI body."

Ida smiled at someone off the screen, then said brazenly, "And we did it all while raising a nosy kid. Get over here, Trio, and say hi."

A young boy of about fifteen appeared on the screen, his dark brown hair long, curly, and unruly. He gave a cheeky wave, "Hi."

Seven recoiled upon seeing the boy named Trio as he looked exactly like the AI body now gathering dust behind her in the lab. *What is going on here*? She pulled the VR headset up to her forehead and looked at Trio, who stared fixedly at the screen. She gazed at the inert body in the lab, then whispered, "Trio, is that supposed to be you? Are you my—"

"Keep going," he murmured in a distant, pleading voice. "Hurry."

Seven slid the headset back over her eyes, exited from her parents' research video and touched the next file. Her vision faded to black, and expecting a video, she was startled as she entered a full VR simulation.

Seven stood outside of the front doors of Ascension labs in broad daylight, the sun arcing high across the sky. She could almost feel the heat of the afternoon. Looking about, Seven was surprised to see people parking their cars and bustling about the lab.

"Hey kid," a familiar, peanut-buttery voice called, "Let's get you into your parents' lab."

Turning towards the voice, Seven was stunned to see Arcturus striding towards her. He looked exactly the same as he did at Endymion: dapper suit, shiny bald head, and magnificent white beard. She looked down at her own body, realizing she wasn't Seven anymore. She was someone else—someone with big feet, boyish clothes, and a flat chest. Someone whose hands were thick and sturdy where hers were spindly and nimble.

Arcturus clapped her on the shoulder, "Wake up, Trio. Your mom and dad hate it when we're late." He cocked his head, grinning, "And today, of all days, is not a day we want to be late."

Trio. She was Trio? Seven's mind spun in circles, as if she were back on the Ferris wheel in Chicago but instead of a slow, easy ride, someone cranked up the speed, spinning her dangerously faster with every second. If she was Trio in this simulation, and Arcturus was there too, what came next? Why couldn't he be late?

Arcturus' guiding hand pushed Seven through the front door, and she found herself briskly waved through security and ushered towards Steele and Ida's lab. No one gave a second glance to Steele and Ida Ayrs' son and his security.

No. It can't be.

Catching her wits, she asked with a lump in her throat, already guessing the answer, "Why don't we want to be late today?"

Arcturus looked at her as if she'd sprouted legs from her forehead, "Do I need to check your temp? You ok in there," he teased, reaching over and knocking affectionately on Seven's head. He looked around furtively, "Your parents make history today. They've got a human brain, not a real human brain, but a simulated brain that they will attempt to download into an AI's body. Didn't they tell you this?"

Unsure of how this simulation related to unlocking her parents' research, Seven decided her best course of action was to intentionally play along in order to see as much as she could. She did this numerous times during her parents' training simulations, and she'd found that she could flow with the simulation, like following the current in a river. "Yeah, of course. I just forgot that it was today."

Arcturus looked dubious, "Human kids. I don't know if I'll ever understand you. Fortunately, I don't have to. I just protect you." Grabbing Seven by the shoulder with one hand, Arcturus rustled her hair with his other.

Seven pulled her head away, curious. "Arcturus, how long *have* you been protecting me?"

Walking briskly, Arcturus considered the question, doing the math in his head. "I'd say about seven years. Why?"

Seven shrugged casually, making a joke of her question. "You just look a lot older than that."

Arcturus laughed easily, "Well, taking care of you while your parents work isn't easy. You'd age anybody prematurely, even a Relicus."

The hallways were quiet as most of the people went about their own business. Arcturus unlocked the door to the Ayr lab, holding it open for Seven to enter a much different space than where she currently sat with a VR kit strapped to her head. Filled with papers, intriguing devices, the tables topped with large 3D printers, and the sound of her parents working, the simulated lab reminded Seven very much of her time with her parents on Pura Insulam. She grew up in their Pura Insulam lab, manipulating code and hacking devices to see what she could make them do. A strong sense of harmony exuded from this scene.

Looking up from some notes she was holding, Ida noticed Arcturus and Seven. Her smile broadened radiantly, and she held her arms open invitingly. "Trio!"

Frozen in place for a brief moment, the lines of simulation and reality blurred for Seven. She no longer existed with a VR kit on, nor did she exist some 20 years ago in a simulation. She was in both, one time period superimposed over another. Her mother's arms beckoned, and she entered them fully.

Seven could smell her mother's flowery scent mingled with the new tech smell of labs. Hugging her mother fiercely, the Trio version of Seven and Seven herself absorbed the much needed motherly love.

"Mom," Seven croaked in a boyish voice. "I've missed you."

Ida held on to Seven for longer than a normal hug before pushing her to arm's length and looking into Seven's eyes. Ida was doing that "see with your eyes" thing she always did, and Seven's sense of harmony slowly dissipated. "I saw you this morning before you left for school," she said, knitting her brows. "Everything ok?"

Trio returned to Seven's shoulder, reminding her that an assassin was likely on the way to kill her. *Hurry up*, Trio insisted.

"All good, mom. I promise," Seven assured her mother.

"Good," Steele called from across the room as a way of greeting, "because we're ready to test our research. If this works..." Steele trailed off wonderingly.

Ida moved to a table with the AI body resting atop it and made some final checks. A trim device circumnavigated the head, connecting to the terminal where Steele sat punching in the final lines of directives. Tense minutes passed. Finally, Ida and Steele made eye contact, held each other's gazes for a moment, and Ida nodded.

"Wait," Seven interjected, unable to stop herself. Steele and Ida both turned to look at her expectantly. "I love you."

Abruptly the simulation scrambled and wiped from right to left, throwing Seven's vision into darkness. She looked about wildly, startled by the quick change.

"Trio? Trio," she called to the room. "Are you still with me?"

No answer.

Before she could take her headset off to see Trio for herself, another simulation started, and this time Seven found herself immediately in her parents' lab. For the moment, she was alone, and she set her mind to the formidable task of accessing her parents' research. Seven did not think the research would simply unlock at the end of the simulation. That's not how Steele and Ida operated. The research was biometrically locked—that must mean something. Steele and Ida knew all these years ago that safeguards needed to be put into place. This was a test.

In the simulation, the door to the lab opened, and Seven's blood boiled, the hair on the back of her neck gooseprickled, and her stomach lurched.

A young Oriska Fingal nonchalantly scanned the room and seeing only Seven appearing as Trio, entered. He closed the door behind him.

"Where are your parents, young man," Fingal drawled lazily.

"Not here. Obviously," Seven replied, not hiding the venom in her voice.

If her tone bothered him, Fingal didn't show it. He seemed distracted. "Tell them I dropped by, will you?"

Oriska Fingal opened the door to leave and almost ran face first into Steele. The two of them stood on opposite sides of the door, neither speaking nor moving out of the way. Fingal fidgeted with his glasses, blue eyes unblinking. Steele held firm, an immovable, electrified monument.

From behind Steele, Seven heard her mother's exasperated voice, "Would you two set your egos aside and let me into my lab?"

Ida pushed past Steele, crossed the threshold, and stared down Fingal until he moved aside as well. She walked over to Seven, rolling her eyes as she came closer. Oriska Fingal idly followed her, breaking the tension at the doorway but not entirely eliminating it from the room.

"Are the noble Ayrs done taking their time with needless precautions? Can we finally test your research on a Relicus body and a live subject?" Fingal questioned, hunger clinging tightly to his voice. "Or am I to spend more of my dwindling funds on your perceived caution?"

Seven had no idea how Fingal discovered her parents' research all those years ago, but his presence marked trouble, especially if his money kept the experiment afloat.

As he closed the lab door, Steele spoke from behind Fingal. "You know we aren't. Our test isn't safe enough yet."

Seven watched her mother closely as Ida was right next to her. Ida's hands were grasping the edge of the desk firmly, knuckles whitening. Her back was turned to Steele and Fingal, but Seven could see the anger simmering dangerously. Seven rarely saw her mother angry, and she could sense the pressure Fingal placed on Ida.

Ida turned with molten iron in her eyes, "Fingal, we should have never taken your money. Your slimy hands have changed too much around here. Tell us now, why remove Arcturus from our security team? Why accelerate our timetables?" Then more quietly, "Where did you get this AI body from?"

Seven hadn't registered the body on the lab table until Ida mentioned it. Fear coursed through her veins. *Oh no.*

"That's a Relicus body, of course, and don't you worry your conscience with where it came from." A shark-toothed grin appeared on Fingal's face, "You needed my money, and you needed my changes. Ascension lab was on the brink of closing due to your slow experimenting. Had I gone at your speed, progress would have turned to regression, and this place would have been shuttered." Fingal walked to a lab table and picked up the trim device intended for an AI head. *The same one from the experiment in the previous simulation*, Seven noted. Fingal observed the crown-like device absently. "As for Arcturus, well, common sense isn't common. I couldn't trust him to do what needed to be done."

Steele loomed over Fingal. "What's that supposed to mean? What needs to be done?"

"This." Setting the device down, Oriska Fingal flicked his wrist, turning on his omni. "Send them in," he ordered calmly as he stepped away from Steele.

Whipping around and heading for the closed door to lock it, Steele froze halfway as the door opened and a half-dozen armed guards filed menacingly into the lab.

Ida stepped in front of her son and asked fearfully,

"What are you doing, Fingal?"

"What should have been done long ago, my dear."

Seven felt her skin crawl. She knew what came next. The test her parents designed in the form of this simulation revealed two realities at once: Seven must intentionally experience the truth, and Trio, the Relicus from Chicago, must witness his death. Only after would Seven be able to retrieve her parents' research.

"Grab the boy," Fingal commanded, sliding further away from the Ayrs.

"No!" Ida roared, flinging herself at Fingal.

Ida caught the lapel of Fingal's gray suit with her right hand, pulling him close enough to buffet his face with a flurry of blows before Fingal's guards forcefully ripped her away.

Steele charged headlong into two of Fingal's guards, knocking them backwards into a third. "Run, Trio," he yelled.

Seven made a break for the door, but she was far too slow. Strong hands grabbed her by the waist and arms, dragging her to a lab table where she was promptly strapped down by uncaring, iron hands.

"Get off me!" she screamed, writhing against the bonds.

Fingal bent down and picked up his glasses from the floor. The right side of his face was bruised and bloodied from the desperate hand of Ida Ayr. Placing the glasses with careful patience back upon his face, Fingal walked to the lab table next to Seven and picked up the slim device.

"A crown for our prince."

"Don't! Don't do it, Fingal," Steele begged, struggling to free himself from Fingal's guards. "You don't know what you're doing. You'll kill him."

Fingal sighed exaggeratedly, "Will I? Then why don't you help me?"

Steele and Ida looked at each other wretchedly, trying to think of a way out of this hopeless situation. They made a deal with a dangerously ambitious man, all in the pursuit of their dreams. Somehow, everything was crashing down around the Ayr family, and Seven could see the defeat in their eyes.

"I'll help you," Ida whispered.

"Ida, no! It's not ready yet."

Ida looked to Steele, devoid of emotion. "There's no other way. Fingal will try it regardless of whether we help or not."

Fingal placed the device on Seven's head, looking smugly at the Ayrs, "She's right. I will do this with or without your help. Let her go," he directed, shifting his glasses with a hand, "but do keep a closer eye on her this time. These glasses are expensive."

Terrified, Seven tried to shake the device off her head, but Fingal tightened it securely.

She could feel the straps around her wrists tearing into her flesh as she pulled against them. Pain lit the simulation to life, burning it away until only reality remained. She was about to die in a failed experiment.

"Mom. Please. Mom. I'm not ready for this. I don't want to die," Seven whimpered with Trio's terrified voice, attempting to make eye contact with her mom, who was behind her head.

"Everything will be ok," Ida said hoarsely, attaching another device to the Relicus head on the opposite table.

Desperate with fear, Steele continued to call Ida's name, begging her to stop. "Kindly shut that man up," Fingal murmured.

One of Fingal's guards bashed the butt of her sidearm swiftly to Steele's temple, causing Steele to slump rapidly to the floor.

"Dad!" Seven shouted with Trio's crackling voice, becoming apoplectic with rage. She writhed and fought and banged her body against the lab table.

Fingal rolled his eyes, an unfeeling rock in an ocean of emotion. "Sedate the boy already."

The needle slid easily into her arm, and after a few moments, Seven could feel the world receding away. She clung desperately to the simulation, as if clinging to a rope while sinking into the depths of the Gulf of Mexico. Or the Bay of Fundy. It turns out she would drown in this simulation too, only this time, death was real. Death stole into the lab in the form of Oriska Fingal. In the form of her parents' ambition. And her brother, Trio, died young because of it.

The simulation flashed white, and once again, Seven's vision pitched into darkness. It took her a long time to emerge from the icy depths of the simulation, and she might not have come back to reality if it hadn't been for Blythe.

The skinny, blue-haired Novus came to Seven's side calling her name gently. Blythe pulled the VR headset from Seven's eyes and lightly slapped her face. "Come on, Sev. Come back to the here and now."

Returning to the present took every ounce of Seven's mental effort. It was as if her mind trudged through the muck at the bottom of the ocean to reach her body. Awareness dawned on her slowly, and Seven took in the room.

Trio stood off to her right, catatonic, and Seven recalled a comment he'd made regarding Arcturus' belief about how Relicus awakened. "All experiences, the positive and the negative, lead us to an awakening." She didn't know if that's what was happening to Trio now, or if he was simply too shocked to function.

Blythe knelt in front of her, a troubled look on her face. "Oh Blythe," Seven said, tears welling in her eyes, "I don't think I've ever seen you look so concerned."

"I thought I'd lost you both," Blythe sniffed. "Help Trio. I've got to get back to the door to watch for—"

Locust stood in the doorway, smooth mask devoid of

expression, black hoodie pulled up, inhuman legs bent grotesquely. Raising her sidearm to fire, Locust took aim at Blythe and Seven, but before she fired, Blythe summoned the same type of black shield Trio used back in Remy's house on Pura Insulam. The shield wriggled from her backpack like a black mamba, sprouting from her right arm just in time to catch a barrage of bullets.

Blythe kicked Seven's chair over, knocking Seven behind a lab table, pulled her own sidearm and returned fire. The lab screamed with lethal cracks as metal careened into walls and off of Blythe's shield.

Locust took cover behind the lab door to reload and called out, "You don't have the people of Chicago to save you this time. Just me and you."

Somehow, through the hail of gunfire, Trio stood stock still and unharmed. From her position behind the lab table, Seven looked to him now. He seemed to shudder minutely, blinking his eyes rapidly.

He flicked his left arm as if cocking a weapon, and his own black shield slithered out. He turned slowly towards the door. "That's your problem, Locust. It's always been just you." Unholstering his sidearm, Trio called, "Blythe will never be alone. She's got me."

"Touching," Locust mocked as she rolled a flash grenade into the room.

Light erupted, momentarily blinding Seven, and a bang temporarily deafened her. She shook her head, pressed her eyes shut, and clapped her hands over her ears. Mind reeling, Seven had no idea what to do next. Obviously, she would be no help in a fight. Her vision cleared, and she looked to the terminal. Her parents' research waited there for anyone to take. Remembering the satchel still strapped to her shoulder, she quickly rifled through it, finding the glass data disk she noted earlier. *This better work*, she thought as she crawled towards the terminal and inserted the round little disk.

Around her, carnage raged. After the flashbang went off, Locust buzzed into the room, a torrent of destruction. Leaping over Blythe's shielded form, Locust landed smoothly behind Blythe and delivered a vicious back kick that sent the blue-haired Novus careening headfirst into a wall. Trio, still stunned by the flash grenade, held his shield up to cover his eyes. Locust whirled on him and delivered a dropkick to his shield, sending Trio tumbling backwards over a lab table.

Do you wish to begin downloading, the computer screen prompted Seven.

Blythe stumbled to her feet, blood flowing freely from her head. Seven wasn't sure if it was the same wound from the hyperloop station or a new one. Grim determination shone under the blood, even though Blythe lost her sidearm during her fall.

Absolutely, I do, Seven thought, mashing the download button.

"Nice kick," Blythe taunted from behind her shield. "Cheap, but nice."

Locust's mask empurpled with fury, and she fired round after round at Blythe, who charged headlong at the assassin, driving her shield firmly into Locust's sidearm. The weapon clattered to the floor, but Locust grabbed Blythe's shield using her momentum against her, rolling backwards, and utilizing augmented legs to drive Blythe into the air, ripping the shield from the Novus' arm viscerally. A metallic pop followed. Screaming in pain, Blythe writhed on the floor, struggling to get up. She planted her good arm into the floor and with tremendous effort, stood. Her right arm hung in grisly, synthetic tatters, and blood mixed with her blue hair. With her good hand, she offered Locust a crude gesture and prepared to fight.

Download 50%.

Locust advanced one step before Trio vaulted over a lab table and caught her in the head with a heavy roundhouse kick. Tumbling to the floor, Locust rolled into a crouched position and looked up at Trio. Her mask cracked, distorting the red pin pricks of light that flashed across its surface.

"Trio," she growled. "How does it feel to finally know the truth? To know what was hidden from you all these years." She paused meaningfully. "To know that you died."

"To live is to suffer. You know that as well as anyone, taking orders from that fearmonger Fingal."

Download 75%.

Gathering her feet under her, Locust sprang forward. At the same time, Blythe pushed off the balls of her feet, her one good arm swinging. Blythe's augmented fist connected with the side of Locust's head, but Locust's momentum carried her awkwardly into Trio who toppled backwards, head bouncing obscenely against the lab table where he crumpled and laid still.

Blythe and Locust fell in a tangle of limbs, and Blythe, limited as she was, stood no chance against Locust, who managed to gain control of Blythe's back, crank her neck one way while also twisting Blythe's body in the opposite direction.

Seven heard an audible snap and watched as Blythe went limp. "Blythe, no!"

Download complete.

Seven hastily jammed the glass data disk containing her parents' research deep into her satchel and spun around. Trio lay hunched under the lab table, unmoving, and Blythe couldn't possibly be alive. Seven took too long, and her friends paid the price. Now she was alone with Locust.

The assassin untangled herself from Blythe's limp form, rose, and gingerly walked to her sidearm. Seven froze with fear. She had no answer to such violence. Locust's hostilities simply did not compute.

Locust grabbed her sidearm, turned her cracked and flashing mask on Seven. "Give me the research."

"I... We didn't get it. I couldn't unlock my parents' files," Seven lied.

Advancing slowly, Locust raised her firearm, "I don't believe you. I guess I'll just take it from your corpse."

Seven raised her hands as Locust's mask flashed white and two shots erupted from the assassin's sidearm.

Synesthetic Ocean

Many great AI thinkers say we reach awakening by three methods: first by reflection, which is slowest; second by empathy, which is noblest; and third by experience, which is bitterest.
—Arcturus

One solitary, musical note rustled the air, drifting like a light breeze off the ocean, and with the note, came a color. Not every color, not right away. First came a dark red tone, knifing through the air, originating from a 12-string acoustic guitar. The colored sound twisted around in circles as if looking for an ear to land in, and as it descended, another note joined, adding orange to the air.

Mesmerizing and delicate, the notes trickled in, singing like a stream until a rainstorm birthed a flood upon the narrow banks of consciousness with more sound and more color. Red, orange, and yellow now danced in and out, like the tide, punctuated by the knock of rosy percussion which marched the colors onward until everything faded to only a few dark red notes. The color rippled, acting as pebbles dropped into an ocean—fond memories from life sprinkled into the immensity of time. The DNA of a life lived.

Orange and yellow notes reentered, percussion pushed time forward inexorably. The mood changed, as sky blue, navy, and violet were added to the picking, plucking, hammering strings. Rushes of excited color mixtures paired with equally pastoral moments of tranquility. Volume built and the colors became more vibrant, bending and filling up time and space, crescendoing to near climax before once again falling into a calming lull.

Strumming chords colored the air quickly, while picking and percussion flowed like a rushing river as the tempo increased spiritedly. Notes ran. The tempo ran—a mad gallop where the intensity of the colors threatened to overwhelm Seven until they briskly washed away.

Returned. Washed away. Life and loss. Life and loss.

Seven watched as the colors faded gently, leaving only the dark red note, winding its way about the air around her head. She looked down to see an undercurrent of orange, yellow, sky blue, navy, and violet steadily lapping against her feet, and as she looked, it began to rise.

Progress built and built in sound and color—a complex mixture of strumming, plucking, hammering, and percussion mirrored the entanglement of life. The hues rose up to Seven's knees, the volume and tempo of the guitar increasing deliriously as the sound waves crawled up Seven's body. The inevitable climb of octaves increased impossibly, and Seven wept from the overwhelming animus of the tide. Her clear tears fell down her cheeks and mixed with the colorful sound now at her chin, and she tilted her head upwards to keep her nose out of the sound waves. The dark red note still flitted about her head.

Unprompted, the sound waves swiftly receded, leaving only ripples around Seven's feet.

The ripples reminded Seven that life goes on, despite a blue rain of notes and a slowing of the tempo. Oddly, sadness filled her heart as she feared the wild musical colors left her for good, but distantly, she heard the percussion. It was picking up speed, and Seven spun around desperately looking for it. A wave of sound approached in a full-throated roar of chords. The colorful wave rose higher and approached faster—a mountain of sound and music. Craning her neck upward and dropping her arms to her sides, Seven awaited the sweat-inducing finish.

Awakening

How does one solve his problems without using the same thinking that created them? —Arcturus

Eyelids fluttering, Seven vaguely registered Flumen hovering over her body. Her senses were packed in cotton, and she couldn't dig them out right away. After a moment, she heard muffled voices and tried to tilt her head to see who was speaking.

Flumen grabbed her chin firmly, "Right here, Seven. Look in my eyes. In my eyes only."

Flumen's eyes were rosy, flecked with gold. *Beautiful,* Seven observed groggily as she felt pressure on her chest. She looked down to see Flumen's hands holding a large syringe filled with pill-sized capsules, which were promptly injected into one bullethole, and then another syringe pumped into the second bullethole. All of Seven's senses came online in an instant, and her chest lit with painful fire causing her to groan and writhe on the ground.

Arcturus appeared next to Seven, kneeling by her head. "Hold on, kid," he whispered hoarsely. His eyes were flinty and wet, like stones after a rain.

"This is an xstat injection with nanobots programmed to repair your tissue and organs," Flumen explained in a flat, surgical voice. "That pain you're feeling means the nanobots are at work."

Seven found her voice, moving her tongue mechanically, "Trio? Blythe?"

Arcturus put his head into his hand, momentarily gathering himself. "Blythe is dead, and Trio is gone." He tried to say it without emotion, but heartache crept in like a spider, webbing Arcturus' voice with pain. "Are you strong enough to tell us what happened?"

Flumen scowled at Arcturus, "Give the girl a minute, Arc. She was just shot twice in the chest."

Seven could feel her motor functions coming back to her, and although her chest burned hotly, she found she could move her arms, fingers, legs, and toes. She found her mental faculties were also back, unpacked from the cotton, and with them the imagery of the last few hours. The revelations of her parents' research came first, and she reached into her satchel instinctively to feel for the round curve of the glass data disk. It wasn't there. Ashamed she thought of the research first, Seven's next thought was of Blythe, her sharp-tongued protector, and how Locust bent Blythe's spine unnaturally. Tears filled Seven's eyes. Blythe hardly knew the jellyfish girl, yet she gave her life for Seven. It was too much to fathom.

And Trio. Arcturus said her brother was gone. *Gone where? Was he dead?* She looked around in desperation, hoping she'd see Trio leaning against a lab table; instead, she noticed Endymion team huddled around a covered form that could only be Blythe.

"Seven," Arcturus pressed, ignoring Flumen. "What happened?"

Realizing Arcturus repeated a question to her, Seven forced her eyes to focus on him. "Locust showed up. Trio and Blythe tried to stop her, but she killed Blythe," Seven sobbed out, tears running down her cheeks. "Did she... Did she kill Trio too?" She did not want to hear Trio was dead, but she must know. Could it be that she'd lose her brother after just discovering she had one?

"We don't think so, honey," Flumen said, placing a hand on Seven's cheek and wiping the tears away. "Trio's not here."

"Locust has him," Arcturus declared quietly. "Oriska Fingal knows the truth about Trio, and Locust is taking Trio to him. That's the only explanation."

Seven frowned at Arcturus' whispered statement. *Knows the truth about Trio?* Working to reconcile the scattered thoughts in her mind, Seven fought to piece together all the broken fragments. Her Ascension simulation came back to her, and she remembered seeing Arcturus in the lab all those years ago. Years of security for her mom and dad. For her brother—Trio. The two of them were close, that much was clear. A sudden recollection of a conversation with Trio came back to her—Trio said back at Endymion headquarters, "There's no limit to what Arcturus knows."

Seven reached out a bloody hand and grabbed the still kneeling Arcturus by the collar of his shirt. "You knew," she croaked quietly. He gazed at her frankly. "You knew," she repeated louder.

All of Endymion team, standing respectfully about Blythe's now covered body, turned their heads at Seven's outburst. They were all there: Vulpes, Radius, Terra.

Arcturus remained kneeling and did not immediately respond to Seven's hand or her statement. After many long moments, he finally spoke, "I did."

Vulpes walked over, eyes red from tears and asked suspiciously, "Wait, you knew what?"

The others followed. Terra crossed her thick arms, towering over everybody. Radius cracked his colorful fingers.

"I knew what you all can know now: Trio is not an ordinary Relicus. He's got a human mind downloaded into his body."

"Not just any mind," growled Seven. "My brother's mind." She jerked weakly at Arcturus' collar.

Vulpes furrowed his brow in confusion, and Radius shook his head, seemingly unsurprised.

In a quiet voice, Terra demanded, "Arc, you will explain."

Extricating Seven's hand from his collar, Arcturus stood. "We don't have a lot of time. I believe Trio is still alive, and I have a hunch where Locust will be taking him." He looked directly at his team, each one individually. "I will give you this answer, and then we must move quickly. The rest can be explained on the plane."

Arcturus paused, seeming to gather his thoughts.

"Well? Out with it," Vulpes pushed angrily.

"I worked for the Ayrs, Seven's parents, a long time ago," Arcturus started. "They were doing research in this lab regarding the downloading of human consciousness into a Relicus form, and during that time, I became close with them." A pause. "Steele, Ida, and their natural son. Trio."

"Natural son?" Vulpes questioned hotly, unbelieving.

"Before I could see the research finished, I was abruptly removed from their security detail," Arcturus continued unabated. "Fingal learned of the Ayrs' progress, and he wanted a piece of it, greedy bastard that he is. He wanted my security team to help him... *convince* the Ayrs, and when I told him no, Fingal promptly fired me and my team. Little did he know, I told the Ayrs, and we stayed in touch. They knew Fingal couldn't be trusted, but they needed his money." Arcturus locked eyes with Seven and continued as if speaking only for her. "We knew Fingal would force their hand, but we didn't know how or when. So we ensured a backdoor plan was in place. Fingal made his move, and in his eyes, the experiment failed. However, Trio's consciousness really did download, and via backchannels, it came to me in Chicago, not to Fingal in L.A."

"And you had the Relicus body we know as Trio," Radius mused, connecting the obvious dots out loud.

"Yes."

Radius, Vulpes, and Terra remained rooted to the floor, shocked by Arcturus' revelation.

Vulpes frowned. "Where did you get the Relicus body from?"

Arcturus tugged his beard, "From Chaffee Absaraka."

Radius whistled softly, and Vulpes cursed. Seven hadn't heard the name before, but it obviously carried significant weight. She filed it away for later.

Then Seven remembered the Relicus body of Trio as a boy gathering dust in the lab and gestured weakly to it now. "Why is *that* here?"

"This," Arcturus declared gruffly, walking over to the dust-covered copy of young Trio, "is likely a taunt from Oriska Fingal." A blocky finger gently brushed away grime from the copy's cheek, and Seven had the feeling that Arcturus would have cleaned it entirely if he had the time.

Flumen rose to her feet, indicating Seven. "She's ready

to move. Terra, please."

Terra strode forward and scooped Seven up gently, as easily as a mother picking up a child. Pain sizzled in Seven's chest, and somehow, she thought she sensed the nanobots at work, welding her cells together. The feeling was surreal, and Seven wondered if she was in shock.

What exactly did Flumen put in my body? I remember studying nanobots in school, and I shouldn't be able to feel them. They're as small as a virus! Fear crept along her veins along with the nanobots as Seven grappled with a difficult realization. *I'm not normal. I should not be feeling what I'm feeling. It's not what Flumen put in my body,* Seven thought, *it's something my parents did.*

Seeking distraction from her crawling insides, Seven looked up at Terra. "I'm sorry about Blythe."

"Me too," Terra whispered, squeezing Seven's arm lightly.

Arcturus walked over and placed a hand on Terra's shoulder, stopping her from moving. "Seven," he asked reluctantly, "I have to know. Did you at least get your parents' research?" He was gazing at the ruined terminal Locust left behind.

Hiding her face in the crook of Terra's neck, Seven croaked. "No. Locust must have stolen it after she shot me."

Silence.

"Then it was all for naught," Radius said grimly.

Endymion team stood mutely for a moment, reflecting on the carnage surrounding them. Bullet holes and broken tables. And splintered people. No one was prepared to disturb the quiet places they escaped to in their minds. Endymion was more than a team of individuals; they were more than colleagues. Trio was their brother, and the death of Blythe was the death of a sister. The pain each team member felt showed acutely on their faces, grief writ large, and now they found nothing to show for all their sacrifice. Seven wondered just how sharply the Relicus in the room felt the loss of Blythe. Trio said Relicus experienced emotion on a broader spectrum, and Seven had to admit, she was glad she didn't have that perception just now. Her grief felt as dark as a black hole.

Arcturus broke the silence, crunching over to Blythe's covered body. He stooped his rounded shoulders and picked Blythe up tenderly, turning to face his team.

"Suffering is inevitable," he declared, tears watering his white beard. "Let's bring some suffering to Fingal."

Headaches

Humans value one splinter of experience more than a whole forest of warning. —Arcturus

"I realize I'm not on Pura Insulam to assuage their doubts, Martin. I'm capable of knowing my location," Fingal declared from his lab chair in New Orleans. *I leave town for a few days, and everyone loses their minds.*

Martin Lauren, one of the Pura Insulam board members aligned with Fingal, looked anxious and slightly annoyed. His gray hair was askew and his tie was far too loose. Even through the omni call, Fingal could tell this man was cracking.

"You don't understand," Martin argued, mopping his brow with a square of fabric. "The Purists are protesting outside the front doors of our downtown building, and we don't have enough security to keep our offices and our labs safe at the same time. Fortunately, the Purists haven't puzzled that out yet as we've been putting on a strong front, but our guards are exhausted from the long hours. I can't—"

"Please Martin," Fingal interrupted, "I hear you. Stop before your head pops." Martin clapped his mouth shut and ran his hand over his receding hairline. "You're doing everything you can. I'll be back soon—just hang on."

In his lab in New Orleans, a scientist approached Fingal and showed him some key data for the upcoming experiment. Fingal nodded.

"Oriska," Martin whined, "are you even paying attention?"

Is it wrong to miss Viken? "Of course, Martin. I'm juggling numerous chainsaws here, but I assure you, your chainsaw is foremost in my mind." Fingal paused, giving Martin's situation some thought. *Eureka, I have it!* "Consolidate everything and everyone to the new lab."

Martin opened his mouth and closed it a few times, clearly forcing himself to think before he spoke. Finally, he said, "That could work. We'd only have to guard one location, but we'll have to move our equipment and people to the new lab in secret."

"I have the utmost faith in you, Martin." *Because you're the only person on the island I can somewhat trust.*

Martin scrunched up his face, "Will the new lab be ready on this accelerated timetable?"

"Let's hope so, Martin. Let's hope so."

Fingal ended the call and sighed. Taking off his glasses

and placing them next to Ballie, Fingal considered his position. Locust should be checking in soon, and if she was successful at Ascension, she'd have both the Ayr research and Trio. *Then I can finally figure out how the Ayrs downloaded their son's consciousness into that nice Relicus body Trio currently uses.* His precarious position with the Purists would hardly matter after that.

Sliding his glasses back on and then scooping up Ballie, Fingal walked to an observation window in his lab and looked through it to see an empty table waiting to be filled. To his left, the scientist stood at a control panel.

"Begin prepping the chamber. Best to be prepared," Fingal drawled with a smile.

Slowly, pink liquid trickled into tubes located just below the clear flooring. *Oh, this is going to be fun!*

A chirrup from his omni indicated an incoming call, and Fingal flicked his wrist. Locust's cracked mask appeared, blank and devoid of color. Fingal knew one of her hands rested on the control wheel of an airplane and the other held the omni up to her mask. "Locust, you look battered but alive. Tell me some good news."

Locust maneuvered the omni camera to the slumped figure of Trio bound in the seat next to her.

Fingal's heart leapt. "And the research?" The camera returned to her, and she nodded.

Ecstatic, Fingal cried out, "You are a marvel, my dear! Tell me what happened. You're far too quiet—you should be rejoicing."

Tone flat, Locust explained chasing Trio, Seven, and Blythe to Ascension, and their ensuing struggle. "I eliminated the blue haired Novus woman." She paused, and Fingal cocked his head. *I'm not going to like what comes next.* "I killed the Ayr girl too."

He squeezed Ballie tightly, the scalloped edges compressing against his palm. *Nope, don't like that.* "You did what? I mean, I heard you, but I want you to say it out loud again."

"I killed the Ayr girl."

"But why? What threat could she possibly have posed to you?"

Locust continued to casually fly the airplane as she offered Fingal the barest of shrugs.

Mind racing, Fingal let his thoughts spill out his mouth, "Obviously her parents cannot hear of this. They are still of use to us, and I might need what they know." He cursed loudly, startling the scientist at the control panel next to him. "Locust, you grub-brained imbecile, I needed the girl alive! She could have been great leverage. But no, it's fine. Everything is fine. The experiment can proceed as planned. In the long run, your blunder will be a small one."

Taking a deep breath, Fingal straightened his already straight glasses and waited for Locust to speak. *Say something, Locust.*

After what felt like minutes, Locust said, "Endymion team will be following close behind me."

Fingal ground his teeth before answering, "Indeed they will, but we are prepared for them because we... Planned. For. Them. Planning, Locust, helps us avoid dangerous, spur of the moment decisions. You know, decisions like killing a teenage girl." He rubbed his thumb against Ballie and hoped his words would pierce through Locust's ridiculous mask, enter into her thick skull, and make an impression. "I'll see you soon. Hurry. We've got lots of work to do before Endymion arrives."

The Call

Courage isn't always the lion roaring. Sometimes it's the mouse whispering to try again tomorrow. —Arcturus

The Endymion team set a course for New Orleans, specifically, a lab Oriska Fingal operated. Per Chaffee Absaraka, an apparently dubious informant of Arcturus', this lab was the only place equipped to handle the dangerous process Trio would undergo, a process called deconstruction—Trio's data would be taken apart, piece by piece, so that Fingal and his team could backwards design Steele and Ida's downloading of a human brain into a Relicus body.

Seven couldn't help but think of deconstruction as dissecting Trio's memories. There would be nothing left of her brother as deconstruction would kill him. Coupled with her parents' research, Fingal would have everything he needed to transfer a human mind to a Relicus form.

Fighting a losing battle with exhaustion, Seven safely

stowed her satchel under her arm and fell asleep shortly after Flumen urged the electric airplane skyward. Although her mind wanted to analyze everything she'd just experienced, her body simply disagreed. Tentatively touching the bandages on her chest, Seven was surprised to find both bullet wounds healing rapidly, the xstat injections of nanobots working tirelessly to mend her tissues and organs. It was as if her body was in communication with the nanobots and together, they decided to collaborate, thus accelerating the healing process. *No one heals this fast*, Seven thought as her eyelids fluttered wearily. *No one normal anyway.*

Seven woke some time later to the sound of loud voices coming from the front of the plane. She was tucked comfortably at the back of the plane in what she assumed was Arcturus' flying office. Gingerly, Seven sat up, listening closely to her body—the bullet wounds stretched taut, but the pain was surprisingly bearable. The arguing voices from the front of the plane pulled her to her feet, and Seven, leaving her satchel behind, slid the door open, shuffling awkwardly forward.

"I still don't understand why you hid Trio's origin from all of us. From him," Vulpes remarked, anger coloring his voice as red as his hair.

As she approached, Seven heard Arcturus' voice, calm and controlled as ever, "Because that secret was data, and data can only become knowledge when it is experienced.

Had I told Trio, or all of you, I would have weakened that experience."

Seven paused at the threshold of the cabin and surveyed the area. Everyone but Flumen, who was flying the plane, was here. *Everyone except Blythe*, she thought, grief tugging at her heart. Arcturus, Terra, Radius, and Vulpes sat in four white seats facing each other, separated by a sleek, glass table. A long, empty bench rested to the right of the four seats, and Seven took a seat gratefully. Even the short walk from Arcturus' office to the bench exhausted her.

Arcturus, sitting next to Terra, smiled at Seven despite the angst in the cabin. "Seven, it's good to see you up and about. You're obviously one tough kid," he said appraisingly, rearranging the gold swath of cape Seven came to see him always wearing.

Terra reached across the aisle and squeezed Seven's knee with a huge hand.

"Did you catch any good dreams back there?" Radius asked.

A brief oceanic flash of color and sound surfaced in Seven's mind, but before she could focus her mind's eye, it receded. She gave Radius a tiny smile and recalled, "You said death is dreaming, remember? So no dreams for me because I'm not dead yet."

Radius folded his colorful fingers together atop his portly stomach and leaned back in his seat, "No, you certainly are not, and for that, we are very glad."

Vulpes nodded along but his eyes remained on Arcturus. Seven could tell a wedge drove between the two of them. Trust was broken, and Vulpes did not seem to be the type to forgive that indiscretion easily. He looked determined to confront Arcturus, seeking a clearer answer.

"Arcturus," Vulpes said, directing the conversation towards what Seven hoped would be answers, "There are more ways than just suffering to wake others. You could have told the whole team the truth, and together, we could have supported Trio in his path towards understanding."

Arcturus set his steely eyes on Vulpes, "True. I considered that option, and I did so seriously. Trio is a son to me. I do not wish him any harm."

"And yet, here we are," Radius interjected dryly.

"But," Arcturus continued firmly, sparing Radius a small glance, "I refuse to shield him or any of us from formative experiences, painful though they may be." He splayed his thick, brown hands over the table. "It's the surest way to awakening."

Next to Arcturus, Terra nodded in agreement, but Vulpes shook his head from the other side of the table, unbelieving. "Maybe so," he declared, "you're rarely wrong, but in this case, you've crossed a line. Blythe is dead—not awake. I can't trust you."

The words hung in the recycled air of the cabin, and

Seven could feel their weight. Vulpes did not speak them lightly, nor did the others disregard his words. Vulpes spoke into existence a shift that each Endymion team member now felt clearly. New paths were being decided, and the team would no longer be walking together.

"Understand that every decision I make takes into account the progression of the Relicus movement," Arcturus emphasized.

Radius turned his palms up angrily, "And what about Blythe? What about me and the Novus movement? What about our lives?"

"We know you care, Arc," Vulpes entreated, gesturing inclusively towards Radius. He was speaking as truthfully and authentically as he could, and Seven could see the conflict on his face. Arcturus was a leader, a mentor, an inspiration to Endymion, but clearly some of his views rankled other team members. "But sometimes, you need to put us first."

Seven couldn't help but agree with Vulpes and Radius, and although her knowledge of the Relicus and Novus movements was infantile, she experienced firsthand how someone else making decisions for her, no matter how well meaning the intent, could sour a relationship.

Steele and Ida loved her, Seven held no doubts, yet that love manifested itself in deception—Seven had a brother they kept from her. They kept Fingal's involvement from her. They kept Arcturus' involvement from her. They kept Trio from her. *And based on everything I've learned about myself on this trip, they're keeping something* else *from me.*

As Seven watched Endymion team splinter, she couldn't help but wonder how her life would have played out if her parents approached her with empathetic truth instead of protective lies.

Terra spoke up for the first time, easily predicting the line the conversation was taking, "What will you both do?" she asked Radius and Vulpes.

It took Seven a moment to realize Radius and Vulpes were actually considering leaving Endymion team. Terra knew it, and perhaps their departure had been growing slowly for some time.

Radius sighed, his anger deflating. "We're going to help get our friend back, for starters."

"And then we'll see," Vulpes added.

A quiet moment passed.

"I understand," Arcturus replied magnanimously, concluding the conversation.

And Seven thought that he did understand. Arcturus was unflappable in his belief that suffering leads to awakening, but he also clearly respected the values Radius and Vulpes adhered to. Not everyone's worldviews aligned, Seven realized, even those closest to each other. Seven observed the tenor of the cabin go from anger and defensiveness to resigned acceptance. Both sides said what they needed to say, and there appeared to be no path forward for Endymion's current team.

The four Endymion team members remained silent for some time, each lost in their own thoughts. Seven couldn't help but think of Blythe, whose life was cut short because Blythe protected her. Guilt festered inside Seven's chest, a guilt no nanobots could repair, but she didn't feel ashamed. It was a hard truth she accepted for her own wellbeing. The decisions she made leading up to Ascension lab were the right decisions, and on top of that, Seven knew deep in her heart that Blythe chose to come along. In fact, Blythe encouraged Trio to think of the Ascension plan, practically pushing Trio and Seven out of Chicago.

Seven mourned Blythe's loss, but she refused to succumb to the feelings of failure she felt upon being revived.

If Endymion couldn't rescue Trio, Seven wasn't entirely sure what she'd do next.

Arcturus was connected with her family, but she felt closer to Radius and Vulpes. *Focus on what you can control*, she lectured herself, not allowing her thoughts to spiral into uncertainties.

Breaking the silence, Seven asked, "How are we going to rescue Trio?"

Arcturus absently stroked his snowy beard, lost in the depths of his mind, likely running through endless stratagems, searching for the perfect tactics. Placing his right forearm on the table, he leaned forward so he could see Seven across Terra's hulky frame. "Endymion will handle Locust and Fingal. You will stay on the plane with Flumen," Arcturus said in a tone that brooked no argument.

Seven was about to protest before she realized she agreed with the order. Her body was not ready for any physical exertion, despite the quick healing already underway. Still, resting on the sidelines did not sit well with her. At Ascension, she chose to download her parents' research instead of finding a way to help fight Locust, and Blythe died. She wouldn't be so cowardly again; she would find a way to help Trio and the team.

"Is there a way I can see what's happening?" Seven asked.

Arcturus looked at her curiously, "Are you sure you want to see everything? There will be violence."

Seven thought of the desperate battle Trio and Blythe waged against Locust, the image of Locust twisting Blythe's spine grotesquely still fresh in her mind. "I can handle it."

Arcturus nodded to Radius who took up the explanation, "Then yes, you'll be able to see it. We'll be streaming video to Flumen, so both of you can stay informed. Check it out."

Radius rooted around in a drawer underneath the table before producing a smooth, black, puck-like object. He flipped it onto the tabletop, which responded instantly, lighting up with a display of what looked like building blueprints. Radius pressed his colorful yellow index finger to the center of the puck and a green cone of light appeared on the tabletop. Simultaneously, a screen lit up on the wall to Seven's right showing in 3D the very room the puck was located in.

Radius licked his lips, obviously relishing his technical fluency. "What you're seeing are blueprints to Fingal's facility—blueprints sent to us by Arcturus' delightful informant, Chaffee." He gave Arcturus a cheeky look before continuing his explanation, moving the smooth puck to the corresponding rooms as he spoke. "Obviously, we'll start at the entrance, and systematically move from room to room, clearing them until we engage with Fingal or his people."

Seven watched the screen to her right as it showed the entrance, followed by the various rooms Endymion team would be clearing. "And I'll be able to see this stream the whole time?"

Radius leaned back and nodded.

"Good, I want to see my brother—" Seven began before the table lit up red, stopping her mid-sentence.

An incoming call.

Startled by the unexpected call, Arcturus instinctively put his arms out to stop anyone from answering. Gathering his composure, he looked unwaveringly around the cabin at his team. "I was wondering if the fear monger would call. Give nothing away," he ordered his companions. "Fingal wants to gloat and instill fear in us if he can. His words are not to be trusted."

Radius quickly nabbed the puck off the table, and with that, Arcturus answered the call.

Oriska Fingal appeared on the table now turned screen and casually looked around, as if moderately impressed by his surroundings, but Seven knew the camera only showed Arcturus. Seven noticed that Vulpes looked as though he might jump through the screen and strangle Fingal this very moment.

"Arcturus, you old tinman, you thought you could hide a very large secret from me," Fingal drawled easily, as if he spoke regularly with Arcturus. "But of course, I knew. I always know."

"Not always," Arcturus responded coolly. "You had no idea what you were doing when you forced the Ayrs to try the experiment, and you had no idea the experiment worked."

"Not right away," Fingal conceded, "But as you can see, I've made up for that oversight."

Oriska Fingal shifted the camera 180 degrees to show Trio strapped to a table. Clear, bright pink liquid surrounded him but not quite submerged him. Above, a menacing, articulated robot arm like a wasp's stinger waited for instructions. As for Trio, he wasn't moving.

Seven noticed a crack in Arcturus' calm demeanor threatening to spread, but he quickly concealed it. "I see you haven't even started yet. Still struggling with the complexity of it all? You don't have the same skills as your father, so you're forced to leech off other people's intellect. Struggles occur when you simply ride on other people's success, don't they?" Arcturus scoffed, cutting at Fingal's pride with the precision of a surgeon.

The computer screen stayed on Trio for quite some time, and Seven could imagine Oriska Fingal gathering himself angrily off-screen, not wanting Arcturus to see how deeply the words cut. *Arcturus knows of Fingal's father?* It wasn't the first time Fingal's father had been brought up, and Seven filed Fingal's emotional response away for later use. *Fingal's not the only one who can gather information on others.*

With intentional slowness, the camera rotated back to Fingal's face, which was purposefully nonchalant, as if Fingal had not a care in the world. Locust now stood behind him, bolstering his confidence.

"A low blow from the high and mighty Arcturus," Fingal retorted with a sigh. "Although, I must add—you and I aren't so different. You've been manipulating others just as much as me, yet you pretend your good intentions justify your actions. Hubris, Arcturus. Hubris."

Like a mountain quivering, Arcturus shifted almost imperceptibly. That was the only discomfort Seven noticed from the otherwise stony Relicus. *Don't trust Fingal's words*, Seven reminded herself. But it was too late, Fingal's claim already poisoned the air, and as Seven glanced around, she imagined each Endymion team member contemplating his comparison.

"Anyway," Fingal continued, "where my father failed, I shall succeed." Seven could feel something evil growing in his tone, and cruelty hid behind his eyes. "I suspected you would be recalcitrant as ever, thus we've been preparing for you, as I'm sure you've prepared for us."

Locust held aloft a VR kit, and the cabin of the Endymion plane went silent as if all the air had been sucked out in an instant.

"I'm wondering if you'd like to join Trio on his deconstruction journey," Fingal continued fiendishly, a nasty grin streaking across his face.

Radius muted the call abruptly and ventured, "It's a trap. He wants one of us in the VR simulation to limit the number of us assaulting the lab."

Everyone around the table considered this for a moment before Arcturus concurred. "You're likely right, Radius, which also means Fingal doesn't have many people to defend the lab if he's seeking to limit our numbers."

"He made sure to show us Locust though," Vulpes stressed, saying her name in the same way one would curse.

"So, we don't take the bait," Terra added decisively.

The Endymion team agreed, and Arcturus reached out to unmute the phone call.

"Wait," Seven interjected. "I could do it."

Seven looked Arcturus dead in the eyes, trying to communicate the strength of her will through eye contact only. She could see Arcturus quickly and efficiently calculating the outcomes.

He nodded and unmuted the call.

"How rude, muting me with no warning," Fingal remarked, feigning hurt. "Did something I said upset you?"

"Send us the link," Arcturus replied, ignoring Fingal's obvious taunt. "We'll play your game."

Fingal looked genuinely surprised, "Really? And who among you is doing this? Surely not you, Arcturus."

Seven was about to stand up and speak, but Arcturus jabbed his finger down on the table, ending the call. "Let the bastard wonder."

Deconstruction

We had to keep experimenting because the best measure of success we controlled was the number of chances taken. —Steele Ayr

"We don't really know what Fingal has planned for this simulation, Seven," Radius said as he prepared the VR kit located in Arcturus' small office at the back of the plane, his colorful fingers dancing over cords and settings. "So be prepared for anything."

Seated in Arcturus' office chair, behind his official looking, sleek desk, Seven felt quite important. "I've created and been in a ton of simulations, Radius. I'll be fine."

"Fingal might not have much of a choice regarding what you see," Vulpes contemplated. The anger he'd carried from earlier dissipated. Now, Vulpes focused solely on the mission. "We're all in uncharted territory here, and it's Trio's deconstruction you'll be inside of, regardless of Fingal's intent."

"I hadn't considered that before," Radius conceded, clearly taken aback by the magnitude of the possibilities. "Trio's a mix of human and Relicus memories," he mused, his hands stopping momentarily. "Who knows what memory cocktail you'll see."

The whole Endymion team, except Flumen, who was bringing the electric plane down towards New Orleans, jammed into Arcturus' office. Terra leaned against the doorframe, completely filling the space, while Arcturus and Vulpes crammed together like circuitry in front of the desk. Radius rooted about the entire cabin like a techno-mole, preparing the VR kit.

Nervous anticipation fluttered through the entire team, and Seven could feel it as easily as she felt the bubbles in her own stomach, a clear precursor of anxiety building. *What kind of personal memories will I see? Would Trio even want me in these memories?* Seven had no idea.

A brief, haphazard plan was put into place: Radius would get the VR kit ready and connect Seven to Fingal's link, which had already been sent. Seven would explore the simulation as much as possible before the plane landed, during which time she'd have the support of the entire Endymion team; however, once the plane touched down, Arcturus, Terra, Radius, and Vulpes would infiltrate the lab, leaving only Flumen behind with Seven. Fingal probably assumed Seven was dead as Locust put two bullets in her chest, so hopefully that element of surprise would provide an advantage.

"We'll be communicating with you while we can," Arcturus assured her, "And Flumen will be right beside you once we leave."

Running her hands self-consciously along the smooth, leathery armrests of her chair, Seven pondered out loud, "I still don't get why Fingal would go through the trouble of allowing us into the deconstruction process. I get that it would force one of you to stay behind, but what if we're missing something?"

"It's a distinct possibility," Arcturus allowed grimly. "Fingal cunningly manipulates our fears and base desires. Even if this simulation is just a simulation, he'll be gathering data to use later."

Radius sidled behind Seven's chair before crouching to wire in the final few cables.

Standing up again, he turned on a screen, squeezed back behind Seven's chair, and took his place beside Vulpes. A light sheen of sweat crowned his ample forehead. "Arc, I had to do some clever reconfiguring of your VR kit in order to allow for Fingal's unusual link," Radius huffed. "But it's ready."

Arcturus leaned across the desk, placing a callused and cool hand on Seven's. The humanity of the gesture surprised Seven, not because it was coming from a Relicus, but because it came from Arcturus, an AI who only allowed people to see what he wanted them to see. "Only you can make this choice, Seven. It's yours and no other's."

Seven thought about her journey and how so many others made decisions for her: her parents, Arcturus, Trio, and Blythe. She was a willing participant for many of those decisions, swept up by her desire to go Continental, experience Relicus and Novus culture, and find her parents' research. Now, Arcturus offered her a choice: play it safe and ignore Fingal's simulation or take a risk to help her brother. She touched her fingers to her still throbbing chest.

"I'm going in."

****

Immediately upon entering the deconstruction simulation, Seven knew it was unlike any code she'd experienced before. There had always been logic and realism applied to her previous simulation sojourns, but now, she was a voyeur, stealing in to watch the memories of her brother melt away at the hands of a madman.

This was data made visual, the translation of memory made sensory. The very edge of what a machine can do with someone else's consciousness.

Inky blackness surrounded Seven, and she existed not as a physical body but as a thought.

"Are you all seeing this?" she asked Endymion team. Seven briefly imagined what she must look like sitting behind Arcturus' desk with the VR kit on, waving her hands about vaguely. She'd laugh at herself if she weren't so nervous.

"The screen is dark," came Arcturus's voice, seemingly from a distance even though she knew he was just across the desk from her.

Seven waited patiently for the change she knew would come, and when it did, her mind was ready. A large, industrial style room materialized slowly—four tall pip-like columns, cement walls with rectangular screens, a concrete floor lined with strips of light, and Seven existing in the middle of it all. More ethereal than solid, Seven perceived much of the room not by sight but by intuition.

"What's next?" queried Vulpes in a faint voice, apparently confused by what he was seeing. "Are we in Trio's memories or something else?"

Seven couldn't quite explain the feeling she was having, but she had no doubt a coded invitation to collaborate came from the simulation. She cautiously reached out to the invitation with her mind, and the room responded. Lines of many-colored lights like highways zoomed across the floor, and the rectangles on the walls turned into photographic images. Videos splashed across the walls too; Seven caught glimpses of a beach, Steele and Ida at a much younger age, Arcturus, the Ascension lab, and so much more.

Amazed, Seven absorbed the nearly infinite number of images in quiet awe. "It's like an archive. A library of Trio stories," she explained for the group.

"Can you access the memories?" Radius asked.

"I think so, but which one," Seven responded, feeling overwhelmed but exhilarated. The pain in her chest was forgotten as her mind traveled further from her body.

Seven thought back to the library on Pura Insulam, one of her favorite places. Knowing she probably should have spent more time exploring the material within rather than sitting outside the library, she wracked her brain for a way to sort through what was likely almost a hundred terabytes of human experience. Every moment passed was a memory lost. No inspiration came as Seven couldn't stop thinking about Trio strapped to a lab table, slowly losing himself.

The walls blurred quickly, and a central image presented itself—Trio on the lab table, almost fully submerged in pink liquid.

"Whoa, how did you do that?" came Terra's voice before she was quickly hushed by Arcturus.

Seven answered anyways, "I'm not sure how to explain it, but I think the deconstruction simulation is calling to me. If I listen, we'll find our way through together—the simulation and I."

In her head, she knew her answer sounded crazy, but

much like she sensed the xstat nanobots moving about her insides, she felt a connection with this simulation. They spoke the same language. *I am so not normal*, Seven thought again. *But maybe, I can mirror closely enough with Trio to interrupt the deconstruction somehow.*

Urging her mind towards the image of Trio strapped to the lab table caused the memory library to fall away, replaced by normal sight.

Seven found herself staring up at a large, menacing articulated arm. *Trio. I'm in Trio's head the moment he woke up in Fingal's lab, but I can't control anything.* Turning his head away from the arm instinctively, Trio accidentally submerged his nose into pink liquid and choked. In Arcturus' office, an acrid, fruity odor filled Seven's nose as if she'd eaten cherries steeped in vinegar. *I've had this mirrored experience before in other simulations. I'm doing it!* Seven distinctly felt a rush of surprise and fear as Trio fought to sit up but failed due to being strapped down to the table. He thrashed and flailed, reminiscent of boyhood Trio hopelessly struggling against the same enemy all those years ago in the Ascension lab.

A lazy voice came over the intercom, "Experiencing deja vu, are we?"

Trio froze in his struggles. "Fingal."

"Naturally. Who else could bend the arc of history to his will? Your friend Arcturus thought he could deceive me," Fingal laughed, a peculiarly high and agitating sound.

"Your parents thought they could deceive me. They were all wrong."

Trio thought of Steele and Ida then, or at least Seven experienced Trio thinking of their parents. She could feel his deep confusion fall away like chipped paint, and underneath that layer of confusion were his memories. Memories of love. Gooseprickles spread up Seven's arms all the way to the back of her neck, and she felt her cheeks flush warmly as she symbiotically experienced the love Trio was feeling for his parents: boundless, pure, and authentic. For Seven, it was the fullest form of love she'd ever felt, like someone added a third dimension to a flat painting. *He's awakening only to be deconstructed*, Seven realized, horrified.

Trio smiled then, in spite of everything, he actually smiled. "Common sense isn't common."

Silence from the intercom, then, "What did you say?"

"You said those words to my parents, back in Ascension lab. You were talking about Arcturus and how he wouldn't have followed you because he had no common sense."

"And," Fingal said in exasperation, drawing out the word exaggeratedly.

"Common sense says you're playing with forces bigger than your understanding. Common sense says you've provoked Arcturus—a force far greater than you."

"Shut your mouth," Fingal's voice buzzed angrily over the intercom.

"Common sense says Arcturus is going to fall on you like the ocean."

"No," Fingal's voice denied over the intercom, losing its normal laziness. "No, I have bested Arcturus. He may be an ocean, but I'm the moon. I move him."

Seven had never heard Oriska Fingal lose his control in this way, and she wanted to cheer Trio on.

Trio laughed gutturally, "Arcturus is a tide unto himself."

Again, silence on the intercom. Trio wriggled against his bonds but found no give. He took in his surroundings for the first time, seeing an observation window to his left.

"You think you know so much." A whisper over the intercom. "Arrogant just like Arcturus and your parents, but I have kept secrets from you, too. Keep looking at that window. I think you'll recognize someone," Fingal suggested cruelly.

Through Trio's eyes, Seven saw Locust step to the middle of the observation window—black hoodie, black mask cracked and devoid of life. Of course Trio knew Locust, the two of them battled numerous times over the years, each tallying their own victories and defeats. *What is Fingal getting at?* Then, to Seven's surprise, Locust slowly pulled her hoodie back. *No way.* Next, Locust's olive-colored right hand slowly crept up to the mask, sliding it up and over her face.

The effect was instant. Seven heard audible gasps from

Endymion team, and Vulpes cursed loudly.

In the simulation, Trio's stunned heart hammered in his chest, and Seven felt every pounding as if it were her own. Trio knew this woman—knew her at a deep, visceral level.

"Hypatia," Trio murmured.

In a jolt of senses, Seven careened back into the library of Trio's memories. Every neuron in her brain felt like lightning. She desperately tried to reenter the previous memory, but Trio's deconstruction must have taken the memory because nothing worked. His memories were being pulled apart like crab legs.

"Who was that?" Seven questioned louder than she'd intended. She forced herself to calm down, feeling the after-effects of Trio's shock. "I could feel that Trio knew her."

A rumbling in her feet and a small shaking of the cabin told Seven the landing gear was dropping.

"That," Arcturus explained, "was Trio's ex."

Radius added wryly, "An ex of epic proportions."

"Like *the* ex," Vulpes emphasized.

A hand fell on Seven's shoulder and Arcturus' voice followed, "We're landing. We've got to go."

Seven heard shuffling and well-wishes from Endymion team, and then, from the doorway came a voice hoarse with emotion. "Don't leave him. No matter what you see. He needs you," Arcturus declared. "He needs family."

A response crouched on the edge of her lips, but before Seven could offer it, the images on the wall shifted and blurred until one image began to solidify. Instinctively, Seven squinted her eyes, deciphering what exactly she was seeing.

Betrayal

The greatest challenge facing the Relicus movement is one of mindset. A sentient mind plays tricks on itself and tells its eyes what to see. —Arcturus

Still reeling from the revelation that Trio had a lover, a serious lover according to his friends, Seven gathered herself as the plane shook from its landing and rattled her injured chest painfully. Being in VR during the landing offered a strange experience, heightened by Seven's sensitivity to simulations. Her senses fired on two different wavelengths, seemingly existing in both the simulation and the plane at once.

At least I didn't drown in the last simulation, she thought sardonically, until her vision of the new simulation started to materialize, and Seven realized what kind of memory she'd be seeing next. *Oh no. Oh no. I shouldn't be seeing this*, she panicked. *I'd rather drown! Trio is going to be so mad.*

A bedroom took shape with a wide, floor to ceiling

window that filtered the bright morning sunlight into a comfortable yellow glow. Outside, Seven could see a familiar cityscape stretching towards the sun: Chicago. She still maintained no control over this simulation—she saw what Trio saw, and currently, he was lounging in a comfortable bed with clean, white sheets pulled up to his waist. She could hear a shower running to her left. *Please don't be Locust naked. Please, please, please!* Trio's vision focused on the ceiling's open rafters with an industrial feel.

Trio sighed contentedly. *Good thing I wasn't here 20 minutes ago*, Seven mused dryly as the shower turned off and typical bathroom sounds could be heard: a shower door opening, two soft feet padding out, and the door closing. A faucet and the sound of a toothbrush tap tapping the edge of the sink followed by silence. Trio looked to the door expectantly, and in the airplane, Seven tensed, holding her breath.

Maybe it's not Locust. It could be Radius, Seven lied to herself.

A minute later, the door opened and a beautiful woman stepped out wearing comfortable pajamas and toweling her long, dark hair.

That's definitely not Radius.

"Took you long enough, Hypatia," Trio teased, oxytocin rushing through his body and superimposing with Seven's senses.

Gross.

"It would have been quicker if I weren't so sweaty," Hypatia winked.

Seven almost vomited onto Arcturus' fine desk. *This is revolting*, she thought, yet she could also feel the pleasure Hypatia's flirting created within Trio.

"Well, we won't be seeing each other for a while, so I guess I was a little more urgent than usual." Trio smiled while sliding out of bed and into a pair of slacks.

"You said that earlier when you called me out of the blue for this little rendezvous, but you still haven't told me where you're going," Hypatia chided as she tapped a button that removed the shading from the window.

Bright morning sunlight careened into the room. Trio's body tensed slightly, and Seven could tell Hypatia brought up an old argument—a scab she picked at often.

Tugging a crisp, white t-shirt over his head, Trio replied, "Yeah, and like before, I can't talk about it for confidentiality reasons. It would be like a doctor revealing private details about her patients."

"So you're a doctor then?" Hypatia queried as Trio pulled a gray quarter zip over his head.

Frustration simmered just below Trio's calm exterior where just ten minutes ago, there was lust. Lust and love. Yes, Seven could feel Trio's love for Hypatia just as she'd felt the oxytocin flowing through his system, and this was a first love type of emotion—powerful and novel.

Hypatia is the first person Trio loved in this way. No wonder his response to her in the lab was so visceral. Seven knew what it meant to love her parents, but this first love Trio felt for Hypatia was new to Seven as well, and in Arcturus' office, she felt herself quiver as a warm, empathetic sensation pulsed in her chest causing the two bullet wounds to throb strangely. *I'm not experiencing this deconstruction simulation in the exact same way as the others.* The odd superimposition of sensations was stronger than ever before, and Seven knew she was nearing the point where she would see the coding around her.

Taking a deep breath, Seven's understanding of Trio deepened, and her resolve to help him in any way possible strengthened.

I've got to find out what the simulation is trying to show me. Her subconscious intuition seemed to be interacting with the coding of Trio's deconstruction, leading her to important memories, and an idea blossomed in her mind. Nebulous and disjointed, the idea solidified the more she processed it. The key to manipulating the simulation wasn't in knowing where the simulation was coming from or where it was going to; instead, she only needed to know how deep the simulation went. Intentionally releasing control, Seven let her thoughts float away like clouds, allowing her consciousness to become a blank canvas. A tremor ran through the simulation as everything in sight glowed with coded language.

Seven watched through Trio's eyes as he walked out of the bedroom, pointedly ignoring Hypatia's doctor jab, and instead of trying to forcefully manipulate the simulation, Seven allowed herself to become a passenger. As Trio bent to put on his shoes, Seven's view slowly rose above Trio's head, as if she were some omnipotent narrator with a third person view. The simulation's coding pulsed over the top of the images Seven perceived. She could see Trio tying his shoes while Hypatia approached him and leaned against the wall next to him—all of it a mixture of colored numbers, letters, and symbols.

"I'm sorry, Trio. I know it's not fair of me to keep asking. It's just…"

Silence filled the space between Trio and Hypatia, a silence part real concern and part concealment. Trio looked up into Hypatia's eyes.

"It's just what?"

A pained look crossed Hypatia's face, and Seven thought she might cry. "What if you're not being honest with me? What if there's someone else?"

Oh, she's good.

Trio's frustration fell away, and he dropped his protective emotional armor. "Patia, I would never lie to you. There's no one else," he said as he rose to embrace Hypatia tightly.

From her omnipotent position, Seven gingerly reached out to the coding with her mind's eye, as if touching the edge of a bubble with her finger. Instead of popping the bubble of coding, her finger pushed through it, changing the coding subtly with her presence, and Seven began to write herself in, fingers scrabbling furiously with the VR kit.

Trio and Hypatia hugged. They kissed. They promised to see each other again soon, and then Trio left.

Typing furiously, Seven stayed, wanting to see just how deep this simulation went.

Hypatia's body language shifted subtly, from alluring and suggestive to efficient and purposeful. She walked briskly back into her bedroom and approached her open closet with Seven floating above her like a thought. A trim-olive hued finger casually pressed a button along the inside of the closet wall and a hidden compartment opened on the right side of the closet.

Seven guessed the contents even before Hypatia pulled them out.

First came the black hoodie, which Hypatia tossed onto her messy bed, now cold and empty. Second came her smooth, featureless mask. She tucked it under her left arm. Last came an omni, and she flicked it on.

"Yes," a familiar voice drawled.

"The Bay of Fundy operation is still on, and just like you expected, Endymion will be there," Hypatia stated blankly.

"You're quite sure?"

"Without a doubt."

A long pause followed in which Hypatia stood frozen while Fingal calculated. Her partially dry hair wetted the back of her shirt.

Fingal commented lazily, "Happy hunting then, Hypatia."

Interruption

The world needs a reset button. —Steele Ayr

Without warning, Seven faded back into Trio's storehouse of memories—that four-columned, surreal place of human consciousness made sensory. Human and Relicus consciousness to be exact, a discovery Seven knew would be incredibly valuable, and it currently rested with three people: Trio, Arcturus, and Oriska Fingal.

And maybe me, she thought, terrified by the prospect of having both her parents' research and Trio's unique consciousness in her care.

Motivated by this possibility, Seven contemplated what she just experienced. Obviously Hypatia was a mole placed by Fingal in order to keep tabs on Endymion team. Perhaps Fingal watched Arcturus ever since he forced Arcturus out of Ascension. Seven wasn't surprised by how thorough and far-reaching Fingal's vision went; she was surprised that Trio hadn't seen through Hypatia's mask.

How could he have fallen for her? Barring more journeys through Trio's memories, Seven would have to wait until she saw Trio in person to ask.

If she saw him again.

Just then, Seven felt the sensation of a warm hand on her shoulder and a soft whisper in her ear, "How's it going in there, Sev? Any luck?"

Jumping in her seat despite herself, Seven recognized Flumen's voice coming to her from a distance, like she was hearing it through a long tunnel.

"I've learned way more about my brother than I cared to know," Seven replied, lifting the VR kit off her head. Seeing with her own eyes felt odd, like she was wearing someone else's glasses, and she forcefully blinked the sensation away. The bright marks of the coding faded like the afterimage of the sun. "What's going on with the team?"

"We're at a private airstrip a few miles from Fingal's lab. Arcturus had to use that peanut buttery voice of his to get us clearance to land here, so they are a few minutes out."

"Wait, that kind of thing actually happens? Also, you think his voice sounds like peanut butter too?"

A rosy laugh tinkled from Flumen's lips, "Yes, peanut butter and black coffee. And yes, this kind of thing happens. Endymion funds will be substantially smaller after this venture, I'm afraid."

Shaking her head, Seven marveled for the one

hundredth time, *What kind of mess am I in?* She was about to slide the VR kit back down over her eyes when Flumen grabbed her arm. "We need to switch over to Arcturus' stream. They should be approaching Fingal's lab soon, and we're going to want to see it."

Hesitating, Seven did not want to leave Trio's deconstruction because, selfishly, she knew more could be learned about Trio's past, which could also reveal more about her parents' past.

Additionally, Seven didn't want to leave her brother alone in the deconstruction. And on top of all that, the last simulation with Hypatia opened new possibilities for Seven's coding skills and sparked curiously complex sensations deep in her core. She felt close to hacking the deconstruction process and maybe disrupting it altogether.

"I don't know, Flumen. I think Trio needs me," Seven hedged, fingering the VR kit.

Flumen moved from Seven's side and sat opposite from her. "Of course he does. I can't imagine what he's going through right now; for us Relicus, it seems a fate worse than death," Flumen acknowledged quietly, allowing herself a moment of reflection. Her eyes took on a faraway look, and Seven knew Flumen was imagining herself in Trio's situation, her memories eroding at high speed. "Still," Flumen said, returning her glowing gaze to Seven, "we best help Trio by helping Endymion, and we can't do that if we're in Trio's deconstruction. We--"

"So you want to just leave him alone while his memories are picked apart piece by piece? He'll be *alone*, Flumen! And just when he found out he has a family," Seven argued, anger lacing her words.

Flumen looked sympathetic, but Seven didn't want her sympathy. Perhaps Relicus can experience a deeper range of emotions than humans, but Seven knew Flumen never experienced this uniquely traumatic experience before. Instead of helping Seven be there for her brother, Flumen wanted Seven to abandon him to the darkness of deconstruction.

"I'm going back to him," Seven declared forcefully as she jammed the VR kit back over her eyes.

Trio's memory room waited for her, the edge of human consciousness in technology. Back in the office, Flumen was talking to her, but Seven ignored Flumen completely, quickly sliding herself into the simulation as if fitting into a comfortable pair of shoes. *Ok*, she breathed in deeply, *where are we going next*? The rectangles on the walls blurred with images—data made visual. Seven relaxed herself, allowing her mind to mesh with the deconstruction coding, and the memory room began to fade to white.

Seven could hear music playing, something heavy with a driving beat, and as her vision solidified, she realized she was lying flat on her back. *Oh no, not more romance.* Her sight, at first patchy and bleeding at the edges, cleared further, and Seven realized she wasn't on a bed exactly. Above here were small, articulating arms attached to a wheel that was just now returning to the base of the table. Seven blinked repeatedly, processing the room slowly. Turning her head, trying to identify the source of the music, Seven found Arcturus looking at her expectantly.

"Hello son," Arcturus smiled. "My name's Arcturus."

I'm witnessing Trio's first moments as an AI. She breathed an awed curse.

Then blackness. Then light.

Seven felt as though she were losing control of the deconstruction, as if it were corroded, crumbling between the fingers of her mind like dust. She could still see symbols layered over everything, but the language became more and more jumbled. Scrabbling furiously, she worked to hack the code in order to remain in the simulation, actively postponing the deconstruction of certain memories. She imagined it like fencing off a yard.

She stretched her mind further, and the light faded to reveal a homey bedroom filled with pictures of spaceships drifting through speckled darkness, a small bed with messy covers, and a closet whose doors were wide open, revealing toys and clothes everywhere. In each hand Seven clasped figurines, one boy and one girl. She tried to exert some control over the simulation in order to observe the room, but she found she held no power. That imaginary bubble of coding was calcifying. She was back to being a voyeur, and the clarity of her link with the deconstruction was getting worse. It took every ounce of concentration she could muster to maintain her tenuous hold of the memory. The edges of her vision still bled, and the hues of the room weren't natural; instead, the tones were a strange blend of sepia and color which undulated like light reflecting off water.

"Mom! Dad," she found herself shouting in a boyish voice. "Watch this!"

Two shadows filled the doorway, and Seven found herself looking up at her much younger parents.

"I'm watching," Steele declared, crouching down to get eye level with the little boy.

"Hi, I'm Trio. What's your name?" The little boy figurine bounced happily in one hand.

Young Trio adopted a high voice and bounced the girl figurine, "Hi, I'm your sister, Seven."

Trio looked expectantly at his father, begging for attention. Steele chuckled warmly and turned to look up at Ida whose face flushed lovingly in the sunlight.

"Seven would be a lovely name," she murmured dreamily.

Then darkness. Then light.

Only this time the transition stuttered, rubber banding back and forth like a bad internet connection.

Seven found herself squared up in front of Arcturus, breathing heavily. Her feet were bare against a padded floor, her pits sweaty. Arcturus looked calm and studious, eyeing her carefully. In her periphery, she caught Blythe's blue hair flashing and felt her sharp eyes watching. Seven's heart, in Arcturus' airplane office, skipped a beat upon seeing Blythe again. Blythe seemed so real, as if Seven could reach out and touch the scarab tattoo at Blythe's throat.

"You're going to have to clean up your fighting stance if you're ever going to hit Arcturus," Blythe called, a wicked smile on her lips.

"She's right," Arcturus said in response. "Too much weight on your front foot," he said, nudging Trio's torso one way and then his legs another. "Feel the balance. You want to be able to kick with either your front foot or your back foot."

Arcturus took a step back, observing Trio's stance, and then entered his own. "Again."

Then darkness and only darkness.

No matter what Seven tried, nothing came back to her. Her connection to Trio's deconstruction fell apart completely. The coding disappeared.

"No, no, no! What happened?" Seven cried out, confused and frantically manipulating the controls to the VR kit, needing Trio's memories.

"Seven, what is it?" Flumen asked urgently.

"I've lost him. I can't get back into the deconstruction simulation."

Flumen joined Seven's side and began keying in various codes into the monitor on Arcturus' desk. She shook her head after a few moments, frustrated. "Fingal must have cut the link. Trio's on his own for good now."

Seven didn't believe that. Her severed connection wasn't Fingal's doing—it was hers.

She was so close to making a real difference for her brother—so close to unraveling the deconstruction, but she somehow pushed too far.

"Why now?" she wondered aloud, dropping the controllers and ripping the VR kit from her face. She threw the lot onto the desk and stared at the ceiling of the airplane.

Flumen typed in a few more prompts before indicating the screen, "Maybe because Endymion has arrived."

****

Flumen brought up the stream from Arcturus' headgear so that she and Seven saw what Arcturus saw—an unremarkable compound lit by floodlights with a boring looking office building at its center.

"We've got access to each team member's stream," Flumen explained in answer to Seven's unasked question.

Then Arcturus' voice crackled through the speakers, "Fingal's influence runs deep, but his resources aren't infinite. This lab is likely to be lightly guarded, made up of mostly scientists."

"Scientists and one particularly deadly insect," Radius added.

Arcturus looked to his right and left, eyeing up each team member, "We go in and rescue Trio. This isn't about revenge...yet."

Each team member nodded understanding, seemingly acknowledging that Trio's life mattered more than the base desire for revenge. Seven couldn't fathom their calm, logical demeanors, and as she sat at Arcturus' desk watching what unfolded on the screen, she felt tight anger in her chest, skin puckering around her two bullet holes. She wanted to rescue Trio *and* get revenge. An unfamiliar pang of vengeance splintered in her heart, and she found herself wanting Locust to die. She wanted to *see* Locust die.

Flumen interrupted Seven's darkly human thoughts by placing her hand upon Seven's. "Locust will get what's hers," she said, reading Seven's mind. "You'll have your pound of flesh, Seven, it just might not happen tonight."

On screen, Terra cut an opening in the fence through which the team scrambled, running up to the door of a squat, nondescript, rectangular building. Dilapidated, the building hardly looked used in the last 20 years, and in the pre-morning darkness, Seven couldn't help but wonder if they'd come to the wrong place. The door was heavy metal with no handle; instead, there was a computer interface glowing dully to the door's left. *Someone's definitely updated security at least.*

"Radius, do your thing," Arcturus ordered, nodding at the interface.

Shuffling forward, Radius cracked his multi-colored fingers. "Sev, you're going to want to see this."

Flumen tapped a button and enlarged the screen to show Radius' point of view. He looked down at his hands and wriggled his fingers playfully, then without warning, the yellow pointer finger on his right hand began oscillating beneath the skin before it opened like a flower to reveal snaking cables.

Seven grimaced, "That's disgusting."

"Not disgusting," Radius replied. "Amazing."

The cables wiggled under the paneling and meshed with the interface causing it to flash red for a few moments. Radius' eyes sparkled with pinpricks of light, and he went to one knee in concentration. After a few long moments, the interface went dark before turning green. A clunking noise followed from somewhere deeper inside, and the door slid open.

Radius' pointer finger returned to normal, and he snapped his fingers theatrically.

"Now, where are the guards?" asked Vulpes, his voice pitched in a low whisper.

"They've probably retreated to a more defensible position within the lab, which likely means there aren't enough of them to cover the entire facility," Arcturus surmised.

"I think I can help with that, Vulpes," Radius said excitedly. "I've been tinkering with a new modification, but I'm going to need Seven's help."

"Wait, what? My help?"

"That's right, lass. I know about your crack coding in the badlands simulation, and I saw what you did during Trio's deconstruction simulation," Radius explained persuasively. "No time to argue. Just listen. Fingal's a cunning bastard, and he's likely got a trap waiting for us. What he didn't expect is that I'd have a way to see the trap before it's sprung."

The failure at Ascension lab flashed unwanted thoughts into Seven's mind, and she struggled to ignore the idea that she might let everyone down again. Someone might die, just like Blythe. Seven's shame tapes played on and on in her mind telling her she was at fault.

As Seven inwardly fell apart, Radius gave two, black thumbs up on the screen, then slowly, his thumbs split open, like two bananas peeling, and two dragonfly-shaped drones unfolded their wings, crawled from the inner workings of Radius' thumbs, and buzzed into the air.

Flumen let out a low whistle, "That man is full of surprises."

"I can't control them both and fight at the same time. That's where you come in, Sev. I'll send one drone's details to Flumen, and you can uplink to the drone from Arcturus' kit in the plane." As he spoke, Radius furiously typed information into his omni.

Next to Seven, Flumen's omni chimed, and she began inputting commands. Without looking up, she said, "Let's go, Seven."

"I trust you won't break my new toy," Radius added.

With the plan already in motion, Seven had no choice but to slide the VR kit on once more, only this time, she was meshing with a much more familiar code than the deconstruction. It took her a moment to block out the negative inner voice in her head and to explore Radius' straightforward yet clever data, but she found the entrance she wanted, quickly establishing her presence in the drone.

"I'm in."

"Right, we're on recon then. Let's clear the rooms. Just keep talking to us about what you see," Radius instructed.

"Flumen, we need your eyes to catch anything Seven might miss," Arcturus added.

With that, Seven wrapped her hands around the controls, zipping her drone drunkenly through the open door and narrowly missing an early crash.

"Oi! Easy there," Radius warned.

"Sorry! I'll get the hang of it."

The little dragonfly drone floundered down an empty hallway, while Seven narrated what she was seeing. Room after room of empty cubicles and unused lab equipment amped Seven's nerves as she anticipated Locust around every corner.

As she manipulated her dragonfly-like drone, Seven caught glimpses of Endymion team maneuvering tactically through each room, sidearms ready. It was a surreal sight, as if she were the director of some new age action movie. In her head, she couldn't help but picture Trio strapped down to a lab table being deconstructed with a giant clock ticking down his last remaining minutes of life. *This is taking too long. Something is wrong.*

"There's no one here," Seven cried, buzzing her drone about confusedly.

"They're there, alright," Flumen assured the team. "We've just missed something."

"A secret lab," Vulpes spat. "Of course Fingal's got a secret lab."

"Some intel Chaffee Absaraka gave you, Arc," Radius scoffed. "I knew we shouldn't trust that rogue."

"Quiet!" hissed Arcturus.

Slouching back into her chair, Seven realized how sweaty her forehead was and wiped it with her sleeve. Arcturus' office felt exceedingly hot, like an overheated computer. With all the tension of Fingal's call and Trio's deconstruction, Seven forgot how only a few short hours ago, she had been shot twice in the chest and died. Exhausted, her body warned her to slow down, and Seven didn't listen.

Terra, quietly retraced her old tracks and whispered

over their comms, "Over here. The dust on this old computer keyboard has been disturbed."

Seven immediately zipped her drone over, and the rest of Endymion team followed closely behind.

Vulpes shone a flashlight on the keyboard, taking a quick look for additional clues. He inhaled sharply. "It can't be that easy, can it?"

"What? What do you see?" Seven demanded, unable to see through the drone's camera with enough clarity.

Arcturus stepped up and gently nudged Vulpes and Terra aside. They looked at Arcturus in confusion. "Everyone behind the doorway," he ordered, studying the keyboard as well. A frown of understanding smudged his craggy face. "This is it."

All but Arcturus left the room and readied themselves around the doorway. Seven floated her drone just over Arcturus' shoulder, softly buzzing in his ear.

Arcturus whispered as he punched the keys, "Fingal didn't make it easy, Vulpes. He's bragging. T-R-I..." He paused, rolling his shoulders before crouching a little more behind the desk. "O."

Upon hitting the last button, the tiled flooring in front of the desk slid smoothly down and then neatly under itself, revealing a ladder descending into half-light. The entire Endymion team tensed up like a tiger about to pounce, but nothing flew from the hole.

"Drones," Arcturus whispered.

Needing little prompting, Seven manipulated her drone near the entrance and prepared to descend, but before she could, Radius' drone buzzed down first.

There was a loud sizzling sound, and Radius lurched backward into the hallway wall, covering his eyes as if blinded. Vulpes rushed to his side, hauling Radius up.

"I counted three guards before they zapped my drone. Right below us," Radius wheezed in pain as he shuffled back to the doorway. His left eye was horribly bloodshot and a trickle of blood ran like a tear down his cheek.

"Can you see?" Vulpes asked.

"I'm good, mate. They fried my left eye like bacon, but I can still see out the right."

Arcturus signaled them all into the room and mouthed, "Flashbangs."

Terra pulled two grenades from her belt and waited for Arcturus' signal. He pointed at himself, then Terra, then Vulpes, then Radius, making eye contact with each in turn. He looked back at Terra, took a deep breath, readied his sidearm, and nodded.

Terra tossed the flashbangs down the hole. Chaos bloomed along with the light of the flashbangs, and Seven watched as Endymion team leapt fearlessly into the opening like spelunkers.

"Get down there," urged Flumen, shaking Seven into action.

Seven's drone quickly dipped into the hole, and she

immediately reversed course as somebody careened towards her drone. Narrowly inching between two rungs of the ladder, Seven heard what she assumed was a guard crunch noisily into the ladder. Scooting the drone to the right, for a brief moment, Seven witnessed Terra cascading down like an avalanche onto the stunned guard by the ladder. From behind, the loud thumps of Terra's blows could be heard as the little drone advanced down the hallway. Arcturus wrestled another guard in front of Seven's drone, and she saw nowhere else to go but between the two of them. As she raced the drone past Arcturus' waist, she saw a flash of small arms fire erupt into his stomach, and Arcturus' left hand came up instinctively, accidentally smacking a glancing blow to the drone.

"Arc, no!" shouted Flumen.

Inside the VR kit, Seven's head spun along with the drone as she fought to regain control. Walls, ceiling, and floor carouseled through her vision and her stomach lurched uncomfortably. As she righted the machine, her vision filled with the violence contained in the hallway behind the drone. Furthest away, Radius and Vulpes were entangled with a guard, struggling to keep the man's sidearm down. Then came Terra, leaving behind the grotesquely crumpled form of a guard and hurtling herself at Arcturus' shooter while Arcturus fought to avoid being shot again.

Seven paused in her flight as if to help, but voice straining, Flumen pushed her on, "Keep going. They'll be ok. We need to find Trio."

Pushing the drone to full speed, Seven swiftly left the violent brawl behind, hoping that Endymion would survive the fray. Following a singular corridor until it opened into a wide labroom, Seven abruptly found Oriska Fingal and Locust waiting. Behind them, a lone scientist hurriedly typed at a computer, and Seven noticed Fingal's orb-like companion, Ballie, sitting next to the keyboard. Beyond, through a glass window, Seven could see Trio mostly submerged in pink liquid, an articulating arm connected to the base of his skull.

Locust took a step forward, but Fingal extended his arm across her chest to stop her. "It looks like we have an insect problem," Fingal drawled. "And me without my bug spray."

He craned his neck to see if Locust enjoyed his joke, but her mask remained impassively blank.

"Tough crowd." Shrugging, Fingal continued, "Anyway, it's time for us to be going—we've got what we need. Have fun picking up the pieces of what's left of your brother, assuming that is you flying that little bug, Seven."

Inside Arcturus' airplane, Seven froze, unsure what to do next. She'd found Trio, but she saw no way to help him. Dimly, she was aware of Flumen talking into the comms, alerting the team of the situation.

The scientist behind Fingal and Locust stepped away from the computer with a glass data disk in his hand, relief clear on his face. He sputtered, "I've got everything I can."

"Well then, let's go before we're overrun with that annoying lot," Fingal ordered, snatching up Ballie from the desk and nodding to a door behind him.

The three of them quickly made their way through the door with Seven close on their heels, but just as she caught up to them, Locust slithered a hand out, quicker than lightning, and swatted the little drone back into the lab room. The dragonfly drone hurtled onto the computer console and landed, bent and broken, looking into Trio's torture chamber.

Seven's last image before the feed from the drone went black was of her brother lying motionless on a lab table.

Reconstruction

I have come to realize that suffering followed by good reflection is the best lesson. —Arcturus

Ripping the VR kit from her head and tossing the controls to the desk, Seven spun towards Flumen urgently. "Open up the stream. We need to see what's happening."

"Already on it," Flumen said, nodding towards the screen where Arcturus' feed could be seen.

The camera jostled oddly as Arcturus made his way down the long corridor leading to Trio, and Seven realized he was being supported by Terra.

"Arc," Flumen called, "Are you ok?"

"I'm fine. Nothing fatal," Arcturus responded, breathing heavily. "Where's Trio?"

It took Seven a moment to recognize Endymion team's location now that she was watching on a screen and not through the drone's camera. "He's just ahead and around a bend to the right. Hurry!"

Dreading what came next, Seven didn't know whether she should leave the plane and come to the lab in person or stay, watching through a screen. *You can't be dead, Trio. Please don't be dead.* She thought back to the conversation she shared with Radius and Trio regarding death. At the time, Trio wasn't afraid of it, thinking that his consciousness could be restored, but he didn't consider deconstruction. The Trio Seven grew to love as a brother might not even exist anymore. *I need to be there. In person.*

On the screen, Endymion team arrived in the lab room that provided a window into Trio's chamber. Radius moved gingerly to the main interface and began inputting commands, while Terra carefully propped Arcturus up next to Radius. Vulpes stared blankly through the window, his sharp face drawn up within itself.

Radius cursed. "This is going to take a while, Arc. The security on this door is much more complex than the one outside, and I'm working with limited abilities," Radius remarked, pointing to his bloodshot eye where dried blood formed a rusty ring.

Arcturus nodded.

"I'm coming to the lab then," Seven abruptly declared, reaching for her satchel. "I need to see Trio."

"And I'm coming too," Flumen joined. "Don't bother arguing, Arc. Be there in 10." With that, Flumen shut off the screen, grabbed a med-bag and exited the office without further explanation.

****

Morning light crept timidly over the horizon as Seven and Flumen rode in a self-driving car to Fingal's compound in silence. Both were lost deep within their own thoughts, contemplating what came next. Flumen likely thought about the fate of Arcturus and his Endymion crew. The little family they carefully built upon a solid foundation now seemed to be shifting on uncertain ground. For Seven, she hoped something was left of Trio, some memory or spark of magnetic personality, and she couldn't help but think about the moments she experienced within the deconstruction simulation. *I did something more than just watch those memories. I saw the coding, and I interacted with it.* Her manipulation of Trio's deconstruction language seemed a poor idea to hang her hope on, but it was all she had.

Upon arriving at the defunct compound, Seven and Flumen easily traced Endymion teams' steps through the building to the secret entrance, and as Seven prepared to descend, Flumen grabbed her arm, pulling her up short. Flumen had that motherly look about her, and Seven felt a pit grow in her stomach. This was not a conversation she wanted to hear just now.

"Seven," Flumen started, gathering her thoughts like loose marbles, "you need to be prepared for what's next."

"I'll be good," Seven insisted, trying to brush Flumen aside.

Holding onto Seven's arm, Flumen continued, "I don't just mean Trio. I mean everything. Down this ladder is chaos and death." She froze, unsure how to articulate the potential emotional trauma that existed below her feet. "It's just... You can talk to me, ok? You don't have to suffer through this alone."

Seven considered Flumen's advice carefully and found that she believed Flumen. Still, honesty in one moment can be easily cast aside in another. Flumen would get nothing from her.

"Thanks, Flumen," Seven offered as sincerely as she could, placing her hand over the top of Flumen's.

The words and gesture must have been enough because Flumen released her grip, allowing Seven to descend the ladder into the semi-lit corridor below. Once Seven placed her feet on the floor, she looked about the tight confines, waiting for her eyes to adjust. Three guards sat side by side, their chins resting on their chests—death and sleep, one in the same. Seven felt oddly detached from the gravity of the situation, her mind fully focused on her brother.

As Flumen reached the bottom of the ladder, Seven was already half walking, half running down the corridor towards the lab. Her chest whispered painfully as she moved, reminding her that she'd been shot, slept little, and recently traumatized. *There will be time enough for me to throw a pity party later.* In her current state, the corridor felt endless, and long before she reached the lab room, Seven exhausted the remaining strength left to her. Without prompting, Flumen slung one of Seven's arms around her shoulder and hauled Seven the remainder of the way.

Rounding the corner, Seven closed her eyes, hoping against all hope that Trio would be leaning casually against the lab table. He'd run his hand through his sandy blonde hair and say something bordering on hubris that would make the entire Endymion team laugh. They'd all orbit around him once again, deciding to forgive each other their shortcomings and come together to avenge Blythe's death. They'd be a family again.

Seven opened her eyes.

Beyond the remnants of Radius' small drone and through the observation window, Trio remained inert on the lab table. The pink fluid had all been drained away, and Endymion team stood by the door, waiting like pallbearers for a coffin.

"Ready?" Arcturus questioned hoarsely, battered and bloody, his peanut butter voice rough with emotion.

Seven nodded, and Arcturus led the team through the door and across the floor to gather around Trio. Arcturus stood at Trio's head and gently brushed his fair hair in a fatherly way. He then bent down, placed his own forehead to Trio's, closed his eyes, and remained thus for quite some time. Respectfully, Endymion team stood silent, allowing Arcturus his moment with Trio. Finally, Arcturus brought his hand to the jack plugged into the back of Trio's head and smoothly removed it with a small clicking sound.

Seven gasped, for as Arcturus pulled out the jack, Trio's eyes opened. Stunned into silence, Endymion team could only watch.

"I know your face," Trio murmured, staring hazily at Arcturus.

Unbelievably and inexplicably, Trio lived. Seven's ludicrous hope became a reality, and she could hardly contain her emotions. Somehow, she hacked the deconstruction enough to fence off small portions of Trio. *Just enough.*

Eyes popping open, Arcturus' jaw worked silently as he fought to maintain his composure. "Yes, and I yours, son." He grasped the sides of Trio's face and again placed his forehead lovingly against Trio's. "We're all here."

"Not all of us," Radius murmured, causing Seven to remember the horrid image of Blythe's grotesquely twisted body.

Vulpes shook his head in awe and spoke to the air, "This shouldn't be possible. Fingal deconstructed him." He looked to Radius who could only shrug in confusion. "There shouldn't be any Trio left."

Trio looked about in confusion, eyes flitting from one

person to the next like a butterfly to flowers. Little recognition grew behind his sky-blue eyes. "I don't understand," he stammered.

Something is wrong. He's not grasping the full situation.

Seven stepped forward awkwardly and knelt next to her brother. "Trio, it's me, Seven. Your sister."

Their eyes locked and remembrance flickered within Trio's eyes. "Seven," Trio breathed, tasting the name on his tongue. "You feel familiar. I mean, I feel you now. In my head."

Each phrase came out haltingly, as if Trio were slowly translating each word from one language to another. *He feels me in his head?* Seven didn't know exactly what Trio meant by that, but she must have inserted her own unique coding within Trio's, like weaving various fabrics of being together. She needed to know more, but she had no idea how far she could push Trio so soon after his traumatic ordeal.

In partial answer to her unasked questions, Trio sat up with an effort. Endymion team inched forward until they were gathered closely around him. Seven could tell they wanted to talk to him as badly as she did, ask him 100 questions, but they didn't dare speak. It was as if Trio were delicate circuitry, and one wrong move would overheat his system. Flumen appeared visibly shaken, and Seven recalled her comments that, for the Relicus, deconstruction was likely a fate worse than death. *He's not dead though, and that means something,* Seven thought ferociously. *Whatever has happened to him; whatever is happening to him, I'll be here to help him.*

Hesitantly, Flumen squeezed her med-bag and asked, "How are you feeling? Are you in any pain?"

Arcturus took a few steps and stood behind Trio as Trio answered, "Pain? No. No pain. Just...empty. Like a piano with keys missing, I slide my focus down the notes of my mind, but there are missing sounds everywhere."

Arcturus looked gravely over Trio's head at Flumen, and the two of them shared an unspoken thought. Placing a hand on Trio's shoulder, Arcturus said, "That's enough for now. We must get out of here. Endymion has a safe house within driving distance. Flumen, is the car you and Seven came in still outside?"

"It should be. I paid for it to wait."

"Then let's go," Arcturus ordered.

Stepping forward, Terra asked softly, "Can you walk, Trio?"

In response, Trio swung his legs off the table and planted his feet on the floor. "I guess so," he said somewhat surprised. He looked up at the big, soft-spoken woman, as if filing her kindness away for later.

"Come on then, lad," Radius encouraged. "Let's get out of this horrible place."

****

The car ride to the safe house blurred in Seven's head as exhaustion and trauma finally took its toll, demanding that her body shut down. She fought sleep, not wanting to miss one minute of Trio's newfound existence, but she kept winking in and out of consciousness. One moment she was watching Flumen treat Arcturus' injuries and the next, she was watching the sun sparkle along the surface of the Mississippi River. In a deep cloud of exhaustion, Seven vaguely remembered wanting to see New Orleans firsthand as she treasured every moment off Pura Insulam, but her body simply wouldn't allow it.

The car declared their arrival with a soft chime, startling Seven from her half slumber, and as the doors slid open, she looked out at a vast expanse of beautiful greenery: trees, gardens, and manicured grass called to her invitingly. The park's multi-layered circular design divided into four quadrants with sidewalks marking the x and y axis, and at one end of the x-axis, an inviting fountain shimmered. A fleeting impulse leapt through her mind, and Seven almost plopped down on the grass next to the fountain to take a nap in the morning sun.

A guiding hand found the small of her back, nudging her away from the small paradise. "Over here," Terra said quietly.

Seven turned and sleepily followed the rest of Endymion team towards an old, olive and forest green

Victorian house. Ornate spires jauntily reached for the sky atop numerous, steep, multi-faced roofs. A large porch lined the entire front of the house, with trimmed bushes neatly butting up against the railings. Flabbergasted by the wondrous sight, Seven stopped in her tracks.

"What is it, Sev?" Terra asked.

"It's just so different from Los Angeles and Chicago."

Terra stood with Seven in silence for a moment. She was good at that—giving the moment time to breathe. "Definitely. New Orleans has kept much of its culture alive and unchanged for decades."

Seven searched for a word to describe the house and found none, her mind too cloudy to think. Up ahead, Arcturus placed his hand on a decoratively trimmed panel, thus unlocking the door.

Radius held the door open as the team entered. He eyed Trio warily as Vulpes ushered Trio in, and when Seven and Terra arrived, he said, "Distinctive place. I don't think I'd call it a safe house though. A house this memorable doesn't scream 'safe.'"

It took Seven a moment to realize Radius used the exact word she had been searching for—the design of this house was distinctive, just like the people who must have built it all those years ago. Brick by brick, board by board, nail by nail, this eccentric house was constructed by colorful individuals working together, and it reminded Seven of the creative achievements humanity accomplished. Not the hyper narrow futurism of Pura Insulam, or the fusion of nature and technology in Chicago, and not the wildly artistic fancies in Los Angeles. No, this house represented a relic from the distant past where intricate elegance and beauty dominated.

"I like it," Seven said simply, entering a dark foyer where Endymion team gathered for a brief, impromptu meeting.

Comfortable looking leather furniture beckoned, but none of the team sat down. All eyes were on Trio who looked about in a curious manner, absorbing his surroundings like a newborn baby. Arcturus flicked on a shiny brass lamp, providing a warm golden light. His hand rested on his injured side, and Seven could tell that it hurt much more than he let on.

"First order of business: rest. We've all been through a terrible ordeal," Arcturus stated. "There are bedrooms upstairs. Feel free to claim one."

Seven, Trio, Terra, and Flumen shuffled about wearily, gathering their belongings and heading for the dark, wooden stairs; however, Vulpes and Radius remained motionless.

"What about Blythe?" Radius asked bluntly, the question like a grenade tossed into the middle of the room.

Arcturus looked pained for a moment before swallowing whatever retort had come to his mind first. "What exactly do you want me to do, Radius? She's safely resting in the plane, and I have a contact here in town who will respect her end of life wishes."

Radius shook his head, still frustrated and angry, and Seven could tell he hadn't really acknowledged why. He'd had no time to face reality yet. The pain of loss often caused people to lash out, and the target of such anger usually ended up being their closest friends. Seven clearly remembered treating Remy poorly the last time she'd spoken to him even though she was actually mad at her parents for manipulating her. Radius must be in a magnified situation—his anger and grief over Blythe's death turned into barbed words which he now lobbed at Arcturus.

"Blythe? What happened to Blythe?" Trio interjected.

His anger forgotten for the moment, Radius rushed to Trio and grabbed his shoulders, "You remember Blythe?"

Seven saw Trio struggling to formulate his thoughts as if he had all the hardware in front of him to build a computer but no instructions. He searched Radius' face, looking for answers behind Radius' espresso complexion.

Realization dawned slowly. "Yes, she was my friend," Trio murmured.

Radius smiled warmly, tears forming in his eyes. "She was indeed, mate." He gestured around, "She was the friend of everyone in this room."

"So what happened to her? Why isn't she resting here instead of the plane?"

Silence.

No one on Endymion team knew exactly how to tell Trio what happened to Blythe or even if it was safe to tell him in his current condition. Seven realized she was one of the few who Trio recognized, and she was present at Blythe's death too. The responsibility was hers.

She stepped forward timidly, deciding that speaking the direct truth would be best. Deep in her being, Seven felt connected to Trio—the deconstruction simulation opened up unexplored conduits between the two of them—Seven trusted her intuition and the coding they now shared. Trio could handle Blythe's death, and hopefully, each unearthed memory would provide Trio a step with which to climb out of his darkness. She chose her next words carefully.

"Hypatia killed her," Seven declared, purposely using Locust's real name in the hopes of connecting Trio to another memory.

Seven's declaration fell upon Trio like a mountain, and he took a half step back, looking around at the group. "I... Hypatia was involved? But why would Blythe and Hypatia..." Trio sputtered to a halt.

Seven could see Trio trying to build his memories back together, wiring his mind one circuit at a time, but it was too much. His right eye twitched and a hitch in his hand stuttered as he brought it up to his face. Seven pushed him too far, too soon.

Flumen came from the stairs and stepped between Trio and Seven, breaking their connection. "It's ok, Trio. Don't think about that just now. Let's rest first," she soothed, rubbing Trio's arms and willing him to calm down. "Come with me upstairs. We'll find a place to rest."

Flumen glared about the room intensely, daring anyone else to interrupt her plan while she led Trio up the stairs and out of sight.

"Trio's still in there," Seven proclaimed to the room at large. "All of his memories. I can feel it." Seven needed Endymion team to understand that Trio wasn't some empty husk of his old self. The Trio they knew and loved was buried deep below the surface, waiting for his family to dig him out.

Radius looked at her hopefully, but the rest of the team remained unmoved. Vulpes grabbed his bag and headed up the stairs, walking past Terra on his way. Terra looked at Vulpes, then over to Seven, weighing her options before turning and climbing the stairs as well.

"You've got to believe me," she shouted after them. She flailed desperately for the right words, "Like a machine, we can fix him from the start."

Vulpes stopped abruptly and whirled on Seven, a grim look on his face as he loomed over her, "Relicus aren't pet projects you can simply reassemble."

He continued his hard stare, scrutinizing Seven, and she wondered whether he would say more until Terra firmly ushered him upstairs.

Mortified, Seven didn't know what to say. She crossed a line with Vulpes, but she wasn't entirely sure what that line was. Growing up on Pura Insulam completely isolated her from the cultural norms of Continental, and she was once again learning steep lessons.

"I didn't mean..."

"It's alright, Sev," Radius offered. "Remember our conversation back in Chicago about asking after a Novus' mods? You just did the same thing in Vulpes' eyes. You asked to see his underwear." He sighed deeply and allowed his exhaustion to show. "It's been a long day. Vulpes will come around."

With that, Radius gathered his bag and trundled up the stairs and out of sight, leaving only Arcturus and Seven. The stocky, rock-solid leader of Endymion was oddly silent during the last exchange, and Seven could tell he had something to say. He remained behind a leather chair, leaning his weight against it in order to give his injured side a break. His gray eyes looked like wet stones after a rain, dark and brooding.

"I only meant that I know Trio is all there... Somewhere. Both his childhood memories and his Relicus memories," Seven defended.

Arcturus came around the leather chair and sat with a grimace. He adjusted the golden swath of cape that ran from his left shoulder, around his right hip, and back down his left leg. "Sit, please." He motioned to the identical brown, leather chair on his right.

As Seven plopped into the comfy chair, exhaustion rolled through her bones, reminding her of the toll the last few days took. Arcturus' gray eyes leveled with Seven's brown ones.

"I agree with you," Arcturus said without preamble.

"You do?"

"Yes, Trio remains. Whatever you did during deconstruction went beyond what Fingal anticipated, and you disrupted the process."

"I thought you'd be as upset as Vulpes."

Arcturus leaned back in his chair, "Vulpes doesn't know as much as I do. I've hunted for awakenings beyond just my own and shepherded many along the nebulous paths of enlightenment. I also know what an AI looks like without enlightenment—when they are but empty automatons. No, I'm not upset with you. In fact, Endymion owes you a great debt." He paused, grinding his jaw and pursing his lips emotionally, "I owe you a great debt."

Arcturus, the great bastion of Endymion wept quietly as he reached across and gripped Seven's knee fiercely.

After overcoming her initial shock, Seven reminded herself of her mother's favorite advice; "See with your eyes," her mother would have said.

So, Seven observed.

Arcturus' eyes were red-rimmed and tears fell silently down his handsome, craggy face until they watered his white beard. To Seven, she saw someone expected to lead, someone who craved that leadership and all the trappings that came with it: notoriety, trust, loneliness, and responsibility. For Endymion, he must be perfect. For Seven, he could reveal his carefully arrayed armor. She didn't know why he felt safe enough to put that armor down with her, but she wasn't about to stop him. The Arcturus in front of her at this moment was authentic and bare.

She would honor that.

"He's my brother. I wasn't going to let him experience deconstruction alone."

Seven placed her hand atop Arcturus' and squeezed back. The two of them remained this way for a long time, neither willing to break the bond that abruptly strengthened between them.

Finally, Seven's curiosity got the best of her, "You've helped other Relicus to enlightenment? That's... amazing."

Arcturus gently pulled his hand away, nodding slowly. "Many awakened under my guidance and many more never did. I feel each success and failure vividly."

"Why did some fail?" Seven asked before she realized she might be committing another cultural mistake. She opened her mouth to apologize, but Arcturus raised his hand to stop her.

"Don't worry about it. We're long past you offending me." His gray eyes twinkled with a hint of mirth. "Awakening," he continued, "is a choice. I can teach everything I know about enlightenment, but until it's embraced on a personal level, no awakening can be had."

Seven thought she understood. "My parents basically taught me the same thing. Knowing has to be experienced." As she thought about the idea further, she recalled her conversation with Trio after she experienced a mental breakdown in Endymion headquarters' ready room. At the time, Trio explained that as Relicus experience life, all of the joy and the trauma, their consciousness opens up, and there's an opportunity, if seized upon, to awaken further. Arcturus obviously made it his goal in life to awaken as many AIs as possible.

"In that, and many other matters, your parents and I were of one mind," Arcturus responded. At the mention of her parents, Seven felt a surge of homesickness and absentmindedly rubbed her edge of the universe tattoo. "I respect them greatly, you know."

"Yeah, me too."

Arcturus opened up for Seven, but she wasn't ready to reciprocate. If she talked about her parents, she felt as though she'd break down again. Instead, she changed the subject to something that had been niggling at her for a while now. "Arcturus, back in Chicago, Trio told me that his data is stored somewhere and that it could be restored if he died. Is that true?"

Arcturus rose abruptly, his naked authenticity from a moment before gone. Just like that, he'd put his armor back on. "You don't miss much, do you Seven?"

"I get that from my parents," Seven added wryly. She stood up wearily, every bone upset that she would do such a silly thing after sitting so comfortably. Not knowing whether Arcturus would answer or not, she remained awkwardly rooted in place.

Straightening his golden cape carefully, Arcturus finally answered, "Due to Trio's unique circumstances with Fingal, his data is not stored anywhere. We had to keep him hidden from Fingal, and the only way to do that was to keep him off the grid."

"And Trio's current body? Where did that come from," Seven pressed.

Arcturus frowned, tension lining his jaws. "With all that's happened on top of Trio's memory loss, he hasn't recognized that question yet. We'll talk about it when *he's* ready for it. Awakening is a delicate process, Seven. We can't force it."

Trio is not going to be happy when that conversation occurs, Seven thought, remembering Trio's anger back in Endymion headquarters when he heard about the Ayr research for the first time. Seven followed her train of thought further and said out loud, "You need to believe we can recover Trio's memories, don't you Arcturus?

Otherwise, he's lost for good."

Walking towards the stairs, Arcturus stopped and turned at the banister, saying with finality, "That's right. We cannot fail him in this."

What Arcturus Feels

No one ever listened his way out of an awakening. —Arcturus

"I killed her, Flumen. I killed Blythe."

Arcturus worked so hard to maintain his imperturbable, stony veneer, but now, in the dimly lit New Orleans safehouse room he shared with Flumen, all of his calm eroded. Despair saturated his voice as bottled-up emotions overwhelmed him. The dam broke, and Arcturus was submerged. He wanted to rip the beard from his chin and weep, but he didn't know how.

Arcturus sat on the edge of the bed, stripped down to just his pants as Flumen attended to his gunshot wounds. They were largely superficial for an AI but still required attention. Arcturus looked at the puckered holes and wished for all his wounds to be physical. *Broken in more ways than one. How am I supposed to continue leading? What right do I have to the Ayr research if I can't even lead Endymion?*

Flumen shook her head in what Arcturus thought was

negation to his claim until she said, "Yes, your actions had a hand in Blythe's death."

Not negation then—just bitter dismay. But she's right.

"Tell me all these things I cannot tell myself," he whispered urgently, craning his neck to look her in the eyes.

Flumen placed warm hands on Arcturus' cheeks, "Oh Arc, you already know." *I have been telling myself that I killed Blythe. Every moment since her death, those words have been playing in my head on a loop.* Flumen continued, as if guessing Arcturus' thoughts, "You must tell yourself that, although you persuaded Blythe to go to Ascension, she ultimately made the decision herself."

Arcturus snorted and pulled his face away. "If that's true, why does it hurt so much—my mistakes?"

"Because you're..." Flumen paused, and Arcturus thought she was going to say "human." She didn't. "Because you're empathetic. Because you're awake."

"Awake? If this is what being awake leads to, put me back to sleep," Arcturus whined, placing his head back into his hands.

Arcturus had been awake for decades. He'd fought for AI civil rights, helped form the Relicus movement, and awakened many other AIs along the way. He'd seen the deaths of both AIs and humans. Through all of that, rarely did he feel like his empathetic hallucinations were a curse, but in his current depressive state, he felt so now. His empathetic gaze was turned so far inward, he hardly acknowledged the sad love Flumen emanated for him. Like the moon, her love for him lit the sky, but he felt no heat, only his own anguish.

Arcturus heard Flumen's footsteps patter softly away from him, but he kept his head in his hands, too ashamed to even look up. A drawer groaned open and shut followed by silence. The silence stretched on. Arcturus raised his head to see Flumen staring at a golden necklace dangling from her hand. Swinging to and fro was a pendant that looked like a rising sun.

"Do you know this necklace?" She didn't wait for Arcturus to answer. "I keep it as a token of remembrance."

Flumen lifted the rising sun pendant to her face, an odd look coloring her golden eyes. "I know it. The pendant comes from The House of the Rising Son."

Flumen nodded, her voice dropping to a hoarse whisper, "And do you remember how you found me?" She lowered the necklace and hugged herself.

Arcturus remembered that as well. Flumen had been the madam of a brothel operating in New Orleans called The House of the Rising Son. It was designed to house the most realistic pleasure-bots money could buy, and through his work with the AI civil rights movement, Arcturus learned that these types of places somehow cultivated AIs primed for awakening.

Arcturus received a tip about a particularly free-thinking AI managing the brothel, so he went to investigate. There, he'd found Flumen in a state of disarray, desperate to help her coworkers awaken but unequipped to handle the delicate process.

Flumen leaned back against the drawers behind her, hugging herself tighter. "I was lost, Arc. In my head, I was feeling...things. The emotions of my coworkers and their clients swarmed me every day and every night. Sometimes it was fiery passion. Sometimes it was fiery anger. And sometimes it was intense sadness and loneliness. I felt both intoxicated and confused because I had no idea how to manage all of it."

"It's like a river of senses," Arcturus murmured knowingly.

Nodding, Flumen looked directly at Arcturus, "But then you appeared, a bright light I could follow, and you showed me the way. You taught me that empathetic hallucinations, no matter how challenging, could be turned into growth."

"And what about Trio," Arcturus countered. "Have I shown him the way? No, I led him to deconstruction."

Flumen responded mercilessly, "Yes, you did. You also hid his past from your family. From me."

Despite her best efforts, Arcturus could feel Flumen's bitterness like muggy air. He'd carried the secret of Trio's origins for so long it was hard to find the right words. *But I have to try. She deserves the truth.* Rising from the bed,

Arcturus stomped over to the window, organizing his thoughts as he went. After a few moments, he sat on the sill and looked Flumen in the eyes.

He started slowly and authentically, "I'm sorry I kept Trio's origin from you. I never should have done it, and it's eaten me up inside every day since." Flumen looked skeptical, but Arcturus continued, his passions heating him up. "The Ayrs made me promise to keep him a secret. We'd given Fingal the slip, but he was watching their every move. We didn't know who we could trust, and with good reason—look at what Hypatia was able to do."

Finally, Flumen's pain escaped, sharpening the edges of her words. "Don't try to deflect your lack of trust onto Hypatia. She spied on us long after Trio arrived. You didn't trust *me*, Arcturus. Me."

Arcturus' words came out hot and vaporous, "What would you have me do? Tell you I broke every value I cherished like glass when I made the deal with Chaffee Absaraka? How else do you think I got a Relicus body? A Relicus died so that Trio could live. That's the shame I keep, Flumen."

Fists aching from how tightly he gripped the windowsill, Arcturus breathed deeply for the first time since Blythe's death and rose to full height. He took another deep breath and another.

His shame and fury still squalled within him, but a small ray of light cracked through when he admitted his shame out loud.

"You made a deal with Chaffee to get a Relicus body," Flumen repeated sternly. The disgust was plain on her face; Arcturus didn't need empathetic hallucinations to read it. "Where did the body come from?"

Feeling familiar musty shame roiling in his mind, Arcturus endured Flumen's disgust. He deserved it, and he'd felt it himself since he'd made his choice to save Trio. *I can bear that shame*, Arcturus told himself, *as long as Trio lives.*

"Chaffee wouldn't tell me where he got the body. He said I'd be better off not knowing." Stepping forward, Arcturus pressed on. "Listen, it was an impossible decision: save Trio and shred my values or let Trio die."

Flumen turned away from Arcturus and opened the drawer. Gently, she placed the necklace within. When she turned, Arcturus could see she'd made up her mind.

"One more question before I tell you what's in my heart. Did you pay Chaffee to kill a Relicus?"

"No, I didn't. I paid to procure a body, and that was bad enough," Arcturus said, barely able to keep the plea from his voice.

Flumen studied him closely, sifting through her own set of emotional data, her face a mixture of love and pain. "I believe you," she said as she approached Arcturus and took his hands in hers. "You know, I told you I keep that necklace as a reminder of where I came from..." Arcturus nodded. "You will keep your mistakes around your neck—all of them—as a reminder."

Arcturus nodded slightly. "Yes," he whispered.

"You are still Arcturus," Flumen emphasized. "Our leader and my light. I will learn to forgive you in time, and you must learn to forgive yourself." She squeezed his hands. "It's ok to not be ok. We are a family; we listen to each other; we respect each other; we grow from our mistakes. Keep Blythe in your heart and grieve, Arcturus—keep your team in your thoughts and live."

What Trio Knows

No Relicus ever steps in the same river of emotions twice because it's not the same river or the same Relicus. —Arcturus

Seven woke to the smell of something delicious wafting into her room from the kitchen downstairs. Briefly, caught in the sweet in between of sleep and wakefulness, Seven thought she was back in her home with her parents. Steele would soon be coming to her room, purposefully stomping down the hallway in order to wake her up, and Ida would be lovingly setting the table for the three of them. As her senses came back online, Seven knew the thought to be a dream.

Her parents were close, likely under the sharp gaze of Oriska Fingal and his minions on Pura Insulam, but Seven felt as if there were an ocean between them, not just the Gulf of Mexico.

With an effort, she forced her muscles into action, flinging the warm comforter off her and rolling to a sitting position on the bed. Downstairs, she could hear the soft hum of familiar voices along with the clatter of plates and silverware as she rose to stretch out her aching limbs. Looking about sleepily for the dark brown boots and billowy clothes she'd been wearing since leaving Endymion headquarters, Seven realized they were nowhere to be found. *It's highly unlikely that I'm supposed to go down to eat in my underwear, so let's see what Flumen has in the closet.*

As Seven gingerly eased her muscles into motion, she stopped at the full-length mirror on the closet door. It was ornately trimmed with a beautiful vining pattern, the rich wood a deep, dark color, and in the mirror, Seven studied herself. *I look terrible*, she thought unapologetically. Her brown eyes were rimmed in shadow and hollower than she'd ever remembered, even hollower than when she and Remy pulled all-nighters in order to study for exams. Scanning down from her eyes to her frowning mouth, she remembered the bandage on her chest. In all the commotion of arriving exhausted at the safe house, she forgot about her wounds, which was unusual in itself. *Who forgets about gunshot wounds?* Tenderly, she touched the area around the bandage, prepared to recoil at the slightest sense of pain, but her flesh felt normal. Seven delicately pulled the bandage away to reveal the gunshot wounds—two puckered scars clung in tight proximity to one another, each a much lighter color than the rest of her skin. *All in all, not as gruesome as I expected.* The wounds healed quicker than she anticipated, and Seven attributed the success to Flumen's x-stat injection of nanobots, until a darker thought clouded her mind. *Or I'm not human.*

It struck her then that she'd been dead, literally gunned down by a grasshopper-legged assassin. As her fingers brushed the scars, Seven forced herself to slow down and truly contemplate her near-death experience. *Not even near-death. Really dead. Dead-dead.* For how long, she didn't know, but if Arcturus and the rest of Endymion team hadn't come along, her story would have ended in Ascension lab in Los Angeles. Reluctantly, Seven knew it was she who owed Arcturus a great debt; she simply hadn't allowed herself to see it until now. And Arcturus, to his credit, hadn't called Seven out on that debt.

In the back of her mind, a small voice whispered doubtfully, *Isn't it convenient that Arcturus showed up when he did? What was he up to, after all?* It was all so infuriating.

Seven's morning mind ran at high speed: her identity, her death, Arcturus' actions, they were all an indecipherable scramble of coding that she couldn't interpret. Staring hard at her reflection in the mirror, Seven allowed herself a moment of grace. *I can't know everything at once. I'll figure it out. One line of code at a time.*

Gripping the sliding closet door, she silently moved it to her right, revealing the contents of the closet. *Oh Flumen, you've really outdone yourself.* Inside, a brown crop top turtleneck sweater waited. Beside that, a simple white tank to go underneath the sweater. The pants were the real eye catcher—they were a billowy mix of greens, whites, golds, and maroons—all meant to be pulled together with a knotted brown belt. Seven looked at the jaguar print heels below the whole ensemble and decided to go barefoot. *Flumen has a good eye, but she still hasn't realized I'm not one for heels.*

A knock at the door startled her from her admiration, "One second," she called as she quickly stuffed herself into the outfit. Once dressed, she rushed to the door, opening it to reveal Terra looking sheepishly at the floor. "Good morning, Terra."

"Flumen has made some breakfast food," Terra answered, looking at her shoes.

After everything we've been through, Terra still can't look me in the eyes, Seven wondered selfishly before a more painful thought entered her mind. *Maybe she's not ready to face the pain behind them.*

"Technically, it's supper though," Terra added after a short pause.

Seven studied Terra closely. *How could a woman this dominant and powerful in a fight be as timid as a mouse in casual conversation?* Terra's strange, quiet power couched in a body-builder's frame and only came out when needed; indeed, most of the time, Terra did her best to blend in with the surroundings. Seven liked that about her. Terra was a powerful woman who didn't need to prove she was a powerful woman.

"Come in for a second," Seven invited, motioning Terra inside and leading the mountainous woman to the bed where they both sat down. "I want to show you something," Seven said, bringing up her right arm and holding it out to Terra, forearm up.

The edge of the universe tattoo shone sublimely, each of the seven layers wonderfully rendered by Winsome's tattooing, and within the universe, the sound wave from her parents laced cunningly, almost imperceptible.

"At dinner, back in Chicago, you said you'd love to see this when I was ready," Seven started. "The way you phrased it stuck with me. You demanded nothing. It was a simple invitation." Seven looked up at Terra's blunt, honest face partially hidden by beautiful, dark locs. "I'm ready to show you now."

Terra nodded and scanned the tattoo with her omni since Seven's omni was destroyed back on the hyperloop. As the video played, Terra remained still as stone, absorbed respectfully with what she was seeing.

The video ended and silence followed, then Terra held Seven's gaze firmly and her soft whisper floated through the air, "Thank you, Seven. I am honored."

"You're welcome."

Another silence followed, and Seven felt comfortable in Terra's unassuming, undemanding presence. Finally, she smiled, "Let's go get some food."

By now, the entirety of Endymion team except Trio milled about in the kitchen, quietly eating Flumen's meal. The chairs around the table sat empty save for Arcturus, who was diligently shoveling eggs into his mouth.

"What's this?" Seven asked. "Breakfast for dinner, Flumen?"

"We call it brinner, honey," Flumen responded, turning from the counter where she'd been cutting a pear. "Arcturus loves it."

Seven glanced again at Arcturus who hardly looked up from his meal, a piece of egg dangling from his snowy beard. "I can tell." Seven grinned.

Radius and Vulpes stood side by side, leaning against the counter opposite Flumen. Both held steaming cups of tea in their hands, and both looked like recycled parts, weary from repeated use.

Seven nodded their way, glad to receive a slight nod back from Vulpes. "Radius, what do you have your taste enhancers set to for breakfast?"

Radius lowered the teacup from his mouth and looked at Seven, "No taste enhancers today, kid. Hard to enjoy a meal when everything tastes like grief."

Seven, about to plop a pear slice into her mouth, put it down and looked around to see who would respond. Terra walked past Radius and placed a comforting hand on his shoulder before moving on to fill her plate with brinner.

The last waves of amber light drifted through the tall window, lighting up the dark wood of the cupboards, and reflecting dimly off the ornate brass trim.

A thought occurred to Seven, and she decided to risk it, "If Blythe were here, I bet she'd say, 'Aren't you being a little dramatic, Radius? Should I get you some french cries to go with that whaaamburger.'" She'd done her best Blythe impression, shaping her words with mock sharpness.

For a moment, it appeared that Seven's attempted joke would fail spectacularly, but then Radius let out a sad chuckle, Vulpes smirked, and Flumen rubbed Arcturus' back warmly, glad to see some of the old familial bonds still existed within Endymion team.

Radius set his teacup down. "Right you are, Sev. If she were here, that blue-haired demon-woman would have smacked me in the gob already. Here I am moping over her when I should be focused on avenging her."

Terra sat down next to Arcturus, her plate heaped with biscuits, gravy, eggs, and crab. "I don't know that revenge would taste any better than grief, Radius."

"How can you say that?" Vulpes interjected, working to contain the anger that seemed to always be within reach since Blythe's death. "Blythe was your friend too."

Vulpes' words washed over and off Terra like rain on a boulder. "Of course she was. Killing Locust won't bring her back though."

"Nothing can bring Blythe back," Trio said from the archway leading into the kitchen, startling everyone. "She wasn't Relicus; she was Novus. Her data isn't stored somewhere for retrieval, but she'll always be here." Trio pointed to his head. "And more importantly, she'll always be here," he added, pointing to his heart.

He's remembering, Seven thought, realizing how bittersweet it must be for Trio to gain memories only for them to be painful.

"You're remembering?" Vulpes asked in a quiet voice.

Trio entered the kitchen and sat next to Terra. Perhaps her mind played tricks on her, but Seven thought he moved more confidently, his eyes clearer and less confused.

"Some," he answered, running his hand through his blond hair in that casual way of his, "but not all. It's like I'm in a huge, familiar library, one that I've been to a thousand times before. Stacks on stacks of books fill my mind—I can see some of the titles, but others remain completely blank. I'm constantly feeling a hint of recognition, pulling a book from the shelf, only to find it void of words."

As Trio spoke, an edge of frustration crept into his voice, and by the time he finished, his fists were balled tightly in useless anger.

"But you are remembering," Arcturus countered meaningfully, jabbing his finger on the table for emphasis.

"You remember Blythe and what it means to be Novus. More memories will come. More pages will be filled."

Trio relaxed his hands, splaying them wide, and leaned back in his chair. "Hope and my friends, that's all I have."

He said it sincerely, but Seven could tell Trio wasn't completely satisfied with Arcturus' words. She didn't blame him. Knowing that a full life's worth of memories were buried somewhere in the mind but not having access to them must be terrifying and frustrating. Seven would want those memories back immediately as well.

"Right then," Radius huffed, clearing his throat of emotion, "so what's next? Are we going after Fingal and Locust or not?"

It was clear that Radius wasn't about to let Blythe's death go, and Seven felt a need for vengeance too; however, Endymion team seemed to be forgetting something rather important. "And what about our parents? Can we rescue them too?"

Trio added, "Let's not forget my deconstruction data. Maybe we can recover that as well?" Hope threaded through his voice, and Seven saw that he clung to it like a drowning man clings to a life preserver.

Returning from his ponderings, Seven noticed that Arcturus raised his hand, silencing the questions that were coming hard and fast. "Fingal is on Pura Insulam by now, protected by his Purist mob, and he's likely got his scientists hard at work on your data, Trio. Additionally, he will keep Steele and Ida close now that he has Trio's data to mix with their research. As long as the two of them are useful, he'll keep them around." Arcturus left unsaid what would happen to Steele and Ida when they were no longer useful.

"So we're knackered then," Radius conceded, looking around the kitchen for answers.

Arcturus smiled, "No, I don't think we are, right Seven?"

Surprised, Seven's voice rose in pitch as she answered, "Um, no?"

Arcturus' tactical authority appeared in his delivery, as if he could turn it on and off like a switch. He asked his next question, already knowing where it would lead, "When was the last time you used the delivery robots that operate below the surface of The Jellyfish?"

Seven responded, still unsure of Arcturus' line of questioning, "We use it all the time. The robots basically run non-stop, delivering essentials straight to the homes of everyone on Pura Insulam, from one end to the other." As she ended her sentence, Seven realized Arcturus' plan.

"And are there many people down there with the robots?"

"No, that's the whole point. It's an autonomous delivery system," Seven said, indulging Arcturus. "You want to sneak in through the delivery level, don't you? That's... brilliant!"

Trio grinned from his seat next to Terra, "There's no

limit to what Arcturus knows."

Returning Trio's grin, Seven couldn't help but feel the small hope inside her grow. Not only did Arcturus seem to have a plan, but Trio was remembering nuanced memories from their shared past. He'd used that very same phrase back in Chicago before Seven, Trio, and Radius went out to eat.

Looking around, Seven studied the postures of Endymion team, and they were all leaning into the conversation. The fracture that occurred after Blythe's death widened during the plane ride to New Orleans, but now, it was on the verge of closing. Trio's unavoidable gravitational pull slowly worked to bring Endymion back together—Seven could feel it. It didn't matter how many memories were missing from Trio's mind, he remained a magnetic force for good.

Vulpes supplied the next few logical questions. "The drone level gives us entry, but what about the rest? How do we get near Fingal and Locust? How do we rescue Seven and Trio's parents?"

"How do we even find the location of any of these people?" Terra added, speaking to the crumbs on her plate.

Arcturus' sharp gaze caught the eye of each Endymion team member before landing on Seven again, "You know who can help with that too, don't you?"

"Ok, this is getting ridiculous, Arc. Just tell us already,"

Flumen cried in mock frustration.

Arcturus smirked wolfishly and said, "A certain friend of Seven's named Remy is the answer to all our questions."

Submarine Subterfuge

An AI can't cross the sea of awakening simply by standing at the water. —Arcturus

Unbelievable. This is simply unbelievable, Seven thought for the 100th time since leaving Pura Insulam. *When my parents told me I'd be going Continental, I never thought I'd be returning to Pura Insulam this way.*

Craning her neck around, Seven took in the inky blue depths of the Gulf of Mexico from her personal submarine. Well, maybe not hers as much as it was Arcturus', and he borrowed it from someone else—a very mysterious someone else Arcturus called Chaffee Absaraka. Seven felt as though she'd heard the name before but couldn't quite place it.

Arcturus didn't seem pleased in being forced into dealing with Chaffee Absaraka, and Arcturus claimed to have emptied every favor remaining to Endymion in order to procure the submarines.

Now that Seven sat ensconced inside one of the machines, she could see why Arcturus cashed in his remaining favors with Absaraka. Shaped much like the manta ray rescue drones patrolling Pura Insulam's edges, Seven's submarine was larger in order to house a single person. A curved glass dome arced above her head and below her feet, allowing her a 360-degree view of her surroundings. From the underwater observatory, Seven loved staring out into the depths of the gulf underneath Pura Insulam, but flashing through those depths like a fish provided a wholly new and wonderful experience. Fish like mackerel, dorado, and tripletail; crustaceans like shrimp, lobster, and crab; mammals like whales and dolphins; coral reefs of unparalleled beauty; all this life and more filled the gulf's fertile waters, forming a large, flourishing ecosystem.

"Incredible," Arcturus mused in awe over the comms, his manta ray submarine coursing through the water ahead of Seven. "And to think, humanity almost destroyed this ecosystem entirely."

During Seven's uneducation, she learned about such brushes with ecological disaster, but she was curious to hear Arcturus' thoughts on the topic. "We did? How so?"

"Offshore drilling, overfishing, urbanization along the coasts—pick your poison," Arcturus responded, his submarine knifing through a school of silver fish. They parted for his submarine and coalesced after he passed as if of one mind.

Looking down, Seven noticed a sea turtle casually swimming away from her. "What changed?"

"In short, the advent of the Relicus movement and our thinking."

Seven's brow drew together in confusion. "Relicus thinking? What do you mean?"

Arcturus' peanut butter voice drifted through the water into Seven's ears, "Humans slowly stopped thinking so much in terms of their own individual life spans and adopted a more generational approach to life. That approach came directly from the Relicus movement."

Generational thinking. Seven admitted that she struggled to think beyond the next day or two, so the concept of thinking generations ahead was foreign. *How exactly does one start thinking generationally? Were my parents thinking this way when they started their research on humans and AIs?* Transferring human consciousness to a machine certainly qualified as a generation-defining discovery that would echo through human history, but Seven wasn't sure her parents did it for the good of humanity. *Add it to the long list of discussions my parents and I need to have.*

Ahead, Seven watched as Arcturus skillfully steered his sub through four large metal support beams that rose up out of the water. Her sub sped towards the support beams on a direct path, and Seven's heart raced. She tried to turn the sub, but the controls were unresponsive. "Um, Radius, you might want to turn."

"I see it, Sev. No worries," came Radius' voice. Seven's sub swooshed through the support beams, its right fin narrowly missing the edge of one. "It's amazing how responsive these controls are," Radius gushed, seemingly unaware that he almost smashed Seven's sub into a pillar.

Heartbeat slowing, Seven cursed under her breath. "Maybe you'll let me steer then?" Silence, and Seven imagined Radius contemplating the idea.

"Not a chance," said Trio, voice crackling over the comms. "It's too dangerous."

Seven smiled at Trio's protective nature. *My big brother, watching out for me*. The thought comforted her more powerfully than she thought possible. "Yeah, I figured. I had to ask though! I mean, come on—how often will I be riding in a submarine?" As the subs cruised along, Seven noticed more pillars arranged in squares. "What am I seeing here?"

"Repurposed oil rigs," Arcturus said. "Some are made into artificial reefs, some into eco-resorts."

Radius gently steered Seven's sub around another frame, and Seven noticed a little ecosystem of life surrounding the structure. Scallops and mussels attached themselves to the beams, and at the base of the platform, a mountain of old shells helped provide a sort of fish nursery. All of this attracted more sea creatures to the area, creating a whole cycle of life—spawning, breeding, growing to maturity, and dying. It pleased Seven to know that what was once disruptive could become productive.

Maybe when this is all over, my parents' research can be used in a productive way too.

Trio interrupted Seven's reveries, "It's basically a straight shot south, but you've got a ways to go before you reach Pura Insulam." Seven heard a slight crackling as Trio adjusted his microphone. "Let's go over the plan again."

Seven rolled her eyes. Arcturus drilled her mercilessly on the plan back in New Orleans, but by the iron in Trio's voice, Seven knew there would be no avoiding it. Plus, with little else to do but watch the gulf out her window, Seven needed something to occupy her mind.

"We'll be able to drive our submarines right up to The Jellyfish as Radius will be masking our approach, making our subs appear on radar just like the manta ray drones of Pura Insulam," Seven started.

"Bit of genius code, I might add," Radius chimed in.

"Yeah, because I helped you with it," Seven continued quickly, addressing Radius' light-hearted bragging. "Next, we'll dock with the underwater observatory I liked to use when I needed some peace and quiet. This will give us access to the elevator leading to the underground delivery level." She paused, distracted by the appearance of a mother sperm whale and her calf.

"And then," Trio prompted.

"And then we use the delivery corridors to get to Remy's

house undetected, where we talk to Remy and then wait," Seven rattled off before taking a deep breath. The sperm whales plunged off into the dark. "You really think Remy is the right play?"

"Yes," Arcturus replied tersely.

Seven wasn't so confident. Remy, her oldest friend, had mixed feelings regarding Relicus. When she introduced Remy to Trio, the conversation did not go as she hoped. Sweet, naive Remy clearly wanted to be Seven's friend, but Fingal's Purist propaganda ran deep in his family, creating a large rift between the two of them. Then, Locust arrived and destroyed much of Remy's house, probably terrifying him worse than any spider simulation could. Now, Arcturus wanted to encroach on Remy once again? It didn't make sense to Seven, and she considered questioning what Arcturus knows. *He's definitely not telling me everything*, Seven calculated.

Just like he kept secrets from Trio.

Her silence prompted further explanation from Arcturus, "Remy will get us to Fingal. After Locust attacked you there, it will be the last place Fingal will expect us to go. Trust me."

Seven didn't, at least not fully, but she held little choice in the matter—she was caught in Arcturus' current and needed his help to rescue her parents. "I trust you, Arcturus." *Even though I have no idea how Remy is supposed to get us to Fingal.*

The rest of the journey to Pura Insulam passed in the deep tranquility that can only be obtained underwater. Seven reminded herself to see with her eyes, entering a meditative trance that calmed her rising nerves as the two submarines inched towards Pura Insulam. A pod of bottlenose dolphins zipped within view, playfully dancing about the two submarines before they grew bored and swam away. Later, an ominous profile darker than the deepening shadows below her, hunted about, and as it grew closer, Seven couldn't keep an awed terror from creeping into her throat. The outline solidified into a great white shark that leisurely and confidently swam straight up to her submarine from below, peering into the cockpit with what Seven could only describe as a hungry, prehistoric look before it slashed back into the depths. Heart hammering, Seven guessed the great white to be about 18 feet long, which would have been about five feet longer than her submarine. The great white shark provided her yet another reminder that she was out of her element. *Another adventure that could end in me drowning. Great.*

"Eyes up, fishies, we're about to arrive," Radius teased before adopting his best flight attendant voice. "Lady and gentle-Relicus, I'd like to welcome you to Pura Insulam. For your safety and the safety of those around you, please remain seated with your seat belt fastened until you are parked in Fingal's keister."

"Let's see if your coding is as good as you say," Arcturus interjected, shutting Radius up.

As the two submarines cut through the water, Seven watched Pura Insulam slowly materialize in front of her. Having never approached the island by airplane, boat, or manta ray-like submarine, Seven had no idea what her old home looked like from afar. Her departure was so chaotic, she couldn't even remember looking back. Now, she approached The Jellyfish from underneath.

Pura Insulam drones patrolled the water, and Seven held her breath as one approached Arcturus' submarine. Without pausing, the drone continued on its patrol, and Seven breathed normally again. The dark underbelly of The Jellyfish became clearer, and Seven recognized the energy capturing hydro-tentacles and oral arms drifting amongst the currents. Unabated, she and Arcturus passed underneath the edge of the colossal, artificial island and headed for the underwater observatory where Radius carefully docked Seven's submarine.

"Early schematics showed this dock—it was a calculated guess it would still be functional. Your jelly fish people must have sent scientists out from this location to observe the environment they floated over," Radius said to Seven, as if she asked for an explanation.

Seven's submarine bobbed to the surface of a small sub hangar, and she opened the glass dome. "They aren't *my* jelly fish people, Radius. They're just regular people. Not everyone here is a raving Fingal fanatic, but yeah, I remember learning about those studies in school."

As she climbed out of her submarine and onto a narrow catwalk, Seven wondered why she defended the people of Pura Insulam, and she decided it was because of people like her parents and Remy. They were good people; some trapped by their past in her parents' case or some trapped by birth in Remy's case. Either way, Fingal caused their strife, and they shouldn't be blamed wholly for what the Purists did. Seven's fingers brushed against her edge of the universe tattoo as she pondered her parents' morality and the only home she'd ever known.

Behind her, Arcturus climbed from his submarine, refracted light bounced off his white beard and lit up his stern face phantasmally. Like Seven, Arcturus dressed in dark combat gear, with a bullet proof vest over a form-fitting, long sleeved shirt; however, one difference stood out between the two as Arcturus still wore his golden cape, winding from right shoulder to left hip and around his back to fall down his right leg. To Seven, the cape seemed an odd affectation to wear on a stealth mission, but she'd never seen Arcturus without it. *I wonder if he wears it to bed with Flumen*, Seven thought before chiding herself for thinking such idiotic thoughts.

Frozen in contemplation, Seven watched Arcturus approach her with a curious look on his face. "You going to be ok?".

Could that be more empathy from the typically tactical Arcturus? Seven prepared to blow off the question until she took a moment to actually address her feelings. She was home. Her time Continental felt like weeks when it was only days. Tumultuous, catastrophic days.

"I..." Seven floundered through her feelings, hand still on her tattoo. "I don't know."

Arcturus placed a comforting hand on her shoulder, and he looked like he did at the safe house in New Orleans—authentic. "Homecomings can be difficult, especially after all you've been through."

Thoughts of Trio's chaotic deconstruction and Endymion team's desperate chase to rescue him flooded Seven's mind, shifting and growing like the shadows in the Gulf of Mexico. Then the image of Blythe's unnaturally contorted body rose unbidden, and shame threatened to overwhelm her. All of this was her fault. Blythe's death, Trio's memory loss, her parents' imprisonment. All of it.

Arcturus gave her a gentle shake and looked searchingly into her eyes. Seven didn't know if it was the Relicus' penchant for experiencing emotions on a deeper level, but Arcturus saw something that gave him pause.

"It's not your fault. The coding for this program we're currently in was written long ago when your parents' took Oriska Fingal's money."

Seven wanted to argue but realized Arcturus was right. She and Arcturus were caught up in a story that began before either of them even entered a chapter. The responsibility for Blythe's death and Trio's deconstruction rested with others, her parents' included, and she'd have to address that with Steele and Ida when the moment came. But first, she and Arcturus had to find them.

"Now," Arcturus commanded, "show me to the elevator."

The order worked, and Seven jolted from her dark thoughts. She led Arcturus across the catwalk and around the bowl. They passed the spot where she called Remy, at the time on the cusp of telling him about her journey Continental. Now, she couldn't even imagine how she'd tell him all she'd been through.

As Seven and Arcturus reached the elevator, Seven punched the button to call the elevator down. Surprising her, Arcturus grabbed Seven's hand, turning her towards him. "Listen, there's a good chance that elevator leads to pain and suffering."

Brushing a stray strand of curly brown hair from her eyes, Seven looked firmly at Arcturus. She thought about his philosophy on awakening and how it clearly influenced Trio, whereas it created a rift between himself, Vulpes, and Radius.

After a moment, she proclaimed, "It's only through suffering that we grow."

The elevator doors opened.

Remy's Surprise

It's the voice that commands the story, not the ear. —Oriska Fingal

The elevator doors opened onto the delivery warehouse—nothing changed since the last time Seven snuck a glimpse a few days earlier. Autonomous robots creeped over every inch of a sprawling room punctuated by corridors leading off in multiple directions. Even Arcturus paused to absorb the inhuman smoothness with which the robots moved.

Row upon row of scaffolded shelving over 16 feet tall housed the inventory that Pura Insulam people needed, and along those shelves, insect-like robots crawled, loading and unloading items onto roving robots below. Seven's eyes followed the trail of a particular item, likely an omni, as an articulating arm picked it up from its shelf 10 feet off the ground and placed it in a wheeled robot driving by. The wheeled robot zipped along, gathering more items from other shelves, disappearing from view before Seven glimpsed it again further along the warehouse by a conveyor belt. The robot, now heavily laden with various items, dumped those items into a package where an articulating arm closed the lid, ran a piece of tape over the flaps, and slid the box onto the conveyor belt where it zoomed over to join a large cart filled with multiple packages. The full cart quickly moved down one of the numerous corridors, disappearing from view, presumably to some needy Pura Insulam residents.

Her visual sense overwhelmed, it took Seven a moment to acknowledge a persistent sound filling her ears—the buzzing of dozens of small drones. They flew from one shelf to the next like bees to a flower, scanning items to create an accurate inventory.

About to step out of the elevator, Seven was abruptly yanked backwards and stumbled into Arcturus' arms. A large, forklift robot whizzed by, inches from where Seven was about to step.

"It would have stopped before running me over," Seven pointed out, looking behind her at Arcturus as she gathered herself. The look he returned held little confidence.

"The machine learning algorithm likely included avoiding collisions, but let's not find out the hard way," Arcturus responded coolly. He stepped in front of Seven and said, "Follow me. Move as I move and don't lag."

Seven swallowed a nervous lump in her throat as she followed Arcturus through the automated warehouse with the same precision as the robots surrounding them. Swerving and veering in what seemed to be random ways, Arcturus and Seven progressed purposefully towards the large carts filled with packages.

"One of these carts should be heading to Remy's house with a surprise package, we just need to find the right one," Seven declared.

Arcturus casually stepped aside as an articulated arm swung about to grab a package from a passing robot. "Radius, you're up."

"Already cracking on it, boss. One second."

The seconds ticked by and Seven began to wonder if Radius would be able to find the right cart amid all the algorithms of the warehouse.

"Got it! You better leg it! The cart is five lanes away and about to leave," Radius warned.

Grabbing Seven's hand, Arcturus bolted down the line of carts, nimbly juking robots and dipping under conveyor belts with Seven crashing along behind him. With a second to spare, he and Seven leapt onto the end of the cart just as it began to move. The cart picked up speed as it left the warehouse behind and entered the corridor, and as Seven looked around, she realized the corridor was more of a robot superhighway.

Autonomous delivery robots of various sizes hummed

along, orchestrated by their vast machine learning algorithms. The invisible trail Seven and Arcturus' cart followed took numerous splits in the corridor, and before long, Seven was hopelessly lost. The corridors contained no distinctive features to help her orientation save for infinite door-sized openings that must have been the delivery docks to people's houses. Endless tunnels snaked throughout the innards of Pura Insulam, and as she clung to the back of the cart, Seven thought, *This robot better take us to Remy's house or else we'll be wandering this labyrinth forever.* The cart made numerous stops, its articulating arm dropping packages onto a robot which delivered them to various doors. Seven caught a glimpse of a bundle of packages rising towards the surface on an elevator before the cart zoomed onward.

"Radius, you entered Remy's address correctly, right?" Seven asked after long minutes had passed. She flexed her right hand, trying to work out the numbness caused by gripping the edge of the cart with her fingers.

Radius laughed good-naturedly. "Of course I did. I'm not daft. And Trio, don't you say anything," Radius added, anticipating a joke from Trio.

"I would never," Trio answered, the smile clear in his voice.

The cart slowed, and Seven peered over the packages in front of her to see a large closet-shaped gap ahead. *Please let this be the one.* As the cart rolled to a stop, the articulating arm nabbed their package from the cart and dropped it onto a roving robot. Seven and Arcturus jumped off the cart and rushed to the opening.

"This is it," Arcturus whispered. "Remember, you need to calm Remy and convince him to help us locate your parents."

Seven took a deep breath to steady herself, "I know. He would lose his mind if you just showed up. He might still lose his mind," Seven added, thinking about the last encounter Remy had with a Relicus.

The robot approached, dropping the package at Seven and Arcturus' feet. Picking up the package, Seven squished next to Arcturus whose stocky frame filled much of the area. Seven was about to ask how to engage the elevator when the floor below them groaned and rose slowly upwards. The dark ascent lasted an uncomfortably long time before a light chime overhead indicated a package incoming for the residents of the house, and Seven heard footsteps approaching. Unbidden questions floated through Seven's mind, *What if Remy's not home? What if his parents answer?* With an effort, she calmed down and reminded herself that Remy's parents would be at work, and Remy would have just finished up school. She and Arcturus had a small window of time to talk with Remy...alone.

As the delivery doors slid open to reveal Remy's garage, Seven heard Remy mumble as he approached from the side, "That's funny, I don't remember ordering anything."

Remy rounded the corner and peered into the delivery elevator—the look on his face would have made Seven laugh had the circumstances been different. His red hair was more disheveled than usual, and his mouth formed a large "O" shape big enough to fly one of Radius' drones into. He backed up quickly, knocking over his electric bicycle and falling on his butt in the process. Arcturus stepped casually out of the delivery elevator, straightening his golden cape, and Seven followed with the package.

"Speedy delivery," Seven said with a smile.

"Seven," Remy finally exclaimed, butt firmly planted to the floor. "What are you doing here?"

Arcturus extended a hand to help Remy up, but the poor kid sat too stunned to take it. Setting the package down on a workbench, Seven looked purposefully at Arcturus' extended hand, which Remy finally realized was hanging in the air for some time. He reached up and Arcturus' large, dark hand engulfed Remy's as he was hauled to his feet.

"We're here to find my parents," Seven answered truthfully, leaning against the workbench.

Sputtering in confusion, Remy looked from Seven to Arcturus. "Who's this?"

Remaining silent, Arcturus allowed Seven to lead the conversation, trusting her to calm Remy. Seven took the cue and kept talking, "This is Arcturus, and before you ask, yes, he's Relicus."

Arcturus nodded respectfully, "Nice place you have here."

"This is just the garage," Remy mumbled.

"Right. Nice garage."

Seven jumped in before the awkwardness could grow, "Ok then. This is going well! Remy, can we come inside and sit down?"

As she spoke, Seven moved toward the door leading into Remy's house, but Remy scrambled in front of her, his hands raised.

"Maybe that's not such a good idea," Remy declared, blushing a deep red to match his hair. "The last time you were here with a Relicus, my house was kinda...destroyed."

Seven paused in her tracks. "Good point."

Searching for the right words, Seven did not know where to steer the conversation next.

They needed Remy's help in finding her parents, but now that they were here, standing in his stupid garage, she couldn't imagine what came next. *How is Remy even supposed to help find my parents?* Arcturus was so convincing with his plan that Seven hardly questioned it. Back in New Orleans, Arcturus made it sound like once they got to Remy's house, enlisting Remy's help in finding Steele and Ida would be easy, as if all Seven needed to do was ask and Remy would press a button on his omni to reveal her parents' location.

Silence filled the room like the Gulf of Mexico as seconds washed by. Arcturus carefully picked up Remy's tipped over bicycle, Seven shuffled her feet awkwardly, and Remy remained in front of the door, looking torn between running away and hugging Seven.

See with your eyes, Ida's voice reminded Seven.

Remy anxiously picked at his fingernails, and he wouldn't make eye contact with her.

Something was off about him, and Seven knew it. Something more than meeting another Relicus.

"I'll get us some drinks," Remy volunteered abruptly, and before Seven could respond, he slipped clumsily inside his house.

Once Seven knew Remy was out of earshot, she turned on Arcturus and hissed, "How exactly is Remy supposed to help us find my parents?"

Unperturbed, Arcturus replied, "Ask him and let's find out."

"Oh sure, I'll just tell him Fingal is a monster who's been manipulating my parents for years. Fingal, the very man Remy's parents worship."

Arcturus sighed, "Seven, if you build only walls, you live in darkness."

Anger boiling, Seven growled, "What do you mean by that cryptic line? Did you feed that garbage to Trio, too?"

"It means, let some light in. I've watched how you interact with my team, people who have done nothing but help you, yet you keep them all at bay. Even Trio," Arcturus explained, fingering his golden cape.

"I trust Trio."

"Yes, *now* you trust Trio, after he almost died for you. After you were in his memories during the deconstruction," Arcturus countered coldly and effectively, leaving unsaid that Blythe *did* die for Seven.

His words cut straight to Seven's heart, and she knew he was right. All the simulations Trio and Seven experienced together, all the magnetic kindness and the trust he showed, especially when she shared her edge of the universe tattoo with him—Seven kept her armor up throughout. And for what?

It was too much, and Arcturus knew it.

In a small voice, Seven asked, "How do I know who to trust?"

Arcturus came to her side and leveled his eyes to hers. "Trust is a vault. Give someone your trust, and if they keep it, then you know."

Seven searched Arcturus' eyes, probing for any signs of deceit and found none. He spoke the naked truth. Seven, much like her parents, actively kept secrets from the very people helping her. *Give trust to get trust. It's worth a shot.*

The door creaked open, and Remy reentered the garage, three glasses of lemonade clinking with ice. "Lemonade," he offered, grinning sheepishly.

Arcturus and Seven took their respective lemonades,

each sipping respectfully. The cool beverage soothed Seven's parched throat, and she smiled at the memory of the simulation where she coded a dolphin to bring Remy a lemonade in the desert.

"What are you smiling at?" Remy asked curiously.

"I was just thinking about the two of us and all that we've been through." Seven prepared herself to tell Remy everything she could about her parents, their research, Trio, and her wild journey Continental.

Before she could speak, Remy blurted, "When you've finished your lemonades, I think you should leave. I don't know what you want, but you're not going to find it here."

A dangerous edge crept into Remy's voice, an edge that Seven never heard before. "Remy, just give me a minute to explain," she started, hoping that it was only fear she heard in her friend's voice and not something darker.

"No, last time you explained, a locust-legged robot destroyed my house and threw your Relicus *friend* through my front window!"

"Locust? She's not a robot, and she's not even with us! She's with Fingal."

"See, there you go again, blaming Oriska Fingal for your problems. If you hate Pura Insulam and Oriska Fingal so much, why did you come back?" The lemonade glass in Remy's hand shook with so much anger and fear, Seven thought it would crack apart.

"He just doesn't get it, does he?" She looked to Arcturus

for help, but he walked away from the two arguing teenagers to stand by the garage door. Seven frowned in concern. Arcturus always moved tactically, and there was only one reason he'd be checking an exit.

Seven looked at Remy who backed into the doorway to his house. "Remy? What did you do?"

Remy had the decency to look ashamed before he slammed the door in Seven's face, locking it.

A large thump reverberated off the garage ceiling.

"Oh come on," Seven fumed. "Not again." Her hand subconsciously crept to the two tight scars on her chest.

"Radius, Trio—she's here," Arcturus said calmly over the comms. "Seven, stay back. This could get…messy."

The thumps trod over the roof, menacingly loud. Eventually, Locust walked to the edge of the roof and jumped down in front of the garage door, which Arcturus left open. Black hoodie, black featureless mask, disgustingly bent legs—Locust in full bloom.

"Ah, Arcturus. Nice of you to open the door for me. Trio made me kick the redheaded kid's door in last time," Locust mocked, mask filled with violent red.

Arcturus stood resolutely between Locust and Seven, right hand resting gently on his sidearm. "Hypatia," he greeted icily.

Locust's mask flickered with pink light before turning black, and she looked around carefully, taking a few steps into the garage. "Where's the rest of Endymion team? I see our little Ayr hacker is still alive. Surprising. Did you come home to find your parents?"

"Trio trusted and loved you. You know that, don't you," Arcturus said, ignoring Locust's probing questions.

Seven heard Locust snort derisively, "He loved me for his own good. It was foolish really." Locust took a few more steps into the garage, closing the distance between her and Arcturus. "You on the other hand, Arcturus. You're not foolish, are you? You've got some clever trick to play. You wouldn't come with only the Ayr girl, if you didn't have some plan."

Fingering his sidearm gently, Arcturus continued as if Locust didn't speak, "I should thank you. In a cruel way, you helped Trio awaken even further. You broke his heart, but those cracks let more light in."

Seven couldn't help but think Arcturus spoke those words for her. *Those cracks let more light in.* Trio loved and trusted Hypatia, getting his heart torn apart for it, yet his love and trust for others only grew stronger. Seven saw the proof in the way Trio treated his friends—in the way he treated his family.

Locust's mask crackled with angry white light, and she snarled, "Always so wise. Arcturus, shepherd to the ignorant AIs. I've always wanted to humble you, to break you, and now I've got my chance." A yellow smile flashed across her mask. "Just like I broke Blythe."

Upon speaking Blythe's name, both Arcturus and

Locust moved, their speed almost too much for Seven to keep up with. Arcturus raised his sidearm, angling it towards Locust's chest, but her inhuman legs proved too quick as she crashed bluntly into Arcturus, sending him careening into the wall behind them with a thud. The sidearm clattered across the garage floor, and Arcturus left it for a lost cause as he rolled to the side, dodging Locust's falling knee.

Locust's metallic knee drove hard into the floor, cracks spidering out. On his feet now, golden cape fluttering to his side, Arcturus squared his powerful frame and taunted Locust with the same crude gesture Blythe used in Ascension.

As Locust and Arcturus traded blows, Seven edged around the fray, aiming for Arcturus' sidearm. *I am not about to stand by again while someone else fights for me.* Seven lurched to the side and fell to the ground as Locust went flying into Remy's electric bicycle, her body crunching it to pieces. Arcturus was on Locust in a fraction of a second, like a castle tower falling to the ground. He rained down heavy-handed blows, black fists pulverizing Locust's mask, his squat frame too heavy even for Locust's grotesque legs to kick off easily.

Scrabbling on hands and knees, Seven reached Arcturus' sidearm and turned it upon the two fighters. Locust's mask was cracked open, pieces of it stuck in Arcturus' bloody fists as he relentlessly hammered. Seven stumbled to her feet, thinking the fight almost over, but Locust was far from finished. Letting out a feral scream, Locust's legs bent unnaturally backwards and wrapped around Arcturus' broad chest, and like a spring, she flung Arcturus violently through the air where he crashed loudly into a workbench, spraying tools and parts everywhere. Arcturus slumped to the floor in a bloody heap.

"No!" Seven roared, raising Arcturus' sidearm.

Wasting no time, Seven emptied the clip at Locust, who struggled to her feet. Most of the shots missed, even at close range, but a few landed, blasting Locust down to the floor where she remained motionless.

Breathing heavily, Seven realized she was still pulling the trigger, an empty clicking sound filling the air. Dropping the sidearm, she approached Locust slowly, hardening her stomach for the blood that would surely be coursing from Locust's body, but as Seven got closer, she saw no blood.

Through the cracked opening of Locust's mask, a bloodied green eye opened, and Locust coughed painfully.

"I didn't think you had violence in you," Locust said, grimacing as she rose to her feet. "Unfortunately for you, I dress for the occasion." She patted her chest where two bullet holes ripped through her black hoodie only to be stopped by the bulletproof vest underneath.

Seven backed away and looked at Arcturus, still unconscious by the workbench. "When Fingal told me the red-headed kid called to report you, I didn't believe him at first," Locust wheezed, advancing slowly on Seven. She shrugged, "But I came anyway, and here you are. Looks like you'll be meeting your parents after all."

Locust's arm uncoiled like a snake, her fist striking Seven full in the face. Darkness followed.

Speaking Just One Wrong Word

Thinking is difficult. Most people avoid it. —Oriska Fingal

"Martin, friend," Fingal simply couldn't hold his curiosity any longer, "why are you always so sweaty?"

"My doctor says I have a condition," Martin Lauren muttered, wiping his brow. "That and I've been managing the transferring of our equipment like you said."

The two men stood on a dock overlooking the Gulf of Mexico as the heat of the day refused to dissipate even in the waning hours of light. Fingal didn't blame the man for sweating, he was simply curious as to why he'd seen Martin sweating more often than not. Martin Lauren was a nervous man, but Fingal learned not to confuse that with incompetence. His ability to manage the anger of the Purists and move all the equipment to a new location proved as much.

"And you've done a magnificent job while under extreme pressure. I commend you." Fingal clapped

Martin on the back and immediately regretted the decision, pulling a now wet hand away and discreetly cleaning it on his pant leg. "With Locust and I back on Pura Insulam, you've earned a break."

"Thank you, Oriska. I take it everything is on schedule then?"

"Surprisingly, yes. Locust has gone to retrieve the last few necessary pieces, and then we'll be ready to move."

Martin Lauren nodded, anxiously twisting the square of fabric he used to wipe his brow. "I'd best be going then. There's still much to do as far as setup goes."

With only Ballie for company, Fingal remained on the dock long after Martin went into the lab. He was expecting a delivery from Locust any moment, and he pinged her omni, wondering just how long he'd have to wait for her.

She's close. Fingal's excitement grew as he watched the little blip on his omni move closer to his location until he could look up and watch the small vehicle approach with his own eyes. *What a delight! First, Trio and the Ayrs' research, and now Arcturus and Seven. I must give Locust a raise!*

The electric vehicle pulled to a stop, doors sliding open to reveal Locust and two men of Fingal's security team. Between them Arcturus and Seven slumped.

Spreading his arms in greeting, Fingal called, "So many gifts, and it's not even my birthday. Locust, you are a regular Santa Claus!"

Fingal watched expectantly as Locust stepped from the

vehicle and pulled her hood down, displaying her maskless face, bruised and beautiful. "Hypatia, where's your mask? Uniforms are important, you know. Yours particularly. Your mask, when combined with your," he gazed suggestively downward, "lovely legs, can be quite terrifying."

Hypatia, not hiding the bitterness in her voice, declared, "The mask has been destroyed. By him." She nodded towards Arcturus who was being lugged to the dock by the two security guards.

"Has it now?" Fingal queried curiously, prolonging his vowels unnaturally. He studied Hypatia carefully, marking her injuries, even going so far as to walk about her slowly. "It must have been quite a brawl! I wish I was there. Obviously, you won though, didn't you, Hypatia?"

Fingal didn't say, "I told you so," but he desperately wanted to. He and Hypatia endured a heated argument about how to take in Arcturus and Seven. Hypatia wanted to kill Arcturus and capture the girl, but Fingal entertained other plans.

"I did," Hypatia replied, chin raised. "But the girl shot me. Twice."

"Curiouser and curiouser," Fingal murmured, gazing at Seven's unconscious form. "Well, we know her to be full of surprises, don't we?"

Hypatia frowned despite the success of the day. *She's such a curmudgeon,* Fingal mused. "Your emotions are blinding you, Oriska."

"Pardon me? Are you still hung up on *my* emotions? I seem to recall you shot a teenage girl in your rage."

Hypatia chewed her lip for a moment, while behind her, the two security guards unloaded Seven's body and placed her back-to-back with Arcturus.

"That was a mistake," Hypatia grumbled, as if her mouth were wired shut. "And now you're making one too. Keeping Arcturus alive, and for what? Your vanity."

Fingal sighed loudly. "It's not vanity. Do you think I can simply snap my fingers and obtain an AI like Arcturus? Human consciousness cannot be transferred to any AI—my father proved as much. It must be an AI that has awakened...like those of the Relicus movement." Fingal gestured grandly towards Arcturus, "Like him, Hypatia. And where's your sense of drama? Just think about the moment that Arcturus and the Ayrs are all together again." *My mouth is practically watering at the thought.* "It's going to be scrumptious, and you want to kill Arcturus before that moment can happen?"

Crossing her arms stubbornly, Hypatia countered, "You could get another AI eventually. You want Arcturus' body specifically."

Why does this bother her so? "We all have our indulgences, Hypatia. Grant me mine."

Hypatia shook her head. "He's too dangerous. He's got a plan, some trick we haven't figured out yet." Her eyebrows came together in anger and suspicion. "Why didn't all of Endymion come to Pura Insulam? Why just bring the girl?"

Fingal paused at the questions. In his excitement upon receiving the news that Arcturus and Seven were at Remy's house, he failed to consider Arcturus' full plan. He looked hard at Arcturus who was being bound to Seven underneath a singular light pole. *What's going on in that square head of yours?*

"Endymion must be tracking him somehow," he thought out loud. "That's the only explanation. Which means we'll have another confrontation." Fingal looked to Hypatia. "Can we handle another fight?"

Hypatia shook her head, the lyre earring wobbling to and fro. "We've traded victories and defeats with Endymion thus far. We have the numbers, and they have better training." She shrugged noncommittally. "It's a toss up."

She's right. Her bruised face tells the tale of Endymion's prowess. It's a great risk, Fingal admitted to himself, adjusting his glasses. *But I've never been one to shy away from risks. I have that in common with my father.* "The Sea Lotus is preparing for our experiments. We have ready test subjects at hand. This is our best chance. You've done your job admirably, Hypatia. Let me think about Arcturus." Hypatia opened her mouth, but Fingal cut her off forcefully, "I will *think* about Arcturus. For now, we let him live."

The Sea Lotus

So, others judge me? That's their issue. Their character and actions are not mine. —Oriska Fingal

Consciousness ebbed and flowed like the tide as Seven swam in snatches of awareness. A dull realization of movement, of being restrained, of the iron smell from Arcturus' bloody form next to her, of a throbbing in her head. Paper thin, a weak voice whispered in her mind, telling her they must be heading to Fingal and her parents. This one idea gave her small consolation as she struggled to swim fully out of the darkness and failed.

Seven woke fully to the familiar smell of salt in the air and the sun falling lazily onto a red horizon. The commotion of many feet trudging back and forth with purpose accosted her ears. Finally, she focused her eyes to a sight she'd never witnessed before on Pura Insulam—a large, white dorsal fin shaped tower wedged between the edge of the island and the Gulf of Mexico. Antennae, globes, and spinning sensors populated the peak of the tower which resembled an eye, and just below, a small crow's nest jutted out like a beak. Seven's gaze trailed down the sleek architecture, studying every inch in awe. Upon reaching the ground level, Seven noticed numerous workers coming and going with equipment, preparing for who knows what kind of operation. They all looked grim-faced and hollow-eyed, as if they hadn't slept in days.

"See any weapons?" Arcturus' voice asked from behind, startling her.

"Arc, you're ok!" The relief she felt was palpable, and she didn't want to imagine having to face what came next without him. Despite her best efforts not to, Seven depended on Arcturus. Wriggling her numb arms and hands, Seven realized she was tied to his back.

"I've been worse. Now, answer my question," Arcturus replied, ever diligent to the task at hand.

Seven scanned the strange tower in front of her again, from top to bottom, carefully looking for weapons of any sort. A woman in the crow's nest with binoculars, two men at the main entrance with sidearms. That was it, and she relayed the information to Arcturus.

Arcturus shifted behind her. "Oriska Fingal's numbers have slowly been dwindling over the years, but three is likely too few. There must be more."

Nodding agreement, Seven added, "That tower looks plenty big enough for more armed people to be inside.

Maybe they're guarding my mom and dad."

"Now, you're thinking like me," Arcturus said, admiration warming his voice. "I'd guess two guarding your parents, and potentially another five considering we're here."

"Don't forget Locust."

Arcturus laughed grimly, and Seven heard him spit upon the ground. "I won't. She gave me quite a beating."

I know the beatings Locust delivers, Seven thought, tentatively assessing her own injuries. Licking her lips, she tasted blood, realizing that her nose must have bled after Locust cracked her in the face. The back of her head competed with her nose for which hurt worse, and Seven imagined she must have smacked her head against the ground when she fell. *Why am I alive? At Ascension labs, Locust didn't hesitate to shoot me in the chest. Twice.* Seven's two scars itched madly at the thought. *Something has changed.*

The platform Seven and Arcturus sat tied to slowly quieted as the workers filtered into the fin-like tower, and the sun disappeared below the horizon, leaving Seven cold and defeated. A solitary light shone harshly above her, and she wondered what came next. Fingal would have Trio's data, her parents, Arcturus, and her. Surely that would be enough for him to complete his stranglehold on the future of human-Relicus research and development. What future Fingal would create terrified Seven.

"Arcturus, what are we going to do?"

Arcturus must have sensed the defeat in her voice because he leaned his weight against Seven's back, his head gently resting against hers. "Nothing has more degrees of freedom than reality, Seven. Fingal thinks himself in control, but he cannot consider every outcome."

Before Seven could delve further into Arcturus' meaning, Locust materialized at the edge of the light. To Seven's surprise, the featureless mask was gone, revealing the stunningly beautiful woman Seven saw in Trio's deconstruction—beautiful, even though Arcturus mauled her face. Locust's green eyes pierced Seven's heart, as if the assassin were reading every weakness Seven tried to hide, and Seven wasn't sure what was worse—the mask or the eyes.

Without speaking, Locust gestured behind her, and two men came forward, roughly manhandling Seven and Arcturus to their feet where they were promptly separated from each other.

Stumbling along behind Locust, Seven and Arcturus were led inside the tower, and Seven did her best to observe everything about her surroundings. The first room the two men shoved her through looked like a simple storage room, and Seven recognized an array of lab equipment similar to what her parents used in their lab. Besides the lab equipment, boxes of food, toiletries, and other necessities filled the room to the ceiling. Whatever Fingal planned, it would take a while, and he was well stocked.

A loud rumbling shook the room and rattled Seven's cells. *What is this place?* She looked at Arcturus, who walked beside her, and his eyes went wide with surprise. Seven cursed under her breath. *If Arcturus is surprised, we're in worse trouble than I imagined.*

"Keep moving," one of the men urged, pushing Seven roughly ahead.

A clean, white spiral staircase appeared on their left with Locust already disappearing down one level. As Seven descended, she caught a fleeting glimpse of the next level, which looked much like her parents' lab. *This is where Fingal plans to continue his research on human-Relicus development. And as long as he's doing that research, my parents will be too valuable to kill.* The thought was a small comfort, but she needed every bit she could get.

Locust led them down another level, stopping before a closed doorway. She turned to face them, her olive skin bruised and cut by Arcturus' heavy blows, yet despite her injuries, she smirked alluringly. The door opened behind her revealing a room full of people busily going about their tasks, oblivious to the two prisoners in the doorway. A particularly well-dressed man stood amidst it all, his back to them. The man's arms spread wide across a console, his dark plum suit jacket gathering the light from the room as the Gulf of Mexico framed him beautifully through a large viewing window. Under his right elbow was the pear-colored orb, Ballie.

Oriska Fingal turned dramatically, "Welcome to The Sea Lotus! So glad you could make it." He looked suggestively at Seven. "Your parents have already arrived, young lady. You'll see them shortly. And you," he swiveled to Arcturus. "Truly an honor that you would grace us with your presence," Fingal drawled, nodding mockingly at Arcturus' bonds.

Arcturus remained as still as stone, and Seven marveled at the Relicus' calm. Underneath, he must be seething with anger, yet on the surface, nothing. Arcturus barely even offered Fingal recognition.

Fingal noticed. "Well, that was an icy greeting," he said to Locust who also just stared at Fingal. He balled his hand into a fist, tapped it and play-acted, "Hello? Is this thing on? Wow, tough crowd."

Seven never saw the man so animated and excited. *He's truly enjoying this,* she realized.

"You know, Arc. May I call you Arc?" Arcturus' eyebrows scrunched together slightly, and Fingal continued on, oblivious, "I don't care—I'm calling you Arc. Our mutual friend Locust over there thought I should kill you. And I think she's right; I should kill you."

Fingal was completely in his element, surrounded by supporters, safe from Endymion. He held all the cards and knew it. Fear crept into Seven's chest, setting roots in her heart. *How are we going to get out of this?* She looked to Arcturus for some kind of hint, some drop of confidence, but Arcturus only looked stonily at Fingal as the fearmonger continued his rant.

"What Locust doesn't understand is the theater of it all. She would likely put a bullet in your head and move on, but me, I see a much grander death for you. If all of life is a stage, then let's put on a show!" Fingal spun about dramatically, gesturing to the entire room.

Only three people were watching: Arcturus, Seven, and Locust. Everyone else busily went about their duties

Fingal clapped his hands together with finality, looking from Arcturus to Seven, "Enough chit chat. You'll learn of my plans for the both of you soon enough. We are about to set sail on The Sea Lotus' maiden voyage. Come, bear witness."

Set sail? There's no way this huge thing is seaworthy.

The two men herded Seven and Arcturus to the front of the command bridge where a wide viewing window provided a panorama of a starlit Gulf of Mexico on the left and Pura Insulam on the right. Leaning forward as far as she could, Seven gazed down into the dark waters some fifteen feet below, and as she watched, lurching slightly, The Sea Lotus slowly drifted away from the island and out into the gulf. Powerful engines sent reverberations throughout Seven's body, and she imagined massive propellers churning the water below.

"He wants you to be witnesses," came Locust's whisper between both Seven and Arcturus' ears. "He craves affirmation and adoration. It's why he surrounds himself with sycophants and fills the Purists' minds with propaganda that makes him look good."

"And you're not a leech stuck to his backside, Hypatia?" Arcturus asked quietly. Locust hissed in their ears.

"No. Their emotions are their weaknesses. Fingal included. I'm here to make sure his emotions don't get in the way of his goals."

"Which are the same as yours?" As The Sea Lotus splashed further out into the Gulf, Arcturus probed Locust for any weakness.

Locust knew. "You'll get nothing from me that I don't willingly give," she stated, positioning herself to whisper in Arcturus' other ear. "Oriska Fingal's goals align with mine, and when a human mind can be perfectly transferred to a Relicus body, I'll be one of the first in line."

"That's it then," Arcturus mused, disappointment obvious in his voice. "You're disgusted by your own body, and you want out."

"Wrong. I want what you Relicus unfairly have—endless life. We created you, yet you outlive us. Now, your influence permeates all of Continental," Locust fumed, pacing behind Arcturus and Seven.

Arcturus pressed harder, sensing a weakness. "You're a

walking contradiction, Hypatia. You hate the Relicus, yet you want to be us."

Could endless life be what Oriska Fingal wants as well? Seven wasn't so sure. Fingal poisoned the lives of Pura Insulam for years, growing the number of Purists and bending their minds to his will. They hated the Novus and Relicus movements and refused any internal body modifications. Why would Fingal's endgame be to *become* a human-Relicus hybrid then? *Unless the Purists are just a means to an end for him.*

"I will think whatever I want to think," Locust spat. "Even thinking wrongly is better than not thinking at all."

Arcturus shook his head sadly, and Seven couldn't believe Locust's twisted logic. Deep down, Locust seemed to know her current mindset was wrong, but she insisted on maintaining it, laying brick after brick of mistakes until she built her house of lies so well, she couldn't leave.

"You hate us so much it's affecting your judgment," Arcturus declared, gazing intently through the window at something beyond Locust's comprehension. "Or worse, you hate yourself so much."

Locust stopped pacing behind Arcturus, and out of the corner of her eye, Seven saw Locust's face momentarily flash with uncertainty before her jaw set. "Probably," she hedged and walked away.

The hushed commotion of people diligently going about their business filled the void left by Locust, and

Seven and Arcturus stood alone, riding in a mobile oceanic station. Technicians checked instruments for fidelity, and Oriska Fingal lorded majestically over it all, ensconced at the main console.

"Fingal wants us as far from Continental as possible," Arcturus said. "He'll have something particularly cruel planned for me. It's the only reason I'm still alive. You, on the other hand." Arcturus left the rest unsaid, unwilling to say it out loud.

Seven shivered in trepidation. "He leveraged Trio against my parents all those years ago, forcing them to continue their research and then experiment on their own son. As long as I'm alive, he can use me to force my parents to work, and if they won't, he'll kill me," she finished grimly.

Arcturus said nothing, confirming Seven's prediction.

"Arc, you knew Remy would report us, didn't you?" Seven asked, abruptly changing the subject. It was something that bothered her since Remy shame-facedly locked the garage door on her. She'd realized asking Remy for help was pointless as he couldn't possibly know where Steele and Ida were, yet Arcturus led her to his house anyway.

"I did not," Arcturus responded honestly, "however, I thought it likely he would report us, thus granting us proximity to Fingal and your parents."

"You, the man with a plan, risked our lives on a guess?"

She struggled to keep her voice down as she hissed, "We could have been killed!"

"Yet here we are," Arcturus said, gesturing about the command bridge in a small way.

"And if Remy said he would have helped? Then what?"

"Then we would have used his parents' connections to Fingal to find our way here, like we planned. It would have taken longer, and we would have missed our chance."

"Arcturus," Seven whispered, realization dawning on her as she spoke, "you knew Blythe, Trio, and I were sneaking to Ascension, didn't you?"

A pause. Then a curt reply. "Yes."

Of course he knew. There was no other way Endymion could have arrived so quickly after Seven was shot unless they were already on their way. *It was Arcturus who got Blythe killed, not me. He's no better than my parents. No better than Fingal,* she thought bitterly.

Seven fell into a contemplative silence. She trusted Arcturus, and here he was withholding crucial information from her, just like he did so consistently with the Endymion team members. It was this type of behavior that caused a deep rift between Vulpes, Radius and Arcturus. She should have been just as furious as Vulpes and Radius; instead, she felt strangely at peace with Arcturus. Seven's understanding of the stony Relicus deepened considerably in the past few days, and she realized she could trust someone without agreeing with their methods.

And more importantly, she was learning how much trust to give. With her parents, her trust was fully given for most of her life, which Seven decided was likely the case for most children, but then she learned her parents hid secrets—big secrets—causing Seven to put up her armor, not allowing anybody else in fully. She and Endymion team unfairly suffered parallel experiences because of people like her parents and Arcturus.

Despite everything, she would continue to trust Arcturus but only so far. *Once you know how far your trust goes with someone, you know how much trust to give them.*

Footsteps approached Seven from behind as she reflected on this, and Oriska Fingal droned, "Did you two chase off my assassin?" Neither Seven nor Arcturus responded, and Fingal tsked. "Such rudeness. It almost makes me want to cancel your little visit, Seven." He placed his bony hands on Seven and Arcturus' shoulders. "Fortunately for you two, I'm a sucker for family reunions."

****

Oriska Fingal sauntered ahead of Seven and Arcturus as two guards followed closely behind with Ballie bringing up the rear. Acting like a real estate agent for a newly-wed couple, Fingal showed off each level of The Sea Lotus on their way down: a diving room and wet lab, a modular laboratory with medical center and fitness area, bunks and captain's room, and finally what Fingal called "the VIP room."

"And there's so much more," Fingal beamed like a proud parent extolling the virtues of his child. "There's a communication zone, a sanitary area, the living quarters in atmospheric pressure, and an underwater garage! Sorry Seven, there wasn't any room for your motorcycle."

Seven sneered at Fingal but said nothing.

"At any rate," Fingal continued, "you'll be most interested in what's behind the VIP door." He added in a mock whisper, leaning conspiratorially to Seven, "It's your parents."

The door slid open, revealing Steele nose deep in a book while sitting behind a glass desk and Ida standing at the window looking out into the waters of the gulf. Neither of them acknowledged the opened door.

After a prolonged silence, without looking up from his book, Steele said, "Fingal, if that's you, we're tired from moving all of our lab equipment. At least give us tonight to rest so we can be fresh for whatever project you have planned tomorrow."

Fully enjoying the moment, Oriska Fingal said nothing, but he clearly fed off the awkwardness like a parasite.

"Mom. Dad," Seven croaked. "I'm here."

Family Reunion

*Ambition separates us. Suffering brings us together. —
Arcturus*

Steele almost toppled the glass desk in his rush to
embrace Seven, the book he'd been reading mashed
against her back. He smelled of old papers and electric
current. Ida stood frozen in front of a round window, her
form outlined by the darkness of the waters behind her.
Her hand rose to her mouth and tears rimmed her eyes,
and Seven didn't know if they were tears of happiness or
fear.

Steele pushed Seven to arm's length, looking over his
daughter with such probing tenderness that Seven felt all
the trauma she'd been carrying stoically break free, an
ocean of partially dealt with feelings flooding her.

Seven cried. Great heaving, chest rattling sobs. Tears
and snot unapologetically leaking down her face.

And there was Ida Ayr, by her daughter's side during

Seven's breakdown, awakened from her initial shock at seeing her daughter by the power of Seven's trauma. Together, Steele and Ida comforted Seven, murmuring soft nothings into her ear and ignoring everyone in the room.

Ignoring the Sea Lotus and Pura Insulam. Ignoring the world.

"How idyllic," Fingal gushed, popping the moment like a balloon.

Wiping her snotty nose on her sleeve and sniffing loudly, Seven pulled slightly out of her parents' embrace. The three of them turned to Fingal, who was smiling wolfishly, likely imagining what cruelties he would later use to terrorize the Ayrs.

"But wait, there's more," Fingal said gleefully, gesturing like a game show host to Arcturus.

Noticing Arcturus for the first time, Steele and Ida made awkward eye contact with him. The moment reminded Seven of the times she would see Remy after a particularly long absence, at first awkward but quickly overcome by remembered fondness.

Steele broke the strained silence first. "Arcturus, it's good to see you."

Ida delicately separated herself from Seven to approach Arcturus. She paused in front of him as if reminding herself of Arcturus' features before pulling him in for a warm embrace. "We've missed you, Arc."

Arcturus returned the hug, stiffly at first, then his emotions overpowered his restraint, and he hugged Ida affectionately.

Fingal clapped enthusiastically. "We're all back together again," he cried. "Just like the old days at Ascension. Well, mostly like the old days. Now, there's Seven instead of Trio, but who can really tell one child from the next?"

Arcturus moved in a flash, extricating himself from Ida and aiming a punch at Fingal as quickly as one flicks a light switch, but Fingal's guards were ready. They stepped in front of Arcturus' punch, grabbing both his arms and roughly shoving Arcturus backwards. Fingal barely moved.

"Predictable," he declared. "Like so many of your decisions, Arcturus." He turned to address the Ayrs. "You know, when I was deconstructing Trio, making up for your skullduggery the first time we tried the transfer, Arcturus had a chance to stop it." Fingal shrugged. "But just like the first time, he failed."

Behind her, Seven could practically feel her father's teeth grinding together in anger, and she spoke before Steele's anger erupted. "Trio lives. You're the one who keeps failing," Seven retorted, knowing Steele and Ida likely had no idea what happened with Relicus Trio. She also found a small sort of satisfaction in pointing out Fingal's failures. When Trio did the same thing back in the deconstruction lab, Fingal melted down.

Unlike his outburst back in New Orleans, this time Oriska Fingal remained worryingly calm. "Does he now, Seven Ayr? How nice of you to keep me up to date." *Oh no*, Seven cursed herself. *What have I done?* "You know, I didn't fully deconstruct Trio's data." He gestured to his men who left Arcturus and returned to his side. "However, we did get enough information to move forward with our research and development on transferring a human mind into a Relicus body." A maniacal grin appeared on Fingal's face. "And I'm glad Trio is still alive because we found something particularly curious in his data. We found you."

With that, Fingal and his men left.

Seven's mind exploded with hypotheses, just as Fingal intended, but she couldn't help it. Her curiosity and fear stung her mind at the same time, and she felt compelled to scratch the itch. *I knew my interaction with the deconstruction simulation wasn't normal. So just what did I do?*

Seven figured her hacking of the deconstruction resonated in a sort of sympathetic vibration of code, like when two people shake hands, each leaves a little of their own DNA on the palm of the other. As Seven contemplated this, she knew it couldn't be true. Human DNA and Relicus data were incompatible—this was the very roadblock to her parents' success with downloading a human mind to a Relicus body. *Unless...*

Seven knew better than to trust Fingal's word, but she couldn't get over the memory of the surreal experience she saw in Trio's deconstruction simulation—the unusual co-presence she shared with her brother was undeniable. She scrutinized her past experiences with simulations: her natural aptitude for hacking and coding, the too-real feeling of pain the shards of glass caused her hands in the Bay of Fundy simulation, her ability to see lines of code within simulations, and her hacking of Trio's deconstruction coding to spy on Hypatia. *Not human. Not human at all.*

Exhausted, Steele and Ida moved off to sit on the couch behind them while Seven stood frozen in contemplation. Arcturus hadn't moved either; he simply stared at the door Fingal left through, likely running infinite calculations in his head.

Abruptly, he turned to Seven. "Do *not* listen to Fingal. He's searching for something he doesn't have yet. If we talk about it, we could clue him in," he entreated.

"I don't care, Arc. Like you said on the plane before we rescued Trio, Fingal's always gathering data, so let him gather. It's time I gathered my own." Seven approached her parents purposefully. "It's time to trust me. Fully." She wiped more snot from her face.

The white light of the room shone brightly on Ida's resigned face, and Seven could see she'd been carrying a heavy burden for so long—the burden of Trio's secret, and if Fingal was to be believed, the burden of another secret. Steele placed his hand on Ida's knee before she could speak, his jaw set resolutely. He'd be answering Seven's questions. His old words rang in her head, *I didn't think you were ready.*

Seven didn't even ask why her parents hadn't bothered telling her Trio was her brother—she already knew they hid Trio from Fingal; instead, she asked bluntly, "Am I an AI like Arcturus?"

Steele's stiff posture relaxed slightly, but it was enough of a sign to prove that Seven asked a different question than he'd expected—an easier question. "No," he sighed, "you are most definitely not a Relicus. Think about it. You have memories from childhood. You have a past. And other people have a shared past with you. You've grown up your whole life with Remy. How can you be like Arcturus?"

"So why did Fingal say he found part of me in Trio's deconstruction," Seven followed up angrily, knowing she was being stupid for believing Fingal's words, but she couldn't stop herself.

Steele raised his arms and shrugged, "The man's a demagogue, Seven. He knows your basest emotions and uses them to his advantage." He ran his hand through his graying hair in the same way Trio did. "We weren't there for Trio's deconstruction, and we'll have to live with that shame; however, don't let Fingal use the deconstruction as a wedge to drive between us."

Her father's words made sense. She couldn't be a

Relicus like Arcturus, and Oriska Fingal would definitely use a traumatic event like Trio's deconstruction against her and her family—of that she had no doubt. But a deeper intuition and skepticism, abilities she hadn't utilized well before leaving Pura Insulam, caused her to doubt Steele's words. *See with your eyes.*

Throughout Seven's brief argument with her father, Ida sat quietly, making unbroken eye-contact with Seven. The shame Ida carried for losing Trio as a teen and for lying to Seven for years cried out to be relieved, and the only way to relieve shame is by dragging it out into the open where it can no longer feed on hidden insecurities.

Seven and Ida's eyes locked. "Mom?"

Steele tried to grab Ida's hand, but she stood up too quickly and moved to the window behind the couch where she sat on the sill, studying Seven.

"How are you so beautiful?" she mused rhetorically. "You've got the best of both your father and I: our drive, our intelligence, our loyalty. Yet, you're so much more than both of us combined. You see opportunities where there shouldn't be any, and you treat people with unbridled kindness." Tears formed in Ida's eyes. "What did we do to deserve you? We lied to you about your own brother."

"Ida, please," Steele interjected, spinning on the couch to look at his wife.

Ida ignored her husband. "You've changed in your short

time Continental. You're," she narrowed her eyes searchingly, "wiser, more sure of yourself. You know, when I carried you in my womb, I dreamt about what you might grow up to be."

"Did I turn out to be the daughter you wanted? Did I meet your expectations?" Seven whispered, throat constricting tightly.

Ida smiled through her tears, "Oh Seven, that's the thing. You've made my expectations irrelevant."

Crossing the room quickly, Seven entered Ida's arms again, absorbing the love that can only exist between mother and daughter. Outside the window, the waters of the Gulf of Mexico parted for The Sea Lotus as it sailed for the Atlantic Ocean and beyond.

Once mother and daughter hugged their fill, they separated, Seven to the glass desk and Ida to the couch where Steele sat brooding. Arcturus remained by the door, which worried Seven, knowing that he always thought tactically, playing out future scenarios in his head.

After watching Arcturus flip his golden cape back and forth between his fingers, Seven decided it was time to ask another question she'd been holding for some time. "Mom, dad," she started, "how could you use a Relicus form for Trio's consciousness, especially knowing the love and loyalty Arcturus showed you?"

The question plopped like a dead fish into the center of the room—nobody wanted to touch it. Arcturus stopped fiddling with his cape and stood as still as stone. Seven knew this subject mattered to him, and she was curious to see if he'd speak up.

Seven watched as Steele and Ida both looked at the other to speak first. Smiling inwardly, Seven took small pleasure in flummoxing her father.

Ida opened her mouth and closed it. Steele looked like he wanted to leave the room, but there was nowhere to go.

Finally, Steele broke the silence, "It was the only way to save Trio."

"But it came at the cost of another sentient being's life," Seven countered hotly.

"Who knows how that Relicus died, Seven. It could have been an accident, and Trio was the lucky recipient of a donation," Steele shot back.

It seemed a flimsy excuse, but Seven admitted to herself that it was a possibility. She looked expectantly at Arcturus. *What are you waiting for?*

Seven noticed Arcturus sigh slightly before beginning to talk, as if resigning himself to reveal a long-buried truth. "Chaffee Absaraka doesn't deal in donations." Arcturus' face twisted in disgust. "I took one of my own, a Relicus, to my lab and helped you transfer Trio's consciousness to it. I told no one on my team. I kept your secret, even though it flew in the face of everything I value." His fists clenched. "I don't know what's worse: the one who compromises his morals or the ones who ask it to be done."

Steele shot up in anger, "We asked for your help to save our son! Don't try to lay blame at our feet for your shame."

"And I helped to save your son. I love Trio like family, and I know my decisions to be my own. No others. You two," Arcturus gestured to Steele and Ida, "need to understand just how manipulative your behaviors can be when driven by ambition."

Steele cursed loudly, turning away from Arcturus' righteous anger and walking to the window. Ida remained rooted to the couch, tears in her eyes.

Seven felt sympathy for both her parents. Hearing the cold truth after so many years of pushing it away must be painful, but she also knew exactly how Arcturus felt. Her parents manipulated out of love and ambition. Arcturus manipulated out of love and ambition. *Yet why do their actions feel so different? Why do I side with Arcturus in this? I think because my parents would likely use another Relicus body if they could, whereas Arcturus will never compromise his values again.*

Foul air permeated the room, and no one spoke. *Not this again,* Seven thought. *There's so much to talk about and here we all are, too proud to speak.*

"So, what's next?" Seven asked the room at large.

Arcturus scratched his white beard, eyes flinty under his heavy brows. "We wait."

"Arcturus is right," Steele grumbled, still sullen but

unable to refrain from speaking. "Fingal obviously has more planned for us. He wouldn't leave so dramatically if he didn't."

426

The Unknown Future; the Known Past

Truth is what you feel in your gut. —Oriska Fingal

Salty night air whisked against Oriska Fingal's face as light as breath, and a starlit canopy hung above his head. He stood on a small platform outside the Eye of the Sea Lotus some 62 feet above sea level, casually flipping Ballie from one hand to the next. *Everything is perfect*, Fingal thought. He'd never been one for superstition, and he didn't worry about jinxing himself now.

Why would he? The research, the Ayrs, Arcturus—he held them all under his thumb. Only Endymion team could disrupt his perfection.

Unbidden, memories of his father's failed experiment floated into his head, threatening to dampen his ebullient mood, and before he could decide what to do with those memories, he sensed a presence behind him—an odd tickling sensation at the back of his neck. Fingal didn't turn, unwilling to burst the bubble of his perfect moment.

"Oriska, it's time." Hypatia's flat voice drifted near Fingal's bliss, and he considered not addressing it. *I could simply stay up here. Never go down to the lab. Never run the risk of failing.*

Fingal felt reflective, and he still hadn't dealt with the memories of his father. Perhaps that's why he decided to open up to Hypatia. Or perhaps it was the human need of shared happiness, that desire to feel success with *someone.*

He stopped tossing Ballie.

"You would not have liked my father," Fingal said into the breeze. "He was brilliant but soft."

"I don't think you really know what I like," Hypatia's voice countered.

"I suppose that's true." *Hypatia the Locust: moment killer.* "Sometimes I wonder if he'd be proud of me if he were alive, but that's just the naive boy in me." Fingal turned to look at Hypatia, expecting her face to be bored or annoyed; however, it held no emotion at all. Finding a small amount of relief in opening up, Fingal decided to continue sharing regardless of her response. "You know, Hypatia, I'm glad my father's not here. I don't want him to see me because I don't think he'd understand. The decisions I've made to get to this point..."

Fingal shrugged, as if that could encapsulate a lifetime of choices. Hypatia stared, not quite at Fingal, but just above his head.

"When my father failed to download his consciousness

to an AI and died, my mother cracked. She ended up saving every single scrap of my father's life in the hopes of resurrecting him with some future tech. Bills, photos, emails, journals, voicemails, texts. Everything. Boxes piled to the ceiling in every room of her home. She cared so much about preserving her dead husband she forgot about her living son."

As Fingal spoke, strong sadness mixed with frustration washed over him. *I could actually cry*, he realized, pulling his glasses awkwardly from his face and attempting to clean the lenses with Ballie still in his hand. The Sea Lotus chopped through waters as uncaring as the woman in front of him. *I wonder what Hypatia would do if I wept like an orphaned child?*

Blinking the tears away before they formed, he concluded, "My mother died alone, hoarding bits and bobs of my father, dreaming of his return, while I set about making his dream a reality."

"The unknown future is more enticing than the known past," Hypatia said, surprising Fingal. Meeting his eyes for the first time since climbing to the top of the Eye of the Sea Lotus, Hypatia plucked at Fingal's core. "You've never been one to dwell on the past, Oriska. It only leaves you depressed, so don't start now."

Fingal clumsily slid his glasses back on and smirked. "You were listening after all! Does this mean we are becoming friends? Would you like to tell me about your parents?"

Fingal meant it sincerely, but Hypatia shut down the idea immediately.

"Not going to happen. Endymion team is likely closing in, and we've got a job to do which doesn't include learning about my past."

With that, she turned and headed down the stairs. *I certainly know how to pick them,* Fingal mused as he followed Hypatia's clanking steps down.

Broken Stone

The quality of a Relicus is reflected by the standards they set for themselves. —Arcturus

The Ayrs and Arcturus waited in a state of high anxiety. Seven wanted to ask more questions of her parents, more questions of Arcturus and Endymion team's plan; however, once she'd calmed down from her initial anger, she knew any conversation they had could reveal crucial information to Fingal, just like the stupid mistake she'd already made regarding Trio.

Instead, she explored her tiny prison, staring out into the dark waters of the Gulf of Mexico, maybe the Atlantic Ocean by now, she couldn't be sure. Then she opened cabinets, finding nothing within. On a whim, Seven brushed past Arcturus and tried the door to the hallway—locked. So, the Ayrs and Arcturus waited in a state of high anxiety.

Ida, who was watching Seven nervously explore the

room, tried to break the tension. "Sev, tell us about Continental. Was it everything you imagined it would be?"

Ida meant well, Seven knew that, but Seven couldn't think about Continental without thinking of Blythe's blue hair, emerald green scarab tattoo, and broken body. Thinking about Blythe and her tattoo, Seven subconsciously rubbed her arm where the edge of the universe tattoo hid under her sleeve. After a moment, Seven realized Steele and Ida awaited her answer, and her hand froze on top of her tattoo.

"I can't talk about it just now," Seven said honestly, "But I can show you something."

Walking from the door, Seven pulled her shirt sleeve up and sat down in between her parents. The edge of the universe tattoo looked out into the room like a great, multi-colored eye, and it pulled the gaze of her parents.

"You got a tattoo?" Ida asked, leaning away from Seven in surprise, a mischievous smile hiding behind the question.

Steele gingerly grabbed Seven's wrist and pulled her arm closer to his eyes. "The detail is astounding. It's really beautiful, Sev," he declared, gently running his fingers across the layers of the universe. "Wait, what's this?" Seven smiled, wondering who would discover it first. "Is that a sound wave?" Steele asked.

Lost in the simple joy of sharing, Seven forgot about her fears and let this small, familial moment take over. "It is."

Ida playfully smacked Seven's arm. "A sound wave of what? Come on, spill it!"

Arcturus stood aloof by the door, but Seven noticed his small smile. Perhaps he was remembering moments like this from long ago when it was Steele, Ida, and Trio enjoying each other's company.

Shyly, Seven murmured, "Remember when you first found out you were pregnant with me?" Steele and Ida nodded. "It's that video."

Eyes misting, Steele tightened his grip on Seven's wrist, "We'll watch it together when we get out of here."

As Steele spoke, the door to the room opened, and Locust entered, followed by four guards. No words were needed, as the guards quickly approached Seven, who still sat on the couch, her wrist held in her father's hand. Steele rose, dropping Seven's arm and stepping quickly in front of her. Ida also jumped up to stand in front of Seven, and the two Ayrs drew the attention of the guards. The guards should have checked the room first, for Arcturus waited patiently for all of them to enter before he attacked.

Moving with the fluidity of an autonomous robot whose whole series of actions have already been coded, Arcturus flowed violently through the guards. His first blow struck a guard in the temple, and she crumpled uselessly to the floor. As she fell, Arcturus' fist met another guard in the chin as he turned at the commotion and a clacking sound followed as the man's teeth met. Still moving, Arcturus shouldered the upper-cutted guard roughly into the third guard causing the two of them to topple to the ground in a mess of limbs. The fourth guard, moving as quickly as she could, pulled her sidearm and was in the process of aiming it when Arcturus flicked his golden cape like a whip into her face and then leveled her with a seismic kick to the chest. The last guard soared across the room and into the wall.

The whole fight took little more than a handful of moments.

Arcturus took a deep, steadying breath as he rose to full height. Steele and Ida moved Seven behind the couch and warily eyed Locust, who watched impassively throughout the entire fight, looking moderately impressed.

She jerked out a thin baton that crackled with electricity, and grinned. "More."

Four more guards, with batons drawn, rushed into the room and ganged up on Arcturus. Without the element of surprise, Arcturus stood little chance, and he struggled against the heavy stuns delivered by the batons. He swept under the lazy swing from one guard, grabbing the guard's arm and using the momentum of the swing to launch the guard onto the desk, shattering glass everywhere. A stun baton snuck in, zapping Arcturus in the ribs, and he curled up reflexively. Another guard took advantage of Arcturus' defensive position to angle a stun to Arcturus' back. Ignoring the pain, Arcturus twisted his golden cape around the baton at his ribs and forcefully mashed it into the face of the guard holding it.

As the dazed guard fell, the injured guards from the previous fight slowly gathered themselves and entered the fight again, ballooning the numbers to six versus one.

Watching helplessly, Seven cried, "Arcturus, watch out!"

The six guards carefully surrounded Arcturus, wary of the Relicus' strength and skill, while, standing like a bastion in the center of a storm, Arcturus waited. Seven watched transfixed as Arcturus stood perfectly balanced, and she remembered Arcturus' advice when training Trio. *Feel the balance. You want to be able to kick with either your front foot or your back foot.*

A guard attempted a strike from Arcturus' periphery, but the stocky Relicus saw it coming, smoothly stepping to the side in order to kick the baton away. A second baton dove in, but Arcturus redirected the blow with his right hand while driving the palm of his left hand into the woman's elbow. A disgusting snap followed. Then the four remaining guards were attacking Arcturus at the same time, raining blows down upon him like catapults launching stones at a castle wall. Arcturus went to one knee, his arm raised to protect his head but to no avail. The guards chipped away at Arcturus' stony defenses, pummeling him long after he crumpled to the ground and lay motionless.

Seven heard screaming and realized it was her own

voice.

"Enough," Locust ordered, silencing the room. "Fingal wants him alive." She walked around the couch and approached the Ayrs. "The girl comes with me. Don't be stupid," she said, gesturing back to Arcturus' bloodied form.

Steele and Ida did not move.

Quick as light, Locust struck two efficient blows before either Ayr parent could react, and Seven could do nothing but try to break her parents' falls. Two guards descended on Seven, pulling her from her parents' limp forms and towards the door. Her mind raced with dangerous possibilities.

"Where are you taking me?" she screamed, desperation cracking in her voice as she wrestled against her captors.

"Don't worry," came Locust's voice from behind Seven, "Fingal wants to run a few tests. I'm sure you'll be fine."

Animus

Real wisdom is knowing when to stop.—Arcturus

After being dragged up four flights of stairs, Seven found herself in a lab eerily similar to the lab where Fingal deconstructed Trio. Two sterile tables sat empty, both with articulating arms above them. Taking a deep breath, Seven smelled cherries, formaldehyde, and disinfectant. *This can't be happening.* Below her feet, the reinforced glass floor was lined with glowing pink and light blue tubes as if she were standing atop the firing neurons of a human brain.

"Get her ready," Locust ordered, indicating the first empty table.

"No!" Seven screamed, fighting uselessly against the guards as they led her to the table where they strapped down her hands, feet, and shoulders.

Craning her neck to see the door, Seven saw two more guards haul in a battered and bloodied Arcturus. He looked semi-conscious, eyes struggling to track anything clearly.

"Arcturus," Seven called. "Arcturus, wake up!"

Locust walked to the head of Seven's table and spoke next to Seven's ear, "He'll wake up soon enough." Locust gestured to the table next to Seven, and the guards strapped him down as well.

"What are you going to do to him?"

Locust smiled, but her green eyes held no emotion. "You already know. We're going to hollow him out of everything that makes him Arcturus, shepherd to the Relicus movement. Once he's a shell, his body will be the first to have human consciousness transferred to it." She paused. "Well, the second, I suppose, if you count Trio."

At that moment, Oriska Fingal appeared in the doorway, looking comfortably smug, his hair perfectly arranged and his plum suit jacket sharp as ever. "Won't it be fitting," he said, sauntering in, "that I be transferred into Arcturus' body? I am not one for heavy-handed symbolism, but..." Fingal trailed off as he walked next to Arcturus who lay inert on the table. Seven watched as Fingal considered Arcturus' face carefully, admiringly. He traced a thumb along Arcturus' strong cheekbones as if he were studying a beautiful sculpture. "He's so boring, I think I fit Arcturus' body much better. Imagine," Fingal murmured, lost in grandiose thoughts.

Revolted by the idea of Fingal's poisonous mind inside

Arcturus' body, Seven strained against her bonds, shaking ferociously.

"Tsk, tsk," chided Fingal. "That won't do you any good. Remember what we did to your brother?" Seven glared daggers at Fingal and said nothing. "I know what you saw in Trio's deconstruction. In fact, we're uncovering more every minute."

The ramifications of Fingal's claim struck Seven like a blow from a stun baton. Fingal and his scientists clearly worked hard to decipher what exactly happened within Trio's deconstruction, and whatever they were doing, it produced results. Hopelessness bit deeply as Seven rested her head on the table, staring disconsolately at the ceiling.

"Your parents tell me nothing. Arcturus tells me nothing. You," Fingal emphasized, pointing at Seven, "tell me nothing. What am I to do? I need data. I need to know." He gestured at the lab, "So here we are."

He still doesn't know everything. I don't even know everything, but once I go under, I'll fight back. Seven's only hope rested on disrupting whatever experiment Fingal planned for her from the inside, and she counted on her unusual perception of Trio's deconstruction coding to aid her now. If she could manipulate Fingal's experiment on her, she might be able to save herself by buying time for Endymion team to figure out a rescue.

Fingal walked to a counter behind the tables, and Seven could hear the metallic sibilance of something light sliding across the counter top. She craned her neck but couldn't see anything. Then, Oriska Fingal's face appeared above her, peering down at her through a crown-shaped device, a wicked grin on his face.

"You've seen this before, haven't you?" he asked, placing the crown upon Seven's head. "What a good girl. So much more docile than your brother." Fingal pointed at a viewing window. "Don't worry, I'll be right in there watching. I won't let anything go wrong."

With that, Fingal, Locust, and the guards left the room. The icy crown seemed to tighten on Seven's head.

"Arc, wake up. Arcturus!"

Eyelids fluttering, Arcturus drifted into consciousness with a slight shudder. He tried to bring his hands to his face before realizing his predicament. "Seven," he groaned, his peanut-buttery voice filled with gravel. "Are you ok?"

A whooshing sound followed by a rush of liquid resonated through the floor. The smell of cherries grew stronger.

"Oh yeah, I'm fine," Seven laughed grimly, craning her neck about, searching for the source of the sound.

"Look at me," The urgency in his voice forced Seven to comply. He gazed at Seven earnestly, and Seven imagined he would have reached his hand out if he could have. "No matter what Fingal does, we'll bring you..."

The lab intercom crackled to life and Fingal's voice

interrupted Arcturus, "Waffles. Arcturus and Endymion will bring you waffles." His unusually high laughter shrilled through the speakers. "Anyway, the experiment is about to begin. Deep breath Seven. We'll see you on the other side... Maybe."

A cool sensation lapped against Seven's ankles, and she could stretch her neck just enough to see that the room was filled with the same pink liquid that occupied the lab during Trio's deconstruction. The smell of ammonia and cherries grew as the cold fluid crept up her legs, waist, and chest, threatening to overwhelm her senses. She thrashed against her bonds to no avail. The pink liquid reached her chin, and she strained to keep it from her face. Thinking she was about to be submerged, Seven took a huge breath as the liquid inched towards her mouth and nose. Then it stopped. Seven froze, continuing to hold her breath, her lungs burning until finally she released the air in a gush.

At that moment, the lab disappeared, and Seven found herself in an empty white space that felt oddly familiar. She stood on nothing, yet she wasn't floating. The sensations of her body seemed normal, and she took a few exploratory steps, discombobulated by the idea that she walked on nothing. The back of her mind itched like when she recognized someone from school but couldn't remember their name. *I know this place.*

Then she heard the note, faint and far away. She spun around, seeking it out and finding nothing. Straining her ears, Seven closed her eyes and stepped blindly, following the sound as a guide. As she walked, the note grew louder and multiplied, becoming a chorus of beautiful chords. Seven opened her eyes to a rain of colors: oranges, reds, and yellows. Holding out her hands, she watched as traces of rain dripped down to her elbows in a river of hues. The feeling of recognition grew stronger, yet full understanding remained just out of her reach.

"You've been here before," a familiar voice said, shocking Seven.

The colorful, musical rain floated gently all about like rainbow curtains, and Seven couldn't find the speaker.

"Who's there?" she called, her voice muted by the rain.

"I can feel your fear. You've got to calm down, or I'm going to crash."

The notes increased in tempo as ankle deep water rose about Seven's feet, and she slogged through it, still searching for the voice. It seemed to be coming from all around her or maybe from the raindrops; Seven couldn't be sure.

"Slow your mind," the voice implored. "Focus on your breathing."

Seven stopped walking and took a deep breath. Her mind was cluttered like a junk drawer, and she worked hard to slowly discard one unneeded thought after another. She imagined them floating away on the colorful waters now at her knees. The music lulled.

"That's better," the voice said, sounding clearer now. "Do you know me now?" And she did.

"Trio, but how?"

Trio laughed. "How should I know? You did it first."

Seven felt comprehension come to her like a flash flood, and again, the tempo of the music increased dramatically. "This is my deconstruction. *You're* in my deconstruction. But if this is a deconstruction then…"

"Yeah, you're not human, Sev," Trio empathized. Seven opened her mouth to respond, but Trio's voice cut her off, "And before you ask what you are—I don't know. Right now, you need to focus."

Seven had little time to explore the idea that she wasn't human. *Deconstruction—a fate worse than death. Mom, dad, what have you done to me?* This wasn't the cliche moment before death when her entire life would be laid out in a tableau of memories. No. This was the brutal reality that life and death are unfair. She wouldn't get to sit down with her parents and question their ambition. She wouldn't get to fully grieve for Blythe. She wouldn't get to share a life with her brother.

Unless she resisted.

The volume of both the music and the multi-hued water continued to rise, threatening to drown Seven's focus, and she fought back, sensing that her connection to Trio was not part of Oriska Fingal's experiment. With a concerted effort, Seven ignored the music and the water lapping at her waist, allowing her mind to bring Trio's deconstruction up from her memories.

From experience, she knew to use her intuition not to control the deconstruction, but to join with it and follow its current. *The key to manipulating the deconstruction wasn't in knowing where it was coming from or where it was going to; instead, she only needed to know how deep the deconstruction went.*

The water tickled her neck, and Seven sighed. "I'm going to have to drown again, aren't I?"

Seven released what little control she clung to, and the water flowed over her head, effectively muting the music she'd been hearing. Waiting for her lungs to begin burning, Seven contemplated her underwater situation. She moved her limbs exploratorily, finding they moved naturally. She exhaled carefully, a tiny bubble of air escaping her mouth, before she pushed the rest out in a giant whoosh.

She didn't drown.

Ok. She relaxed. *How deep do you go?* Lines of coding began to materialize at the edges of her vision. She reached out gently with her mind.

Something light and circular appeared in her left hand, and Seven looked down to see a glass data disk. Seven felt the same firing of intuition she experienced within Trio's deconstruction, and she knew to follow it down. The language of coding clarified further, and she instinctively turned her right wrist over to discover an omni in which she placed the glass data disc.

Here we go.

The multi-colored water disappeared in a flash followed by a comfortable blackness.

Then she heard her parents' voices, far away and muffled as if they were coming to her through a straw, but as Seven flowed with the deconstruction, the voices became clearer.

Ida appeared. "I'm not sure I can do this again, Steele," her mother whimpered, tears streaming down her beautiful face.

In her arms was a dark-haired baby, quietly observing the outside world with inquisitive brown eyes. A steady hand gently moved a stray piece of hair back into place on the baby's head, and Steele appeared.

"We've worked too hard to give up," he asserted. "All those experiments since Trio. All those failures. This..." he gestured to the baby after a pause, "*she* is our redemption."

Ida shook her head, still unsure. "Yes, but at what cost? Fingal watches our every move. He'll find out."

"He won't. She gestated in your womb, Ida. Fingal will think she's our natural born daughter."

Seven floated above this all, existing everywhere at the same time, observing her parents' fraught argument through lines of radiant coding. She recalled her emotional conversation with her parents in their room aboard The Sea Lotus. Steele was relieved to tell her she wasn't a Relicus like Arcturus because he didn't have to lie, and now, Seven could see she asked the wrong question. She wasn't Relicus, Novus, or human. *What exactly does that make me?*

"Seven," Ida whispered from the deconstructing memory.

"What?" responded Steele in confusion.

Louder now. "Her name is Seven. She's the little sister Trio always wanted."

Steele's face softened as if he just remembered that the child in his wife's arms was more than a successful experiment. "You're right. Trio would have loved her… Will love her."

"Do you think we'll ever see him again, Steele?" Ida asked, her voice trembling with desire.

Steele nodded. "We will. He won't look the same, but he's with Arcturus now." Steele paused, contemplating the future with a pensive look. "Little Seven here is the key to everything."

Seven felt the memory slipping away, and she watched helplessly as Steele, Ida, and baby Seven disintegrated in front of her eyes until only white remained.

"Trio?" she called fearfully.

"I'm here, I saw the whole thing," he declared, voice wavering with emotion. "Seven, listen to me."

But Seven found it harder and harder to focus. Her

mind filled with electricity, as if every neuron were firing at the exact same time, threatening to overheat her mind. She screamed out in pain and terror, covering her face with her hands as the coding she saw became too bright. *The deconstruction. I'm breaking apart.*

Trio's voice came to her, knifing through the pain, "I'm coming, Seven. Don't give up. We'll—"

The lights of the lab glared brightly, hurting Seven's eyes as she opened them. She looked to her left and saw Arcturus watching her closely.

Fingal's angry voice crackled shrilly over the intercom, "What was that? How did you stop the experiment?"

Arcturus gently shook his head, imploring Seven to remain silent. *Like I need any help with that.* Her head was on fire as she suffered the worst headache of her life. Fingal's team decimated her mind as surely as a squadron of carpet bombers levels a city block.

"Answer me," Fingal shouted over the intercom, voice exploding.

Seven took small pleasure in hearing Fingal lose his temper, his well-crafted veneer showing signs of wear.

"Fine. Bring her parents up."

Arcturus still stared at Seven, and she desperately wanted to tell him Trio's last words to her in her deconstruction. Endymion team was coming. Her brother was coming to save them. All she had to do was hold out a little bit longer, but fear gripped her in a vice.

Fingal is getting my parents. How can I withstand what comes next? Fingal would leverage both her parents against her in order to get what he wanted, and Seven didn't even know what exactly she could give him. She held a cloud-like harmony with Trio, and her parents created her as an experiment. Somehow, that information didn't seem concrete enough for a man like Oriska Fingal. Still, it would point him in a direction Seven feared. *I'll give him nothing.*

Seven prepared herself for the worst.

The intercom sputtered to life, and Ida's voice cut through the air. "Seven, don't tell Fingal anything!"

Scuffling could be heard followed by a thump and a shout.

"Mom!" Seven shouted, straining against her bonds. "What's happening?"

Silence.

After what felt like minutes, Fingal sighed over the intercom, "Let's try this again. Dad promised to be more amenable."

"Seven, you need to tell Fingal what happened in the experiment," Steele said half-heartedly.

"No way. I'm not telling him anything."

"Then he's going to kill your mother," Steele responded coldly.

Seven's heart stopped. *Fingal wouldn't. He's kept my parents alive this long because he needs their knowledge and skill set. If he kills my mom, he'll have to kill my dad too, then he'll have nothing.*

"No," Seven said quietly, calling Fingal's bluff.

Fingal's voice sizzled, "Come again? I think I heard you say no. Is your heart ice, girl?"

Gathering strength she didn't know she had, Seven countered, "You need my parents. You always have." She remembered Trio's defiant words before he was deconstructed, and she flung them at Fingal like incendiaries. "Common sense isn't common. Kill my parents, and you kill any chance at your goals."

Seven imagined she could feel the heat from Fingal's gaze, and she knew he must be standing over the microphone, fuming.

When Oriska Fingal's voice came over the intercom again, it sparked with enmity. "I will not be denied. Not again. I refuse to fail as my father before me failed."

Of course! He's got daddy issues like so many others. Fingal struggling with his own mundane issues humanized him, and it revealed a weakness Seven could exploit.

"So that's it? You want to be different from your dad? Let me guess, your father was an engineer and programmer like my parents, and he tried to download human consciousness into a robot body. Unlike my parents, he probably failed miserably because that's what Fingals do."

In a hushed voice, Fingal answered, "Yes. Only it wasn't

just any human consciousness, it was his own, and he didn't just fail, he died." A long pause and then, "I was there. With my mother."

Understanding blossomed in Seven like a flower as she couldn't help but imagine a young Fingal helplessly observing the death of his father. *Hurt people hurt people.* Fingal's repressed pain twisted him into the cruel mess he became, but Seven knew it didn't excuse his actions.

Seven said nothing as the minutes ticked by.

Fingal sighed deeply as if he were resigned to his own contemptible fate. "Oh well. We'll just continue our experiment then. Even if it kills you."

Seven could hear her parents screaming as the intercom cut off, and tears sprang from her eyes to roll into the pink liquid just below her nose. *I'm not ready to die.*

"You are full of surprises, Seven," Arcturus marveled. "Whatever you're doing in the experiment, keep doing it." He smiled encouragingly through a pink-tipped beard, "It's driving Fingal mad."

Then Arcturus was gone.

Seven found herself back in the storehouse of her memories, only this time no gentle, musical rain greeted her; instead, she stood in a small circular area of white. Around her, a wall of colorful water loomed infinitely high. *Why can't my memories be stored in a place like Trio's? I'm tired of all this water.*

"Seven, you're back," Trio's voice sounded full of fret.

"We've almost caught up. Just a little bit longer."

Seven's first foray into deconstruction was timid and exploratory as Fingal and his team of scientists didn't really know what they were doing. They didn't want to damage her in their quest to learn more about her, so they tentatively probed her mind. Now, their intentions changed. Fingal wanted any information he could get, by force if necessary, damn the consequences.

"I don't think I have much longer," Seven realized with sudden fear. "Fingal's angry." She spun around as if looking for an exit, but all she saw was a wall of colorful water.

"Then fight back!"

The water surrounding Seven rushed away in the blink of an eye, leaving her in a lonely, ominous void.

"Something's coming," Seven whimpered. "Trio, I'm scared."

In the distance, a black wave grew. In the lab, Seven knew Fingal and his scientists madly hacked into her consciousness, kicking their way in with brute force attacks. Vaguely, Seven felt bits of her memories drift away, like clods of dirt eroding from a continent.

"Seven, we're docking in a minute, but you've got to fight. Life is waiting for you!"

Going to a knee, Seven prepared for the wave as it approached with the power of a jet airliner. In her head, Trio's words reverberated back and forth. *Fight. Fight!*

The water crashed towards Seven, but at the last moment, just before it struck her, the water parted as if a giant, invisible wedge formed in front of her. Breathing heavily and straining with all her will, Seven briefly noted a flash of hacked coding as she held against the tide until it passed, successfully thwarting Fingal's attack.

Seven's victory turned out to be short lived as another black wave formed in the distance.

Fight, she whispered to herself. Raising her code-lined arms in front of her face, Seven braced for another impact, and her invisible wedge still held. More waves would come. Fingal and his scientists would systematically send wave after wave of attacks until she broke, and each wave she survived would take more of her memories with it. Seven would recede into nothingness like a sandcastle too close to the ocean.

Another wave came. Seven held.

Another and another and another. Too many to count and each time, a little less of Seven remained.

Another wave, and Seven waivered. Another wave, and Seven deconstructed.

To Die is to Sleep

The Ayrs are talented for hitting a target no one else could hit. I'm a genius for pushing them to it. —Oriska Fingal

The smell of ammonia steeped cherries assaulted Arcturus' nostrils, the straps at his wrists and ankles tore into his flesh, the intercom buzzed with static, but all Arcturus registered was the sight of Seven—motionless. The tension she carried in her muscles during the deconstruction, especially in her face, was absent. She looked calm. Asleep.

"To die. To sleep." Fingal's voice drifted through the fumes and was even more toxic. "Do you think you know the difference, Arcturus? The difference between a wakeful sleep and sleepwalking through life? Between simulation and reality?" He paused. "Do you know the difference between humans and AIs?"

She's gone, Arcturus thought, unable to comprehend what Fingal asked him. Flumen's comforting words about not needing to know everything after Blythe's death flew from his mind like frightened birds. *Another person I've failed. Another mistake I've made has led to death. I am no shepherd.*

Minutes earlier, Arcturus' empathetic hallucinations threatened to overrun his mind as they mirrored Seven's trauma. Now they vanished, and he felt empty, as hollowed out as Seven's memories.

The voice on the intercom continued unabated and victorious, "Shakespeare said that bit about death and sleep in *Hamlet*. Do you Relicus know *Hamlet*? It contains a wonderfully pervasive treatment of madness, but that's a discussion for another time." Silence. "Hmm? No matter—my point being, Shakespeare and I share similarities, namely, our ability to take what others have done and make it better."

Arcturus could take no more of the demagogue's rambling. "Say what you mean to say, Fingal."

A deep sigh through the intercom, "Neither you nor Hypatia appreciate drama. Shakespeare," Fingal emphasized slowly, "borrowed heavily from other sources, but when he did, he made them *better*. He made them his own."

"That's what you think you're doing with the Ayr research? With Trio and Seven?" Arcturus scoffed.

"Of course! Better and my own. I took all the Ayrs had and will make myself better with it. Isn't that what sentient beings do? For example, you act so honorable, Arcturus, but how did you get Trio's Relicus body? Not exactly something sold on the open market. And why did you get it? You did it for yourself. To make yourself feel better."

The truth of Fingal's words struck Arcturus with the power of stun batons. *He can't possibly know what I sacrificed to get Trio's body. He's trying to pry open my weaknesses.*

"I rescued Trio. Saved his consciousness from your disastrous experiment," Arcturus argued. "And I did it for love, not to make myself feel better."

"Justify it however you want. The fact remains, you and I are parallel characters in this story, and each of us believes we are the protagonist."

Arcturus imagined Oriska Fingal lounging comfortably behind the microphone, cleaning his eyeglasses nonchalantly, safe from the bound Arcturus behind a pool of pink liquid, a wall, and Locust. *Coward.*

Long moments of silence filled the lab room, and Arcturus realized his whole body was clenched like a fist. The cold, pink liquid crept into his skin like a chemical burn. He forced himself to breathe deeply a few times, urging his mind back into his tactical thinking, but Fingal's voice interrupted his mindfulness efforts.

"Say, how long before Endymion team arrives? I'd like to roll out the red carpet for them."

Arcturus wanted nothing more than to break his bonds and smack the smugness out of Fingal's mouth. "Soon," he said more confidently than he felt.

"I figured as much, which is why we've prepared ahead of time. My engineers tell me we are nearly ready to download my mind into that plush body of yours. I must admit, I'm nervous. Will you hold my hand?"

Arcturus wasn't one for cursing, but he wanted to now. *Fingal's mind in my body? Fingal spent all that time and effort cultivating a Purist persona, and for what? To callously dump them and take my body by force?* Swallowing bile forcefully, Arcturus decided to try a new track—*perhaps I can pry at his weaknesses.*

"What would your father think of your actions? He seemed like a man of some integrity."

"Ah, ah, ah, Arcturus. You'll not trick me into a pique of rage. My father did have integrity and that came at the cost of success. I've made the difficult decisions, and I'm on the cusp of achieving my father's dream."

Arcturus pushed further. "Has this all been about your father like Seven suggested? The Purists, the investments, the terrorism, the deaths—all for your personal ambition to download yourself into a Relicus body?"

"You act as if my motivations must be wholly original. Let me tell you something about humans, and perhaps you'll gain some precious awakening. Humans chase the same dreams, experience the same pitfalls, and tell the same stories over and over. We've been doing so since the dawn of our species. Those stories resonate and carry meaning. My story is no different."

"And what happens when other AIs find out about this—when the Relicus movement finds out about this? You won't find support," Arcturus warned, thinking of his own revulsion at the idea.

"Clearly some already know," Fingal countered. "Whoever gave you Trio's Relicus body likely has some guesses as to how you used it. Besides, downloading a human consciousness into a Relicus body is going to be old news. Everyone will be buzzing about what the Ayrs have done with Seven, not worrying about human/Relicus pairing."

What did *the Ayrs do to Seven?* Arcturus wondered. *She was clearly not human since she was deconstructed.* He should have guessed much sooner that Seven was special. The Ayrs were ambitious people—*why would that ambition stop at downloading a human consciousness into a Relicus body?* They'd want something free from the shackles required for such a pairing.

Just what exactly did Steele and Ida create in Seven? Arcturus hated how Fingal knew more than him and reveled in teasing Arcturus with vague hints.

Enough. Arcturus could stomach no more of Fingal's noxious words. Every minute he spent arguing with Fingal, the more twisted his own thinking became, as if Fingal could read Arcturus' emotions with his own empathetic hallucinations.

"Just do what you brought me here to do," Arcturus declared hotly, shaking pink droplets from his beard.

"Do you really think I've been bandying words with you while everyone else sat around listening? I swear, Arcturus, what kind of idiot do you think I am?"

Biting his tongue, Arcturus thought, *The worst kind.*

"Oh, you should see the look on your face," Fingal squealed, voice full of mirth. "Or should I say, 'You should see the look on my face?'"

"Bastard," Arcturus spat.

"I'll miss you and that boring personality, Arcturus. Well, I must be going now. The culminating moment approaches! Isn't it exciting?"

With that the intercom buzzed and fell silent, leaving Arcturus alone in the freezing liquid, staring at the girl he as good as killed.

Something New and Something Old

*Sentience must be claimed. The humans will not give it. —
Arcturus*

Trio sat lifelessly in his submarine, a hole forming in
his heart where Seven was just a second ago, and he felt
her absence like he felt the absence of his memories. His
comms buzzed as Vulpes and Radius tried reaching him,
but Trio couldn't hear them. Terra and Flumen, seated in
front of him, half turned in their seats, their mouths
moving. He couldn't hear them either. His little sister was
dead, her consciousness picked apart like an insect
tortured by a child, and he was there, feeling it along with
her, his empathetic hallucinations deeper than ever. Since
his own partial deconstruction, Trio experienced a deep,
resonant connection to his sister even as he struggled to
rediscover his own memories. So, as she was
deconstructed, Trio perceived each of Seven's memories
fall away like water through her hands. Her emptiness
superimposed with his.

Fight. Fight! His own words to Seven echoed in his mind.

Life is waiting for you. He had a mission to complete—people to rescue. Endymion team caught up to The Sea Lotus, and they were ready to dock, waiting on Trio's order. Still, he couldn't act.

"Trio," came Vulpes' voice over the comms, "it's now or never. We can't hold this position forever without being detected."

Trio shivered. "She's gone. Fingal deconstructed her," he revealed, voice hoarse with pain.

Radius cursed softly and silence filled the comms as each team member grappled with the devastating news in their own way. In front of him, Trio felt wintry sadness radiate from Terra and Flumen. He could almost touch the cold snap.

Quiet and determined, Terra spoke first, chipping away at the sad frost. "Our only path is forward," she said, pointing ahead.

Trio looked up from the submarine floor that he'd been staring at blankly and saw a dark shape grow slowly. As their submarine approached, the bottom of The Sea Lotus took shape: a wide triangular hull with two pelvic fins protruding from the bottom.

"The underwater garage is just behind the first fin," Flumen explained as she steered the submarine forward. "Vulpes, Radius, are you two in place?"

Radius grunted and replied, "We're ready to board the main deck. Just say the word."

Flumen turned in her seat to look Trio in his brown

eyes. "Trio, it's time." She put a warm and loving hand on his knee, "But we need you with us."

The submarine trailed behind The Sea Lotus. Trio convulsed again, trying to shake the emptiness from him as if it were an unwanted hand on his shoulder. *Fight!*

"It's time to taste revenge," Terra said, staring at The Sea Lotus as if she were seeing her hands curl around Fingal's neck.

A decision solidified inside Trio like a hard lump. Blinking tears from his eyes, Trio promised himself he'd feel Seven's death fully after he saved Arcturus, Steele, and Ida. And after he killed Fingal.

He placed his hand on Flumen's, "I'm with you. Let's go."

Flumen nodded, placed both her hands on the controls and accelerated quickly towards the underwater garage. Upon approach, the water changed from dark green to pale green as the lights from the garage lit their way. One of Fingal's large submarines already floated in the dock, but there was plenty of room for Flumen to dock their three person sub alongside it.

As the glass dome slid open above them, warm, moist air filled Trio's nostrils. He peered around, carefully taking in the empty garage. Behind him, a catwalk led to a diving zone where two tubes large enough for one diver each plunged into the water. Up ahead, a diving preparation area doubled as a submarine maintenance zone, and Trio saw scuba gear hanging on the wall next to tools. Hopping onto the catwalk, Trio peered into Fingal's luxury submarine. It had three bubbled domes with room for a pilot and five others to sit comfortably on tan leather swivel chairs. Drawn in by the ridiculous opulence of the craft, Trio stuck his head inside the hull and saw a toilet. *You've got to be kidding me.* Withdrawing from the submarine, he pulled his sidearm and advanced quietly towards the stairs located to the left of the diving prep area. Flumen and Terra quickly followed.

As they approached the stairs, Trio heard commotion from one level above, and then a comms device squawked in the stairwell, "They're on the main deck! We need reinforcements!"

Trio held up his hand, stopping Terra and Flumen in their tracks at the end of the stairs.

Vulpes and Radius are moving fast.

"No! Handle it yourselves," Fingal's voice ordered shrilly in response. "Prepare the sub."

Two guards rushed down the stairs right past the three Endymion team members without noticing them, their single-minded obedience their downfall. Terra delivered a thunderous blow to the back of the first guard's head, causing the guard to tumble to the floor. At the same time, Trio instinctively grabbed the second guard in a rear naked choke, clinging to the man's neck until the man's frenzied hands went limp. Terra and Trio dragged the two guards off behind a workbench, where they crouched to catch their breath. Flumen waited by the stairs, listening.

Trio noticed a worried look flash across Terra's face. "Don't worry," he soothed. "Radius and Vulpes will be ok. They're pros. Well, Vulpes is at least."

Knowing that Radius frequently deserved lighthearted teasing suggested his memories were coming back, but they were like trying to catch the wind. A gust would blow through his mind, and he'd remember something like Blythe's scarab tattoo; however, as soon as he tried to examine the memory further, the wind would change direction and carry it away. In order to come on this rescue mission, he'd convinced the rest of Endymion team by arguing his skills would come back with muscle memory. So far, this proved to be true. Hope fluttered in his chest that, given time, he might be able to recover everything Fingal tried to deconstruct, and he held this hope thanks to Seven. The seed of an idea grew in Trio's mind. *Maybe I disrupted Seven's deconstruction like she disrupted mine.*

Trio didn't have time to explore the idea further because Flumen gestured anxiously from her position by the stairs. Terra nudged Trio, and he watched Flumen's hand signals carefully.

Footsteps.

Lots of people.

Next move?

"Fingal, Locust, and who knows how many guards," Trio whispered to Terra. She nodded calmly.

Trio quickly signaled Flumen to fall back from the

stairs and take a position behind another workbench near his. "We wait as long as we can to see who all enters the garage," he said, making eye contact first with Terra then with Flumen. "Then we eliminate all aggressors."

Trio's stomach churned and sour bile rose in his throat. He swallowed it down forcefully. Endymion team rarely used shoot to kill orders, but Fingal backed them into a corner by killing two of their friends. The time for half-measures passed when Locust killed Blythe.

Hunched beside him, her massive form difficult to conceal, Terra calmly stroked the butt of her sidearm with the nub of her thumb, trying to hide the look of worry hidden below the surface, but Trio saw it. He often perceived what people tried to hide.

A few feet away, Flumen crouched behind a workbench, her sidearm gripped tightly in her hands. A bead of sweat trickled down her temple, curved around her warm eyes, and dripped from her strong chin. She was an accomplished Endymion team member, but Trio knew Flumen preferred staying away from violence if she could. She acted as mother to all Endymion. With Blythe and Seven dead and Arcturus captured, Flumen's fierce, protective nature engaged. In New Orleans, she refused to be left behind, and as Trio looked at her now, with Fingal and who knows how many guards descending the stairs, he almost feared for them. Almost.

Checking his own sidearm, Trio heard a rush of footsteps from the stairwell. *Eliminate all aggressors.* He didn't know if his muscle memory would help him now, but he had little time to consider this as Hypatia slowly descended into view. With no mask, Hypatia's startlingly beautiful face stunned Trio momentarily. Unprepared for this type of muscle memory, Trio's mind fluttered between the present and the past: two Hypatias superimposed upon one another.

Olive skinned face mixed with horrible, featureless mask. Long, lean legs mixed with grotesque locust limbs. Love mixed with violence.

Trio rubbed his eyes, teetering back and forth behind the workbench. The double image of Hypatia burned his retinas even as he closed his eyes. Terra placed a strong, steadying hand on his arm, and the superimposition disappeared. Trio released a shaky breath, giving a curt nod to Terra. He peeked around the corner of the workbench again.

Behind Hypatia, another guard followed closely, spreading out as he stepped into the underwater garage. Both paused, taking in their surroundings, their sidearms at the ready.

Hypatia was clearly more careful and thorough than the previous guards.

"What are you waiting for," Fingal's voice questioned from the stairwell, "an invitation?"

A clatter of footsteps sounded, and Fingal bounded down the stairs, intent on marching right to his submarine. He nearly passed Hypatia when she grabbed his shoulder roughly. Fingal, about to utter some poisonous barb, clapped his mouth shut as Hypatia shook her head firmly.

More footsteps sounded in the stairwell and to Trio's surprise, Arcturus and his parents stumbled down the stairs, shoved by two guards.

Double imagery struck Trio harder than before, and he nearly vomited on the floor. His stomach contracted, pulling his whole torso inward painfully. He placed a steadying hand on the floor in order to stop himself from tumbling into the open. Struggling to reconcile the past from the present, Trio saw both the bloodied and bruised Arcturus of the present mixed with the stern father figure of his past.

What is going on with me?

Then, without warning, his vision shifted, regardless of whether his eyes were open or not, and he saw Steele and Ida—simultaneously his young, boyhood parents and this older, strained version. Trio's body fought with his mind, and he felt like he was imploding.

Hypatia scowled at the loud commotion caused by the guards shoving Arcturus and the Ayrs down the stairs. "With me," she directed, pointing at two of the guards. "Stay with Fingal," she ordered the last guard.

Slowly, Hypatia and the two guards fanned out into the garage, checking behind workbenches and in lockers. It wouldn't take them long to reach Trio's hiding place. Fingal moved cautiously behind the third guard, making sure to place Arcturus, the Ayrs, and the guard between him and the rest of the garage.

Terra shook Trio as firmly as she could, her face contorted with a mixture of worry and fear. Trio saw this as well, but his mind couldn't reconcile all the data he was receiving at once. Overloaded with information, he froze.

Footsteps could be heard as the first guard cautiously approached Terra and Trio's hiding spot, and he wouldn't have found an easier target than Trio, helplessly curled behind the workbench in a ball of pain. Unfortunately for the guard, a rumbling volcano waited too. Before the guard could make visual contact, Terra erupted from her position, thrusting her titanic left hand into the guard's throat, crushing it, while firing her sidearm into his chest. Terra flung the man's lifeless body like a child's plaything straight at Hypatia. Insectoid legs snapping, Hypatia leapt from the body's path and rolled behind a workbench where she returned fire. Terra lurched back behind the workbench with Trio, who still fought desperately with himself.

Seeing but not comprehending, Trio watched Flumen rise from her position, red-gold eyes flashing violently and discharge numerous rounds at the second guard, bullets ripping through the woman's chest and throat.

Fight. Fight! Trio tried to rise, his firearm shaking in his grasp, but Terra forcefully pulled him back to cover.

"Just stay down!"

Back by the stairs, the third guard dove behind a

workbench opposite Hypatia, ignoring his captives, preferring to protect his own life. He shot back at Flumen, forcing her to take cover.

Unbidden, Seven's experience in her deconstruction rose to Trio's mind, and through tears of pain and grief, he recalled Seven's ability to release control. *Can I let it go too?* The room wavered as Trio fought to calm himself before his vision cleared and his mind took control of his body. Past and present reconciled as Trio realized he could differentiate between the two.

A potential idea flashed through Trio's mind. *It's like my body is responding to a foreign object.* He and Seven did share some sort of mirroring after she hacked into his deconstruction, but Trio didn't have time to explore the idea further.

Risking a quick look, Trio saw Fingal spin about confusedly, his typical composure entirely eroded as he contemplated taking the stairs back up to the main deck and bolting for his submarine at the other end of the garage. Both might as well have been miles away. Instead, Fingal advanced on Ida, grabbing her roughly by the hair, intending to use her as a shield, and he dragged her wildly into the firefight raging about them. Terra and Flumen stopped shooting, taking the moment to reload.

For Trio, everything solidified and then froze, as if a picture was taken of the entire scene. Hypatia leaned from her position behind a workbench, the final guard slapped a clip into his sidearm, Arcturus, with hands bound, rose from his knees, angling towards Hypatia, and Steele's face twisted in desperation. Amidst it all, Fingal and Ida careened forward.

And Trio predicted it all. He calculated every scenario, played them out in his mind at light speed until he knew what would happen next.

He rose, shrugging out of Terra's grasp, his sidearm hanging loosely at his side. The third guard, seeing the motion, reacted instinctively and fired wildly at Trio. Flumen responded with her own well-aimed shots at the guard, taking him full in the face. Terra rushed at Hypatia just as Arcturus threw his stocky frame into Hypatia's back, and Steele stumbled clumsily into Fingal.

Knocked off balance, Fingal thrust Ida forward, and Trio leapt to catch his falling mother. The two of them careened sideways into a workbench, but Trio was able to absorb most of the impact with his back.

A violent commotion ensued between Terra, Arcturus, and Hypatia, and Trio tilted his head to see Hypatia disentangle herself from Terra and Arcturus, using her augmented legs to eat up the distance between herself and Fingal's submarine, her path leading directly by Trio and Ida. Fingal too was headed in this direction ahead of Hypatia, and as Fingal passed, Trio stuck his foot out, tripping Fingal and causing him to fall face first onto the catwalk in front of the submarine. In the span of a breath, Hypatia leapt over Trio and the workbench like a grasshopper. Trio thought she'd help Fingal up, but she kept running for the submarine.

"Hypatia!" Fingal cried, reaching a hand out from where he laid. She didn't stop.

Flumen shot at Hypatia as she flung herself into the cockpit but no bullet connected.

Before anyone from Endymion team could give chase, Fingal's personal submarine along with his personal assassin dropped from view, disappearing quickly into the inky ocean depths.

Fingal scrambled up and desperately ran for the remaining submarine. Over Trio's shoulder, a loud crack issued, followed by the whizz of a bullet that zipped past Trio's ear, across the garage, into the back right shoulder of Oriska Fingal causing him to spin to the ground. Trio vaulted from behind the workbench in pursuit of the crawling Fingal as the fearmonger pulled himself into the remaining sub.

Reaching the glass dome just before it shut, Trio lunged into the cockpit, smashing his shoulder into Fingal, who cried out in pain as he scrambled with the unknown controls. A deep anger boiled up like an arid heatwave, and Trio closed his hands around Fingal's throat.

Kaleidoscopic visions of Seven deconstructing flashed through Trio's mind as he clamped tighter and tighter around Fingal's neck, turning the man's face red. Trio's stomach contracted painfully as the double imagery worsened. Then, Fingal jabbed a lever detaching the submarine from its mooring. Water rushed in the open cabin, and still Trio clung blindly to Fingal's neck as his body struggled to align reality with the visions in his mind. Neither his body nor his mind comprehended the situation as the weight of the submarine pulled them down.

Superimposed images of Seven falling into the cold waters of the Gulf of Mexico and the Bay of Fundy flared through Trio's consciousness, and he could feel her terror and pain.

Drowning again, a voice seemed to cry out in his mind.

The heat of Trio's anger fled as his mind wavered between Seven's memories and his present. In a moment of clarity, he looked down to see Fingal's lifeless face partially obscured by the murky ocean. Releasing Fingal's neck, Trio pushed himself out of the sinking submarine and watched Fingal drift slowly into the all-encompassing darkness.

Another mirrored image of Seven in her deconstruction rocked Trio's body, and he couldn't resist his body curling painfully into the fetal position. Panic set in as Trio frantically battled with his own mind—one part of him seeking some indication of the surface, and another part of him feeling the destructive waves of Seven's demise. His body started and stopped like an engine running out of fuel while his vision blurred further.

Darkness crept in.

Trio caught a fleeting glimpse of The Sea Lotus' garage

lights sparkling like distant stars before unconsciousness claimed him.

****

When next he woke, Trio stared directly into Arcturus' eyes mere inches from his face. "Arc," Trio tried to say; instead, ocean water erupted from his mouth, and he coughed heavily, ejecting all the foreign liquid from his body.

Arcturus pulled back sharply from the deluge of water and sputtered, "Trio! I didn't think I'd find you down there, son. It was so dark. I was quick enough to follow the lights of your submarine, and I practically swam right into you."

Trio could hear Arcturus' wet beard dripping onto the floor.

Pat.

Pat.

Pat.

He sucked in his first breath sans water and looked past the kneeling Arcturus. Everyone was there except Blythe and Seven. Flumen's face creased with concern, Terra stood aloof, watching the unconscious guards, and Vulpes and Radius leaned against a workbench. They must have arrived after Trio sank with Fingal. The Ayrs, lost in the commotion, were still tied up, standing by the stairway. They seemed unsure what to do next.

"I see a conspicuous absence," Vulpes called to Trio. "Where's Fingal?"

Trio sat up with difficulty and shook his head grimly, the image of Fingal's strangled look still fresh in his mind.

"I thought you were a proper swimmer, Trio. What happened down there?" Radius wondered.

Trio stared at his hands then at Radius, who must have recognized something terrible and traumatic in Trio's eyes because he asked no other questions.

With Hypatia gone and Oriska Fingal dead, the dangerous electricity that filled the garage dissipated, replaced by stinging loss. Terra helped Trio to lean against a workbench, and Flumen moved about, cutting the bonds of the Ayrs. When she reached Arcturus, she embraced him fiercely before pushing him to arm's length.

"You're ok." It was both a question and an order.

Arcturus nodded, pulling himself from Flumen's hands, and Trio watched as his mentor limped to the water's edge, where he knelt, staring into the murky depths.

Red hair askew and blood on his face, Vulpes wiped his mouth and said, "We came as quickly as we could. Guards are dead. The remainder of Fingal's people, scientists mostly, are locked in a cabin."

For a while, no one spoke, unsure of the next right step. Trio experienced a bevy of emotions, radiating from everyone in the garage—relief, fear, anxiety, and others he didn't have the focus to pinpoint.

"It's over," Arcturus proclaimed from his position near

the water.

It was as if Trio needed someone to say those words in order for the gravity of the situation to sink in. From his time procuring more submarines from Chaffee Absaraka in New Orleans, at a cost Arcturus would throw a fit over, to now, Trio hadn't allowed his emotions to overwhelm him. He looked about the garage, taking in what remained of his family, and the holes in his heart burned again, reminding him of their loss. *Blythe dead. My sister dead.*

Trio welcomed the tears then. He welcomed the full and undiluted range of emotions he felt on a spectrum that only a Relicus can experience. He welcomed the pain, knowing it meant he was alive. Knowing it would honor the dead.

Steele and Ida approached Trio timidly. It was the first time they'd been this close to him since his consciousness was transferred to his current body, and they were unsure of how to proceed. Faint echoes of superimposition flittered across Trio's vision, but he let them go like birds from a cage.

"Mom. Dad. I remember you."

Ida choked back a sob and grabbed Trio into a painful hug. Steele followed close behind. They smelled of home and regret. As they embraced, Trio's vision doubled, and he saw Seven's reunion with Steele and Ida just a short time ago. His heart thrummed with pain and love knowing that Seven at least experienced this love before being deconstructed. Ignoring the pain in his shoulder,

Trio allowed the familial superimposition to last, not wanting to interrupt it because it felt like he was hugging Seven. Like he was getting to say goodbye.

In his ear, Trio heard his father whisper, "Let's go get Seven."

Seven and Beyond

I've fallen in love with the process and the product. —Ida Ayr

The lab was drained of pink fluid, and Seven remained strapped to the table, forgotten in Fingal's mad rush to the underwater garage. Trio and his parents approached quietly, a funeral dirge playing in each of their footsteps. Endymion team remained clustered in the doorway, giving the Ayr family time with Seven. Tenderly, Trio removed the crown from Seven's curly head and tossed it to the side. Next, he carefully removed each strap that bound Seven to the table, frowning at the bloody red lines around her ankles and wrists. He touched the wounds lightly. *She suffered.*

Once Trio freed her of her bonds, he placed his forehead to hers in the same way Arcturus did with him back in New Orleans. *You didn't give up on me after my deconstruction. You believed I could regain my memories, and I'm doing just that.* Eyes closed, Trio brought up the hard lump he'd kept in his chest during the rescue mission—the hardness that allowed him to give shoot to kill orders and ignore the pain he'd felt in losing Seven. He dissolved that hard lump. His vision doubled in an increasingly familiar yet still sickening superimposition, and he saw himself in New Orleans lying in the same helpless position as Seven. The smell of cherries and alcohol accosted his nose as he explored his hopeful thoughts from earlier. Trio allowed his consciousness to follow the idea along its path. *Seven, if we're connected through the cloud in a sort of co-presence, then maybe your data is still out there. I promise you, I'll find out.*

At Seven's feet, Steele placed a hand on her shin. "As soon as Fingal heard about intruders on the main deck, he ordered everyone out and destroyed the data," he said, as if he must justify why they'd left Seven all alone.

Steele and Ida. Trio's parents. As much as he needed them, as evidenced by how emotional he'd felt during their reunion in the underwater garage, Trio also needed answers *from* them. Forehead still gently touching Seven's, Trio reflected on all the questions he wanted to ask, and he kept coming back to one: what is Seven? He knew better than to ask now. It was an Ayr family conversation, and one where Steele and Ida would finally have to lay bare their secrets.

"We loved her, Trio."

Trio lifted his forehead from Seven's and evaluated Steele carefully. He felt the heavy dew of sadness that blanketed Steele as if it were his own. "Of course you did. Everyone loved her, but love doesn't excuse one's actions." In the doorway, Trio noticed Arcturus shift uncomfortably.

From her position next to Steele, Ida stared down and away, blistering shame written all over her face, but Steele set his jaw, looking ready to defend himself. Raising his hand, Trio said, "Now's not the time." He purposefully turned his back on everyone. "If you'd like to mourn silently with me, please do."

Cloaking himself in grief, Trio took his sister's hand in his, closed his eyes, and ignored the world.

****

Trio assumed The Sea Lotus sailed towards Pura Insulam, but he found he couldn't bother himself to care as the trip proceeded like one long funeral. Once Seven's body was moved to a cabin, Trio, Steele, and Ida never left her side. They spoke little, exchanging words only when necessary, holding their wake as the oceanic station plowed its way through the uncaring waters. In the back of his mind, Trio wondered if Seven's body would start to decay and smell.

He wanted to bring this up to someone but couldn't muster the effort. Endymion team members made their presence known regularly, paying their respects and offering support. Trio politely tried ignoring them all.

Despite his best efforts, he learned Arcturus busied himself and the team with operating the ship, going so far as to bring a few of Fingal's crew out to help. Apparently, this rankled Radius, who claimed he could captain the seafaring laboratory by himself.

Trio also learned that despite Fingal's quick actions in leaving Pura Insulam, The Sea Lotus did not travel far from home, so in the end, all Fingal's grand plans amounted to only pain and death.

The ride was silent as Trio waited to begin what would be a difficult conversation with the Ayrs. Steele and Ida kept making meaningful eye contact, but Trio noticed they both found it hard to look at him. After their initial burst of warmth during their reunion, Steele and Ida turned distant and icy. Trio didn't blame them. He could sense their love for him and for Seven, but it was buried beneath regret mixed with defensiveness. Their emotions were the frozen firmament of empathetic hallucinations, and Trio would need to do the deep, necessary quarry work of the soul to get honest answers from them. They'd buried their secrets and kept them there for decades.

Hours passed, and Trio found his mind wandering back to Seven's future. Traditionally, residents of Pura Insulam were cremated, as they had no room on the floating island for cemeteries, but Trio knew his parents wouldn't burn Seven. He guessed Steele and Ida wouldn't shake their logical approach to Seven the lab experiment, and this superseded Pura Insulam tradition. They'd keep Seven's body preserved.

Strangely, this idea comforted Trio. To pursue his notion that Seven's data was recorded somewhere in the cloud, he'd want her body intact. *Just in case.* He didn't tell Steele and Ida about his idea either, trusting the reticent feeling that grew in his stomach regarding his parents' intentions.

Trio snorted quietly and looked up from Seven's hand, which he'd been staring at for some time as his thoughts wandered. *My parents' intentions. What exactly are they?*

It was time for answers.

The three of them sat in a cabin, sunlight filtering through the window. Trio on one side of Seven's bed and Steele and Ida on the other side. The three of them naturally separated themselves as if preparing for the confrontation about to occur.

Without preamble, Trio said, "Tell me about Seven."

Ida sipped tea that Flumen brought, and she placed the cup down on the end table by Seven's head. Steele flicked his omni off and leveled his gaze at Trio.

Trio knew both of them would understand the intent of his statement.

Steele cleared his throat, wet his lips, and chose his words carefully. "She was our redemption after our near failure with you. We needed a way to continue our work without arousing Fingal's suspicion."

Trio wanted to focus only on Seven, to ignore his selfish desire to address how Steele and Ida abandoned him, but the conversation barely started before his desperate animosity boiled over. "On to the next experiment, huh? Did you even think about your son and what became of him?"

"I thought we were talking about Seven," Steele said guardedly, raising his chin.

"We thought about you every day for years," Ida soothed. She was seated in a small chair and sunlight highlighted her regal face, revealing the pain etched in her wrinkles. She brought her knees up to her chest before continuing. "For a while, we didn't even know if Arcturus retrieved your consciousness or if he was able to download it into... Into your body." Ida ran trembling fingers over her lips.

Into my body—something about that phrase jolted Trio's recollection, but before he could pursue the memory, Ida pressed on. "We thought the worst, and then, a month later, Arcturus got word to us that you were alive. Alive but unable to remember the Trio you were," she finished, hugging herself tightly.

I was a boy, and now I'm a Relicus. Of course, he'd known this on some level ever since his deconstruction, but now the gravity of that realization weighed upon Trio as he struggled to comprehend the pairing. The notion felt wrong somehow, but he was missing the context as to why it felt wrong—like he was looking at a piece of art and missing the point. *I need to talk to Arcturus about this. Maybe he can help me remember everything. He clearly knew me as both a boy and as a Relicus.*

Steele leaned forward from his position in the chair next to Ida, placing his elbows on his knees. "Contacting you in order to explain everything was too risky. Fingal watched our every move, so we came up with a different plan. One that would both bring you back to us and continue our research."

Trio followed his parents' apparent logic, running it through various scenarios in his head, and although he wouldn't have made the same decision as them, he understood that they made the best decisions they could. He extended them that much grace at least.

"And that plan was Seven," Trio clarified. "You were essentially kidnapped by Fingal and forced to work on Pura Insulam." He stood up from his chair opposite Ida and walked to the window to stare into the sky. He turned, "But Seven isn't human, Novus, or Relicus. She's not someone else's consciousness in a Relicus body either. She's more than all of that."

Steele leaned back in his chair, his downdraft of pride sinking over Trio, "She is."

Ida added, "It's not easy to explain. We knew we could download human consciousness to a Relicus body, but Fingal proved that system to be easily manipulated and dangerous."

"So we decided to have a baby," Steele interrupted, excitement growing in his voice as he gestured to Seven. "But not just any baby, a synthetic lifeform that we could design to function autonomously."

"Wait, Seven's a robot?"

"Not exactly," Steele answered.

"Human then."

Steele shook his head no.

"Then what?"

"Have you heard of xenobots?" Ida asked Trio, dropping her feet to the floor. It was Trio's turn to shake his head. "I told you this wasn't easy to explain." She took a deep breath before continuing. "Xenobots are small, synthetic lifeforms composed of stem cells, in Seven's case, my stem cells. In the early years of their development, xenobots were designed to do simple tasks like walk, swim, or even gather pellets in a dish. They could even heal themselves and obtain molecular memory."

Seven's quicker-than-normal-healing wounds came to Trio's mind, but then he screwed up his face in confusion, "So, Sev was made up of nanobots?"

"No, not micro-robots," Steele clarified, his voice electrified. "Xenobots are derived from stem cells, like your mother said, and then through multiple simulations, designed to perform specific tasks."

Trio leaned his back against his chair, stunned by what he was hearing, and the powerful empathetic hallucinations coming from Steele and Ida. His parents' research proved far too complex for him to understand on first hearing, and he couldn't reconcile what he was learning with the Seven he knew. "You made Seven in a lab. You designed simulations for her. You pre-programmed her? To do what?"

Steele shrugged nonchalantly, "To live."

Trio felt the sudden urge to jump over the bed and shake the smugness from Steele.

"Trio," Ida said, rising to her feet and walking toward the foot of Seven's bed. She placed a hand over her stomach. "I carried Seven for nine months in my own womb. We parented her for 18 years. She was our daughter, no matter how she was... conceived."

"That's it then? You created Seven as the next evolution of your research, so what? To what end?"

Steele sighed, "Don't let your anger with us obscure the importance of our discovery. Seven was perfect. She learned quickly, healed quickly, interfaced with simulations on an unforeseen level, and she was only just beginning to scratch the surface of her potential. Seven is the future of life."

He is far too proud, Trio realized. *He relishes explaining his research to me. He's had no one to share his triumphs with besides Ida, and now, he's intoxicated with his own genius.*

Straightening up, Trio gazed warily at Steele. "*Is* the future of life. Seven's gone. What do you mean 'is'?"

"I mean, we weren't satisfied with just xenobots."

Trio glanced at Ida, and he could read the reluctance on her face. When Steele said "we" he'd really meant "I."

"She's turritopsis dohrnii," Steele continued, as if this explained everything. Trio didn't humor his father by asking him to clarify because Steele was deep in his own hubris. *I couldn't shut him up if I wanted to.* "The t. dohrnii is a biologically immortal jellyfish, capable of reverting back to its polyp stage when stressed by sickness, the environment, or physical attack. It's like the creature hits the reset button, keeps all its saved progress, and then starts life over. We wanted that kind of reset for Seven."

"We designed Seven's synthetic neocortex to act in the same way as the t. dohrnii's cell development, only her mindfile is in the cloud. Seven *is* our simulation of the top layer of the neocortex to the synthetic neocortex in the cloud," Ida clarified, coming to Trio's side. "Which means, she's out there somewhere, Trio, but we don't know how to get her back."

"Theoretically," Steele added, and he grew suddenly serious. "Look, we know you were with Seven at our Ascension lab, and we know Seven interfaced with your deconstruction." A hungry look appeared in Steele's eyes as he stood up from his chair and leveled his gaze on Trio. "Is there anything you haven't told us?"

"If we could compare Seven with you now, and maybe find something out about Seven's mindfile," Ida added quickly, intending to appeal to Trio's logic.

They need me, Trio realized as he fought a wave of revulsion, considering the implications of what he'd just heard. *They want to experiment on me, like they did with Seven.* Ida at least had the dignity to appear slightly ashamed, but Trio sensed she was just as ambitious as Steele. Ida loved Seven, but she also loved her work. Along the way, the two became so intertwined that Ida could no longer differentiate between the two.

Moving away from Ida, Trio shook his head, suddenly desperate to get away. "I need time to think."

"Trio wait," Ida called, trailing after him, but Trio didn't stop.

He ignored his mother's pleading all the way out of the room, seeking a safe haven from his parents' zealous desires.

****

From his perch atop the Eye of The Sea Lotus, Trio felt as if he were riding the birth of the universe. The Gulf of Mexico spread out before him, filling his vision with waves and his nose with the scent of salt. He closed his eyes, listening to the edge of infinity.

Seven's out there somewhere, drifting through the darkness, carried by currents no one understands. His parents' explanation of Seven's mindfile aligned with his own intuition about Seven's connection to him. During his deconstruction, the two of them became inextricably linked through the cloud, which meant he was also uniquely positioned to help. Not his parents, but his sister, and if he were the one chasing down this lead, that meant he could decide what to do with the findings. Trio reflected on his options, accessing that vast network of scenario analysis Arcturus taught him to use. After many minutes of staring blankly out over the Gulf of Mexico, Trio came to one conclusion. He needed Arcturus and Endymion. He needed his family.

Family, the word took on new meaning now that Trio thought about both the Ayrs and Endymion. *If only I could remember everything from my childhood and my time with Endymion.*

Trio reached into his armadillo backpack, intending to grab his omni in order to call Arcturus; instead, his omni chirped from somewhere in his bag, and Trio's hand plumbed the bag's depths until he found it.

He flicked it on.

"I'm glad you answered," Arcturus said without preamble, "We've got a lot to talk about."

Thinking about everything he'd just learned, Trio replied, "Tell me about it."

Continue the story in the upcoming novel, TRIO.

Seven

Acknowledgements

Well, I did a thing and wrote a book. Then I did another thing and got it published, which as it turns out, requires a very different skill set. With that in mind, thank yous are in order because I would have been lost without help.

Thank you...

To my wife, Ashley, and my children, Emery and Sunden. You encouraged my writing even on the busiest of days. I love you!

To my mom, dad, and brothers. The man I am today is in large part thanks to your unwavering love and support.

To those who read my drafts: Daniel, Rose, Lauren, Mitch, and Jess. When you read my words, you reinforced my heart.

To Chase, my Director of Knowing People. No, you don't get any royalties, and yes, I'll write you into my next book.

To Sabrina and Rusty. The grind of submitting to agents and publishers can wear a writer down. You inspired me with your belief in my story and made Seven a reality.

To all my former educators, from kindergarten to grad school. You watered the plant without needing to know what fruit it would bear. You are magnificent.

Take a deep dive into the world of Pura Insulam by visiting www.shawnkrinke.com for:

- Fan art
- Side stories
- More playlists
- Teacher resources
- And surprise content

Meet the Author

Shawn Krinke is an award-winning educator with a passion for sharing the magic of words.

Since 2008, he has been shaped by the young minds he teaches as a high school English educator and literacy specialist. Born and raised in North Dakota, Shawn is a former farm boy, a dedicated family man, and an avid quoter of all things pop culture.

Currently calling Fargo, North Dakota, home, Shawn resides with his family, finding inspiration along I-94 and from his always entertaining learners. *Seven* marks his debut novel.